Immortal

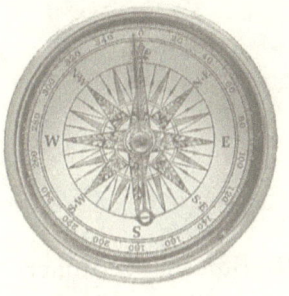

THE TRELAWNEYS OF WILLIAMSBURG

BOOK TWO

ANNE MEREDITH

With gratitude for the freedoms I enjoy
to those who fought for liberty
in this great land, when they themselves
were not afforded her privileges
In their bravery and selfless sacrifice,
they were not Africans,
nor free men, nor slave.
They were mere Americans.

And, as always …
with love …
for Joshua

Notes from the Author

This novel is the second in *The Trelawneys of Williamsburg* series. Although there are no cliffhangers between these books and each story is a complete "happily ever after" tale, there is a complex revenge murder mystery played out across the books.

Consider first reading *Tender* before beginning *Immortal*. Each book contains plot developments that put in motion events of the next book, as well as revealing events that occurred in previous books. Reading the books out of order may not be the optimum reading experience.

A list of major series characters is provided at the end of the book, in case you need a refresher on a character introduced in *Tender*. (Family trees are in development and will be posted on my website at www.annemeredithbooks.com.)

THROUGH airy roads he wings his instant flight
To purer regions of celestial light;
Enlarg'd he sees unnumber'd systems roll,
Beneath him sees the universal whole,
Planets on planets run their destin'd round,
And circling wonders fill the vast profound.
Th' ethereal now, and now th' empyreal skies
With growing splendors strike his wond'ring eyes:
The angels view him with delight unknown,
Press his soft hand, and seat him on his throne;
Then smiling thus. "To this divine abode,
The seat of saints, of seraphs, and of God,
Thrice welcome thou." The raptur'd babe replies,
"Thanks to my God, who snatch'd me to the skies,
E'er vice triumphant had possess'd my heart,
E'er yet the tempter had beguil'd my heart,
E'er yet on sin's base actions I was bent,
E'er yet I knew temptation's dire intent;
E'er yet the lash for horrid crimes I felt,
E'er vanity had led my way to guilt,
But, soon arriv'd at my celestial goal,
Full glories rush on my expanding soul."
Joyful he spoke: exulting cherubs round
Clapt their glad wings, the heav'nly vaults resound.
Say, parents, why this unavailing moan?
Why heave your pensive bosoms with the groan?
To *Charles*, the happy subject of my song,
A brighter world, and nobler strains belong.
Say would you tear him from the realms above
By thoughtless wishes, and prepost'rous love?
Doth his felicity increase your pain?
Or could you welcome to this world again
The heir of bliss? with a superior air
Methinks he answers with a smile severe,
"Thrones and dominions cannot tempt me there." ...
- *Phillis Wheatley, A Funeral Poem on the Death of C.E. ...*

Prologue

The man they knew as Michael Johnson leaned on his walking stick, huddled around a fire with the other sailors in a public house on King Street. Only a few knew him by his given name: Crispus Attucks. Tomorrow he would become memorable; tonight, he was a simple seaman of no import, wanting nothing but to warm himself before they weighed anchor again.

The older he got, the more he loved a roaring fire. His joints felt the cold. He'd grown up in this land, and his mother's people had lived here for millennia, but how he hated the cold. He yearned for his captain's home in St. George's.

Tonight had been the crew's last night in town. Any shorter, and they'd get restless and behave badly. Any longer, and they ran the risk of abandoning the sea altogether.

As the men dreamed about island girls who could warm a man's flesh, he recalled Antoinette. He'd helped her escape in Spanish Town long ago during a Caribbean voyage. How they'd loved! He'd delivered her to the Adamses, old friends in Boston who'd helped him escape his own bondage years ago.

These Adamses weren't as well-known as John or Samuel, but they loved this land. With the gold he left them for her

1

care, they'd helped her build a home where she raised their daughter. Camisha Adams had changed Antoinette, saved her soul, made her insist on marriage and faithfulness. Faithfulness, he could abide; life on dry land, he could not. He loved the land, but he could no longer live on it. Escaping slavery decades ago had given him a restlessness he could not conquer.

Yet how he loved Antoinette and their child, Marie—now a grown woman with children of her own. And the memories of Marie, of Antoinette, warmed him where the fire failed.

An urgency filled him. *Go this second. Find her, take her with you, build your home in St. George's. Or even her hometown in the West Indies. But marry her, man!*

"Michael!"

The voice jarred him from his reverie. "Back in Spanish Town again?" He merely stared back at the young face teasing him. Of course it was Rashall, Camisha's son.

As he looked at the others, he smiled. The remaining levity drained away as they waited, absorbing his intensity. Men took this humble mulatto man seriously because he cared. A person couldn't help caring when they were around him.

"Raven, 'twas my mother who taught me to love this land. You boys can roam the seven seas all your days. You can touch distant pink shores seeking treasure. You may be seamen, but you cannot make me believe you do not love these shores.

"You are not an Englishman, Elias, nor you an Irishman, Johnny, nor you a free Mozambican, Obadiah. You are all Americans. Look within your hearts and, beneath the love for sea air and salt water, you'll find you hunger for the sight of the prairie, for the craggy mountain, that fire in your veins that is your love for this land and for freedom. Freedom that beats not in the heart of any other land except this."

This made them titter. He'd known every man here since their days as callow youth, and they knew him to be the occasional sentimental fool. He'd practically raised their very own captain, and Adams, here, himself, if knot-tying were schooling and sea shanties, lullabies. The captain, at 17, had approached him with the offer of a quartermaster position on board their *Adventurer* seven years ago. His bravado hadn't fooled Michael, but his combined pluck, bravery, and earnestness had charmed him into accepting the offer and helping him outfit a ship. Within a few years, as the captain had promised, all the sailors Michael had scared up to follow the young captain were rich as Croesus.

The captain came to be known as Hawk, roving the seas and plucking treasure from Spanish and English ships. The days of the pirate were long since passed, but there were riches enough for those unafraid of hard work and long hours.

Hawk's boyhood friend, Camisha's son, called himself Raven, and he and Michael ultimately shared the quartermaster position, with all three men in a similar place of authority among the crew.

And even as he thought of him, that young captain filled the doorway five feet away, stamping his feet free of snow. He wore a heavy wool coat, but his blond head was bare save for a knot of leather tying his hair in a queue.

How he loved that lad. He was his captain, his good friend, and more like a son to him than most men's own sons.

Hawk gestured at Michael. Michael nodded in response and the seamen headed out the door, eager to get underway. They hurried down the street toward the harbor, and Michael stopped. He had forgotten to settle up with the tavern wench.

"Be along straightaway."

As he returned to King Street, a rabble of boys and men and redcoats crushed in upon him. He stepped into the tavern and paid for their drinks, then returned to the street. The crowd had stopped, and a boy of perhaps fourteen years stood, confronting a British soldier at least twice his age and size.

"He owes my lord, the wigmaker!" the boy cried.

"I told you, begone! All of you! Disperse!" This from the soldier as he inched backward away from the crowd.

But they encircled him. "Lobster-back! Lobster-back!"

The soldiers raised their bayonets to force back the crowd. They were outnumbered—but they did, after all, have weapons. The boy had only an invoice for payment.

Another, deeper, British voice rang with authority in the night: "Do not fire! Don't fire, I tell you!"

Michael shoved through the crowd. The boy persistently thrust an upturned palm toward the soldier. The soldier pushed back with the bayonet, making the boy jump away. Michael lost all patience; what madness, for the cost of—what, a *wig-dressing*? He would pay the boy himself.

He raised his walking stick and with it nudged the barrel of the musket away. The nervous soldier almost dropped the gun. Michael pushed the boy out of the way, taking his place.

"Wasn't the death of the German boy last month enough to satisfy your bloodlust? Let's see what happens when your cowardice is met by a full-grown man."

Michael faced the soldier, unafraid, mocking the soldier's badgering of the boy. "Then fire, damn you!"

And he fired.

Michael felt little but a fire deep inside. He touched his stomach and found a mass of viscous wetness he recognized to be his innards. And then his legs betrayed him, and he fell.

Presently, he saw the captain's anguished face before him, heard him shouting *Michael!*

"Go, boy."

"Get a surgeon," the captain urged the British soldiers. They stood mute.

In a moment, Michael knew he was dying.

"I will not let this pass, Michael. I will fight—"

"Fight for the land, boy. For the land of your mother."

And as he said the words, he was in his heart a child again running through that land, the spring sun on his dark shoulders and the wind in his face, the coolness of the Charles River on a hot summer day, laughter singing in the air. He was a young man loving Antoinette and their daughter. And in a blink he was old—on the deck of the *Adventurer* with this young captain, the heady salt breeze filling his lungs and stinging his eyes.

Life—how endless we think it!

The captain drew him back into his life as the glow and the sting of the wood fires burning in the cressets began to leave his eyes and his nostrils, as the terror in Hawk's voice went silent on the cry of *Michael.*

He wished too late that he had told him the truth of his name. At least Antoinette knew. And he hoped in time she would find in her heart the kindness to tell their daughter how much he had loved her. He was not a perfect man, but he had tried hard for them, as he never had for anyone else.

And even as he wished, as his earthly eyes and ears saw and heard no more, the sound of his mother's voice came to him—the ancient sound of a Natick Praying Indian. Her visage, her beloved face with the same high cheekbones as his, the same strong, blunt blade of a nose—the face he'd loved as a child and missed as a grown man, when she passed on—now warmed him at last as she held out a hand to welcome him. "Come home, Crispus. 'Tis time to come home."

Chapter One

Present day Richmond, Virginia

The day's work had been long and hard at the dig in Norfolk, and Marley had arrived home aching and sore and filthy. An eighteenth-century ship, unearthed at a construction site, was the most exciting discovery she'd been involved in during her short career. Early tomorrow morning her team would finish scanning the site. The construction contractor's timetable added pressure to what would otherwise be a more comprehensive physical effort—but the computer-generated 3D images of the site would help their research efforts.

Now, she stood in the kitchen, freshly bathed, in her nightshirt and slippers, enjoying the quiet of the house. The milk boiled, and she poured it over her own hand-ground, gourmet cocoa mix in an oversized mug and placed the pot in the sink to soak. She watched the mixture continue to boil and steam inside the cup as she stirred. A moment later the mix was dissolved.

Dropping in marshmallows, she set the mug aside. She washed her hands scrupulously, rinsed until they squeaked, and rubbed them on a tea towel until they were dry as parchment.

Then she retreated with the cocoa to the window seat in the old stone home outside Richmond where she lived with Nan.

She placed the cocoa on the deep ledge alongside the window to cool. She turned on the reading lamp, closed the heavy drape around the window seat, and curled up inside. It was a luxuriously cushioned place almost as big as a daybed. With any luck, she'd fall asleep here. Her grandmother's house was nearly 300 years old, and with all its charm, she loved most the window seats where she could usually be left alone.

She fluffed the pillow and stuffed it between her shoulder and the window frame so that it cradled her head just so, and she inhaled the sweet smell of the spring rain. She started to sip her cocoa from the dissolved puddle of marshmallow, but it was still scalding hot—she'd let the milk boil. She set it aside and, just for a moment, she stopped to love life.

And then, she retrieved the leather book from the display case on the shelf above. How many times as a child she had been scolded away from it. She was ten years old before she was allowed to touch it and then, only wearing white gloves. As a historian, she had seen and loved many old volumes, but none were as treasured, as doted on, as the one she held.

As she grasped the heavy book, she looked at the binding.

THE TRELAWNEYS OF WILLIAMSBURG

Truth to tell, it was a collection of leather- and cloth-bound ledgers, expanded to add pages as time passed. The book ran for hundreds of pages, from 1746 well into the twentieth century.

Just one volume was missing, from perhaps the most meaningful, exciting period of time in American history—late 1775 through July, 1776. She didn't let that noteworthy flaw keep her from enjoying the priceless treasure.

The outer binding was a leather-encased cedar box, hand-tooled by freed slaves, as beautiful as any jewelry of royalty. They had fashioned the binding with the future in mind, allowing room for the volumes that would annotate over two centuries of their history.

The cover contained small portraits of family members. In its center was the lady who'd begun it, a woman named Ruth. Underneath the portraits was an engraved banner.

For our children's children.

That gave her a bit of guilt for the wealth she held in her lap. She was not a Trelawney. One day, she hoped, she would either donate the book or see to it that it was returned to the last surviving Trelawney—wherever they might be. But it didn't belong to her, it belonged to Nan.

She opened the cover and withdrew the oldest volume, the most fragile of them all. On the frontispiece was written:

This is the diary of Ruth Freeman Trelawney of the events beginning July 4, 1746.

She turned the page and began to read, loving each lark of spelling, each hard-won new word selected by each home-schooled author. Back in those days, even college graduates spelled creatively.

July 7, 1746

Mr. Godfrey Hastings has been teaching me to read & write. He gave me this diary as a school lesson. He says it will get better over time, but I have to write every day in it. I have a powerful strong story to tell, soon as my spelling gets better. If houses have hearts, our house's heart is broken.

That's all for today.

July 8, 1746

Mr. Hastings tells me spelling don't matter, and that what matters is that I catch all the thoughts and the happenings around me.

I was sad already that my friend Camisha was gone, sailed up to Boston to be with her husband's family. Then two nights ago the awfulest thing a person could imagine happened. There was a fire up at the house, and by the time we saw it, we couldn't do nothing but watch it burn.

I got there just after my Dan. We all brung our pails to try and help, we all lined up in two lines from the river, and it was just a mess. The noise, the heat, people going every which way.

None of us know Mr. Thomas much. But, first we knew something was wrong, we saw him screaming and crying and running like a crazy man behind the house, and his little baby screaming and crying and Dan and the other men had to keep him from going in the house. I had to take the baby from him, I was so afraid of what he might do.

Then we found out. Mr. Grey, and Miss Rachel, and poor, sweet little Emily—they was in that fire. Those good people, they died in that fire. It just makes me hurt all over. I don't know how to tell little Dan and Sukey, they loved that child like she was they sister.

Come to find out, Old Nate saw the whole thing! He was coming back from visiting family at Westover, and he saw that James Manning, that devil of an overseer Mr. Grey ran off. Well, Old Nate saw him sneak into the house with a torch and a kettle of whale oil. And not long after, out came the family, looking for something. Then, by the time Old Nate got close enough to tell anybody what he saw, little Miss Emily went and ran inside, like she forgot something. Mr. Grey ran in after her. Miss Rachel, she ran in after him. I expect if he hadn't had the baby, poor Mr. Thomas would have gone in after all of them.

I feel for that man, I do. He's rich as sin, and he's lost every last person he loved, except for that little baby boy. And in sparing that little baby boy from man's sinful destruction, God is merciful.

Marley reached for a tissue and wiped her cheeks. Each time she read this, the story of loss broke her heart all over again.

July 9, 1746

I have just wondrous news, the kind so good you want to blurt it right out. But Mr. Hastings he says it makes for a better journal if you say these things in time order. He has a pretty word for it, but I forget it.

Mr. Hastings gave us leave for the funeral. The saddest part to me was, there wasn't no bodies to bury. Dan, he says the fire must've been that hot.

Some wagging tongues are saying awful things, that they didn't die at all in the fire, that they ran away. Do they think Old Nate is bearing tales? Do they think poor old Mr. Thomas would have been carrying on so, if they didn't die there? 'Tis not a decent way to talk about the dead.

Poor Little Sukey, she dreamed Miss Emily came to visit last night. She woke up talking about her just as if she'd just left the house. "Don't worry, Mamma, she be all right now. She in a better time."

But the best news of all came after the funeral, when Mr. Hastings came to visit us in the cabins. I wish I could get down all the words he said, he's such a pretty talker. I reckon I'll use my own words.

Well, he says, Mr. Grey left behind some papers. In it, he wrote a message to every last one of us workers. He said he was sorry. Sorry for enslaving us. Sorry for keeping all the money he said we rightly earned over the years. And he said things that you could tell Mr. Hastings didn't want to read, the way he got real quiet and had a hard time speaking. (I won't embarrass Mr. Hastings about this, case anybody else reads this, so we'll just leave it at that.)

But he did say Mr. Hastings was a smart man and thanks to God for that. Mr. Grey left so much for us, you see. He gave us our freedom, though he said he never had a right to keep it from us to begin with. He gave us each a little bit of that money back, and said he wished it was more, but that the wealth was in our homes, in Rosalie. So he gave us our homes, and the land here on Rosalie, and he gave us all jobs, as long as we want to live here. And we'll be paid for it, Mr. Hastings says.

And he's made my Dan the new overseer, except he calls him a foreman.

He's also made me the new school mistress. Now that's the blind leading the blind, but I'm trying hard to learn.

I don't know how to explain to my children what this all means. But I know it is right that a man, and a woman, too, is born owing nothing to nobody except God, who gave us life. I remember now when Camisha told me what it was like being a free woman. You just decide what you want, and then you work hard to get it, she said. It seemed like a puzzle to me.

Now I think when you become a free woman, you become in your heart the real person, the full person, God made. Because I decided what I want, and it was easy as looking up and seeing the sky for the first time.

I want my little Sukey to go to school and be smart like Camisha. I want my little Dan to grow up and be strong and seek God, like his father, and to work like Ashanti for the freedom for other people, other little children like him.

Dan and I and all the other plantation workers have made a decision to honor this day and the man who gave us our freedom by taking his name. A lot of workers have the surname of cruel men who work them hard, till they die in the field. Mr. Trelawney was a good and fair man, and he took people with all kinds of scars from all kinds of plantations and he made us a family.

Today, we are now all the Trelawneys of Williamsburg.

I praise God for this day of freedom, this exalted day. I will never forget this day, and I will never let my children forget, or my children's children, either. I find I'm walking taller, my shoulders back, my head up as the woman God meant me to be when he made me.

It is good to be a free woman.

Only a few pleasant minutes had passed when Marley heard the crunch of tires on gravel in the driveway, and her stomach knotted. She quickly placed the journal back into its leather box, but she had no time to lock it in its display case. She tucked it beside her in the window seat.

The screen door slammed, and she turned off the lamp and curled up into a ball. She shut her eyes tightly in the dark and pretended to be asleep.

"Marley? Where you at, girl?" Jimmy, her grandmother's …partner, companion, acquaintance—she just couldn't use the phrase *her grandmother's boyfriend*—called from the kitchen.

He sounded harmless enough tonight, but you never could tell. He had taught her one lesson in life, and that was to avoid confrontation. For a man she'd known most of her life, his moods were impossible to gauge. She knew kindness lived somewhere within him, for she'd seen it once, perhaps twice, when he was sober and took them sailing on his small boat; but what she knew of him was bitterness and rage.

The back door closed, and she heard the hushed rumble of voices, ending in the louder male voice. "I *told you* I didn't want to talk about it!"

Then a quick, sharp pop, followed by Nan's cry.

Marley's breath came faster, and she bit her lip. She had missed the slight slurring of his speech in his first call to her. But she heard it now, even as she pressed her hands over her ears, trying to blot out the noise that followed. He was drunk, and taking it out on Nan.

Once, years ago, Marley had tried to intervene. It had only made him angrier, anger that he took out on her grandmother. Now, she tried to blot out the noise, and the shameful knot in her stomach, knit there by her cowardice.

For cowardice it was. Nan had made her promise never again to try to defend her. But she was no longer the lonely child cowering under a blanket in her closet, as she had for so many years. She was a grown woman now, well-educated and well aware that this man should be in jail for his abuse.

Marley had no photographs of her grandmother as a youngster—Nan said her family had been too poor for such luxuries when she was a child. But she had a small, old-fashioned miniature of a young woman that she didn't quite believe was the same woman, so joyful and carefree and vibrant was she.

She heard nothing, and she sat up slowly, listening. Then came the heavy thud of Jimmy's work boots. He flung back the drape around the window seat, and she cowered from him, trembling in terror.

"Leave her alone, Jimmy!" Nan snapped, rushing at him. He backhanded her across the side of her head, sending her into the china closet. Only the angle at which she'd landed had kept her from smashing into the glass or knocking the whole thing over on top of herself.

Paralyzed with fear, Marley quaked in the corner of the window seat, staring at her grandmother. The rain still fell, just as peacefully.

"What a snot-nosed coward you are. Close the goddamned window. Don't you give a damn what people think of us?"

With quaking hands, she started closing the window.

"Hurry up!" She stood up for more leverage but her shaking legs gave out underneath her and she fell beside him. He kicked at her thighs—hard—and she cried out in pain as she scrambled away from him on the floor.

Nan rushed at him again, and he turned his fury full on her. He slapped her across the chest, as he always did—leaving his scars unseen. "You think you're so tough?" he asked, slamming his fist against her ribs.

For the first time in her life, something snapped in Marley. If she didn't do something, he might well kill them both.

Still trembling, she reached for her oversized mug of cocoa. And she walked the few steps to them. She chose her angle carefully. And when she flung the twenty-four ounces of scalding cocoa over his face and neck, not a drop landed on her grandmother.

His anguished screams were not enough for her. She bashed the heavy ceramic mug into his temple, and he collapsed.

"Marley!"

Her trembling grew violent as she collapsed in a heap. It was the first time that she'd stood up to this man who'd terrorized them for two decades.

Nan took her in her arms, holding her close. The older woman wiped her tears away. "Don't cry, lass."

Her English accent—that musical trill that reminded her of her own mother, that sound that she'd thought had been washed out of the woman when she became a Virginian—comforted Marley.

She withdrew from Hannah, looking at the man, who still lay where she'd cold-cocked him and destroyed her favorite mug. An ordinary mug wouldn't have done this much damage; this, from her employer's gift shop, was stoneware, more like an ale tankard. God bless colonial craftsmanship.

"Is he dead, do you think?"

Nan leaned over him. "No, more's the pity. He's passed out. Likely better off than us, won't even remember it tomorrow." She straightened. "Nor will we. Get dressed and get your bag. We're leaving. And be sure to pack the book."

She didn't have to say which book.

As they stood on the gravel pathway under the shelter of the ancient oak in the front yard, Nan looked back at Stonefield, the simple stone home where her family had lived for three centuries. The night was silent, but for the chirping of crickets.

"We'll have to get a court order to get him out," Marley said.

Nan turned and smiled as if she hadn't spoken, holding out a hand toward the car. "Shall we?"

Chapter Two

In the dank coolness of the night, Marley pulled the car to the side of the deserted road long enough to make a phone call. She called her employer in Williamsburg to find out if there were any empty rooms she might book at a discount. There were several in their finest hotel. Even at a discount it was beyond her budget, but this was vacation—and it was during Publick Times, so she was lucky to get anything. So she refused to dwell on distractions like finances and reality.

Neither woman noticed the bell captain who stood at the door watching their approach. He'd held this job for half a dozen years and had acquired an appreciation of expensive suits and jewelry and luggage. He had seen Marley turn into the drive in a fifteen-year-old sedan and bypass the valet, and when he offered to have someone take their luggage, he did so warmly but without insistence when the younger woman declined.

Sarah, the desk clerk, welcomed them, recognizing Marley. They had attended orientation together three years ago and remained cordial co-workers. "Oh, having a staycation?"

"Just thought it'd be nice to see how the other half lives. We're headed to Florida tomorrow."

Sarah glanced around and leaned forward to whisper. "I slipped in a VIP package. You get Godiva chocolates and flowers and a bottle of wine."

Nan's eyebrows rose. "How lovely! And you get to share these romantic trappings with your grandmother!"

The women laughed, and Marley felt the oppressiveness begin to leave her. It seemed she'd spent the past ten years worried about either money, or Jimmy, or both. She deserved a week off.

"Chris!" snapped the clerk.

The bell captain, inside now and behind his stand scribbling in a book, looked up.

"Well what are you *waiting* for?" she asked with a slow smile. "Take these ladies' bags to their room."

He leapt forward, apologizing at his oversight, even as Marley sent Sarah a scathing look. Sarah merely raised her eyebrows and smiled.

On their way to the room, she dug in her purse for a tip. He opened the door, handed her two passkeys, and walked before her into the room to place the suitcases horizontally on two folding stands.

He walked to a table in a small seating area and removed the champagne from its bucket.

Frozen by the opulence of the place, she continued to stare.

"May I?" He held out the bottle for her inspection.

"Oh, please!"

Nan watched him anxiously. He poured a splash into a glass and gave it to her. After a moment, she tasted it. "Thank you."

"Is it to your liking, madam?"

Tears came to Nan's eyes as she bowed her head and nodded silently.

He filled her glass and Marley's, then replaced the bottle in the bucket.

"Enjoy your stay at the Williamsburg Inn."

When she attempted to press two dollars into his hand, knowing it wasn't enough, he smiled at her with genuine warmth. "No, it's truly my pleasure. Have a relaxing evening."

He closed the door behind her, and any lingering bruised pride she might have felt was soothed by the very aura of the room. The mugginess of the tidewater was gone, and a faintly pleasant aroma she couldn't identify lightly scented the air. The lighting was just bright enough to reveal the gleaming antiques, and just soft enough that she could feel the stress physically leaving her.

An arrangement of tulips and daffodils, brilliant red and yellow, stood on a low-boy underneath a gilt-edged mirror, a focal point in the large room full of 1930s era finery. Two full mahogany beds with sea foam and sea glass dressings filled one side of the room. A loveseat and two chairs comprised the small seating area, their paisley cream-on-cream embossing elegant and inviting.

She had looked forward to their road trip tomorrow for months. They were traveling to Florida, and staying in a unique seaside hotel in St. Augustine. Supposedly, it had been created from an actual shipwreck from the late 1700s.

She had invited her stepfather, grudgingly, and had been thrilled when he mocked the invitation. "Do I *look* like a sea captain?" he'd asked.

No, she agreed, that he did not.

Which was ironic, considering that the man loved sailing, and the few pleasant memories she had of him were when she was younger and he taught her to sail.

But as much as she had looked forward to tomorrow, at this moment Marley simply stood there enjoying *now*. She breathed in deeply. And for the second time that night, just for a moment, she stopped to love life.

The women both showered quickly, reluctant to waste a moment of the luxury. Now, Nan sat on the loveseat, peering at the label on the small bottle of complementary hand lotion. She squeezed a dollop into her palm and set the bottle aside.

Marley stood at the window, peeking past the drapes into the parking lot below. "Are you sure Jimmy was okay?"

Nan smoothed the lotion over her forearms and into her elbows. "Yes. Come and sit down. I have a small gift for you."

She sank to the loveseat beside Nan, resting her hands at her sides, moving her fingertips over the softness of the elegant upholstery.

Nan withdrew from her purse a small, round silver box, perhaps an inch and a half in diameter, and half an inch deep. Marley had seen it many times over her life, but she had no idea of its contents. She'd asked as a child. Nan had replied that it was a "silver repousse pillbox." After a series of follow-up questions, she understood in more detail that *repousse* was French for *none of your business, Miss Nosy.*

Now, Nan held the box in her hands. She raised it to her lips, as if it were a religious relic or icon. When she held it out to Marley, her eyes glistened.

"Remember when I used to say, 'when you're older'? Well, the time has come."

Marley opened her hand, and Nan placed the box there. She wasn't sure what to make of Nan's emotional state; it might have everything to do with this box, or she might simply be upset over Jimmy. She gave a small smile, waiting for Nan to explain, but the woman only gave a nod toward the box.

Marley pressed the fragile clasp, and the top opened.

The sound of her mother's voice echoed in her memory as she read to Marley the engraving on the back of a locket she'd once worn. *As time is, so beats our hearts—tender, immortal, forever.*

Marley had repeated the phrase until she had it committed to memory, thinking it magical. Then, when her mother cuddled her, Marley would take the small locket in her chubby fingers and turn it over, pretending to read it. *"As time is…"*

How her two daughters had loved it when their father had given it to their mother that Christmas. It was the grandest thing, shaped like a Valentine! Rachel, especially, held it and stroked it as if it were the dearest thing in the world.

Now, Marley once again saw the portrait she'd thought never again to see, cradled within the pillbox. It was quite like the portrait she already had of her grandmother. In a moment she traveled back in time more than two decades to a hot summer night in a farmhouse.

She shouldn't still remember those days; she'd only been three then. She'd been like any middle sister, not big enough to do the things Mama allowed Rachel to do, but too big to be cradled and doted on like little Juliana.

But those last days with her sisters were as clear as yesterday.

She and Rachel had traded off looking after Julie while the other stole into the chicken house at the farm next door, borrowing eggs. They knew better than to steal, and they were sure that as soon as Mama and Daddy came for them, they would be so happy to find their girls that they would gladly pay the farmer for the eggs.

They never came. But eventually the girls were rescued and taken to a place where they were all together. And then—and then, the unthinkable. Someone had taken Juliana away. Then Rachel. Nan had come, but it was too late. The only one left was Marley, crying endlessly, terrified of the dark for months, then years. She still avoided it.

And then, fainter, came a happier memory.

"Do you remember what I did?" Marley asked.

"You pilfered the locket from your mother's jewelry box, for your sister's birthday."

They laughed together. "I didn't really know what stealing was, then. Rachel sure straightened me out when she opened my present. She was only six, and she was already a bossy thing. I didn't know! I just knew how much Rachel loved the locket. Mama was so kind about it, just letting her have it."

"How did the portraits get separated from the locket?"

Marley sobered. "Rachel gave them to me to cheer me up before we left the house. I put them in my pocket. And now, I guess there's only this one left. I truly don't know where the other one went. I don't think I lost it. Rachel had told me to make sure and take care of them until Mama and Daddy came, and … oh, Nan, she was so smart, such a good big sister! She was just distracting me from my grief. We really did think, back then, that they were coming back for us."

Nan's tears were silent, as they'd come to be over the years. Marley suspected she did it to keep from upsetting her. In a way, it worked. She had no idea how often her grandmother cried.

She closed the pillbox and moved to the other bed, comforting Nan, sharing their sorrow. "I'm sorry, I know it was hard for you, losing your own daughter."

"And I loved Rob as my own son. He was a fine and brave man. And Marley, they loved you so. You're just like your father, interested in things that mattered in history, trying to help people, clever and true."

They fell silent, and Marley again opened the pillbox, withdrawing the portrait and examining it. Her older sister, as a happy young girl—the portraits completed before the birth of their younger sister. The lost miniature had been of Marley.

"I just wish—" She arrested her own speech.

"Wish what?"

"It doesn't matter. But I do wish I knew, somehow, where they are, Rachel and Juliana."

Nan looked at her a little too quickly. "Marley, how much do you remember of your childhood?"

"Everything."

"And when I came to get you ... just after that?"

"That's a little fuzzier. I do remember being pretty clingy. After everything that had happened, I was terrified something might happen to you. I remember you holding Julie, but that must have been ... well, before. And I remember you putting her down and then running back after you, thinking you were leaving us. That must have been a bad dream."

Nan nodded, swallowing down emotion, patting her hand. "You have been my only joy for the past twenty years. I miss your parents and your sisters as you do, my love."

"I've looked for both of them, but I can't find them. No Rachel or Juliana Hastings anywhere in Virginia. At least, not the right ages. With social media, I'd think I'd be able to find them almost anywhere in the world."

Nan wiped her eyes. "I will never understand why the state agencies made the decisions they made. But I am grateful for the blessing you've been in my life."

She patted Marley's shoulder on her way to the restroom. When she emerged, she left the light on and pushed the door only partway closed.

Despite her excitement over the portraits, Marley quickly fell asleep. And she dreamed, for the first time in years, of the sisters she'd loved—and still missed.

They were back in the old deserted farmhouse where they'd hidden. Marley and Rachel were playing games with Julie as their very own, real live doll. The girls waited patiently for their mother and father to come and pick them up.

And eventually someone had: police officers, tending to them with gentleness and kindness, something in their eyes as they looked at the three little girls, something that made Marley feel uncomfortable. Although she thought they meant to comfort her, it only made her feel bad. Years would pass before she understood that the emotion in the officers' gazes was *pity*. And it became a look she could not bear in life—anyone's pity.

Then came the next day, the worst day of life Marley could remember—after all, she'd mercifully blotted out that other, awful day. No, the worst day she could remember was the day she realized she was alone, that Rachel and Juliana were both gone. The only part of the day that softened the blow was when Nan took her home, broken-hearted when she wasn't allowed to take the other girls.

She awakened early in the unfamiliar luxury of the hotel, plagued with the memories of her sisters. Nan still slept as she left for a short morning of work, and she had to shake away the lingering realism of the dream. For in her dream, she and her sisters were together—and they were playing in that same, ancient, rock house she had left the night before. Playing with their parents, just as they all had before their parents were murdered.

Chapter Three

The sun was high and bright over the Virginia tidewater. In the distance, a cannon boomed. Marley strolled down Duke of Gloucester Street, a wide-brimmed, beribboned straw sunbonnet shielding her from the heat. Charcoal-gray skirts, covered with a white apron, brushed the dusty street, and she smiled at two women as they passed.

Perhaps her age or a little older, the women strolled along the street with an older couple, talking and laughing. Both statuesque, they looked like they'd stepped out of a sophisticated women's business magazine, dressed in elegantly casual clothing. One of the women was a stunning African-American beauty with short hair, joy beaming from her face.

The other woman met Marley's gaze when she smiled at her, then they moved on. She was riveted to the spot, however, and captured in the moment when the woman had looked directly at her. Something about her was familiar; she knew her. It was more than the riotous dark curls bundled up into a French twist. She knew those eyes, that laughter.

Marley shook her head. The woman hadn't given her a second glance, no recognition had sparked in her hazel eyes. And then she knew who she reminded her of.

Rachel.

She couldn't have been Rachel, because her sister would have recognized her, wouldn't she? Even after all these years, she would have known her face. She had been the older girl when they parted; at six, she would have remembered Marley.

The very idea made no sense, and with a bit of embarrassment, she swallowed down the old grief as it came to her. They'd kept telling her—her grandmother, her doctor— that eventually she'd get used to it.

They lied. She never adjusted to losing her family. Her sisters hadn't died—they'd just been taken away, without warning, by people who determined Nan wasn't capable of raising three young girls. Just Marley, it seemed.

As a small child, too young for such things, she'd begun observing her sisters' birthdays. Even though she was no longer exactly sure of the date. Even though both her sisters had new families now, she never gave up hoping to see them again. Rachel was twenty-eight by now. Juliana, twenty-two.

So, in fact, it did make sense, in an unsatisfying logic, that she'd imagined seeing her own dear sister in the streets they'd once run along as small children with their parents.

She shook off the memories and made her way to the tour group waiting for her in front of Raleigh Tavern.

"Ladies and gentlemen, you stand before a simple colonial tavern, and an important historic landmark. It's the first building that was reconstructed as a part of John David Rockefeller's philanthropic effort to save Williamsburg. It also happens to be the location where members of the House of Burgesses met after they were dissolved by the royal governor. And it was *also* a place where Patrick Henry, Thomas Jefferson, and other patriots just liked to hang—mostly to discuss how to avoid *being* hanged."

Polite chuckles came from the crowd.

"Construction in the nineteenth and twentieth centuries damaged many of the archaeological footprints that would have aided our research. However, there are still many underlying treasures that tell us how life was lived in the eighteenth century.

"Let me tell you a little about myself. Growing up, I always loved Williamsburg. In fact, it was here that I first discovered archaeology and its ability to help us time travel, if you will, into the past, where we can learn more about ourselves. And it was archaeologists who enabled us all to enjoy Williamsburg as it was nearly three centuries ago."

A young boy of perhaps five years old was intent on her, a sheen of sweat on his pink cheeks from the morning's humidity. *Poor little guy, trying his best to understand her gibberish.*

A smile lit his face as she looked at him, and she reached into the cooler left on the steps for this purpose, quickly passing out icy-cold water bottles to her group. The boy was interested and eager-to-please—or else simply charmed by her weird outfit.

"If the children in the group would like to come forward." She smiled, gesturing them toward her.

Their parents hastily shepherded them into a small group. There were three young boys and two young girls ranging up to perhaps twelve years old. A boy of about 10 fiddled with a video game, and his mother took it away from him. Marley expected a scene, but he merely glowered at his mother.

She cast a glance toward the edge of the historic street where they stood and noticed an old, smashed bottle cap, embedded in the dirt. *Thank God for litterers.*

"You there, young man."

Gameboy glanced up, startled. "Me?"

"Pick that up for me, will you? There, in the dirt."

He found her target. "It's stuck."

From her pocket she produced gloves and a small trowel. "Here. Wear these to protect your hands."

The other children gathered around him.

"Dig at the dirt. Avoid the spoil."

"Spoil?"

"As in prize, or loot. Have you never heard of pirates?"

"Yes! I have a video game!"

"Ah, I thought you might. What you're doing now is what archaeologists do at a dig. What have you removed there?"

"Just a bottle cap."

"I see. Might someone use it to cap a drink now?"

"No, it's old and used and dirty."

"Now, pass it around to the others, then pass it back to me. Who can tell me something about the person who tossed that bottle cap there?"

After a moment of expectant silence, the boy who'd dug it out said, "They liked root beer."

"How do you know that?"

"It says 'root beer' on it. So either they liked it, or the store was out of everything else."

"So you examined the artifact. Then you correctly deduced that they drank what they enjoyed, or what they were able to find. People can't survive long without liquids."

She accepted the cap from the last child who examined it, and she held it up vertically for the children to examine. The outer ridges had been pressed completely flat.

"What else? Do you think someone dropped this bottle cap this morning?"

One by one, the children shook their heads. "Why?"

Silence, filled in finally by an older girl. "It's flat and worn. A lot of people have walked on it."

"Does anyone know what this is?"

"Rust," said the same girl.

"Do we know what causes rust?"

"Water!" sang another girl, perhaps eight years old. The man behind her, likely her father, smiled.

"Very good!" Marley said, impressed.

"My daddy's a mechanical engineer," she gushed. The older girl looked down at her, nudging her to shut up, clearly her older sister.

The youngest boy who Marley had first noticed cried out over her, "He's my daddy, too!"

Marley was one of those guides who loved the moments when children overran the conversation in excitement. It meant they were engaged. Likely, the precocious younger girl rarely got a word in edgewise in a family of smart children.

"Does steel rust overnight?" she asked.

The brainiacs went silent. The older sister shook her head.

"That's right, it takes longer for something to rust. So we know that this has been here a while. Is there anything else we know about the person who left this behind?"

"They don't care about the earth." That middle child chimed in again, walking right up to Marley. "One time my cousin got a drink that had rust on the bottle. Where your mouth goes. My aunt yelled at the store guy."

Several people laughed, and the father picked up his little girl.

"Yes. It tells us this person littered. Perhaps they were thoughtless, or they tripped and lost it. We can't always judge what's in people's hearts by the evidence they leave behind. But we can tell how they lived. We can tell what they ate, how they cooked it, the pots they cooked it in, and the dishes they ate it on. In just a few minutes we'll be up at the Prentis Store. Those of you who are interested in digging at an actual archaeological site may do so there. In fact, although the dig exhibit was created with children in mind, we're surprised at the number of adults who enjoy participating."

The tour continued until they arrived at the Prentis Store, where they stopped to allow those who wanted to join the next dig session. And something happened that she'd never seen before.

Her entire group left for the dig. Marley concealed her disappointment as the family with the four children passed.

The mother, a woman perhaps in her late thirties, paused, resting her hand over Marley's upper arm. "Anyone who can engage my Noah with a simple bottle cap is nothing short of a miracle-worker."

With that reassurance, Marley headed back to her office, eager for some lab time.

Just that month, in an area not far from an old battle site in the Great Dismal Swamp, an ancient ship had been discovered square in the middle of a construction site. The project was beyond the scope of her employer, but she had been drafted to quickly capture the site by scans. The fresh history dropped into her lap was too much to pass up on.

In the office, she removed her sunbonnet and placed it on the hat rack, then opened her laptop, logging on.

She loaded the latest scan, one a co-worker had taken early that morning, and began scrolling through the images.

She slowly panned through the ship as best she could. Much of it had collapsed one level on the next, however, like a house of cards flattening. One image, just below the top deck, captured her attention, and she zoomed in on the area.

Enlarging it even greater still, she peered at what she thought she saw. Indeed, it appeared to be human remains, near the stern. She could see a cracked skull and a ribcage.

After looking up the number, she reached for the phone and dialed. "Coroner's office, Seth speaking."

When she finally got the medical examiner on the phone, she introduced herself. "I'm working on a scan for the Norfolk dig. An eighteenth century ship was found there."

"Yes, I've read about that."

"Well, it appears there may be human remains in the ship."

"Really?" He received this news much as Marley had received the news about the discovery of the ship.

"Yes. Of course, the owner of the land is on a contractor's timeline, so they're anxious to have this resolved."

"Oh, don't worry about that. I'm always ready to get my hands down in the muck. Does it look to be recent remains?"

"I can't tell. I'm looking at the 3D model. But I doubt it."

"Fine. I'll head over there in just a few."

She hung up the phone and decided to go, too. This might be the last time she was allowed in the dig—if indeed she were. Medical examiners had a way of shutting things down, turning a dig into a crime scene—as if the seaman had died last week.

But she had one last bit of research to do before she left the office. She wasn't sure why she hadn't thought of it before. She'd certainly used the database for research while attending school at William & Mary, but the relevance of the eighteenth-century Virginia Gazette archived there to the story of the

Trelawneys who'd once lived in Williamsburg had simply never occurred to her. What must have happened during the period of that missing journal had distracted her for years. It had covered possibly the most exciting period in American history.

She tried a few searches with no relevant results. *Rosalie Plantation* (and every imaginable variant), *Ruth Trelawney, Trelawneys, Rosalie 1776, Trelawny, Trelawnie ...*

She leaned back, staring at the database screen in frustration.

With a sigh, she began searching random words. *Rachel, Julie, Marley, Hastings. Rosalie.*

Trio vanish.

Her heart skipped a beat, and she clicked on the article. None of the girls' names were there—apparently *Hastings* and *Rosalie* had brought it up.

> *Three people disappeared from a tobacco plantation in the area according to a man said to be visiting the manager of the plantation.*
>
> *The man's story could only be backed up by a Negro woman who works for Mr. Hastings, a woman named Ruth. Although she corroborated his story, she provided few details beyond what the gentleman said:*
>
> *"I was at a distance, approaching the house where my associate lives and conducts business. The Negro woman was shouting after them—I couldn't understand her, but one of them turned and pushed her quite forcefully. Entirely without provocation! She lost her balance and stumbled several yards away. Then they commenced to cross over the threshold and into the ruins of the old Rosalie mansion and disappeared. The Negro woman scrambled up, screaming, and ran away in affright. I have no explanation for what I saw."*
>
> *Those at Rosalie rebuffed our overtures to learn more.*

Marley shut down her laptop, bewildered. What was she to make of that? People disappearing into thin air?

She headed to Norfolk quickly and arrived at the dig, finding it cluttered with police cruisers and a county van that likely belonged to the coroner. She parked beside the van just in time for a pair of men to emerge carrying a covered stretcher. She eyed it eagerly.

"Ma'am, you can't be here," an officer said, approaching.

"I'm with the archaeology team working on the site."

"Until the M.E. is finished, you'll need to leave."

"Yes, sir." At that moment a young man walked along toward the van, gazing into a plastic bin he carried.

"Seth?"

He looked up, and she introduced herself, glancing casually into the bin as he arrived. It looked like just a handful of items. An ancient knife of some sort, a pistol, and some mud-stained jewelry—a cross and a dove, on a chain.

This area of Virginia had been teeming with navy vessels in the eighteenth century, primarily the Royal Navy. She would have liked another look at the pistol he'd unearthed—although she could certainly view it in the scan, it was an entirely different experience to have one's hands in the earth, on the items that our ancestors had once used.

"Are you through with the site?" she asked.

"No, not yet."

"Can you tell anything about the remains?"

"Looks like a man, probably the ship's captain. In the stern, he might've been in the captain's cabin—or even standing on deck when the ship went down. Beyond that, we won't know anything this afternoon. And you'll have to notify the State Archaeologist. I'll have these items in our office when they're ready for them. We're calling him the Lost Sea Captain."

Chapter Four

Marley headed back to the hotel. The legends of Rosalie, the tobacco plantation on the James River, had charmed her for as long as she could remember. Considering she'd grown up in the area as well as attending school here, it was striking that she'd never visited the place. But when she read the legend of the disappearing trio—and Ruth Trelawney's involvement— she was afire with curiosity. She still wanted to stop by before they left for Florida, but she was already running late.

She found Nan in their room on her phone. Their suitcases sat at the end of the bed.

"Jimmy, I just don't think I can do that right now. And no, of course I'm not upset that you're still alive. To tell you the truth, I knew you were passed out, and so …"

And so it goes, Marley thought as Nan glanced at her.

Marley pointed at her watch. Nan nodded absently, and she looked once more through their small room. She wished she'd had more time to linger this morning over coffee in one of the soft robes that came with the room—the sort of thing Audrey Hepburn wore in old movies.

Even the toiletries were brands she'd never have bought herself. She swept the counter free of the extra soaps and conditioners. Then her face stung, and she put them back where she'd found them. Was it so much? Just a little shampoo. They smelled so sweet, as she imagined an island paradise. She'd heard it was included in the price of the room.

Nan would disapprove, though. At times, she resented Nan her good heart. But it was that good heart that had taken care of Marley these twenty years. So she set it out of her mind and returned to the bedroom.

She closed their suitcases and placed them by the door. Nan ignored her, caught up in Jimmy's false promises. She crossed her arms, tapped her foot. Nothing. Then she lugged both suitcases down the hall, the muscle between her shoulders knotted. At the front door, the bellman—a different one, this morning—held the door for a striking silver-haired man who stepped aside when he noticed her.

Blinded to her approach by the wealthy man at the door, the bellman misunderstood the man's hesitation and leapt into the doorway to take his luggage. She sighed at the exhausting niceties of chivalry and civilization and waited.

The older man touched the bellman's sleeve, pressing him aside so she could pass. "Oh, miss! Let me get those for you!" the bellman, embarrassed, said. "I'll be right with you."

"Thank you, I can manage."

She locked the suitcases in the trunk and headed back inside to wait for Nan. Glancing at her watch, she resisted the temptation to go back upstairs.

Finally Nan appeared at the grand staircase. Never had her regal bearing shown more clearly than as she descended the stairs. Marley moved into line behind the well-dressed gentleman she'd passed earlier in the doorway.

"Yes, Mr. Sheppard," the clerk was saying. "Your daughter Rachel's checked in, but I believe they're in the historic area this morning. No one's answering."

"Could you call my cell when they check in for messages?"

Another clerk appeared and gestured to Marley, someone she didn't know. "We're ready to check out. Room 1746." She slid the passkeys across the counter to the woman, and the woman scanned the key and began printing a receipt.

The gentleman glanced over. She met his gaze. He smiled and nodded in acknowledgment, then looked away. So did she. Yet she could still feel his gaze on her still.

Nan appeared in the doorway. "I'm quite uncertain why you're in such a hurry. It isn't as if we're on a date with destiny. Colonial shipwrecks aren't going anywhere."

The man—Sheppard—turned to look at Nan as if the Queen had arrived opposite him. Marley couldn't see his expression, but his body language spoke volumes. He froze, as many men did around Nan; she was a stunning woman who still turned heads.

Marley accepted the receipt from the woman and turned away, folding it and slipping it inside her bag.

With an expectant half-smile, she approached Nan, glancing back at the man to catch his expression. Then her smile slipped away as she saw the subtle exchange between them. They knew each other.

"Nan?"

But her grandmother had already turned away as if she hadn't seen the man, tying a scarf over her hair and walking to the door.

"Excuse me," Sheppard said. "I think you worked at my company?"

She sent him a withering glance and spoke with an affected Southern accent. "Begging your pardon, sir, you are mistaken. Good day."

Her grandmother was afraid of this man. And as much as she knew about Jimmy, an abusive lunatic who Nan *wasn't* afraid of, what did it say for this guy? They had to get out of there.

She smiled at the man as she ushered Nan toward the door. "You've confused my mother with someone else. She works only in philanthropy. Enjoy your day."

"My mistake," he said, giving a courtly half-bow that somehow disturbed her. It was the sort of old-world gesture that usually charmed her.

And with that, they left the lobby.

"We need to get out of here—quickly," Nan whispered.

"Who is he?"

"Not now. Let's go."

She felt his eyes on them even as they climbed in Marley's old Camry. Not exactly the conveyance of a pampered philanthropic princess. As they headed toward the exit, Sheppard loped toward the front of the car, waving.

In a heartbeat, Nan leaned over and pressed Marley's right knee, flooring the accelerator. With the other, she grabbed the wheel, jerking the car away from him. The fender brushed the man's blazer and the car drove over the opposite curb.

"Go!"

A gardener leapt out of her way, sending a tray of red and yellow pansies flying like colored shards in a kaleidoscope. Fear and adrenaline flooded her. She yanked the wheel in the opposite direction, landing Nan against her own car door.

Marley righted the car as it lurched drunkenly down the drive and gunned it toward the exit, her breath coming fast.

"What the hell?" she cried as they turned out of the elegant entryway, narrowly missing an oncoming truck.

Disoriented, she had to think fast to remember where she was headed, and she made a left.

Nan shrieked. "Where the devil are you going?"

"To Florida! Weren't we?"

Nan's green eyes had a fire that Marley had never seen. In fact, she had never seen any of this side of Nan before now.

"Oh. I thought—you were going home. It's the way home. Well then. Look out!"

A careless tourist nearly walked right in front of her on his way to Christiana Campbell's tavern. He stopped short, then took a few steps backward, glaring open-mouthed at her as she went by—as if she were indeed insane.

She looked in the rearview mirror, saw nothing but an empty street, and slowed down before she continued on toward Richmond.

"Are you all right?"

Nan nodded, staring out her window.

"What was that all about?"

"Just go! He's right behind us."

"There's no one behind us."

"You don't see him, but he's there. He's always there."

They were only halfway to the freeway when once again, Nan's scream rang out. "There he is!"

Marley looked in the rearview mirror. Sure enough, a black sedan grew progressively larger there.

"Please hurry!"

"Who is this man?"

"Marley, you'll learn soon enough. For now, please just *hurry!*"

She floored it as she took the curve to the freeway, and fortunately traffic was light. When she looked again behind her, the black sedan was gone.

A rock song rang out on Nan's cell phone. *I Fought the Law.* Jimmy's ringtone.

"Hello, dear!" Nan sang into the phone.

Marley's guts were like a basket of cobras. Her grandmother might have been sitting in a parlor having tea and crumpets with the bastard who beat the crap out of her every night.

Her face a mask of indifference, Marley pressed a stiffened index finger on the Down power window button, lowering the front windows at once. The highway breeze rushed in, startling Nan. Marley lightly took the phone, switched it to her throwing hand, and flung it over the car toward the woods at the edge of the highway. Aerodynamics took care of the rest. In the rearview mirror, with satisfaction, she watched it fly, land, and shatter.

She mashed the Up button and exhaled slowly and audibly, relieved that the rush of adrenaline was at last spent. The windows closed, enclosing them in silence.

"I'm sorry about your phone." Nan had so very little.

"It was wicked of you."

"Yes, it was. And it's wicked of him to keep you on a leash twenty-four seven. You deserve better than that awful man. I am too old for the denial and the drama. I simply want peace. Don't you?"

"What would you have me do, Marley? Poke about for gentlemen callers on your computer?"

"No. Just do things that interest you, and maybe you'll meet someone with those interests. Why do you have to have a man, anyway? They seem to be more trouble than they're worth."

She couldn't say the words, but it seemed some women put up with an awful lot to avoid being alone. Nan had proven herself to be one of them.

Nan gazed down at the palm of her hand, rubbing it with her other thumb as if blotting out a stain.

"Jimmy was there at a terrible time in my life. I hoped he'd be a good father for you."

"You have got to be kidding me."

"He *is* a good man when he's sober."

"Which is when?"

Nan sighed. "Fathers are important in a young girl's life. As a lass growing up, I didn't know mine. But later I lived with my father-in-law, and he was the best father anyone could know. He wasn't perfect, either—distant and brusque. But I loved him, and I hoped the same for you, in Jimmy. For years I have only pitied him. There is no love for him in me."

"You don't ... ? Well, what the ..." *What the hell is he doing sitting in our house guzzling beer and chips right now?* Marley cut off the pointless question.

"Child, you are not like me. You are complete, independent, resourceful. You do not need a man."

She bristled at this, even though she knew Nan had meant it as a compliment, considering their conversation. She might have said she lacked the hunger to be held and loved.

"You've always supported that guy! I don't know anyone more resourceful than you. You run a daycare and a staff of half a dozen, *and* you somehow eke out a living doing it."

"Money is but a meager resource when inner fortitude is lacking."

Marley sighed. Bromides were code for *end of discussion.*

So she retreated into her thoughts, her search for logic.

Only when they were on the other side of Richmond—when Nan had folded a pillow underneath her head and snuggled under a throw, snoozing against her door—did Marley remember she'd forgotten she wanted to stop by Rosalie on their way out of town. Darn. It would have to wait until they got home from their adventure.

And only much later, when they were well into Georgia and stopped to fill the tank one last time, did she connect two troubling details. She remembered that moment this morning when she'd glimpsed a woman who'd reminded her of her lost sister, Rachel. And past that, to the mundane conversation between the desk clerk and the man Sheppard.

"Your daughter Rachel's checked in, but I believe they're in the historic area this morning."

Chapter Five

The storm came upon them without warning. They all had good excuses for not noticing, but still it came.

Marley had two decades of self-defense walling her off from the modern world and its threats, and she was intent on relaxing. Just one week to herself without fear.

Nan had no choice. Marley had destroyed her only link to an illusion of control. Without her phone, she was adrift.

The ship's crew followed their captain, a capable and arrogant sort who had little use for the opinions of his men.

And the captain? Well, his wife was in New York visiting her mother, and he was in his cabin impressing his mistress.

So the ship's dozen passengers began their cruise lounging about the sloop as they approached Mayaguana, one of the few unpolished jewels left in the Caribbean.

Virginia Beach was the only beach Marley had ever known, and her lowered expectations made the Bahamian waters the most pleasant of surprises. Virginia Beach's usual state, after all, was gray. Gray clouds matching gray aircraft carriers and destroyers cruising in and out of the gray port of Norfolk. Even the sand was gray.

By the time she retired to the deck with sunscreen and a spy thriller, the Caribbean palette of turquoise and aqua emerged.

She sat on the deck of the *Island Girl* with a plastic cup of rum punch, recalling trips to the beach with her family. They would sit under an umbrella in the sand and count the sails glimmering on the water while Mama reapplied sunscreen and fed them chicken nuggets and sliced oranges and watermelon.

Once, a gull had swooped in out of nowhere, grabbing Rachel's finger sandwich. She had shrieked, hunger sharpening her surprise into an angry howl. Then Marley had screamed with laughter at the absurdity of it all—not helping matters.

Sometimes they buried Daddy in the sand while he recounted to them the historic trivia surrounding Norfolk. He had once been a sailor, as had his own father, and he told them of the early days of the sword that was the American Navy, forged in Boston, hardened at Norfolk, and tempered at Yorktown. As much as Rachel had loved her father, she had never cared for their earliest college lectures. *"Daddy, let's go to the amusement park! Please? Last time you said ..."*

Daddy had no interest in such frivolity. And so Rachel retired under the umbrella with Mama, leaving Marley to the important task of heaping piles of sand upon their father. It had been on one of these trips that her father had begun to teach her how to hold her breath underwater for long periods of time. She loved their ocean trips for she had his complete attention, and she soaked up every word as he explained the simple story of people who weren't treated fairly by their king.

For Marley, these stories were like fairy tales, complete with brave-hearted knights and villains and pretty ladies. John Adams and his cousin Sam, Patrick Henry, George Washington, Crispus Attucks. Abigail Adams, Martha Washington, Sally Hemings. The villains, King George, General Gage, Admiral Graves, Governor Dunmore, and General Cornwallis—all rich and well-dressed and angry with the pesky little farmers and peasants who dared to raise their voice against the King and demand equality.

The only blot in the romance of the stories of America's founding was its slavery—and these stories, Daddy told with such striking realism that they made her cry. He spoke of small children on slave ships, and the death and disease the people encountered on the middle passage between Africa, the Americas, and Europe.

Sitting here now as a ribbon of dark clouds formed far on the distant horizon, Marley marveled. Why had it taken her so long to realize why she had become a historian?

Where many children found historic dates to be dull, meaningless numerals signifying nothing except stressful exams, they were for her like dollhouses or toy garages opening to a world of philosophy her father had taught her to love.

Nan had summed up such things with the brusque admonition, "Marley-love, you're an odd bird."

She wasn't odd, she thought as she rose to her feet for a refill. She was her father's daughter.

"Careful, love, you're not a drinker. And would you refill mine. Please and thank you."

Marley stopped to grin at her.

"What? I am most certainly a drinker. Can't you see?"

She returned and passed Nan her cold pink punch and sipped her own. Calypso and zydeco music filled the air, and she lay back in her lounge, stretching in the warmth of the sun.

"Nan?"

"Yes, love."

She turned to see Nan's reaction, obscured though it was behind oversized sunglasses. "Who's Rachel Sheppard?"

Only the slightest lift of her head betrayed Nan's lie. The idea of Nan lying disappointed her, she didn't hear her words.

"I'm sorry, I missed that."

"I said I've never heard the name before."

That much must be true. Surely she wasn't so adept a liar.

"Why do you ask?"

She gave her a direct and utterly inscrutable smile. "No reason. Just wondering."

Nan closed her book. "Yes, but why were you wondering? It's rather an odd question, out of the blue."

"The fellow you're so afraid of has a daughter named Rachel."

"And?"

"It's an odd coincidence, don't you think?"

"How so?"

"Nan, do you have any idea how frustrating it is to ask you the simplest of questions?"

"What do you mean, dear?"

Argggh.

A man in an elegant, pale blue seersucker suit carrying a martini hesitated at the seat beside Nan. "Is this lounge taken?"

Nan raised her head to see past the brim of her straw hat, and Marley watched with interest. Tall and slim, he was dressed with effortless, understated style. He looked like a kindly grandfather dressed for a summer wedding. Exactly the sort of fellow Nan needed.

"Please, join us. I'm Marley, and this is my …" She held out her hand as he sat.

Nan rose, silencing her with a touch of her hand. Then she smiled at the gentleman. "Feel free, I was just going inside."

And with that, she did.

"If you'll excuse me, I must …"

Go get my grandmother's head examined.

They found privacy in a guest lounge off the dining saloon. Nan sat in a stiff-backed chair, removing her hat and setting it aside, then resumed her reading. Marley closed the door and sipped again from her drink.

"Don't you think you've had quite enough of that?"

Her disapproval would have been enough, on any ordinary day, to have shut Marley down. None too ironically, seeing the world through rum-colored glasses showed a view less inclined to guilt. She sipped the drink again, meeting Nan's gaze.

"First you interrupt an important phone call. For the first time, Jimmy truly regretted his actions."

Marley snorted. "You're joking. He does that *every* time."

Nan gazed at a painting of a seagull. "Then you take a phone I can't afford to replace and destroy it in a tantrum."

"I am sorry for that, and I'll replace it. Wait. No, I'm not sorry. At least for a few days, we have a respite from that—that animal. Isn't it nice to relax, without worrying about him pestering you? Without flinching each time he raises his hand to pick up his beer?"

Nan looked at her, clearly surprised that Marley could observe the obvious.

"And then there was that perfectly nice man just now—"

"Oh, yes, that unctuous character with his flimflammery!"

Marley laughed, then immediately stifled herself. "You mean, 'is this seat taken?' That flimflammery?"

"Marley, I am not a young woman looking for the pretty lies of happily ever after—"

"Well, Nan ..." Marley bowed her head, then met the older woman's eyes. "I am."

Nan stared back at her, the anger draining away.

"You're beautiful and men have loved you. You've raised a daughter and a granddaughter. But Nan, I'm so tired of being alone—of hiding in a dark closet. All of my classmates are marrying, having their first child—or second—or traveling the world, visiting exciting places. All I've done is work and study and live in the past. I've been working for 10 years now. I'm not beautiful, I'm ordinary and plain and odd—"

In a fluid motion the woman rose and placed her palm over Marley's mouth. "Hush. Anyone who would dare call you odd, even in jest, should have her head examined."

She lowered her hand.

"What a pity you didn't grow up with your father. He would have taught you what a lovely young woman you are. He would lead you to the mirror and show you how to look beyond that serious studiousness, to the hunger for adventure and love for a clever joke that lurks in your eyes.

"You've grown up in a small community with small minds shaped by a small idiot box. Yours is a beauty rare and exotic. You look like your grandmother."

She looked nothing like Nan, and her confusion showed.

"Your father's mother. She was a beauty from a faraway land, and in your lovely dark eyes are her laughter and her tears. Be patient, my darling. It takes a certain kind of man to begin to know how to deal with a woman like you. You will find him. And whatever you do, don't let him go."

She kissed Marley and lifted her chin. "Now. Why not have a short nap? I'll lock the door and we can enjoy the quiet peacefulness of this lovely lounge before we reach the island."

Marley acquiesced with a yawn. She couldn't remember the last time she felt well-rested. It seemed as if even Nan's best days turned into high drama.

Nan found a light blanket in a chest and arranged it on a plush sofa, and Marley slipped her beach cover-up on, then curled inside the cocoon. She noticed the large chrome clock on the opposite wall—12:30, it said—just before she dropped off to sleep.

The flat, nasal peal of an alarm startled her out of a deep sleep, and she opened her eyes, disoriented. The clock on the opposite wall said 2:15. The cabin was as dark as if it were night, and the walls shook with winds blasting the ship.

The alarm screamed just outside the door, and she shoved back the blanket and staggered to her feet. *Ah, the rum punch.*

Where was Nan?

The room lurched, and she toppled toward the wall. She righted herself and stumbled to the couch. The furniture looked to be fastened to the deck. At the next swell, her bag and the couch's pillows went flying, and she grabbed at the handle of her bag, barely catching it. The cacophony of the storm, of screams from another room, froze her in place.

The door opened, swinging on its hinges. Nan stood there, drenched in a life jacket, clutching another, her face ashen. "Didn't you hear me knock? You missed the muster drill."

"Muster—?"

"No matter. We're to shelter in place. The other passengers are secured in other guest rooms. Marley, a fearful storm is upon us. I saw the waves like Triton rising in the sea."

At that moment the cabin slid sideways from underneath her. Marley grabbed her with one hand even as she clutched the couch with the other. Between the two of them struggling against the pitching cabin, Nan made her way to the couch.

"Sit down and hang on." Marley trembled with fear and with the raw fury of the storm. The soft light from the sconces was dark. Only the brash light of a fluorescent emergency light at the foot of the door relieved the darkness—and for that, even, she was grateful.

"Quick—put this on."

Marley slipped one arm, then the other, through the holes of the life jacket. She fumbled with the connectors. Finally they snapped into place. She tightened the straps just as the next swell hit.

"Oh, dear God, protect us," she whispered.

Nan wasn't religious, but her daughter had been, and for a moment Marley closed her eyes and felt her mother with her. The decades melted away and she was a child again, kneeling beside her bed at night, with her mother's head bent over hers.

And then she felt an arm strong around her shoulders. Just as if she'd been asked, the older woman had looped an arm about her shoulders. "Chin up, child. Where's the pillbox?"

"In my bag. I'll not lose it."

"Put it on your chain. In case we're separated."

"Nan, don't—"

"Do it. Now."

She dug out the pillbox, finding its small bail. She slipped it on the chain and inside her clothing, against her heart.

The women huddled together in the dark underneath the blanket, listening to the wind rise and the waves crash over the ship. Marley trembled, trapped in the darkness and her fear.

"Nan, do they have lifeboats?"

"Of course. It won't come to that, though."

"How do you know?"

Nan stroked her hair without speaking. Rather than comforting her, it terrified her. Could lifeboats even be lowered in these conditions? She couldn't imagine how. The ship they were in now was being tossed like driftwood. If the winds got any stronger—

And then, as if her fear had given it new power, the scream of the wind filled the room.

She looked at the window as water crashed there. A wall of seawater high enough to sink the ship had washed over the ship—higher than its main cabin. The sloop bobbed in the turbulent sea as if it were a toy. The water receded, and the ship righted itself once more.

"Nan, I'm so afraid." She buried her face in her grandmother's throat.

"Hush. There's something I should like to say."

She opened her eyes and gazed at her grandmother in the eerie flicker of the emergency light.

"Forgive me for being cross this morning. That man we encountered is a man I knew long before you were even born."

She was grateful for the distraction. How little it mattered now, how silly her suspicion. "Was he in love with you?"

Nan laughed at that, bringing the sparkle to her eyes. "It was a long time ago. And no."

She took Marley's hand, absently examining it in the flickering silver light. "Poppet, once I loved a man—someone you don't know. I was a young frightened woman, with none of your accomplishments, none of your clever book learning. I knew only the talents of the girls of my era—er, my age."

She stopped, gazing vacantly ahead in that otherworldly way of hers. At last, she went on.

"He loved me and he was so good to me. But it was in another time. Life was far simpler, much sweeter. Then I—I lost him, through my own foolishness. And I lost that life, that love—forever. Do you remember your Grandfather Spencer?"

"Was that Papaw?"

Nan laughed. "Yes, I believed you called him that. I met him years later, and he loved me and we married. Then he, too, died. And my life became a waking nightmare. Jimmy was there when I had no one at all, Marley. No one. Forgive me, I beg you, for allowing him to hurt you."

"Nan, he never laid a hand on me. You made sure of that."

"He bruised your spirit. He mocked you for things beyond your control. He is a hateful man. And he made sure that small child cowering in the darkness stayed there."

"I don't judge anything you did for *me*. I just think how much better your life could be, with a man who loves you."

"Stop worrying about my choices and consider your own. Make those choices wisely. We can never turn back the hands of the clock. I made so many mistakes, keeping you away from others, leaving you no childhood friends at all.

"But if I have protected you, 'twas only because I'd seen the terrors life had to offer. They were fresh in my mind and my heart. Do not pity me. I have known love. For the rest of my life, if I need companionship on a cold winter's night, I need only take out a single memory of that love to warm me."

With the next crash of a wave, the window shattered and water rushed in. Marley froze. "What now, Nan?"

"Just stay calm. Perhaps there's a drain in the floor."

There was not. Aside from the thirty-foot waves battering the ship, driving rain poured in. Soon Marley felt the water pooling at her ankles, then her shins. Then her thighs.

"Nan, we're going to have to get into one of the other cabins."

"Make me a promise."

"Please, not right—"

"All we have is now."

She waited, surprised at her grandmother's sudden calm.

"You've always taught me that, Nan. Stop in an ordinary moment to love your life. For as far back as I can remember. 'Listen to that chickadee, it's calling to you, *hey, sweetie!*' Take just a few moments each day, and stop and love your life.'"

"Yes, because I let our home become dangerous. Now, I want you to promise you'll stop being fearful.

"And the best secret I can tell you is still: Life lives in this moment. That's all. Not the regrets of yesterday, not the fear of tomorrow. If we make it through this, swear to me that you will *live*. Live with courage. Do it for me."

"Nan!" Marley cried.

"And I will do the same for you, child."

Marley understood what that meant: No more Jimmy. "All right, then. I promise."

The next wave crested, and she clutched Marley's hand, pulling her through the deep water to the door. When they pulled it open, the water rushed out. The wind caught the door and slapped it through the water and into the room then closed again, tossing the heavy steel door in the wind and water as if it were a playing card on the breeze.

She opened it again, hanging onto the inner edge of the door to keep it from swinging around. She peeked out.

Marley's pulse raced as she tried to look past her grandmother. She saw only gray. Gray skies, gray rain covering the ship, ocean swells daubing the ship's details into gray. A broken beam—a spar, a mast, she did not know—dangled in the air not far above them, and she gave it a distrustful glance. One gust of breeze, and it would become a killing projectile.

Nan moved out into the wind, and the breeze slammed against her. She staggered a step or two before steadying herself. Marley gripped her hand, now wet with rain and saltwater, and moved out just enough to feel the wind against her. With her free hand, she gripped a rail along the side of the cabin. The cold rain sweeping the deck drove her breath away and pelted her neck in stinging sheets.

Nan yelled something she couldn't hear for the banshee wail of the wind. She led her toward the next cabin over. That door, facing the ocean, was a good twenty feet away in the gale-force wind.

Nan, hurry, please.

They turned the corner and found the cabin locked. They both pounded, Nan crying out. "Please let us in!"

The door swung open. A man held it open, grabbing Nan to help her in. It was an awkward position, and instinctively Marley released her to help her inside so Marley could follow.

But at that moment a wave tossed the ship and the deck pitched. Marley slipped, she lost her grip on the rail, and in that suspended moment she watched each person's reaction in the doorway. The man inside fought indecision, and in the next movement, when Nan would have bolted after her, he swung out a beefy arm to trap her inside.

She knew what came next by the terror in their faces—Nan's and that of the unknown man who'd saved her. She knew it from his step backward as he slammed the door shut, leaving her to the storm. She may have screamed; she didn't remember. She recalled a flash of sky as she lost her footing.

Facing the cabin, she didn't see the ocean cresting twenty feet above the gunwale behind her, nor did she see the massive wave as it engulfed her. And as terror of drowning swept her, the instinct for survival that her father, the sailor, had drilled into his two oldest daughters kicked in.

In the ensuing minutes, she thanked God that she'd had the presence of mind to take a deep, long breath as that door to her salvation slammed. And that her father had taught her to swim, and to hold her breath, and that she'd done so for the past twenty years, training for just this moment. Last she'd checked, she was up to four minutes and forty-five seconds.

But even with all that preparation—done without exertion and fear gobbling the oxygen stored in her blood—she soon realized the danger surrounding her, burying her beneath an ocean churning with sea life fleeing into the deep seeking shelter from the tropical storm. Without knowing her destination, she swam into that primeval darkness on the face of the waters, into a time before time.

All she had left to do then was remember—as she had for twenty years—and listen to her father's voice as she tried to orient herself and swim toward the surface. As she tried to see any light in the darkness. *Hold on.*

In a moment she feared—she knew—she was dying. If she continued without oxygen, she would pass out, she would reflexively inhale, and she would drown.

And then, the moment transformed into something else. She still held her breath, the sea still stung her nostrils and roared in her ears. But no other feeling she'd ever known compared with what she felt now. The cold gray darkness had vanished, replaced by soothing, warm waters, by sunlight directly above. But even as she enjoyed the warmth, she felt faint, light-headed.

Hold on!

That ungodly sense of otherworldly peace filled her—a lie that could only be demonic, whispering that in the depths of the sea she was safe. Dear God, she needed to breathe, and she couldn't begin to see the surface. For all she knew, she was swimming away from the surface.

How life's dreariest moments sparkle with meaning when one faced death. Greeting their letter carrier as she delivered the junk mail; cheered when someone let her merge in front of them on the freeway; a stranger at the grocery store loaning her a quarter when she came up short paying.

Revolting against the desperate thoughts, she tried to kick her legs with the frog-like strokes her father had taught her, but she felt weak. Then a pressure gathered in around her even as the churning water grew warmer and calmer. Even as her strength failed her.

Hold on, darling.

She recalled the days when she and Rachel dove beneath the cold surface of the ocean, or the local pool, smiling at each other as the air bubbles escaped, rushing only to the surface when their bodies begged for oxygen.

"Hold on, darling," Daddy would coach from but a few feet away where he supervised them, treading water at the surface. "Pretend you've just escaped a pirate ship, and you're swimming for your lives." He would growl amusingly, and down they would go again, darting away from him like minnows. *Hold on.*

And then, later the same day, they cuddled within their mother's embrace, bathed and cozy in the window seat in their room, reading *Peter Pan* and clapping for the lives of fairies.

"Why don't we ever have any fun?" Marley had asked.

Mama had laughed. "Ah, my Merri lass, we spent the whole day today at the beach. We left only when you fell asleep in the surf."

Rachel spoke. "But that's not adventure, not real adventure. Not like the ladies in Williamsburg, in their fancy clothes and bonnets."

"Every day of your life is an adventure. We wake up not knowing what may come our way. Eggs or Cheerios or even donuts for breakfast, who can say?"

The girls protested in unison. "That's not a-venture," Marley said, echoing her sister and scowling at her mother's betrayal.

Their father, watching from the easy chair nearby, had laughed and grabbed her close, kissing her forehead. "You'll have a-ventures. The likes of which your mother and I have never known. And believe me, we've known adventure."

Marley noticed her mother and father exchanging one of their secret smiles.

These memories flashed in a moment before her now. And as the water around her warmed her and grew ever brighter, pure happiness rose within her as they appeared before her. So many years remembering the laughter, the love, the happiness. They looked just the same as all those years ago, gazing at her with loving encouragement.

Please, take me with you.

Her father reached out for her. Even as she tried to move into his embrace, her mother stopped them both. Marley stretched toward them with both arms, easily spanning the physical distance between them. Yet she couldn't touch them.

"Hold on."

"I'm so tired," she cried, reaching for him again. "And I miss you so much. Please let me come with you."

"Soon, my darling Merrilea. You'll see how fast it all passes. For now, your place is here. Your sisters still need you."

Merrilea. The name her father had given her, and that her grandmother had changed—why, she still didn't understand. She had actually forgotten it until now. She'd been so young at the time, she thought she was just saying it a little differently.

But now, when she heard the forgotten name after all these years, she thought she knew. Perhaps it was simply less painful for Nan to hear. How easy it would be, to take one deep breath and relax into their embrace. She was so tired. She just needed a moment's rest. She closed her eyes.

Hold on, Merrilea!

She opened her eyes, watching in detachment, welcoming peace—dear God, such a divine reward, against life's constant fear and struggle! Her eyes felt no sting from the saltwater.

"Swim for the light, darling. Always for the light. And we'll be back before you know it."

There it was, that reminder of the last time the girls saw their parents before they left them with the babysitter—that last night.

Her parents began to fade. She cried out, but the surreal, shifting nightmare of the cold and the warmth and the light and the darkness shut out her protest.

And out of that light and darkness he appeared, just as she felt herself giving in to the sea's mightier strength.

Was it her father? No. No. The form she saw was much stronger, much larger, much more muscular than the kindly bespectacled philosopher she'd first loved as a child.

This fair-headed hallucination must have been brought on by her lack of oxygen, and she welcomed him, so weary of her futile kicking. He grabbed her, covered her mouth with his, and exhaled deeply into her mouth, filling and soothing her burning lungs. Even as he shared his oxygen with her, he looped an arm around her and kicked toward the surface with long, strong strokes. Her last thought as she passed out was whimsical.

Like Triton rising in the sea.

Chapter Six

Sleepless for the third night in a row, the captain stood at the wheel of his *Adventurer*, wondering at signs and dreams and omens. No reason everyone should suffer, he'd thought, and he'd taken the wheel to give his helmsman a break. To free his mind from uneasy presentiment.

Foolish things, superstitions, but he was the son of a son of a sailor, of a man whose beliefs found wisdom in numbers and tea leaves. And so, truth to tell, Hawk was unsurprised when the cry came from the lookout. Their first night at sea, just a few hours out of St. George's.

"Sail ho."

The subdued call of the lookout, however—a sailor's *sotto voce*—was a tone that struck fear in his heart. The threat sailed near enough to hear them.

How did I miss that? Why had they stayed so close to the island? And what fool gave me that sobriquet of mine to begin with?

Hawk raised his spyglass. Close enough for him to see the scars on the seamen, a British warship loomed out of a fog covering the south side of the island.

Raven leapt around the dazed captain, grabbing the wheel and turning the barque aside to avoid broadsiding the brigantine. "Recognize anyone in the boarding party?"

"I cannot see past those ludicrous bonnets they call hats."

"Well, they're not firing on us. So far, a victory."

Hawk sighed. "'Tis early. Is everything stowed?"

"Just as you directed." Raven watched the landing party in the boat as the barque began to turn away from the brigantine.

"Send them down."

The captain disappeared down the hatch, grabbed a lantern, and walked inside a cabin. He inspected first with his nose. Despite the distraction of odors lingering in the air including the whale oil lantern, he'd thought as he descended that he still detected the faint scent of charcoal. It might well be his own imagination he smelled.

He handed the lantern to the sailor stationed at the door to the room. "When they enter, come as far as this, but no closer. Insist on protecting the modesty of the ladies."

The light dimly illuminated the women, restless in the dark.

Their restlessness was nothing compared to his worries. Transporting the women was part of the trip, but it would be hell, keeping his men away from them during the voyage.

Kit, his island childhood friend, sat with the rest of the women on the edge of the gaily colored contraption they'd decorated, a light quilt folded beside her.

The huge bed looked quite like a traveling troupe's trunks had exploded and fused over a gigantic mattress, large enough to accommodate the dozen women taking refuge in the cabin. Which was quite close to what had, in fact, happened.

"Up."

Those nearby clambered off the platform and stood aside, watching him as he peeled back the edge of the quilting. He lifted the wooden lid on the box beneath and peered inside. Silently, he reassembled everything and gestured at the women.

"Into bed with the lot of you. Brits preparing to board. I need not tell you again to keep quiet. Tender-hearted pilgrims and maidens such as yourselves have never seen such a display. As a result, you are shocked to silence. Am I understood?"

Kit had been uncharacteristically quiet during the voyage from St. George's. Now, she only watched him.

"The bottle."

She dug an unwieldy bottle of perfume out of a box against the wall and handed it over. He smashed it against the deck then dug a broom out of a closet and handed it to her.

She gave him a sour look. "You have your fun and leave me to my own. We might be seventeen again."

The captain ignored that. His inspection ended at the older woman who sat in the corner, rocking, eyes half closed. Beefier than most, gruffer than most, Mother Barbary was the guardian of this pack, and you couldn't locate a finer heart in any church from Boston to Bombay.

"Mother Barbary, are you well?"

With a single nod, she returned to her meditation.

Up on deck came the clatter of men boarding. He climbed the ladder and joined the noise, his shoes thumping on the freshly holystoned and sanded planks.

Four Royal Navy officers stood awaiting his arrival.

"Gentlemen, your business?"

The leader, a lieutenant of perhaps 35, took a step forward. Unlike the rest of his men, he wore a powdered wig.

Hawk and Raven exchanged a quick look: *Ass.*

"You know quite well that we patrol for smugglers. Can you tell me your purpose in Bermuda?"

"My father, a subject to the throne and a former burgess in Williamsburg, owns an estate in St. George's. We have supplies for the Massachusetts colony and brides for their respectable young farmers and merchants."

"I see. We'd like to inspect, if you have no objection."

"Not at all. However, as I said, I have young maidens aboard, and no wish to introduce them to seamen's manners by terrorizing them."

Certain that the officers would expect him to attempt to distract them from any evidence of wrongdoing, he led them directly to his most precious cargo, where the women had packed themselves under the covers like salted sardines. The women squealed in mock terror, in righteous offense, when the Navy officers descended.

Hawk watched without reaction. The stage's best, these weren't.

"What's that smell?"

"We're at midway point on a long voyage. Could you be more specific?"

Kit spoke up. "I'm sorry, captain. I broke a bottle of perfume. Knocked it over in the dark."

"Perfume, eh?"

Hawk stood aside, his arms folded across his chest in irritation. The ladies sat up, clutching their quilts to their chins.

Two of the men carried lanterns, and the captain disguised his dread, watching as one of the two bumbled about the cabin, looking for contraband. He stopped before the ladies.

"Ladies, er—that is, if you don't mind, we would be grateful if you could—erm, perhaps, if not too much trouble, move aside."

They sat gaping at him, agoggle. Several climbed off the bed, pulling their nightclothes to their throats. Mother Barbary watched from her chair in the corner, murmuring to herself, her fingers moving over prayer beads. One hand closed more firmly over the club plainly visible in her skirts.

Near her lay a thin, sickly looking woman who made no attempt to move.

"What about her?"

The captain watched the exchange, his breath shallow.

"She's lame," Kit said. "We can lift her aside if you like."

They left the woman unmolested.

A man held the lantern aloft while another threw back the cover and revealed the crates. They opened three crates, found nothing except Bibles, used dinnerware, and old glassware.

Under the lame woman, the captain knew, was a different matter. No dinnerware concealed their cargo in those crates.

"Nothing here except housekeeping items, sir," the officer said, replacing the quilt and nodding to the ladies. Then he moved back into the passageway to search the rest of the ship.

"Where is your home port, Captain?"

"Norfolk, Virginia."

"Then I suggest you get there with all due speed."

"She's a ship, *sir*," the captain said with a smile that stopped short of his eyes. "Her very *joie de vivre* is sailing."

"We are here for your own protection, *sir*."

"Then would you ask your officers to kindly stop ogling the young maidens here, if all this protecting has concluded?"

The lieutenant had the decency to struggle for words. He turned toward the door, turned back long enough to tip his hat to the ladies, and bowed.

Hawk exchanged a grim glance with Kit as he followed the officers down to the hold, where they found nothing besides salt pork and beef, lemons, limes, and water for the journey— and a good store of salt, sugar, and molasses for the colonies. And an occasional rat.

Finally, he escorted them to his own cabin, where he produced tax documentation.

"Everything looks to be in order. May your voyage be safe to the British colony of Virginia." And he bowed—again.

"God save your king," Hawk said with an even lower bow.

"And *yours*."

As if we need any reminder of that daft lunatic.

When the officers were safely in their boat, headed back to the warship, Raven spoke. "You white folks sure know how to host the enemy. 'I shall smite thee, sir.' 'Well, not before I smite thee, *sir*. Would you like some tea with your smiting?"

Hawk sent him a withering glance.

"I take it a stop in Norfolk is out?" Raven asked.

"I believe I should like to see New England in the autumn."

"Straight into Boston harbor, then, with our ladies and their many crates of finery."

"Wait." Hawk hesitated, listening for something he thought he'd heard. "Silence." His order echoed over the deck, and every seaman stood still. "Did you hear that?"

"Naught but the tick of the clock and the pull of the tides. The winter cold draws nigh with every moment we tarry."

In the shards of moonlight shattered on the water he saw the glisten of a—what, fish?—flopping near the surface.

"Do you see that?"

"'Tis a marlin."

"A marlin. I could throw you to the shore from here."

"For identifying a fish?"

"A marlin, this close to shore? What does it look like to you?"

"You mocked my last answer. So I'll say ... a mermaid. Well. Truthfully it does resemble a mermaid."

Stepping up to the rail, he peered in the darkness for a glimmer. If he thought he'd had trouble sleeping before, he dared not leave behind one of Kit's women who'd managed to have fallen overboard.

But she wasn't even calling out for help.

Good God, man, go!

He stripped off his shoes and dove over the side, swimming to the area where he'd seen her. Or *it*. If she were a woman, not calling for help, she was drowning.

He stopped to orient himself as pale blue flashed in the moonlight: a slender arm. Raven squawked in surprise and to alert him, and Hawk waved once then swam toward her.

Just before he dove, he filled his lungs with air. He'd seen no movement from her—just being tossed about by the waves.

He had to dive further than he expected—perhaps twenty feet. Then he felt her, and hope filled his breast as he grabbed her limp form into his arms. He supported her head and fitted his mouth over hers, exhaling fully, filling her lungs as best he could underwater. He felt a piece of jewelry, a locket or somesuch, floating away over her head, and he grabbed it. Strapping an arm around her waist, he swam to the surface, praying their lungs held out.

As he reached the surface, he took in great gulps of air, appreciating the mysteries of life. He reached the ladder on the hull and found his crew gawping, craning their necks like a yard full of chickens contemplating a worm. He shuddered to imagine their reaction if they glimpsed the form he'd held when he pulled her from the water. He would have a mutiny of randy sailors on his hands.

"Throw down a covering, quickly—"

"What do you want? A blanket? A nice monogrammed towel?" This from Raven.

"I don't care if you send your breeches. No, *don't* send—"

A remnant of an old, salvaged sail was already on its way down and splashed on the water beside them, and he bundled her into it. Tossing his lumpy bundle over his shoulder, he grabbed the ladder and headed up. As he neared the gunwale, Rashall reached over to grab the bundle.

"My cabin. Put the boy there and leave him."

To the men standing there gawking, he said, "Back to your posts! It's merely a cabin boy fallen off the British warship."

Deming, the boatswain, gave him a suspicious side-glance. "That was no—"

Hawk silenced him with a look. He grabbed his shoes from the deck and descended to the women's cabin. The seaman at the door, fighting fatigue, rose and stepped back.

Hawk tapped briefly on the door, and it opened just wide enough to reveal Kit, relieved to see him.

"Are all present and well?"

"Yes. Why?"

He had no interest in attempting to explain someone who defied explanation. That the woman was a stranger was not good news.

"Just making sure. I trust no Englishman. Good night."

He made his way to his cabin and barred the door behind him. Raven already knelt over her on the deck. He'd folded back the duck only enough to free her head and shoulders, and he'd tipped her onto her side to let the water spill out.

Hawk knelt on her other side as Raven worked, as Raven's mother had taught them both years ago—as soon as they grew old enough to get into trouble. That woman had more home-grown lifesaving tricks than any doctor he'd ever known.

"Compressions. There's no heartbeat."

Hawk obeyed. The two traded off performing compressions and breathing for her until Raven raised his head. "She's breathing."

Relief flooded him. They'd used this technique more than once, and as rare and magical as it had seemed when they learned it, there was no certainty to it. The times it had worked were few.

"Why isn't she …" Hawk gestured toward her.

"Moving at all? She's got that Sleeping Beauty thing going on, doesn't she? Maybe just needs some rest."

Hawk frowned. The color in her face, at least a bit of it, seemed to be returning.

"What do we do with her now?"

For that, he had no answer.

"Where could she have come from?" Hawk asked.

"You know where."

"Perhaps she came out from shore on a smaller boat and it capsized, or another ship was wrecked, or …"

"Yes. Enough time passed for a ship to sink, but she was still out there floating around." Raven gave a nod. "Or maybe she lives out there with her two sisters on a rocky island, singing the poor sailors to their deaths. Or maybe—"

"Very well. Leave us. Have Jem sleep with the crew. And make sure we get safely away from that blasted British brig."

Raven skipped up the narrow ladder, then stopped short and descended again, pulling the door close. "And you will not pass her off as a boy. Trust me."

Hawk glared after him; that much, they'd both figured out during the compressions.

He only laughed as he raced up the ladder, calling out to the seamen: "To Boston!"

When they were alone, he sighed. Found a clean shirt and breeches in his wardrobe. Steeled himself for the next few minutes. Lit another candelabra to enjoy it.

He stepped out of his wet clothes, slung them in the corner, and slipped into the breeches. Dropping the shirt over the foot of the bed, he turned back the covers.

He knelt beside the girl, faced with the daunting task of clothing her. It wasn't the idea of covering her nakedness, but the idea of confronting it. He should have had one of the women do it, but Hawk trusted none of them enough to select from among them.

She had a pleasant enough face, framed by hair still damp with seawater. He couldn't quite tell the color, but in the candle's flame he thought saw a tinge of copper, and a texture of springy curls.

Even in distressed repose, she seemed to be on the verge of smiling. He found something about the shape of her lips provocative, as if a tiny dimple were placed at each corner of her full mouth. She inhaled deeply, coughed twice, turned her head toward him as if in instinct, then opened her eyes, gazing at him peacefully, as if he were a friend she'd always known.

Between the lanterns and candles in his cabin, there was just enough light to marvel as she gazed at him. The palest brown eyes—was it hazel?—he'd ever seen. A color that reminded him of an exotic flower he'd seen in the black hair of a girl while visiting Siam. And he'd seen it in the sunset, and on the ocean at a typhoon's approach. But whether the color had a name, he did not know.

Then she did smile at him, a small smile as if of gratitude, and a single dimple in one cheek creased. A moment later, she returned to her slumber. Hawk stared, smiling back stupidly.

Good heavens, man. Go below, grab a woman, and end your suffering.

Whether to put her to work dressing this woman or undressing him, at this point he cared not.

The captain had traveled the seven seas since infancy, captained his own ship for a dozen years, and he'd known beautiful women from every continent. He'd had his fill of those enamored of their own feminine charms, and had developed a taste for those who weren't.

Perhaps becoming a man in its true sense meant learning that the excitement of a woman existed in her spirit. And one could never learn the extent of a woman's spirit until he saw her laugh.

This woman had barely cast a shy glance at him and he couldn't compose a thought. Except one: he wanted to make her laugh.

Brushing away his puerile brainlessness, he removed the duck sailcloth from her and tossed it in a far corner. As he turned back, he realized he'd closed his eyes.

What is wrong with you? Get it over with. Now.

He opened his eyes.

Raven was right. Pretending she was a boy wasn't an option.

Earlier, he'd been so preoccupied with getting her out of the ocean that he'd scarcely been aware of her nakedness. Now, as he gazed, unable to move, he realized that despite the number of women he'd bedded, he'd never had the occasion to investigate one so clearly, to admire her so completely.

He grabbed the shirt and touched her shoulders. At the first touch of her skin, cold under his fingertips, he grew ashamed of his base instincts. And the captain in him took over, wrapped her in his shirt, lifted her into his arms, and placed her in his bed.

He shoved more wood in his stove, disentangled and removed his necklace, and placed it in his top drawer. Climbing in bed beside her, he curved his body around hers, throwing a thigh around her shivering lower body and warming her. Relieved he'd donned the breeches, he rubbed her skin briskly through the thin layer of his shirt. His own bare chest was hot against her cool back, and he leaned over her head, placing his face against her cold cheek.

He stroked the length of her cold thighs, his other arm tucked around her from underneath, stiffly stroking her arm to conduct his warmth. He exhaled warm breath along the length of her throat, and she gave a soft cry of delight, turning toward his mouth.

He went still, drawing her closer even as he ignored the response of his own unruly body. As she began to grow warm, he had no choice but to notice the softness inviting his own hardness. She was a woman full grown, and beautiful.

She wriggled against him, unconsciously inviting his touch, and he held his breath until she stilled. He rearranged himself around her so the fit wasn't quite so tempting—a challenge in itself—and lay his face against hers, then rested his palm over her throat, where her racing pulse went calm and even.

He removed from his own neck the necklace that he'd caught when it had nearly floated away from her underwater, and he slipped it over her head, settling it between her breasts.

And despite anything he would've believed, as he lay there with her body growing content and warm under his, with her heartbeat steady and calm as if regulating his own, with his ship's sails singing a seaman's lullaby, Hawk dropped into a deep sleep and rested through the night.

Chapter Seven

Marley awakened into what could only be a dream—of that she was certain.

The rolling rhythm of the bed, the occasional creak of wood, told her she was once again on the ship—then she stopped short. She couldn't be. They'd shut her out during the storm—and she'd soon been lost in the depths of the ocean.

Now the storm had passed, leaving only the motion and sound of the ship moving through the ocean.

She opened her eyes to an unfamiliar room. This place was alive with richness of detail and old-world charm that the modern day *Island Girl* had lacked.

The thin gray of approaching dawn lit a bank of tall windows opposite the bed, slanting outward. Each window, perhaps four feet wide by eight feet, held a dozen panes. The mullions holding each pane, as well as the carved casement, were all natural wood—perhaps teak. The walls were lined with the same gleaming woods, the windows trimmed in gilt wood carvings and draped with heavy, crimson and gold curtains.

On a wall adjacent to the windows stood the bed in which she lay. On the other stood an alcove with a recessed daybed with inviting pillows, also gold and crimson, edged with gold cords. Above the alcove daybed hung a gold-carved mirror.

That was Marley's first clue she was dreaming, that she imagined a window seat like those she loved at Stonefield.

She drank in the details of the room, impressed with the imagination of her own unconscious. As much as she loved and knew history, she hadn't thought herself capable of conjuring up an eighteenth-century pirate ship. Well, maybe not a pirate ship—most of the big-ticket spoils had been plundered before that time period—but your average fisherman or merchant couldn't afford this kind of opulence.

Mounted on either side of the daybed alcove was an array of polished swords, daggers, and pistols. Above these displays, on each side of the daybed, was a brass candle sconce.

This pageantry, bringing to mind the weaponry arrays in the Governor's Palace where she often lectured, was her second clue that she was dreaming. At either end of the row of windows, in the upper corner, was a carved bird in mid-flight, each painted in lifelike detail. A hawk and raven.

Facing the bank of windows was a large, ornate wooden table, legs curving down into four lion's paws. On it lay a ledger of some sort—perhaps a ship's log. The matching chairs had been arranged around the cabin—except for the captain's chair, which stood between the table and the windows, facing the cabin. Above the table hung half a dozen lanterns.

The cabin's aromas were strong, not at all unpleasant—and quite male. The faint sweetness of beeswax, the fecund tang of saltwater and sea air, the faint odor of fish she'd associated with the ocean her entire life, and a surprisingly agreeable scent of cigars. Infusing it all, an earthy aroma quite like cedar. Teak, likely, on a ship.

She couldn't recall a single time she'd ever dreamed of smells, and she turned over to snuggle deeper into her pillow.

There she found irrefutable evidence that she was dreaming: a man, the breadth of his chest a supple and welcoming pillow. Startled, she drew back.

Life lives in this moment.

She embraced Nan's admonition. She stretched out her fingers, inhaling the scent of him and moving her cheek against his chest. His breath, deep and even, told her that he, too, shared her dream.

Marley had never touched a man's bare chest before, but this was exactly as she would've imagined it in her best daydream. So she opened her eyes and raised her head just slightly to see what she'd been missing.

The skin beneath her cheek was sun-browned, muscled, and held a tempting pattern of light brown hair.

She let her fingernails play there lightly and dropped a chaste kiss, her lips lingering and parting. His skin tasted of sea spray, as a pirate's would.

She laughed aloud at the thought. The sound intruded in the quiet room, but not enough to awaken her from her dream.

"I amuse you."

A shiver went along her skin at the sound of his voice—low, gruff with sleep, and amused, as well.

"Enlighten me."

She only smiled. "You must be Lilu, come to seduce me in my dreams."

Now he laughed, and she felt the delighted rumble of his chest tingle throughout her body. "You think me an incubus?"

So, he had a brain to go along with the impressive chest.

"Ordinary mortal males cannot be as beautiful as you."

His hand captured hers, and he kissed her fingers lightly. She drew it away, and it came to rest over his taut abdomen. Again she explored there, certain that few men could have a chest this hard yet pliant, as sculpted as Michelangelo's *David*.

Her fingers wandered lower, then stopped shyly as she encountered the sheet.

She heard the sudden race of his heart, and excitement coursed through her at the thought of her power over him. The very idea of her having power over any man.

She plucked the sheet away. Disappointed, she observed he was wearing pants—but they dipped tantalizingly low on his slim hips. Between the solidly muscled rise of his pelvic bones, swelling the front of his breeches, was the hard rise of an erection.

Harder still his heartbeat as lower still went her hand, finding the depression of his navel. She stroked her middle fingertip down over the pattern of dark hair below it. His abdomen rose and fell as she explored, and she grasped the sheet to fling it away.

He caught her hand again and in one smooth, sure motion he thrust her onto her back, his fingertips laced in hers, pinning her down. The nightshirt she wore, unbuttoned, fell away from her in the movement, baring her body to his gaze.

The rising sun flashed through the windows and in his eyes—the pale blue of high noon she'd seen in the Sargasso Sea, with the faintest tinge of pale green. He scorched her with the gaze that roved over her, lingering on her breasts, then rising to her own.

"Who are you?"

She laughed, and the sight captured him, held him immobile.

"It's my dream, I don't have to explain a thing."

A reluctant smile lifted a corner of his mouth. "So you hold to the theory you're dreaming of an incubus?"

Marley, my girl, this is one humdinger of a phantasm. He was splendid.

She could feel an almost painful pleasure growing deep within her as she ached for his touch.

She lifted her face toward his for a kiss. He settled his weight on his elbows, still holding her fast to the bed as it rocked under them. But rather than kissing her, he lowered his mouth to her throat, to her ear.

"Who are you?"

The question was a demand. A husky purr tickling her ear.

She found herself unable to answer at the pleasure of his breath in her ear, his tongue tracing her earlobe, his teeth lightly nipping.

She turned her face toward him, hungry for his mouth on hers. With matter-of-fact denial, he lifted his head away.

The mouth he denied her was open slightly, the lips full and inviting, the tongue touching his lower lip in steady calculation.

Again she lifted her mouth toward his, like a baby bird hungry for the first taste of life.

He moved his head away even as he smiled, his teeth a white flash in his suntanned face. And without warning he lowered that mouth to her breast, his dark blond, sun streaked hair falling over her, one hand releasing her as he cupped and molded her other breast. He stroked her hardened nipple with a callused thumb, then moved his mouth there.

She cried out—loudly—at a pleasure she'd never imagined. Without even slowing his pleasured assault on her, he covered her mouth with his hand.

Released from his grip, her hand slid through his silken hair, encouraging him.

Then, as abruptly as he'd begun, he raised his head. "You're a virgin."

Ah. Eventually, all dreams turned dark.

"You don't know that."

"I know the sound of a woman who's never known pleasure." His gaze raked her breasts again. "A sin against humanity, in this case."

She blushed, ashamed at the fact that no one had ever found her desirable enough even to court, let alone bed.

His gaze raked her body, stopping at the dark purple bruise high on her hip—from when Jimmy had kicked her that last night at Stonefield. "Who did this to you?"

Her mouth opened and closed, then: "I fell."

He examined it, then gave her a dubious look.

"And I am not. A virgin, that is."

One eyebrow shot up. "Oh? Shall I prove it?"

Answering his challenge, aroused at the prospect of what that might entail, she raised her chin. "Yes."

His hand slipped down between their bodies, his palm easily parting her thighs. Her excitement grew. His hand lowered, his fingertips explored, and he gave a surprised sigh at what he felt there.

Marley had no idea what surprised him so, but his fingers lingered, roaming delicately in that center of her pleasure.

"That is—so nice," she whispered. "What are you doing, and how in the world does it feel so exquisite?"

He gave a soft, low laugh. "I'm a sea captain. I've been tying knots for twenty years. Requires a manual dexterity that means I'm quite good at untying them as well."

Distracted with her reaction to him, he continued to play there—then seemed to remember his original purpose. When he started to insert a single finger, then two, he moved it within her, and the feeling changed.

"There. Feel that? Not fun anymore, is it?"

She wanted more. Of his touch, of … of what, she was unsure. As he made to withdraw, she arched her hips, instinctively capturing him within her.

At this he hesitated, then continued touching her and shifted aside to watch her response. His jaw hardened as his gaze roved over her thighs, her belly, watching her tremble in innocence at his touch. The pleasure he drew from her began a swift, steady climb.

"I beg of you," she whispered, lifting her mouth to his ear, delighted to see him catch his breath as she mimicked the way he'd breathed in her ear. "*Don't* stop."

He drew away from her kiss, withholding his own pleasure with an iron will even as he allowed hers. Almost gallantly, as if to help end her suffering.

He watched her face instead, as his fingers continued to play on her. He knowingly stroked, his face grim, troubled, even as a sensation she'd never known washed over her.

As she collapsed within his bed, he slowly withdrew his fingers, covering her with the sheet. "Happy dreams, Morgana," he whispered.

And with that, her knots unspooled and her pleasure spent, she fell into the deepest sleep she'd ever known.

Chapter Eight

When Marley awakened again, her fear went deep. She was convinced she was trapped in a nightmare without end. The only other options she could imagine were that she had been rescued from the ocean and was in a hospital, comatose.

Or that, perhaps, she had not been rescued.

That this was reality, she could not consider.

Same captain's cabin, same bed, same nightshirt. No man, this time. For this, she was equally relieved and crestfallen.

She threw her legs over the side of the bed and rose—and nearly collapsed within it again. Her head throbbed with a pain she'd never known—and yet, it encouraged her. How could she feel pain if she were comatose—or dead?

Equal to the pain of her headache was the heaviness in her head, as if she'd been drugged. She shook her head, trying to dispel it. She sat on the edge of the bed—a huge bed, she saw now, her feet not touching the floor—for a full minute, until the worst of it passed.

The sun had risen, and the brilliance in the windows caught her attention. This was far too brilliant, far too painful, far too beautiful to be a dream. She stood up more slowly, glancing around the cabin. Were her clothes stored somewhere? She looked through the closets and armoire but found only men's clothing, neatly hung.

And where was Nan? It would help to know where she was, but she was just as concerned about her grandmother. After all, she might be somewhere worrying over Marley.

She quickly made the bed then padded to the windows, looking for any clues about where she might be. The rolling of the ship disoriented her, and she grabbed the large table strewn with maps. They were the sort of thing she'd never seen outside protective glass: hand-drawn maps of ancient lands. But they looked as new as a road map bought at a truck stop.

She ignored the treasure trove of documents, turning to the windows. And there she saw an endless expanse of ocean and a long beam—a spar—protruding from the ship. The back point of a taut sail extended out perhaps a dozen feet above the windows. The cabin was at the back of the ship—the *stern*, she reminded herself—where captain's cabins were always situated.

Two windows stood on each adjoining wall, and she peered out each window: no land anywhere.

A wooden edge jutted into her hip, and she moved away far enough to see shelves of books running under the length of all the windows. Not a huge library by anyone's standard, but certainly larger than most at sea. She bent down to get a closer look.

Iliad, Oedipus, Republic, Aeneid. On the adjoining shelf, as if withdrawn and hastily set aside, lay *Argonautica.* The story of Jason and the Argonauts.

Other books included philosophy, art, architecture, science. Fiction from Daniel Defoe, Henry Fielding, Jonathan Swift, Horace Walpole. All of these were eighteenth century. None of these books had been published past perhaps the 1770s. They were cloth and leather, all of these specific books published using eighteenth century technique.

And all of them were nearly new.

Surely she was hallucinating, for these books closely mirrored selections from the library Thomas Jefferson had donated to recreate the destroyed Library of Congress. And no one except she would have such an arcane fact committed to memory.

As she reached one end of the books, she noted that the window on that side was in fact set into a door. She peeked out and saw an old-style toilet there, merely a hole in a wooden seat. It was a reminder that she'd like to use it. She opened the door and walked out.

With a gasp, she looked around at the stunning view. The deep azure of the waters, the fresh cool ocean air, the sails taut with that same air filling her senses and—

She ducked back inside and closed the door just in time to avoid being seen by an entire crew working in the rigging and the deck. Mortification struck her at the thought of dozens of men glimpsing her in the toilet.

Curiosity drew her back to the maps, and she sat at the desk, studying the notations there. Dates and abbreviations whose meaning she didn't know. *Saltpt 10 ck 18 Oct 75*. Several similar notes by the island of Bermuda, the Bahamas, and Boston. Still other dates around Norfolk and, far across the ocean, on London and Paris.

The thunder of feet overhead told her the cabin lay just under a deck filled with busy sailors; yes, the quarterdeck. She quickly buttoned up the nightshirt, a man's shirt that hit her mid-thigh.

Something nagged at her from her glimpse of the men working in the rigging. Every last man there had been dressed in period costume, as if she were cruising in an authentic eighteenth century ship.

Then, before she had a chance to do much else, the cabin door swung open. She stepped behind the captain's chair, embarrassed at her attire and at the man who stood there with a tray.

"Hey, you're up. Mind if I come in? I've brought you some breakfast," he said, glancing over his shoulder before closing the door behind him.

She scarcely had time to react.

The man was young, perhaps only a few years older than she. His long, curly black hair was woven into a club that hung down over his shoulder. He wore a shirt similar to her own, and breeches down to his knees, with stockings and shoes below. In one ear was a diamond stud earring. His skin in the morning light looked like raw mahogany that had been sanded and oil-rubbed to a subtle sheen, his eyes the same color.

He, too, wore late eighteenth century dress.

He crossed the distance between them, placing the tray on an empty corner of the table without fanfare. He lay a napkin alongside it, then adjusted and patted it with the awkward grace of a man unaccustomed to serving.

"All right, 'tis not the finest fare, but it is bug-free. Mostly." He shooed away a fly.

She looked over the contents of the china plate. "Modest boasts from the chef, I see."

He laughed, his eyebrows lifting merrily. "Oh, you're clever. No wonder he likes you."

"Who?"

"Never mind." Grim once more, he glanced around as if they were being spied upon. "I've said too much already."

A smile came to her lips. He was like an old childhood friend, familiar without threat.

"Do you know where my grandmother is?"

"Your grandmother? Were you with her?"

"Yes."

He hesitated, then: "Maybe you'd better ask the captain about this. Oh, by the way, he asked for you to stay inside the cabin and away from the side windows. The men may spy you otherwise."

She hesitated, glad he'd brought it up, and yet still unable to ask him.

He recognized her discomfort and began attempting to guess, as if she were mute or spoke no English or was perhaps a cocker spaniel. "Need something? More butter? Dear God, tell me 'tis not tea. Oh!" He thumped himself in the forehead as if to dislodge his own stupidity. "There's a chamber pot in the closet."

She gave a deep sigh of relief and extended her hand. "Thank you. I'm Marley, by the way."

He smiled and accepted her handshake. "Raven."

She lit up in recognition, turning to point at the bird in the corner. "Oh, that's you?"

"Well, I guess so. Which would make that Hawk."

"Hawk?"

"The captain."

"Oh," she said. "Are you and he …" She wasn't sure how to make the suggestion.

He waited, absorbing her awkwardness then finally tilting his head and, with deep suspicion, drawing his chin in. "Are me and him *what?*"

She laughed at his expression. "Okay, I've just never seen two men that close."

"Closer than brothers, best friends since we were about eight. He's a year older than I am. Where are you from?"

"Not far from Williamsburg, Virginia. Why?"

"Yep. So's my mother. You talk like her. She speaks like nobody else in the whole wide world. It's messed me up. Everybody treats me like I'm a freak because I speak so differently. You know what a freak is?"

"Sure. But …" Who didn't? "Look, I'm really worried about my grandmother. Her name is Hannah Hastings. We went out on a day trip to Mayaguana and got caught in the storm."

For the first time, his joviality left him, replaced by suspicious confusion. "Mayaguana is in the West Indies. You were found not far from Bermuda. They're a goodly distance apart."

"Where was I found? I mean, in the water, or what?"

"Yes. In the water, in the process of drowning. The captain happened to notice you, and fished you out. Look, I've got to run. Captain'll be down soon, and you two can figure it out. Just sit tight. Don't mess with his maps."

With that, he disappeared, locking the door behind him. Marley rushed to the closet and located the chamber pot with deep relief. She found a small pitcher of water and knew from its size that it was for drinking, but she indulged the splurge, dampening the corner of her napkin and scrubbing her face and hands as best she could.

A ravenous hunger descended on her, and she moved to the table, dubiously considering the biscuit. It was then that she began to contemplate the impossible reality before her. She had never dreamed of hunger, nor the smell of boiled coffee, or of sweet butter, or of thick bacon, still warm from the fire.

She saw neither electronics nor evidence of electricity.

Marley, you're a bright girl. What are those clever eyeballs of yours telling you?

Perhaps it was a theme cruise, dedicated to the eighteenth century, reserved for the very wealthy. People paid well for grueling weight loss boot camps and river cruises. If she had even a small bit of money, this would be the sort of place where she would indulge. Maybe she'd been lost in the water so long she'd been separated from the first ship, and this ship had rescued her.

Had she been lost in the water all the way from the Bahamas, she would have become fish food long before reaching Bermuda.

She realized how hungry she was, distracted as she was by the oatmeal, bacon, and the biscuit—which looked a lot like an English muffin. She'd seen photographs of these before, and almost all of those images, recreated for the sake of education, did include bugs. Despite Raven's assurance, she broke this one up in small pieces before spreading a dab of butter on a piece, then realized it must've only recently been baked.

She tasted it—as if it were the first food she'd ever eaten. The butter was a white puddle of glistening, salty oil that brought to life a dense bread that otherwise would have been quite dull. The coffee—thank God for it, to clear her cluttered, aching brain—was hot and strong and sweet, and she smiled at the thought of Raven adding sugar for her. Already she had a soft spot for the jester of a man. Knowing little about him aside from his kindness and intelligence, she knew in her heart he was a good man.

The oatmeal was thick and chewy; the bacon was the sort of bacon served in England, a meaty portion resembling ham. That she'd learned, also, from Nan.

None of it made sense! *Where was Nan?*

She looked around the table, now avoiding the verboten maps. A foot or so away, she noticed a stack of newspapers, all folded in sections as they'd been read and set aside, and joy filled her. She glanced over them, then went back and read more carefully.

These were the stories her father had first taught her to love. Not warriors, but farmers and fishermen whose courage fueled their fight for freedom. The stories went backward from August to March 1775, summarizing a skirmish between two American schooners and a British sloop-of-war; Bunker Hill; the battles at Concord and Lexington; Patrick Henry's stirring "Give me liberty or give me death" speech; and Lord Dunmore's craven theft of the gunpowder stores in Williamsburg.

She set aside the stack of papers, her breakfast finished, then noticed one clipping, much older and weathered, slipped underneath the layer of glass that topped the table:

> *"BOSTON. For some days bypast, there have been several affrays between the inhabitants, and the soldiers quartered in this town.*
>
> *"Last Monday about 9 o'clock at night a most unfortunate affair happened in King Street. The sentinel posted at the custom house, being surrounded by a number of people, called to the main guard, upon*

*which Capt. Preston, who was captain of the day, with
a party, went to his assistance; soon after which some
of the party fired, by which the following persons were
killed and wounded.*

*"Mr. Samuel Gray, ropemaker, killed. A
mulatto man named Johnson, killed. Mr. James
Caldwell, mate of Capt. Morton's vessel, killed. Mr.
Samuel Maverick, wounded, and since dead. A lad
named Christopher Monk, wounded. A lad named
John Clark, wounded. Mr. Edward Payne, merchant,
standing at his entry door, wounded in the arm. Mr.
John Greene, tailor, wounded. Mr. Patrick Cole,
wounded. David Parker, wounded.*

*"Early next morning, Captain Preston was
committed to gaol, and same day eight soldiers.*

*"A meeting of the inhabitants was called at
Faneuil Hall that forenoon and the lieutenant-
governor and council met at the council chamber, where
the Colonel Dalrymple and Carr were desired to
attend, when it was concluded upon, that both
regiments should go down to the barracks at Castle
William, as soon as they were ready to receive them.*

*"We decline all present, giving a more particular
account of this unhappy affair, as we bear the trial of
the unfortunate prisoners is to come on next week."*

This story of the Boston Massacre had meant a great deal
to the person who had placed it there. Likely the captain, since
this was his cabin.

Remembering her promise to Raven, she moved around the
table, looking at everything *but* the maps. In a drawer, she
found a ledger and opened it. A ship's log.

Thursday – October 19 – 1775 – Lat North 32.38, West 64.67 – Departed St. George's. Winds westerly.

The spidery handwriting was difficult to read, but—

The click of a key in the lock alarmed her, and she closed the book, slipped it into the drawer, and spun away toward the window just as the door opened.

She turned, meeting the gaze of the man who stood there. And she felt her face flood with heat.

This man, she could not have imagined. This man was real and she knew him. He had saved her from the depths of the ocean and had pleasured her beyond her dreams—except for refusing her his kiss—in the most sexual dream she'd ever known.

I'm a sea captain. I've been tying knots for twenty years. Requires a manual dexterity that means I'm quite good at untying them as well.

Chapter Nine

Marley thought she had imagined this man when the bitterly cold ocean had grown warm. But she was certain she had dreamed of him—but how, if she didn't know him?

Was *this* the captain?

"Sleep well?"

Her face flamed brighter—as if he knew her dreams.

"I was just—looking at the view," she explained, unnecessarily. "It's quite beautiful out there, and the ship seems to be quite historic."

Stop talking.

He didn't reply.

"Thank you for the breakfast. It was quite good. Much better than I expected on board a ship. And the coffee was delicious, even without milk."

Marley, for the love of Mike, please stop talking.

His physical size made the spacious cabin seem tiny, especially when he closed and barred the door behind him.

Her pulse went rapid at the sudden intimacy between them. Why had he locked the door? He stood a good twenty feet away, but the space felt like a tiny closet. She gulped.

"I've read about biscuits served on historic ships, but in everything I've read, they talk about the bugs. Little worms, and larvae, and—" *Stop talking!* "But this was delicious! And the bacon, just like my English grandmother always talks about. Please, do you know where she is? Her name is Hannah."

He crossed the distance to the table before she could blink. He grabbed a chair, swung it around backward, and threw a leg over it, crossing his arms along the back. He sat perhaps four feet away, looking up at her with humor lurking at his mouth.

"Go on."

"My Nan. Where is she? She was on the day trip with me, and there was a storm, and a wave washed me overboard."

"And this was where?"

She ducked her head, remembering what Raven had said. "Just off Mayaguana. I'm told that's a long way from where I was found. The last thing I remember is ..."

You. Pressing his mouth over hers, sharing life-saving oxygen with her as she passed out. She risked a glance at him.

He bit his lip, a smile at one corner of his mouth. Even as she noticed the smile, he sobered.

"Who are you?"

The color returned to her cheeks at his voice, as deep and demanding with the question as when he had seduced her in her dream. She must have heard him speaking to someone else while she slept—that could explain how she knew what his voice would sound like, and the comfort it would carry.

"My name is Marley," she said. "I'm from Virginia."

He raised his head, considering her truthfulness.

"What does your father do there?"

"My father and mother died when I was young. My sisters were taken away. I only have my grandmother. Please, do you know where she is?"

His face underwent a transformation as pity moved him, as quickly masked by indifference.

"I do not. You were within thirty feet of my ship with a British warship on the other side of you. Can you explain that?"

What was he accusing her of?

"I—no, I—I don't remember anything about it. I remember imagining things, while I was underwater. My parents were there, talking to me, telling me to hold on. And then I remember you grabbing me, and …"

"And what?"

"You saved my life. Thank—"

He stood and turned away, visibly upset. He opened various doors and drawers, and at last she suspected he was checking to see if she'd stolen anything. She glanced down at the shirt she wore. Where would she have hidden any spoils she might have plundered?

"Are you English?"

"Do I sound English?"

"Are you?" he asked again, taking her joke as evasion.

"I'm from Virginia. Which I thought was obvious when I opened my Southern fried mouth."

He continued to pore through his belongings.

"Can I ask you a question?" she asked, her voice no more than a whisper.

"Certainly."

"What year is it?"

He laughed, a hearty sound. "1775."

At last he abandoned his search, turning in time to see her shock.

"I've traveled back into history," she said.

"Traveled where?"

"Not where—when. I've traveled back in time."

His lips—so lovely when relaxed—went tight. "All right. I've known unrepentant liars before, but usually they're much more beautiful."

His words stung in every way imaginable. That they came just after she'd admired his mouth made it worse.

"I'm not lying. I was born in 1991. I grew up outside of Richmond, and I work at Colonial Williamsb—"

"Desist." His voice rose to a roar.

She shrank away, bowing her head and closing her eyes. She heard him slowly exhale. "Any other questions?"

"Where are we going?"

"You're going nowhere. You'll stay in this cabin for the duration of the journey—at least several weeks. Are you certain you don't work for Kit?"

"Kit?"

He scrutinized her, then lifted a hand. She steeled herself against flinching, trembling as he touched her chin and lifted it. "Plain indeed, but Kit hires no hags. You must set a man afire when you smile. Reason enough to make you laugh."

His nearness made her breathless—whether with fear or anticipation, she wasn't sure.

He did not release her, holding her in place, her face uplifted to his. She could feel the warmth of his breath faint on her skin. Her eyes closed.

"Open your eyes."

She obeyed. The same pale, blue eyes of her erotic dreams. The same hair. The same man. But—how?

News flash, Marley—it wasn't a dream!

"Why do you shrink from me?"

She gulped and ducked away, embarrassed at her thoughts.

He let her.

"You fear me. Why? Who lied to you about me?"

She shook her head.

"Look at me."

With the same roughened fingertip that had tilted up her face to his, he rubbed his lower lip. "I am no gentleman, but I can be gentle. As you know well by now. I will not hurt you. And as alluring as I find you, I'll never force you."

He rose, his gaze still on her face, and walked around her to the maps. He rolled them up and locked them in a wall safe. "You are not to leave this cabin—unless you would prefer to bunk with the women in the cabin below."

"Yes. Yes, I'd rather stay with the women."

He laughed, and despite his mockery he grew even more attractive. "'Twas a joke. They're whores, more dangerous to you than I ever could be. Kit, especially. She'll recognize the spirit that lurks in you. A beautiful woman like Kit hates nothing more than a seemingly plain woman whose spirit makes her irresistible."

She had no idea where he'd gotten that idea. Just moments ago she had flinched from his slightest movement.

"I am a coward without courage. Other children rightly called me Mousy Marley."

He laughed. "That, my darling, you are not. Intelligence and boldness flash in your eyes, and when you give them their head, you'll overcome the fear life has taught you. I pray I'm there to watch your first flash of courage. It shall be no squeaking mouse, but the roaring lioness."

For that moment, his gaze on her was utterly gentle, and something moved within her. His mouth softened into a smile.

"Do you know the feeling you get when you're most afraid? When you tremble and shake?"

She nodded.

"That is naught but God's invitation to courage. His power within us to do what we must. That you have not been taught this is no fault of yours. When you encounter it, take a deep breath to harness that power. Find a battle cry, and use it."

She gazed at him in wonder. Was he truly teaching her, or mocking her? A battle cry, from mousy Marley?

"I'll return by dark. Do you know how to read?"

"Of course." Did he think her dull as well as plain?

"Then I invite you to avail yourself of my library." He reached the door. "Are we agreed? If you leave this cabin, I'll chain you to my bed."

"You lock me in. How am I supposed to go anywhere?" Then she heard his last sentence again and warmth flooded her at the idea.

His eyes lit with lighthearted threat at her retort. "I fear you might persuade my halfwit partner."

She laughed at the thought of Raven.

His smile went deeper, and he caught his lower lip in his teeth, a habit she was growing fond of. "Ah. I was right."

"Please, can't you just tell me where we're going? Won't I see when we arrive?"

"Boston. And you're traveling on the ship *Adventurer.*"

As he locked the door behind him, Marley accepted that she was neither comatose, dreaming, nor dead.

What, then, might explain all she'd seen this day?

For the moment, she was done with wearing a shirt and nothing else. She rummaged through the closet, looking for something resembling pants. Lacking other options, she chose a pair of the captain's breeches.

She looked over them. He was a slim man, but they would still swallow her. Taking them back to the bed, she turned them over and found adjustable lacings. She tightened those as much as she could.

She slid into the pants and buttoned the front. They weren't so bad after all. The hems hit low on her shins, almost as long as pants. Still comically baggy, they made her look like she was costumed for Halloween as a vagrant pirate who'd fallen on hard times. She tucked in the shirt to further thicken her waist, then walked across the room, delighted that they stayed up.

She found a vest and decided to put that on under the shirt. At best, it looked weird. But it gave her some small bit of support, and for that she was grateful. After a short search, she found a small sewing kit and went to work taking in the vest. The rest, she left loose for now. Lacking shoes, she dug in a drawer until she found a pair of stockings that looked well worn. He wouldn't mind loaning her these.

And, because she'd been ordered to do something that any reader would consider a fantasy, she selected a stack of books and retired to the sumptuous daybed and quickly lost herself. Occasional notes scrawled in the margins, in the same handwriting as that on the map, amused her—the same observations any booklover might make.

She paused to consider how different he was from the sort of man she'd thought she might expect in a ship's captain— even one, presumably, for a theme ship for the uber-wealthy. For surely that could be the only explanation, could it not?

She remembered his claim that it was 1775. He had answered her matter-of-factly, without embellishment.

She set the books aside at one time, stopping to marvel at the construction of the daybed. The trim was ornate and carved by a master craftsman. When she touched the back wall, she noticed a small panel that seemed separate of its construction.

Pressing against the panel, she was startled when a small chamber opened. A hidden safe.

Hesitating, she listened for footsteps but heard nothing. She was certain she would hear anyone descending the ladder from the quarterdeck. She reached in and found a stack of papers and another ledger, similar to his ship's log.

The papers looked like legal documents, and she set them back into the safe and opened the ledger.

> *Thursday – 19 October 1775*
> > *18 casks gunpowder*
> > *30 casks saltpeter*
> > *24 cords firewood*
> > *32 muskets*
> > *12 bayonets*
> *Monday – 12 June 1775*
> > *8 carronades & shot packages*
> > *8 demi-cannons*
> > *1 ton 32 lb. round shot*
> > *1 ton 16 lb. round shot*
> > *10 casks gunpowder*

Two more pages later, she found *Inventory of HMS Glory, unescorted frigate, 28 August 1775.*

Among its spoils were a variety of cannons and other large guns; bayonets, muskets, gunpowder, shot, and a whole list of practical foodstuffs, liquor, and firewood.

She turned the pages, her spine tingling. Could it be? This was no prop for tourists. This was indeed the work of a pirate.

No. A *privateer*.

Chapter Ten

By the time Marley heard the key at the door that evening, the sun had begun its slide into the water beyond the horizon.

Hawk entered, his glance lingering on his clothes on her. "Fetching."

"Here's your supper, sir—" came the voice of a young boy in the passage, before the captain slammed the door in his face.

Opening a drawer, he grabbed a knit cap and threw it to Marley. "Stuff your hair up under this."

She did so, awkwardly. The long waves, unruly with sea spray, did not go willingly, but as he reached for the door, she finished up.

The tow-headed boy who entered might have been fifteen or sixteen years old, and he looked around until he saw Marley, his curiosity easy to read. He inspected her and found her wanting.

"Jem, this is Marley. He'll be traveling with us on this voyage."

After a long moment, he said, "Hullo."

At the table, he arranged two places for supper. He opened a bottle of wine with surprising expertise and half-filled two glasses, then set the bottle into a clever brass fixture on the table that looked to be placed so for this very purpose.

He padded back to the door, casting a glance at her as he passed, and fetched two full pails of water, placing them beside a washstand. He half-filled the basin and set the bucket aside.

As he readied to leave, he stopped near the captain. "Anything else for you tonight, sir?"

"No. Just the equipment I requested. And for the rest of the voyage, please sleep with the men. Marley shall tend to my needs."

The shock and anger on the boy's face burned bright. "But, sir—is there something I—"

"That'll be all, Jem." The words were kind but firm.

The boy bowed stiffly. "Aye, sir."

He left the room and, presently, he hauled in from the passageway an armful of rigging that looked like a large net. He trudged across the cabin and placed it near the windows.

As he headed out the door, Hawk stopped him. "Jem, how long have you been with me, son?"

He straightened to his full height. "Three years this past July, sir. I'm nearly sixteen now."

"Indeed you are. How would you like to become a seaman?"

The boy's face went blank. "Truly, sir?"

"You'll train your replacement, beginning day after tomorrow."

"Do you mean I'll get to—"

"Yes, Jem. Powder boy, firing the big guns, all the joys a boy's head can hold."

He thrust out a hand to the captain. "Thank you, sir. Thank you. I won't let you down. Oh!" he added in sudden afterthought, glancing back toward the table.

"Forget something?"

He shook his head in embarrassment and ducked out of the room. The captain barred the door behind him.

"The boy's like an adoring son. But I'm too soft with him, and it does him no favors. Another captain would terrify him."

Turning to Marley, he plucked the cap away, smirking at her outfit. "So you'll take my clothing as well as my cabin?"

A flush moved up her throat as she retorted, "Would you have me naked instead?"

"Is that an option?"

She laughed.

As he drew away, watching her with surprising shyness, he gestured to the basin. "At sea we use drinking water only for drinking, but I thought perhaps you'd enjoy at least washing up a bit. Mind if I open a window?"

"I didn't know you could open ship windows."

"On this ship, you can."

She leapt at his offer of clean water, scrubbing her face and hands and throat and upper body with the small cake of soap there. It was decadent, the clean water splashing over her skin.

She dabbed herself and the washstand dry with a small towel he offered. "What should I do with the water?"

"Leave it." He gestured toward the table setting, and she claimed one of the glasses of wine as her own and moved to the open window, intoxicated by its richness. Cool, crisp sea air filled the room, along with the lap of the waves cresting and falling behind as they sliced through.

She sipped the wine, stopping—for the first time since the shipwreck—to love life, even as peculiar as hers had become.

She leaned on the edge of the window, laughing with delight at the stars—more brilliant than any she'd ever seen.

"Careful. Not sure I could capture a mermaid twice in this lifetime."

Her face was flushed with pleasure as she turned back to the cabin, and she went still at what she saw.

He had stripped off his shirt to wash. He placed something—perhaps a piece of jewelry—in his top drawer, and he turned to the washstand. His casual acceptance of her presence during such an intimate act intrigued her, and she sank to a chair, silently sipping her wine.

Then, thinking perhaps he assumed she'd stay distracted with the stars, she turned away from him. And yet there he was reflected in the candlelight in the windows, and temptation grew too great.

With undisguised appreciation she turned and watched him. She had never known anyone who enjoyed such an everyday task as if it were the most sensual experience available.

The joy of life's simplest pleasures. Fresh water was a luxury that in her time was no longer relished as such. Certainly that would be different with the captain of a ship.

He walked to the basin and bent over it, washing in the same water she'd used. His action bore the frugality of a sailor who'd known thirst. That he'd allowed her to use the water first, as small a gesture as it seemed, touched her. At the end, he dipped his head into the water and scrubbed his head with the soap, his long fingers massaging his scalp.

He rinsed like a child playing in the bath, and a smile turned the corners of her lips. He opened a drawer and withdrew a shaving mug, stirring up a lather and dabbing it over his heavy stubble. Then he quickly whisked it away with a straight-edged razor.

He glanced at her, then paused. "What?"

She shook her head silently, looking down at her glass of wine and sipping as he shaved. The shave had revealed a face that belonged on a man far more vain than he.

Rinsing, drying, and storing the blade, he withdrew a sponge and dipped it in the water, scrubbing his chest and neck. And as he turned his head, stretching his neck in enjoyment, he caught her smiling at his ablutions. His gaze on her simmered with blatant sexuality.

"Care to scrub my back?"

Certainly he was teasing her. "Seriously?"

"I never joke about a lovely lady scrubbing my back."

He held out the sponge to her.

She sipped the rest of her glass and rose with deliberate slowness. When she arrived, she saw the amusement in his eyes glimmer with invitation. He held out the sponge in an upturned hand.

"Are you sure you don't want fresh water?"

"Yes. This is more decadence than I've known for months. You weren't nearly as filthy as you seem to think."

"Well, you were," she said, dipping the sponge and squeezing out the gray, hair-flecked water.

He chuckled as he turned, presenting a broad, muscled back for her viewing pleasure. His skin was tanned a deep reddish-brown.

The wine had stirred her mood, sweeping away her fearlessness. She scrubbed firmly, enjoying the supple give of his muscles, kneading and massaging him.

"Ah. Were you a different woman, I would request a back rub."

"Were I a different woman, you'd already be having it."

This pleased him, and she enjoyed the sound of his laughter.

At the narrow curve of his waist, she continued washing. Her ministrations fell to the edge of his breeches, and she saw the paler strip of skin revealed below, untouched by the sun, and it took little imagination to imagine the firm roundness of his narrow hips.

Abruptly he took a step away, quickly towel-drying his hair and, sadly, reaching into a drawer for a clean shirt.

"Thank you." He cleared his throat and buttoned the shirt.

"My pleasure."

"But a luxury for a man like me, without a wife."

And utter joy swept her. She smiled at the silliness of that.

He grasped her by the shoulders—as would a big brother, she suspected—and steered her back toward the dining table. She sat, contemplating her empty wine glass sadly, more reluctant to appear a lush than to be one.

He lifted the basin and walked to the door of his private toilet—head, she corrected herself. She leaned forward to learn the proper method for discarding the water, but it wasn't much of a surprise. He dumped the filthy water into the toilet, which likely had a direct outlet into the ocean.

When he returned, he once more drew the damp towel through his hair, then shook his blond locks into place. He gave a long sigh of pleasure, and Marley found herself echoing it.

Glancing at her, he paused, then hung the towel over the small rod at the side of the washstand.

Damp, his hair curled loosely around his freshly shorn face. The curls gleamed like molten gold and bronze in the candlelight, and he met and held her gaze as he tucked his shirt into his breeches. Then he held out his hands, posing for her approval.

"Fit for dinner with a beautiful lady? Try to ignore the bare feet. I did at least wash them on deck."

She tried to come up with a clever quip. Instead, she held out her glass. "May I have more without seeming like a drunk?"

A rumbling chuckle came from his chest and warmed her even as he drew near with the bottle, pouring. "You're dining with a sea captain, and I have a hold full of more, should this run out. Does that help?"

"More than you know."

He raised his glass. "To mermaids and sea witches."

She raised her own. "To sea captains in days of yore."

"Ah, the pirates," he said, taking the captain's chair. "A bloodthirsty lot to be remembered as romantic as they are."

She remembered the hidden ship's log she'd found this afternoon and felt suddenly awkward—as if she'd betrayed him. At what point had she stopped fearing this man?

Had it been the moment she learned he was a privateer for the young country at war with the most powerful army, the greatest navy, in the world?

When he saw to her comfort before his own?

Or when she watched him play as a child in the water, knowing how he must have looked as a child coming to love the ocean?

She didn't know. She knew only that she no longer feared him. That instead he had awakened a nurturing instinct in her. He seemed so terribly alone, no one to fear at all.

And that miscalculation should have terrified her.

They found in their dishes a rich beef stew with root vegetables, and Marley could only eat perhaps half her serving.

He nodded toward her plate. "Jem thinks you're a growing boy like himself."

"Would you like it? I'm quite full."

He declined, unlocking a drawer and withdrawing a cigar. "Do you mind?"

She shook her head.

"Would you like one?"

Laughing at his teasing, she shook her head. Only then did she realize it had been a serious request. "May I try some of yours?"

With a knife he cut off the tip, then lit it with a piece of tinder at the stove.

"Why not just use a candle?"

"You get the taste of the candle—whale oil."

He took several puffs, then held it out to her with that gaze she already was fond of—a combination of seriousness and flirtatiousness.

"Don't inhale. It'll turn that lovely skin of yours greener than the olive already there. Just puff—like a kiss underwater." His eyebrow raised, bringing to mind that moment deep within her, the moment he had saved her life, sharing his oxygen with her.

This man is a rake.

But no matter how her common sense heckled her, she was transfixed. She took the cigar, hefting its weight, its symbolism of the sort of man she'd daydreamed about for the past ten years.

He reached into a glass-fronted liquor cabinet for a bottle and glasses and poured a generous splash into each, pushing one over to her. "Don't be afraid. Kiss, taste, blow."

She obeyed, turning over what he'd just said.

When she blew the smoke out, she sipped from the glass—rum—rolling it, too, around in her mouth, mixing it with the tastes of the tobacco.

"Where are they from?"

"West Indies. Cuba. That wine's also fine with this cigar. What do you think?" He sipped the rum.

She perched the cigar between her teeth, grinning a roguish smile, and he choked with laughter on the rum. She had no idea what she looked like, but it had pleased him.

"You need a gold loop and a parrot," he said, reaching into the drawer for another cigar. With it came an ashtray that he placed between them.

Marley was inordinately pleased at his implicit approval, then recalled something he'd said earlier. "What do you mean, olive skin?"

"Your coloring. Just a bit of olive. Any Roman ancestors?"

She shrugged. "I'm American. They could be from anywhere."

He shook his head. "If you're American, they're likelier to be English, Spanish, Dutch, or ... well ..."

"What?"

"Natives or ... forget it, you're likely right about having Italian blood."

"What?" She was just relaxed enough to push the subject.

"All right. African."

"I don't have any black in me," she said, laughing at the idea. "You haven't seen me dance. My grandmother is English—the rest, I don't know."

That was odd, she thought. With all her father had taught her about the distant past, he'd never mentioned his own parents.

"You say it as if I insulted your honor. My best friend, dearer than a brother, happens to be descended from Africans. And likely a white or two somewhere along the way."

"I did not. I have the dullest, most uninteresting lineage of any person ever born on this continent. If anything, I was insulting *myself*."

"Nonetheless, lascivious masters have had their slaves since the beginning of slavery. Is it so unlikely that there are lascivious mistresses as well, giving birth to the children of strapping slave lads and passing them off as planter aristocrats?"

"I know that, but ..."

And then she remembered Nan, speaking of her grandmother coming from an exotic land.

His eyes narrowed through the cigar smoke as he watched her, but he said nothing. He gathered up the remains of their meal back onto the tray Jem had left, set it all outside the cabin, then barred the door. He returned to the table. "Up."

Marley rose, and he placed his cigar in the ashtray. He drew the chairs away from the windows and opened another window, locking it into an open position, and it was almost as if they were under an open sky.

Then he lifted the contraption Jem had brought in and separated it into two piles of rope. Grasping a loop at one end, he slipped it over a hook in the ceiling, then did the same at the other end.

Marley smiled in pleasure. It was a hammock. Moments later, both were in place, swaying in the slight breeze from the windows and the motion of the ship.

He walked around the cabin blowing out candles, leaving only a couple burning near the bed.

Moonlight poured into the cabin and lent him a dark, almost sinister aura. He walked to her, took the cigar and placed it in the ashtray. He arranged a small table between the hammocks and there he placed their drinks and cigars.

Standing at one of the hammocks, he held out a hand to her. "Care to view the constellations?"

Delight filled her, and he spread the hammock apart for her. "There's really no graceful way to do this. Just throw a leg up, and then ... well, no, not like—wait."

He quickly saw it was too tall for her, and he lifted her in his arms. She spread the sides of the hammock apart, relaxing into it. "Okay, I've got it now."

He stepped back—for only a moment.

"Oh!" Her panicked cry came just as her rear end popped through the ropes that had been severed there. She was bent nearly double, stuck, her stockinged feet flailing in the air, her riot of curls bouncing everywhere.

He laughed until he, too, was bent double.

For the most fleeting moment embarrassment stung her, until she imagined what she looked like.

And—even more so—when she noticed the look in his eyes, no mockery at all, simply delight.

She reached for her cigar and puffed it, propping her elbow on her knee as she peered up at the sky. "Ah, yes, I believe I see Orion's belt."

Here he roared with laughter.

From the open window came the cry: "Will you two pipe down? Some of us are trying to sleep. I had to eat down here in second class, I won't be reduced to a groundling at a second-rate play. And you better not be smoking my cigars."

Raven.

Laughing, Marley set aside the cigar and attempted to leverage her way out of the hammock. "A little help?"

"Hm. This way I would know you won't wander off." He rubbed his chin thoughtfully.

"I'll scream rape." She was unsettled by Raven knowing she was alone with the captain this time of night. Why, she didn't know. Where else would she go?

"He knows better." He lifted her clear of the sabotaged hammock. "That rotten lad. I didn't know he had such mischief in him."

"Who?"

"Jem. You've made an enemy, I'm afraid. He'll likely apologize tomorrow, he regretted it before he ever left."

He crossed to the other hammock, testing it, glancing at her. "If you don't mind sharing ..."

She blushed in the pale moonlight. And then she nodded.

He swung into the hammock and reached for a walking stick nearby, anchoring the hammock with it. With his other hand, he grabbed her around the waist and swung her up. "Watch out for the table."

She squealed and landed face down on him, spread-eagled, in an intimacy that swept them both with excruciating pleasure.

His rakish humor left him as he held her hips in place—presumably to keep her from falling out of the hammock.

"Careful." His voice was a low command against her throat. "Focus. Moon and stars."

His hands smoothed over her hips as if in appreciation, but then he easily lifted her, working against her nervous fidgeting, and tucking her to his side.

"Hand me a cigar, darling, and a glass of rum."

She smiled as she did so, then did the same for herself.

"What?"

She shrugged. "It just seems quite—intimate. All of this."

"Marley, you have no secrets from me."

"You don't know me at all."

"I know enough. Hush. Exhale. Behold."

She looked into the sky, realizing that the windows he'd opened included a skylight. The night sky was open to them, the windows placed so the sails didn't obscure their view.

The moon rose into a cloud as ethereal as gossamer, lighting it into an apricot glow. Presently the clouds passed, leaving only the moon and the stars.

The stick clattered to the floor. "Oh, shall I get that?"

"Just a walking stick. Not to fret."

"Why does a man as young and virile as you need a walking stick?" She heard, too late, the suggestion in her words.

But he ignored that. "It belonged to someone dear to me."

"Your father?"

"Oh, no." He laughed. "My father is equally *virile*, if not quite so young."

She smiled. "Oh, a shooting star!"

"A babe sent from heaven."

She stopped to think before speaking, then, knowing the answer to her unasked question; a sea captain would indeed be superstitious.

"Where does he live?"

"He owns a home in Williamsburg and a tobacco farm with a good deal of land. He also owns properties in England, and an estate in Bermuda—St. George's."

"Do you look like him, or your mother?"

"My mother."

"She must be a beautiful woman."

He blew smoke rings into the air. Finally he responded, "She was. She died when I was born."

"I'm so sorry. Did you grow up in Williamsburg?"

"My father suffered a string of terrible losses there that year. He could no longer bear the place. Everywhere he looked, he was reminded. He tried for a time to live on my brother's plantation, but was no happier there. So he purchased a sloop, hired a crew, learned to sail himself, and loved it. He built the home in Bermuda. He became a new man, as sea-loving a sailor as any salt who ever drew breath.

"He refuses to discuss his life in Williamsburg. What little I know, I learned from servants. And only recently has he taken to visiting the town again. Truth is, he's there now, waiting for me to arrive and carry him back to Bermuda. But enough of this." He flicked ash into the ash tray and sipped his rum.

She enjoyed him telling her about his father—but curiosity still nagged at her. "But—what about that walking stick?"

He sighed. "It belonged to the man who taught me how to command my own ship. He, too, is dead."

"What was his name?"

"He went by the name of Michael. Ah, I suppose it doesn't matter now. His name was Crispus."

"Crispus Attucks?"

He went still. "How do you know that name?"

She blew away the smoke, then sipped her rum, content. Truly, how little they still knew of one another, yet.

"You've already said you don't believe me."

"Then try once more."

"He was the first man to die for the American Revolution, dying at the Boston Massacre in March of 1770. An escaped slave whose mother was of the Massachusetts tribe. They were known as Natick Praying Indians.

"All things I could have learned from any local Boston newspaper, but I did not. I learned it from my father, who was an American history professor before he died in 1994, then learned it again and again in the classroom."

"Right. I'd forgotten." He gently took her glass of rum and drank it down. "Here, put that back on the table. If one of us is going to be a drunken raving lunatic, I have the poorer imagination."

She giggled at his dismissal of her confession as drunken blather.

"I told you that you wouldn't believe me. I didn't smoke much of this, I'm afraid." She tamped out the cigar in the ashtray and turned carefully, facing him, looking into the sky at another angle. "What's your name?"

"Hawk."

"I mean your real name. Your Christian name. I want to say it."

"Ah, I'd like that, too. But the less you know when we arrive in Boston, the better. Michael gave me that name, and Raven his, to protect us. It has served us well, especially this year."

"Why this year?"

He sipped his rum, making a thoughtful noise. "It has been a *busy* year. Well, you should know that, being the time traveler. Lunatic monarch, a crowd of treasonous colonials, Brits with big guns, and all that."

She cuddled against his throat, brushing her lips against the pulse under his ear.

"Have you ever been in love?"

He laughed. "Have you, sweet Marley?"

Her mouth opened against his throat, and she drew her tongue upward to his ear. "How old are you?"

Suddenly she was so sleepy, she abandoned her kisses and snuggled into his neck, relaxing.

"Twenty nine—I turn thirty next July fourth, if the fates spare me."

"What do you mean?" she asked, her clarity fading away.

"You're sailing on a doomed ship with a man cursed to die before his thirtieth birthday."

She didn't hear him. She only felt him draw her close to his heart, and drop a chaste kiss on her forehead as he stared up into the stars—as if searching for an answer there.

Chapter Eleven

Marley awakened in the captain's bed with an aching head. In the faint light, she saw Hawk seated at a chair, fastening his shoes. When he noticed she was awake, he rose.

And then she noticed that the warm, easygoing man she'd come to know, to trust, was gone.

"What's wrong?"

He walked to the daybed and turned back to her as he slapped open the panel concealing the safe. He withdrew the contents and dropped them into the leather seat of a chair.

"Without lying, if you are able, how much did you read?"

Cold dread swept Marley. She sat up, swinging her legs over the edge of the bed.

"I saw the papers, but I didn't look at them."

"Ah. Kind of you to leave my will alone. And the ledger?"

"I read it all. That you're a privateer, and quite good at it."

"You did not see the Letter of Marque?"

"No. I assumed it's with the Continental Congress since you're not English."

He exhaled, pointed anger glimmering in his eyes. "One need not speak the idiom of the King to be a loyalist."

After a slow moment, she stood, trying to appeal to his reason. "Are you suggesting I'm a loyalist?"

"You have proven it yourself by prying in matters that were none of your concern—after I forbade you."

"That was not my intention. I was sitting in the daybed reading, like you told me to. I admired the carvings in the wall and touched one—and the panel opened."

"And how, I ask once again, did you arrive in the water where I found you?"

"I've already explained that as best I can. I know it makes no sense."

"Tell me the truth!"

His rage shook the room, and she dropped to the edge of a chair. He took a step closer. "*Now.*"

Trembling, she rose, trying to swallow her terror, facing him. Her voice quavered as she spoke—but speak she did.

"My parents were Robert and Cassandra Hastings. They were murdered when I was three. I had two sisters named Rachel and Juliana, and they were taken away. My grandmother is Hannah Hastings. She and I took a pleasure trip, a day cruise, from Florida to the Bahamas. There was a terrible storm and the last I remember is you rescuing me. You know the rest as I know it."

She swallowed, and he remained silent. When she found the courage to look up at him, he was staring at the ship's log and papers he'd tossed on the chair.

"I have spoken nothing to you but the truth. If I were you, I wouldn't believe me, either. But you have no cause to fear me."

"You are correct in one matter. I do not believe you." He walked to the door. "Since you cannot be trusted below deck, you will work with the men above. You have an hour to tailor the clothes you wear to better fit you without revealing that you're a woman. Then you'll report to Raven. You will replace Jem in his duties and be glad of it. If you were a man, this hour I would have you whipped—or perhaps worse."

With that, he closed the door behind him.

But, she noticed with delight, not locked. The disappointment she felt at his anger and distrust was softened by this. Exhilaration filled her with the freedom promised in his action.

She nibbled at breakfast, drinking down her stout black coffee. No sugar this time, but it was growing on her. She wondered how a cigar would taste with coffee. Not that she'd ever likely taste another one of Hawk's.

The memory—was it just last night?—made her face grow warm, with him holding her in his arms as they watched the stars and smoked cigars and drank rum. Not the silly stuff of romance as she'd imagined it, but far more powerful, for a woman like Marley. He had invited her into his world and shared its best with her.

Would this act of imagined treachery end their growing intimacy? She couldn't see any other option, judging from his anger.

Her borrowed clothing was already tailored as best she knew how, but she tied her hair into a ponytail then wound it into a knot and stuffed the knit cap over it. She emptied the chamber pot into the toilet as she'd seen Hawk do it, then spent the rest of the hour tidying the cabin.

She looked at the cotton stockings she'd borrowed from Hawk. They were already showing dirt, and she hadn't left the cabin. She brushed them, pulled them up underneath the pants, and unrolled her sleeves down to the wrists. She tightened the collar as much as she could, trying to hide her missing Adam's apple. Finally, she gave up.

The caffeine in the coffee further energized her, and she grabbed the tray of dirty dishes, heading up the narrow ladder.

If any doubts about the truth of her strange voyage lingered, they vanished as she reached the top step to the main deck. She gasped at the view. The sun was rising into a blue sky studded with white clouds, the air pristine. No land on any horizon. The wind pulled at her cap, and she tugged it back into place.

The men she saw—everywhere, it seemed—were not actors. They perched in the rigging, trimming sails and studying the horizon. They knelt on the deck, holystoning and sanding the wood with methodic care. The man nearest her, a raw-boned, shirtless fellow wearing a brown scarf tied around his head, sang a lusty shanty as he hammered at a structure, perhaps doing carpentry repair.

He looked up at her just long enough to observe the new boy before he opened his mouth to belt out another verse. Around the edges of his teeth was a line of gray discoloration showing decay. And, as excitement filled her, just for a moment Marley stopped to love her life.

"Watch your step!"

She lost her balance trying to avoid a mop the man nearby was slinging in long, wet strokes on the deck. He jumped back, alarmed, as her tray teetered, as she stumbled, and the men nearby turned to watch her dance a clumsy jig before righting herself.

"Marley! Over here!"

Even as she turned to look for the speaker, Jem arrived. No longer hating her guts, he was cheerful and even ready to be helpful.

"Galley's below. When you're on deck, keep your head down and steer clear of the men. You're liable to get your noggin walloped, if you don't stay out of the way."

He led her to the galley, and she found it trickier descending with the tray than coming up. She dreaded serving dinner, and what that might entail.

She heard Cook before she saw him. He muttered in an Irish brogue as if to someone, but they arrived to find him alone in a galley stacked with dishes.

"Why did the crew leave you alone with all this, sir?"

He threw up his hands in disgust. "I sent 'em away. I'd rather do it meself than put up with the likes of them. Get to work."

"Sir, I have duties to the quartermaster up above now, but the new boy here, Marley, he can help you."

He clapped her once on the back before vanishing.

Marley looked around at the piles of battered metal plates and tankards. How many men were on this ship, anyhow?

"Don't just stand there, boy, get going. Them potatoes are waiting for peeling, too." Then, as she stared: "Argh. You ain't never been a cabin boy."

She shook her head.

Cook pointed out two empty tubs. "For washing. For rinsing. I'll help ya by getting the saltwater for washing. You get the fresh for rinsing. Are you simple, boy? In the hold, down below. Hurry now. Wait—don't forget the buckets."

She scurried away with a pail in each hand. Noticing Jem nearby, busy oiling a squat, fat cannon on a slide, she asked, "How do I get down to the hold?"

He directed her, and she raced down three narrow sets of stairs, finding the hold. The casks of water stood to one side, and she filled both buckets. Gripping the pails—perhaps thirty pounds between the two of them—she mounted the first step of the ladder.

Well, nervousness will do you no good, Marley.

And at that moment a rat raced along the rail to her left. She stifled her own scream, but her reflexive jerk toward the right unbalanced her, and down she tumbled, back into the hold, dropping the buckets.

Great start here. Bruised rear, soaked legs, and wasted freshwater. As she refilled the pails, stinging from pain, she focused on how it could have been worse. She could've broken her tailbone. She could have spilled the water all over, rendering her disguise useless. She plucked the clinging pants away from her thighs and went on counting her blessings as she stiffened her spine and headed up.

At the top, she almost shouted for joy—until she spied the remaining two flights.

Up she went.

In the galley she found Cook scrubbing the plates, occasionally sprinkling in a handful of sand. When she carried her buckets to the rinsing tub, she saw it already filled.

"Almost forgot." He gestured to the other wall. "There's two casks of fresh water, here."

She stared from the casks to Cook, scratching one soggy calf with her other foot, the toe already poking at the threadbare stocking. The wiry old man grinned at her, baring exactly four teeth.

"Ah, that'll teach you, lad. Listen to your master, but use your head. You can't always trust your master. He may be a wicked old man ain't been to Confession since he was a wee one."

With as little expression, as little pitch that might reveal her as a woman, as possible, she asked, "Sir, what's your real name?"

"Padraig. Got tired of mealy-mouthed boys calling me Paddy, so I go by Cook. Why do you ask?"

She took the dish he was feverishly scrubbing. "I don't know anyone on board, Padraig. It's good to have a friend."

He gave an impatient noise and a dismissive wave. "When those dishes are clean and dry and stacked away, get going on those potatoes."

She set her mind to getting through the chores as quickly as she could. Fortunately she'd learned the joy of work as a child, and she found enjoyment passing the next hour.

Jem reappeared just as she was placing the peeled potatoes in a gigantic kettle.

"Sir, can you spare the boy while I show him some of his other duties?"

With a scowl and a wave of his hand and a sparkle in his eye he couldn't conceal, he dismissed his helper. "It'll be waiting for ye when ye get back."

Jem led her down one deck and down the passage. "Now usually most of your duties have to do with the captain. But this voyage is different, seeing as we have ladies on board. The captain doesn't like traveling with ladies, but we didn't have no choice in the matter. The colony needs marriageable ladies. So the thing is, he don't want 'em up on deck. So everything they do—eat, shit, piss—it all goes on in this room."

Delightful.

They arrived at a door, and the noise inside set her teeth on edge. Even in school, she had disliked giggling girls.

"Your duties with the women are to take them their meals, empty the chamber pots, swab the deck. There'll also be laundry day before we make Boston. I'll help you with the chamber pots this morning, but this evening, it's all yours."

When Jem opened the door, the feminine voices rose in feigned sexual interest. Instinctively, she knew this was likely to be the toughest part of her job.

A dozen or so women were scattered around the room, half on crates, playing cards. The rest sat alone, grooming themselves, or in pairs, chatting. When they glimpsed Jem and her, their voices rose, no doubt relieved from the tedium of solitude.

The women swarmed them. "And who's your handsome young friend, Jem?"

This from a woman who appeared to be their leader. She propped one foot on a crate and eyed Marley with frank sexual interest.

"This is Marley, Miss Kit. He'll help you from now on."

"Oh, he looks helpful indeed." She straightened, bringing her boot to the ground with a bang and then sauntering toward Marley. Her eyes glimmered with desire.

Holy cow, this was awkward. Marley knew her acting skills were dismal, and she lowered her eyes, noting with great sadness how filthy this floor was. What did these women do all day, have spitting contests?

She raised her eyes again to the woman named Kit, startled at her beauty. Jet-black hair and luminous gray eyes. However, this was eclipsed by the sudden confusion in the woman's gaze, as if she didn't know quite what to make of Marley.

As if she knew the truth.

At last, the woman laughed, pinched her on the rear, and turned back to the tittering women. "You can have him, girls. He can't be more than 12 or 13."

The women screamed with laughter.

Marley exhaled as quietly as possible. These were *not* well-bred ladies. Perhaps they'd leave her alone.

"Go on, now, ladies," Jem said, awkwardly placing an arm between them and Marley. "He's here to work, and he's already scared as a little bunny. He don't need your help there."

Two huge chamber pots stood in the corner, and Marley was relieved they were at least covered. They were also quite full, however, and the smell choked her.

Jem showed Marley how to empty the chamber pots directly into the ocean without splashing their awful contents everywhere. He then directed her to take a pail full of seawater and mop back with them. "When you do this tomorrow, take the mop and pail with you when you go. Save you a trip."

"Do the women never leave their cabin?"

"No. It would be easier, wouldn't it?"

She nodded at him with wide eyes.

"Captain says there would be anarchy. Plus they couldn't use the head anyway. Men would be gawking."

"What about their beds? Do they make them themselves?"

"Captain says no one's to touch their beds. I'll leave you to it, and be back soon for your last morning chore."

As she mopped around the base of the beds, she realized the structure wasn't a bed. They slept on crates, covered with thick quilts.

Sudden understanding swept her. These women weren't faint-hearted Christian maidens; they were prostitutes, ensconced over the crates as decoys.

Here, she was certain, was the gunpowder she had read about in Hawk's hidden ship's log.

She finished scrubbing a corner then walked to retrieve her bucket and leave.

One of the women kicked over the bucket—slyly, as if by accident.

Another woman squealed. "Mary! 'Tis the first time this floor—or deck, or whatever you call it—hasn't been sticky all week. You—"

And a fight was on, with the women scratching and clawing and sliding down into the filthy water, yanking at each other's hair. Marley was alarmed to see one hand come away with a clump of hair, until she realized it was a hairpiece.

"Stop it, now." The quiet voice in the corner boomed into the fray.

She noticed the older woman dozing there. Apparently a housemother of sorts, watching over the young ladies.

She sighed and started mopping up. Again.

Padraig had the midday meal ready for the women, and Marley delivered it to the table set up in their cabin, hastily setting out the dishes. Jem followed behind with two heavily laden trays stacked with tankards of beer.

"One thing I forgot," Jem said as they left the women. "Never take a candle in there. Do your last visit before dark."

"Why?"

"Don't know the answer to that. I think the old hag who watches over them is afraid of fire. She growled at me one time when I forgot."

Confirming Marley's suspicion about the gunpowder.

Her final chore of the morning took her back to where she'd started. The great cabin of the captain.

When Jem knocked and heard a deep voice greet him, he ducked his head inside. "Didn't know you'd be in here, sir. We can come back later."

"No. We're finished."

"Sir, we're so sorry. The women's cabin took longer than we expected, and …"

Hawk waved them in. "Don't give it a second thought, Jem. We scraped out a meal, as you can see."

He sat in the captain's chair, one ankle crossed over the other knee, drinking from a tankard. Raven sat at the table, across from a man Marley didn't know. All three were drinking, enjoying an inside joke of some sort. The unknown man met Marley's gaze and gave a brusque nod.

Hawk spoke with distant politeness. "Philip Deming, this is Marley, my new cabin boy. Jem is training him."

Marley noticed the same lingering glance from Deming that she'd seen in Kit—as if each of them knew a secret about her that even she didn't know.

She ducked her head and bowed stiffly, as she'd seen Jem bow to the captain the night before.

She avoided the captain's gaze, troubled to realize that the reminder of her was painful to him. Not only did he no longer trust her—through no fault of her own—he clearly regretted his intimacy with her. At the moment, he seemed unaware of her.

Between her aching back, her blistered feet and hands, and the low blood sugar from her empty stomach, she was able to put him out of mind, although he was less than ten feet away.

She'd only thought she'd tidied the room this morning. Jem showed her otherwise. First she dusted the room and his books and instruments, then Jem gave her a small pot of wax and set her to polishing the teak covering nearly every surface in the room. Then, she changed the bed linens, replacing them with fresh linens from a cupboard. By the time she began sweeping the rug and mopping the rest of the floor, the men and Jem were gone. She stacked the men's dishes and glasses on the tray, straightened their chairs, washed and polished the table, and left the room with the heavy-laden tray.

A time for lunch failed to present itself, and she found purpose and distraction in the never-ending work on board the ship. By the time the dinner dishes had been done, she realized she was weak from hunger, but was also way too tired to care.

The captain's cabin was dark and deserted when she arrived, as spotless as she'd left it. She stood in the center of the room in the waning light of sunset slanting through the window, uncertain about what she'd intended to do.

"Oh. Right," she said to the room.

She shuffled into the hallway for a lantern, brought it into the cabin, and lit a candle. Quickly she lit a few others along with three lanterns over the captain's table. She replaced the whale oil lantern on its hook in the hall, then sat in the daybed to await the captain's further directions for the day.

All simple details of living in the eighteenth century that she'd known academically in her old life, but that she had learned firsthand today as she grew acquainted with this huge, insatiable mistress of a ship and her constant demands.

For a moment, all the aches in her body cried out against the simple action of sitting down. Then, a moment later, the rush of joy over resting filled her, her head clunked against the wall of the alcove, and she fell asleep sitting up.

Chapter Twelve

A weary, moody Hawk worked through the second dog watch, until the sun vanished into the water and the moon rose high overhead. He'd worked harder that day than he'd worked in years, purely to exhaust himself. He wished for the dozenth time in the past week that he'd never stopped to fish that awkward, impossible, beguiling woman from the surf.

The thought of her disappearing unknown into the surf left a little hole in him. An awkward, impossible little hole.

Today had marked Marley's second day serving as a cabin boy. Last night he had stayed in Raven's cabin—as lavish as his own, one deck below—to avoid her. He had slept little.

He'd seen her, bedraggled and limping, descending toward his cabin at the end of the day, but he wanted to be too tired to do anything near her except sleep. Yesterday morning, he'd thought his anger greater than anything he'd ever felt toward any woman. He'd awakened and with the daylight was able to see his hidden compartment ajar, the papers inside in disarray—and he knew her betrayal.

She knew everything. Nothing could explain her actions except treachery.

Then he'd watched her, yesterday and today, without her knowing, watched her tote pails and tubs almost larger than she, watched her hurry to obey Jem's orders without complaining. He'd watched her labor today, unaided and unbidden.

She'd never spotted him, simply going about her chores quickly and quietly—as hard a worker as any man here. He'd watched her on her hands and knees in his cabin buffing the teak carvings around his windows and bookshelves. And his admiration—his affection—for her had deepened.

His cabin indeed. When he'd brought Raven and Deming to his chambers the day before for the noon meal, he'd seen her everywhere. A room where he'd lived for over a decade now. He had watched the stars countless times with Raven, with Michael, the same way he had with her.

Now that isn't quite true, is it?

Good God, no. He'd been delighted that night when he'd learned Jem had knifed the second hammock, had lain awake watching the stars with her sleeping contentedly against his side for hours before he rose to take her to his bed to sleep. And again holding her that night, he'd slept a better, sounder sleep than he had in years.

There was no logical explanation for her appearance than that she had come from the British warship—and yet nothing in her spoke of anything except a desire to please him.

So, he told himself, she was competent at treachery.

There. With that thought, he was ready.

He headed below.

His cabin was nearly dark, aside from lanterns she'd lit over his table and a single candle. His bed was still made.

Where was she?

He peered around the room, then lit a candelabra. There she was, nearly hidden in the daybed, curled into a ball in the corner, her head at an awkward angle, as if she'd fallen and gone straight to sleep. Her face was nearly covered by her pathetic knit cap. He lit the candle in the sconce there and stooped beside her, planning to move her to the bed.

She was filthy.

He touched her fingers, feeling blisters and dried blood where a nail had broken into the quick and bled unnoticed. He removed her cap gently. Dust and grime covered her face. Her hair was sticky. What the hell had Jem had her doing?

At the door, he called to a sailor on watch. "Have a hot bath brought up."

"Sir?"

"Fresh water. Rouse Jem if you have to."

"Aye, sir."

Presently the bath was brought into the room, and she slept through the ruckus that entailed. An extra bucket of warm water sat beside the filled tub, and Hawk closed and barred the door. He dropped a towel over a chair near the tub, then approached the daybed.

He knelt at her feet and slipped his fingers into the tops of her stockings—an old, worn pair of his—and pulled one down. Where the sole had been before, it was now tattered strips and threads, and utter filth. When he sought to draw the piece all the way off, it was stuck. He tried to find where it was caught on her breeches, but he went still. A strip of the tattered sole was embedded in her foot. He gently tried to pull it loose, and she cried out.

He stopped.

She'd worked for fourteen hours today and the same yesterday with no shoes. For most of the crusty salts on the *Adventurer*, it posed no threat. But she was a woman, no doubt accustomed to finery. Like perhaps decent shoes.

He stripped off the other sock without incident, but he touched her feet lightly, finding them covered with broken blisters. He quickly removed the rest of her clothes, took her to the tub, and almost set her down in the water. He noticed the pillbox she always wore, and he removed it and slipped her into the water. She gasped and splashed, her legs sprawled out of the water. He ducked away from her flailing limbs.

"Shh." He stroked her hair, then tucked her foot with its dangling sock attached into the water. "Relax. Go back to sleep, if you like."

"Just so tired." She yawned and was asleep again.

He leaned her head back against the lip of the copper tub—

it couldn't be comfortable for her, but she was mostly submerged in the water, at least. He slipped a knife from his boot and trimmed her broken nail, as best he could.

With gentle patience he soaped her face and hair, then moved down her body. By the time he reached her feet, the soaking had loosened the stocking, and he dropped it beside the tub.

He'd known women in Paris who had delicate, decadent soaps they guarded as if they were cherished pets. He wished he had those soaps now to tend Marley's wounds. The soap he had was neither decadent nor delicate.

He worked up a lather and washed her hands and arms, then her legs and those abused feet. When she was clean and the water grimy, he trickled the fresh water in the pail over her, through her hair, leaving her clean and well-scrubbed.

He gently twisted the towel around her thick, unruly hair, then whispered her name, bringing her to her feet. She stood there sleepily, her head hanging.

The candlelight glistened in the droplets of water clinging to her, the curve of her throat, the fullness of her breasts and hips, the slimness of her waist.

Would that this were a different moment.

He toweled her off and had her step out of the tub where he dried her feet. He lay her in the center of his bed, then found a fresh pair of comfortable stockings—some of his favorite—and a tin of ointment. He daubed it on her blistered feet and covered them with his stockings, then just a bit on her palms.

She reclined on a pillow, an arm over her head, lifting her breasts in unconscious invitation to him. The peaks were erect, pale pink, hungry for his kiss. He trailed a hand between them, along the curve underneath and even as she gave the faintest, unconscious murmur of pleasure, shame filled him at the sight of his work-stained hand against her firm, luminous flesh.

Good Lord, you cur, she's dead to the world!

He stripped off his clothes and scrubbed in the cooling bathwater, and when ten minutes later he found himself still aroused at the sight of her, he released that tension. He rinsed, stepped out, and dried himself, then rubbed the towel against his wet curls, watching her, aroused all over again. But at least his earlier release had relaxed his exhausted body.

He realized the room had gone cold. They were into the Atlantic now, Bermuda's warmth far behind them.

He started a fire in the stove, stoked it well, and turned, relishing the reality of this woman in his bed. Loyalist or spy, time-traveler or lunatic, mermaid or sea witch—

She was his.

Who knew how much time he had left here—or she—but he would waste no more of what he had with her.

He threw another quilt on the bed and blew out the remaining candles. He climbed in beside her, kissed her throat, rested his hand over her shoulder, and rubbed gently. She lifted her head aside with a soft moan.

He turned her over onto her stomach, straddled her hips, and rubbed her shoulders and back until he felt the tight knots loosen. His naked body's desire to find his pleasure within her was fierce, but his greater desire was to protect her from all—including himself. With her much more safely asleep on her stomach, he lay beside her and pulled the covers up over both of them. He returned to his side, resting his palm over her back.

Moments later, she turned back on her side and wriggled backward into his embrace, as she had that first night. Then again, that night, he hadn't been naked. He sighed, enflamed at their intimacy, her firm, womanly hips cradling him.

Again he spoke her name, but she replied naught save collapsing a hand over her shoulder. He obliged her, taking her hand and kissing her fingers lightly, then wrapping an arm around her, his hand between her breasts, over her slow, steadying heartbeat.

He dropped light kisses from her shoulder to her ear. "My name is Bronson, my darling."

She stirred in his arms, turning her face toward him. "Hm?"

He kissed her ear lightly. And with his own heart's other half tucked against him, once again he dropped into a perfect sleep he'd known only with her.

❧

Hawk awakened to the sound of waves crashing against the hull, the rain pattering against his windows, and a moment later, the cry of the lookout.

"Sail ho!"

He quickly dressed, slipped on an oilskin coat, and left Marley sleeping in the room.

"All hands on deck," Raven shouted, followed by the squeal of the pipes and the thunder of feet on deck.

Hawk rushed up the ladder. And there he found Raven staring through a spyglass. "King's colors, as if you couldn't guess. Two, I'm afraid."

Hawk leapt upon the slide to a carronade, holding out his own glass to look. A schooner of good size, still some distance off, accompanied by a frigate. But they were bearing down hard.

And the Hawk and the Raven began to work in tandem the way Michael had taught them. As if they were a single organism—nature's cooperation that Michael had first observed in them.

"Furl the mizz'nmast sails," Hawk ordered.

Two sailors scrambled into the rigging.

The captain and his quartermaster exchanged a glance, and the captain nodded. "Close reach starboard," Raven called, and as the riggers worked, Carter, the helmsman, turned the wheel.

The sails filled in the rainy gust and plowing surge of the sea, and almost immediately, the *Adventurer* began to pull away from the British ship.

The sound of cannon fire caught their attention, but the shot fell several hundred feet short. The ship continued after them.

Hawk climbed into the rigging, tacking a sail a bit more to his liking. From there he raised his glass, peering at the ship through the storm. "Don't we know that schooner?"

Simmering rage filled him, then, and he gave a bitter, imaginative curse.

"Tell me it isn't." Raven had echoed his partner's perfectionist's leap into the riggings to tweak one of the mizzenmast sails. Now, reading his mind, he, too, looked at the other ship.

"The devil's own, Stephen Falligan, on the devil's *Delight*. Accompanied by a frigate and sailing low in the water, she's heavy with spoils."

"He will not let us go."

"We still owe him for the indignity of delivering his last ship as a prize. And we'll have this one, too."

"Oh, captain, sir, we seem to be headed in the wrong direction for that task."

"Too far from shore. And we don't have the element of surprise on our side necessary to contend with that frigate. So for now, live to fight another day. You can wager he's headed to Boston."

For the moment, they continued to gain distance, and the rainstorm turned out to be a boon to them. The escort had to be having a tough time loading and firing in this soup.

When they were a good ways out of sight, Hawk dismissed Raven, who'd been sailing through the night.

"How's your cabin boy?"

Hawk shot him a look. "He's in a sad shape. Didn't I ask you to keep an eye on him?"

"I told him to slow down. He was trying to prove something to the other men."

"A lack of intelligence?"

"More's the surprise, he outworked at least two of them together. And besides, you saw him as well as I did. Small miracle you didn't fall off the rigging yourself, focused as you were on that lad's smallest movement."

Hawk turned away from him. "Go to bed."

"I accept. Mind if I borrow yours?"

"Do it and die."

Raven laughed, then exhaled with a chortle deep in his chest, loudly mocking as he headed toward the hatch. "Rescue the drowning boy. Save the drowning boy. Put the drowning boy in the captain's cabin. What could go wrong?"

Chapter Thirteen

Marley awakened, sore but well-rested, to the faint streaks of an early morning sun shining through the windows of the captain's cabin. The tap at the door caught her attention, and she blinked in confusion.

"You awake?"

"Yes," she called.

The door opened, and Raven entered with a tray. He moved a table beside the bed and placed the tray there. Over one shoulder hung a pair of shoes, and he set them on the table beside the tray.

"What's this?"

"Breakfast. Captain thought you might feel better by now."

"How long have I been asleep?" she asked, huddling under the covers.

"Best I can tell, about 36 hours. I don't suppose you're …" He gestured at the covers.

She blushed and shook her head.

He hastily stepped away to the door, looking into the passageway. "Just wanted to check and see how the shoes fit."

"Raven! Did you make these for me?" Holding the blanket around her, she sat up and reached for what turned out to be a pair of new, hand-tooled moccasins.

They were unlike similar shoes she'd seen before, with a lip of the soft leather rolled tightly into a cuff of sorts and buttoned at the ankle. Unrolled, they could convert into boots. Leather laces went through hand-punched holes. The interior of the shoe was lined with fur.

Her feet were already in comfortable stockings, though she couldn't remember donning them. She slipped her feet into the shoes, marveling at the perfect fit.

"Not to say I *couldn't* have, but no, I didn't."

"Well who did?"

"Prayers to God above, could you please put on *something*? I'm only a man, and I don't wish to die."

Only then did she realize a cold draft swept in from the door.

She spotted a thick, dark shirt near the bottom of the bed and scrambled into it. It was heavenly. And when she snuggled her face into the collar, she smelled Hawk and smiled.

"All right, come in and close the door. Sit and eat with me."

"Thank you, no. I only want to explain the shoes."

"I can see. This part can be unbuttoned and turn it into a boot. Can you teach me how to do my hair like yours?"

"The captain might well kill me."

"Why?"

His eyes lowered with a smile. "Ah. Well, your cap helps disguise your lovely face."

"It falls in my face all the time. I can't see very well. Grime gets all over me. I walked into a stovepipe the other day."

"Oh, all right. Put your coffee down." He sat beside her on the bed, and she turned, presenting her back. "You have the nappiest hair I've ever seen on a white woman."

"I know. The captain told me. He thinks I'm black."

Raven laughed. "He just likes black women. He wishes he *were* one."

"A black woman?

"Well, no. Just black. Don't think too badly of him. Aside from having the sad habit of being enslaved by other human beings, 'tis a fortunate lot indeed."

He crossed to the captain's dressing chest and yanked open a drawer, withdrawing a warm red scarf. "Don't think he'll miss *this* much."

He smoothed his fingertips through her hair, then tied it at the nape of her neck in the scarf. Then he worked quickly, and in no time her hair was wrapped into a neat club hanging down her back.

She turned to him, beaming.

"How are your feet?"

She wiggled them. "Much better. Thank you for whatever you did, they hardly hurt at all. The other night, I could barely walk."

"Again, 'twas not my doing. Now, I've duties to be about. The captain suggested you help the ladies if you felt up to it. However, no galley duties."

"But I like Padraig. He's my favorite part of the job."

"Who?"

"Padraig. The gentleman who does your cooking."

"Look. Marley, we're simple folk. He calls himself Cook, so that's good enough for me."

"But I can't visit with him anymore?"

"Visit all you like. Just don't tote water or wood or anything to hurt yourself." He headed toward the door and looked back at her, eyebrows raised in emphasis. "Understand?"

"Begging your pardon, Mr. Raven, but if I want to tote wood, I shall tote wood."

"If the captain has to waste another night performing ladies' maid duties, tweezing your pretty fingers and nursing you, your behind will be the next thing that needs tweezing."

His words became the harmless roar of a lion cub that made her laugh. He opened a drawer, withdrew another cap, and placed it over her head. His face was grim as he gazed at her. "And Mr. Raven is my father, thank you."

With that, he slammed the door behind him. She noticed, again elated, that he left it unlocked.

She found her clothes where someone had left them washed and dried over a chair. She quickly dressed and admired her new shoes once again. Marley had grown up the kind of girl who could spend a day in a bookstore, but who visited shoe stores only when her own were worn thin. Loving shoes was a female phenomenon she did not comprehend.

But these shoes—practical, comfortable, and clever—she loved.

She spent the morning, once more, mucking out the alleged ladies' cabin. When she brought their lunch, she brought along a small gift.

Despite their mockery of her, she pitied them. They stayed here all day and all night, with no light except that of one small porthole high above. Were she called upon to do the same, the darkness would have driven her mad by now.

So, after much debate, she found a small dish, filled it with water, then placed a lit candle in the middle of it and placed that by the door. Kit watched her in dismay. "You know the captain doesn't allow us to keep candles in here."

"Aren't you tired of all the darkness?"

Kit looked up at the low beam just above her face, then shook her head. "Dear God, I am. But the weather tells me we'll be in Boston soon, and—" She suddenly studied Marley. "Where did you get my scarf?"

"Your what?" Unconsciously, she touched her braid.

"You thief," she growled, crouching as if she were a wild animal preparing to pounce. Instead, she reached out to snatch the scarf away, dismayed to find it embedded in Marley's hair. Instead, the cap came away.

"Give it back. That was my scarf, a gift to the captain. 'Tisn't yours to wear. 'Tis a woman's scarf, anyway. Aren't you ashamed?"

"But I thought it was the captain's."

"Did he lend it to you?"

"Well, no, but—"

Kit tried again and failed again to disentangle it from Marley's hair. Grabbing her by the thick, heavy adornment, she went into a litany of enraged squeals. "Give it back! 'Tis mine, not yours."

"It's the captain's," Marley gritted out, pulling on the top half of her hair, pecking her head away from Kit in an attempt to escape.

Good heavens, in another ten seconds she'd be dragging her around by the hair like a caveman.

"What, pray tell, is this?"

The voice behind Marley sent dread deep within her, and she looked up from the floor against which Kit was busy attempting to bang her upper body.

The captain's rage was focused on the lit candle, which he blew out. Then he looked at the scene, and his shoulders sank in defeat. He grabbed Kit and set her aside, then pulled Marley to her feet. She spotted her cap on the floor and quickly yanked it over her head.

"What's the meaning of this?"

Marley shrugged, trying to pluck the tightly knotted scarf out of her hair; it was impossible. "I guess I had a scarf of yours I wasn't supposed to. I apologize."

He looked around her at the disheveled dressing hanging down her back. His hand spread over the lower half of his face, rubbing downward, and she wondered if he was trying not to laugh. *Not bloody likely.*

"I thought you loved the scarf. 'Twas a gift for your birthday." Kit was on the verge of tears. Under her dreadful cap, Marley rolled her eyes.

He looked at Kit with a calming, paternal smile.

"Isn't it clear this is Raven's doing? No doubt his idea of a joke. You know I love it."

"Then why would you let this common boy wear it?"

"As I said, I didn't know. He'll remove it, won't you, boy?"

Marley nodded once, her eyes downcast as she wondered what kind of relationship these two had shared.

"Now, what's the meaning of the candle? I've been clear this room is to have no candles. 'Tis crowded and *hot* already."

Inwardly she groaned. How had she forgotten? She'd pitied the women so, she could've blown them all to Kingdom Come.

Hawk's expression was veiled as he grabbed her upper arm and jerked her out of the room. As she glanced back on her way out of the room, she noticed Kit's scrutiny—as if Marley were a puzzle she'd grown weary of trying to figure out.

He strode toward his cabin, his stride long. She flew after him, trying to keep up.

Inside his cabin, he barred the door, sat on a chair, and yanked her across his lap, face down.

Marley blushed at the indignity, flailing to find a surface to push herself back up. His left hand held her back in place. "What are you—"

"Were you not warned about candles in that room?"

She fidgeted, uncomfortable at his focused scrutiny, at his hand firmly clutching her upper thigh, his thumb trailing innocently between them.

"Answer me."

With his left hand, he raised the shirt that she'd left untucked, revealing the shapely curves of her buttocks. With her legs stretched out, she felt the tightly drawn fabric of his old, worn breeches across her rear end, revealing all.

"Yes, but I'm a grown wom—"

"Aye, that I can see."

He smoothed his hand up over the roundness of her buttocks, then suddenly smacked her there.

"Stop that! It hurts!"

His palm roved over the curve of her buttocks, one finger tracing the line between down to where it disappeared between her thighs.

She lifted her hips in invitation to his touch. She moved one leg, parting her thighs slightly.

His hand came down again in a lightly stinging rebuke to her carelessness. She noticed the difference between the first and the second.

"Do you truly want to kill us all?" His voice was low in her ear, almost strangled. She wriggled in surprised pleasure at his teasing spanking, and against her hip she felt his own hard arousal.

She shook her head as she turned her head toward the sound of his voice, but the cap had fallen over her eyes.

In a moment, the tension left him, and the exasperated sound he made was half laughter, half despair. He drew her up, across his lap, and pulled off her cap.

He held her immobile, his arms around her, his face against hers in desperate tenderness. She could taste his breath, could feel his heart racing under her hands, yet he did not kiss her. He only held her close.

"Up," he whispered.

She came to her feet, shaky with arousal at his touch. He rose, turning away, feet planted, fists on his hips.

When he turned, his eyes were bright with emotion. He gestured toward her hair. "The scarf."

"Oh." Thanks to Kit's attack, the scarf was in a knot. She fumbled with the knot that fixed the club in place, which was now a tight, tiny mess with her hair strung through it.

Hawk sighed. "Sit."

She obeyed, sitting in the chair where he directed.

He worked at the knots, freeing strands of her hair with gentle patience. "'Tis clear this is the work of a seaman."

"I just liked how neat his hair always is. I thought it might make it easier to—"

"Silence."

Staring at her feet, she asked suddenly, "Did you make my shoes?"

He exhaled wearily as he continued to work. That he didn't pull her hair at all spoke of his dexterity with knots—and she remembered hotly that morning when he'd first touched her and had first mentioned untying knots. At last, the twisted scarf fell to the bed.

"I just wanted to thank you, if you did. I love them more than any other shoes I've ever had."

"No need to mock."

"I wasn't. I do love them. Did you, then?"

He didn't respond.

"And I did not know the scarf was dear to you."

"It isn't. I had forgot it. 'Twas merely pouring oil on troubled water."

Reaching for a drawer in his chest, he withdrew a small bottle. A few moments later, he began working long, relaxing fingers from the ends of her hair to her scalp, releasing a luxurious, romantic aroma.

"What is this?"

At last, he said, "Tahitian jasmine. It reminds me of better days."

"What do you mean?"

"I traveled to Polynesia first with my father, as a boy. I traveled there last with Michael, as a man. My father no longer sails for enjoyment, Michael is gone, and the world is at war. Is it any wonder a bit of floral elixir can bring a man joy?"

He turned to his dresser, and she rose, feeling the soft, tamed curls. "I keep it in this drawer, but 'tis yours now."

"No, I couldn't—"

"Stop," he pleaded. "'Tis a small gift—and a selfish one—from one who has to tell you the impossible."

She waited, the simple pleasure of his gently dressing her hair dampened.

"You cannot leave the cabin for the rest of the voyage."

She was surprised at how that stung.

"But I worked so hard. My fingers—"

"I know. I dressed your wounds."

"Then why—"

"You took fire into a room containing enough gunpowder to destroy every English ship lurking in Boston harbor. Can you at least tell me why?"

"Will it change anything?"

"For you getting out of this room, no."

She hesitated, knowing how stupid she was about to sound. "I felt sorry for the women, staying in that dark room all day and night."

"It is not forever. Are their needs not met?"

"I would be terrified, in the dark."

"Perhaps you did not know the powder was there."

"I suspected it, the first time I visited. I simply thought if I left the candle in a dish of water, they would be grateful, and would be careful."

"Be careful of what? They have no idea they're sleeping on gunpowder."

"What?"

"High treason! Not something I generally confess to strangers."

"But they surely know what you do for a living."

He laughed, his skylit eyes now darkening to sea-azure. "I do this not to survive, Marley. I do it not for the profit, but because I saw a lowly, simple man, a man who had no rights in this society, display more courage than any king has, by standing up for injustice, standing up for a boy he didn't even know. I do it to honor his courage."

She watched as he spoke, as his gaze rested on the walking stick leaning against his dresser. He licked a corner of his lip thoughtfully, then raised his gaze to hers. "Perhaps you can help me? How would you explain that to the lady who was ripping out your hair over a scarf?"

"Can't you forgive me for the candle? I'm so sorry."

"My Marley, I'm coming to realize I could forgive you almost anything. This isn't about punishment."

"I don't understand."

"A ship on its best behavior is a dangerous place for a woman. A ship full of unpredictable women of questionable character is far worse. Add in a load of gunpowder and a woman whose own courage unnerves me, and I can scarcely focus on what's in front of me, let alone threats out there awaiting."

He walked to her and rested his hands on her shoulders. "I do it not to punish you, but to protect you." His hands slipped down her back to the curve of her waist, drawing her against his chest. "Forgive me for striking you."

"It didn't hurt," she said softly, her breath brushing the bare skin of his chest where the shirt opened. She raised her lips to his throat. "It excited me."

His gaze kindled. "A captain does hate to encourage disobedience." With that, he teasingly swatted her behind again as he kissed her hair and drew away. "Please don't set the place on fire while I'm gone. Tonight, perhaps, I'll finish what we've started here."

Marley pressed smiling lips together, unable to speak as he gave her a fiery glance.

Tonight, perhaps, she would ask him why he wouldn't kiss her.

Chapter Fourteen

Raven sat in the mess with the men finishing a game of dice, filled with anticipation, filled with thanksgiving.

First, they were almost home. Despite the cold, Boston was his family's home, he'd been gone for months now, and he had missed them. Unlike the rest of these misfits, he had a home and he disliked being away almost as much as he loved sailing. Perhaps not quite as much, but he loved and missed his family.

Helen, the next oldest, would have given him another niece or a nephew by now, and he missed being the amusing uncle. Not that Eston was likely to garner that distinction, with his nose always in his law papers. And Parks, his baby sister. When they'd sailed out of Boston, she was still gawky and giggly, all legs and arms. Now, he couldn't wait to see her. Times were uncertain, and he feared for them all.

The older he grew, the more he enjoyed his time on land. The more he yearned for a proper home of his own. Somehow, during their time in Boston, he was going to have to find a way to tell Hawk that soon, he would give up the sea. The thought broke his heart.

Second, it was nearly time for Thanksgiving. Although many of their neighbors celebrated the days of thanksgiving appointed by the colony, nobody did it up like his mother. She turned no one away, she invited strangers who soon became friends, and last year in their modest two-story home, she'd fed fifty. She would roast turkeys, and bake hams, and prepare crab cakes and macaroni and cheese and sweet potato pie. Only a seaman could understand how he could sit at a table gnawing a leathery piece of beef for an hour and still be hungry. The seaman, after all, understood better than anyone the luxury of fine food.

Third, it would be nice to get away from Hawk for five minutes. He wasn't sure what was going on with that man, but he'd ignored Raven's pleas to improve his mood by taking one of Kit's wenches into his cabin for a couple of hours. Now that place was occupied fully by their visitor—and there, Raven was fairly certain, the problem lay.

Aside from Raven, no one understood the captain. Women took one look at that ungodly pretty face and thought him to be a rake and a flirt, someone they knew well how to hypnotize. But he had been reared by an older man, a serious and well-educated man who had made his own share of mistakes, and he had taught the boy all about life's finer virtues early on.

Intense. That was what women who took the trouble to know Hawk, said about him—and not complimentarily. Raven couldn't tell; he'd known him all his life, so as Mama would say, Hawk just was what he was.

And while Hawk did indeed enjoy frivolity in its time— often when they arrived back in Bermuda after a long journey, when he would find a girl he liked and spend several days with her—he had no use at all for silly women.

He suspected that their mysterious guest on this voyage had unwittingly captivated Hawk the first moment he saw her in the surf. She reminded Raven so much of his mother it was a little disturbing. She was like a wildflower, hardy yet tender— and bright, apt to blossom again when one least expected. And she had that flavor of beauty that could keep a man enchanted the rest of his life. Imperfect. Unique. Huge light brown eyes—again, like his mother's. And she rarely spoke at all.

"You're getting as absent-minded as the captain," Deming said. "What is he about, lately? Does he have a fever?"

Raven harrumphed. "If you're so concerned about his well-being, ask him yourself."

But Deming was right. Hawk's concentration wasn't a fraction of what it used to be. If he knew Hawk, he might be lost already to Marley. This, he wouldn't mind—as long as they all wound up settling in generally the same locale.

If only they could successfully navigate the murky waters of treason.

Surely, if Hawk decided to marry, he would give up his ship. Women and ships, they just didn't mix. This voyage had proved it better than most.

The thought gave him pause. If ever a woman might work out well on a ship, he thought, it might be Marley. If she could keep from getting herself in trouble. She had too much energy to be left below for weeks at a time, and too much earthy appeal to bring on deck. He himself had a hard time dismissing her from his baser musings.

He was so mired in thought he lost his next throw. And then came the lookout's cry, along with the chirp of the pipes.

"Sail ho!"

They hastily turned up the table and fastened it to the wall, then hurried above.

Hawk arrived straightaway and they examined the ship on the horizon, growing larger.

"*Delight* again."

"Unaccompanied?"

"Appears so." Hawk put down his glass. "What do you think? Up to a little tussle?"

With all his thoughts of home fresh in his mind, he was loathe to entertain visions of cannon fire blowing a hole in his midsection. He hesitated. "So close to home."

"Never a better place. She's lost her escort."

"How do you know? Perhaps she lurks just beyond the horizon."

"She would be sailing ahead."

"And us with a hold full of whores."

"Come now, is that any attitude to have toward our comely patriots?"

After long consideration, he said, "You know my mother's not many miles off, fattening turkeys."

Hawk clapped him on the back with warm affection. "I do know that. We'll be there in time to fight over the drumsticks."

With that, the orders rang out over the ship and the men went into motion. They ran clattering down to the mess hall where they pulled down tables and with sheer brute force wrangled the cannons into the portholes. They scattered over the main deck, sliding the carronades into place.

And one of the men hurried to send up the commander's brand new ensign: *Appeal to Heaven*.

As Raven watched the flag rise and fly in the wind, hope and fear warred within him. They were one of only a handful of ships authorized to wave the flag, courtesy of the Commander-in-Chief of all military forces, thanks to the Continental Congress. Not that Congress had much of an idea what Washington was up to, from one minute to the next.

"You are forging a new country, son. Never lose heart. In all things, have courage."

The memory of his mother's earnest, quiet plea when last he'd seen her, stirred his heart. And then, as he always did during such moments, he remembered the man who'd taught him through his own example courage beyond any free man's imagination.

Michael would have been pleased.

Hawk stared into the distance in dismay. Falligan was attempting to flee. This, more than any other piece of evidence, assured him that they'd lost their escort. It would take long, hard sailing—and luck—to catch him.

But catch him, they did. Without a single shot. The *Delight* had dropped anchor when they arrived, and Hawk sent Raven, Deming, and half a dozen of his men out to man the *Delight* and escort Falligan back. As the boat headed across, he strode over to his cabin and looked inside.

Marley sat in the daybed, *Gulliver's Travels* open on the bed beside her, her eyes alert on him. The worry on her face was clear. She was fully dressed, her hair fastened underneath the cap, her back ramrod stiff. The reading was a ruse.

"Stay here. We're taking an English merchant ship and will be adding passengers, some of whom will dine with us this evening. You'll remain here throughout."

She came to her feet with sober attentiveness. "Yes. I won't be serving?"

"No. You'll be sitting quietly in the corner, not drawing attention to yourself."

"Yes." She returned to the daybed.

"Marley."

She waited.

He fought the urge to hold her—perhaps one last time, these things were always fraught with risk—and raised his head.

"These men and I have a history, and it isn't pleasant. If anything goes wrong—hide. The daybed is as good a place as any, as I'm sure you've discovered. Do what it takes to avoid capture. Tell me I don't need to explain why."

"No." Her voice had fallen to a whisper.

He closed the door behind him and ran down to the room where the girls were hidden. "Mother Barbary, a word?"

The mother hen padded to meet him at the door. "We're capturing a prize. The captain of the ship is Stephen Falligan. Perhaps you recall him."

She hummed. "Perhaps, perhaps. We shall keep a lookout, captain."

He gave a nod, locked the door behind him, and headed back up.

Watching the exchange of crew members through his spyglass, he noted Raven directing the return boarding party.

Falligan descended into the boat, followed by two others. One, he didn't know. Then he made out the face of the third, and his gut clenched—it was that perversion of humanity, Percy Snaveling. He debated on whether to put Marley in with the other women. They would be safe from Snaveling, whose appetites were barbarous. But dressed as she was, she would be brutally raped before he learned the truth.

Why the hell was that bastard still alive?

Perhaps she would have the sense to hide in the daybed—he had no idea whether she'd found it by now, but she was a sharp girl.

Hawk barked at his next in command, and Conrad hurried forward. "Yes, sir."

"Keep your pistol trained on them. Relax your guard at no time, no matter how harmless they seem."

Conrad joined another armed seaman on the quarterdeck. As Falligan and the others prepared to board, Conrad stood behind a carronade and braced his forearm over it, leveling his flintlock at Falligan.

Hawk called the next man over. "Falligan will remain heavily armed, even after he's surrendered several. Stay alert."

The boat arrived, and the officers from the *Delight* climbed the ladder, followed by half a dozen of their seamen.

Falligan, the taller and darker of the two, eyed Hawk in disinterest. "So we meet again, you grimy bastard."

"And under equally pleasant circumstances. Strip. All of you."

The breath caught in Falligan's lungs for a moment, and then he laughed. "I can see your hospitality is as fine as ever. That field hand you sent to board already confiscated my weapons."

Hawk ignored his slur on Raven. All a ploy to gain the upper hand.

"Do it. Now."

"Damn that accursed, useless escort to hell. Had he an ounce of gray matter between his ears, you'd all be dead."

Hawk removed the dirk from the scabbard at his waistband. "Shall I cut them away? Clothing over there. Carefully, now," he added, as Falligan removed his coat. "There are half a dozen muskets and pistols trained on you, and it would be a shame should one trigger finger slip."

Falligan's black eyes glowered as he threw the coat.

"You, too, paederast," Hawk said.

Snaveling observed him, a cool smirk lingering at his mouth.

"By the way, shouldn't you be dead? Is your partner so desperate for the despicable?"

Snaveling ignored him.

"And you—your name?"

The third, younger than the other two but with a gaze Hawk found untrustworthy, muttered, "Hayworth."

Their coats tossed aside, the men waited.

Hawk laughed. "Keep going, boys. We're long at sea and short on amusements. Take it down to the long johns, if you have them. If not, ah, well. There might be a breeze."

"I refuse."

"Very well." Hawk tossed his knife in the air and made as if to approach. Falligan had seen Hawk and his men handle knives, and he knew each was an expert knife fighter.

"Stop. Give him everything, men."

The men reached into each boot and their waistbands, producing a small arsenal of knives.

"That did no more than prove me right. Down to your long johns. If we find no more weapons in your clothes, we'll return them to you. If we do, you're in for a chilly trip."

Anger crackled from both men. Snaveling's cheeks went pink, but Falligan had paled in anger. Hayworth simply glowered. Still, off came their shoes, shirt, and breeches, joining the growing pile of clothes.

They stood in long johns, shivering with the cold of a late fall day in the North Atlantic.

"Mr. Janssen, you'll recall your impertinence to me last evening when I ask you now to inspect these men's persons for weapons. Beware of bugs."

Although a jest, the seaman seemed loathe indeed to frisk the men. Still he did so and gave the captain a solemn nod.

"Mr. Conrad, will you and Mr. Cooper and Mr. Janssen escort these gentlemen to the cable tier and secure them there?"

"Aye, captain."

Hawk shook his head and sighed as the men passed. "My word, I can recall a day, not too long ago, when an honorable privateer could entrust his scurvy guests to honor their own white flag. 'Tis a shame, indeed, what's become of the world."

And with that, he waved a signal to Raven, who watched the exchange from the *Delight*. That ship's crew manned the capstan to raise the anchor, and Hawk led them on toward Boston.

Chapter Fifteen

As darkness fell over the *Adventurer*, Marley lit all the candles in the captain's cabin. At least a dozen times in the hours since they'd taken the English merchant ship, she'd closed her eyes and whispered a short prayer for courage. She'd stopped to slow her breathing and calm herself.

But as the hours passed without Hawk's return, she grew anxious. The only weapon she had to fight the darkness was the candlelight.

Only when she'd noticed that the cabin had grown cold did she realize the fire in the stove had gone out. *Pull yourself together, Marley.*

She hastily swept out the little stove and built a fire, slowly adding more wood to the fire. In time, the cabin grew warm.

For lack of anything better to do, she found a cleaning towel and some polish and buffed the already gleaming table. From the linen closet she found clean dinner napkins. Unsure, she put down four. As she laid out the napkins, she noticed the trembling of her hands.

And then Marley remembered what Hawk had told her— the source of courage. She knew now it wasn't nervousness snaking through her veins, making her shake; it was full-on adrenaline, ready for a fight, without release. Had it been not her fear, but her reaction to it, that had kept her at the mercy of creeps like Jimmy her entire life?

Unsure how to release—or bottle—the adrenaline, she did a bit of shadow-boxing, finding this useless and silly. Then she did a bit of shadow kickboxing which ended when her soft-shod toe encountered the base of the daybed.

The front panel fell away, broken, and she groaned. Now was not the time to be doing light carpentry.

She knelt to investigate the break, and she heard Hawk's voice again in her memory.

Hide. The daybed is as good a place as any, as I'm sure you've discovered.

It was a false bottom, meant for hiding. This one hadn't been as easy to open as the hidden panel of his safe.

The safe! She leapt to her feet, opened the safe and emptied it, then stashed all the papers in the bottom of the daybed. Hiding wasn't called for yet, but taking the precaution of relocating the details of his escapades made sense.

She took a quick glance around the cabin, searching for something that might be perceived to be of value, were the safe discovered. She found his official ship's log and stashed it there, closing the panel firmly. It was a simple ruse, but for now she hoped there might be no need for any of this.

She looked around the cabin, trying to imagine the worst. She noticed Hawk's array of weaponry above the daybed and quickly dismantled it, pistol after pistol, sword after sword, dagger after dagger. This, too, she piled away under the daybed, stuffing it in tightly in case she, too, had to fit there.

The only essential piece missing was a possibles bag, which might have a supply of gunpowder and wad. Ironically so, considering the endless hours she'd spent learning to shoot over the past few years, at work and after work. It had started as a hobby, but she'd evolved into a crack shot.

At last, she heard clattering in the hallway. She thumped the false bottom back in place with some effort. Grabbing *Gulliver's Travels* once more, she hopped onto the daybed and centered herself with four deep breaths.

Slow. Down. Breathe. Now.

As the door opened, she looked down at the book, noticing it was upside down, and calmly righted it.

She raised her eyes to the group who entered. She saw a flash of gravest warning in Hawk's eyes before he turned, genial and generous, to the three men behind him, followed by one of the senior seamen—Conrad, they called him—his face without expression save vigilance. His hand rested over the stock of his pistol, hanging in a strap around him. His other hand rested at a knife in his waistband.

Hawk seemed as if he were hosting a dinner party; Conrad, an execution. Perhaps they were one and the same.

The strangers wore navy uniforms bright with copper buttons and stripes aplenty. They were faded, however, the cuffs frayed, a button missing. She couldn't imagine officers in the British Navy presenting themselves so shabbily, and she was certain the uniforms were a pretense.

The man who entered first was taller and darker, his coloring and expression menacing for its utter pallor. He equaled Hawk's size and physical beauty, but he was a lesser version, as if tainted and twisted by hatred and bitterness.

He seemed almost an otherworldly being, perhaps a vampire, if she believed in such things. He gave her the notice one might give a chair or a muddy shoe. Were it left up to her, he would've stayed under lock and key until they were safely on shore. Only her trust in Hawk's judgment reassured her they were safe.

The second man gave her an unclean feeling of uneasiness. He had a soft, shapeless face, like a glob of dough thrown on a counter to rise. Colorless eyes noticed her as he entered, with a nervous friendliness—as if he feared being observed. That alone solidified her distrust of him.

The third man was dark, his face drawn; and far too interested in the details of the cabin. This man was not trustworthy.

"Make yourself at home, gentlemen. My steward is in the process of preparing our meal."

Interesting how he'd referred to Jem as a steward, as if he were an older man. What was he up to?

Hawk removed tin cups from his liquor cabinet and poured a dollop of whiskey into each. He raised his cup, and the others followed suit.

"To old friends," Hawk said.

The first man gave a short laugh at this, then drank.

Hawk refilled their cups. Standing on the other side of the table, he acted as if he'd only just noticed Marley seated in the daybed. "Seems I've neglected to introduce to you a passenger I have on board. He's the son of a London lord who's a friend of my father. We call him Master Terwilliger."

She pressed her lips together, fighting her amusement at the yarn. The rest of the men turned toward her.

"I should warn you of his nerve disorder. He's quite easily upset, and has the tendency to erupt in wild shrieks and flailing about if someone attempts to touch him. Other than that, tragically, he's entirely mute."

They gave her startled looks—except for the stoic Conrad. But from behind them, the look Hawk gave Marley was disturbingly intimate—even affectionate.

"Boy, this is Captain Falligan, our guest this evening, and his quartermaster, Mr. Snaveling. And this is Mr. Hayworth."

She flashed crazy eyes from one man to the other, underscoring the distrustful loon persona he'd given her. Hawk pressed his lips tightly together and raised his cup in a private toast, then set his glass aside, untouched.

She edged backward into the daybed and opened her book. The rumble of thunder sounded in the background. At the same moment, the cabin began pitching, as winds buffeted the ship. A storm was upon them.

Jem entered and served the men, serving hers at the window seat. He met her eyes in warning before turning back to the room to finish pouring wine. He quit the room silently.

She saw that Padraig had served the same cold fish stew and biscuit they'd had hot for lunch, and she wondered if it had been selected to avoid arming the men with knives.

She ate quickly to focus her attention on the men, then held the bowl tightly on her lap.

Conrad made no move to eat, but merely sat at his place watching the proceedings with calm detachment. Hawk caught his eye and nodded toward his bowl, and the seaman tapped his biscuit on the table, watching his dinner companions.

The storm worsened, a moan rising from the windows.

"I see neither of us is making use of those sheepskins we earned at William and Mary," Falligan said.

"Speak for yourself. My studies of maritime law serve me daily. No doubt yours in banking surely helps when calculating how many barrels of smoked herring will fit in your hold."

"No need to calculate anything in piracy, I suppose."

"Falligan, you of all people should know. It isn't piracy if you have the King's permission."

"As I recall, you no longer have a King."

"I no longer recognize the sovereignty of a tyrant to impose laws that supersede the Magna Carta and when leaders consider martial law a reasonable response to men crying out for relief from this tyranny."

Falligan sighed. "God above, I'd forgotten how you love the sound of your own voice."

Hawk laughed. "Nor I how poor you are at rhetoric."

"And this, the orator so gifted that he finds a living in roaming the seven seas to abscond the ships of the Royal Navy simply for the pleasure of it."

His voice rose from a petulant rumble to a shrill shout.

Hawk tilted his head in perplexed amusement as he taunted Falligan. "You simply cannot let that prize go, can you?"

"Your theft of the *Sharon* cost me my commission—were it not for my father, I'd have been court-martialed and executed."

Hawk sipped his wine and raised an eyebrow. "Stephen, 'tis high time you let it go. That bitterness will burn a hole in your gut faster than the scotch you love. It was a joke. How was I to know your Admiralty Court would take it so seriously?"

"And that old mulatto you had with you back then, tutoring you in your abysmal trade. I didn't see him today. What happened? Did you sell him off to your father's plantation?"

For the first time in the weeks Marley had known Hawk, she saw deadly anger enter him. She'd seen him annoyed with her, she'd seen him irritated with her, she'd even seen him angry at her. But the rage she saw now was beyond compare.

His face lost all expression, and he leaned toward Falligan with an intent gaze. "Listen well."

At that moment, a wave lifted the *Adventurer*, and every candle in the room flickered, then went out, doused in its own melted wax.

And a cacophony of confusion rang through the darkness. Hawk had gone silent.

Falligan, now: "Now you listen well. Snaveling has a knife at your bosun's throat. Try anything, and you'll both die."

At the next crash of lightning, Marley kicked open the daybed panel and rolled underneath, slamming it closed in the camouflaging noise.

For only a moment, the darkness closed in on her—until she realized the scope of true threats surrounding her. She feared what had happened to Hawk—but she knew without a doubt that the tables had been turned. That now Hawk and his men—and she—were at the mercy of three men without conscience.

As she hid, she felt her pulse hammering with adrenaline, and she listened again to Hawk's voice in her memory. *That fear is naught but God's invitation to courage. His power within us to do what we must. When you encounter it, take a deep breath to harness that power.*

And she lay, quietly and calmly, biding her time. Closing her eyes, she listened for Hawk's voice and she imagined she lay in his arms, staring up at a starry sky.

Chapter Sixteen

Hawk awakened with an aching head. And he remembered. Like a helpless infant, like the most shameful coward, he had delivered his ship into the hands of his worst enemy.

The expressionless face of Percy Snaveling came into view. In a moment, he struck Hawk across the face with a cudgel.

"Aside from your own savagery, what do you expect to prove by delivering me beaten?"

Snaveling sneered, proud of his rotting teeth.

"Where's ..." Hawk asked, looking around, then stopping short. If Marley had hidden herself, he didn't want to ruin that.

"Falligan's on deck, establishing the order of a good English ship—if it can be done on this foul tub."

Hawk tasted blood; his lip was split. He spat into a plate. At least all his teeth seemed to be in place—for now.

The storm continued to pummel the ship, but the *Adventurer* was sturdy and heavy-laden, and this close to Boston, she would do fine. Under whose command was yet in question.

As for his own fate and that of the rest of his crew, his only chance was to outwit Falligan, for he knew the only mercy he could hope for was a quick death. With these two, that would be doubtful.

Had Raven yet figured out the truth? In the dark, with the storm, visibility between the ships was close to nonexistent. Yet Raven was sharp-eyed—and at the moment, his only hope.

Truth to tell, his greater hope was simply that Marley would stay hidden. He could not bear for her to watch the humiliation that Falligan was likely to put him through just for the pleasure of it. He was likely to drop anchor here and torture everyone to death, including Marley.

Snaveling checked his own knots again, fixing Hawk in place, then headed to the door. "I'll be back in two shakes, so don't try any tricks." Then he snorted at the sight of the bound, helpless captain, turned and left.

A moment later, he tried to rock the chair and realized it, too, was fixed to a table leg, which was fixed to the deck. And as he attempted to loosen his numb fingers even a bit, he heard the false bottom of the daybed give way. Marley rolled out and leapt to her feet.

Hawk went pale. "Get back in there."

"I won't. I have your knives and pistols, hidden in the daybed. I'll get you free."

After a moment, he asked, "Are you all right, then?"

She raised her eyebrow. "Why would the well-being of an English spy matter to you?"

At this reminder, his humiliation was complete, and he had to look away from her, thinking of all the indignities she'd had to suffer in the past few weeks. "Not my cleverest deduction."

She went digging for a knife and withdrew several. She quickly hid them with pieces of dirty silverware under a used napkin.

"You *don't* have time. Hear that? He's on his way back already. Close that up and grab some dishes, pretend you only just entered to finish your chores. Then go below with the women and lock yourself in there."

"I won't. I will save you."

He saw her working to steady her slender hands, to take a deep breath, and that stirring he'd come to know as hers alone began deep within him. How proud he was of this terrified girl.

"Marley, these men are savage. Falligan is a threat only to me and the men, but Snaveling is a degenerate who rapes boys. I know you're an innocent lass who can't imagine how that could happen, but it can. Why he hasn't been—"

The doorknob jiggled, and she collected herself and began stacking the dinner dishes in the dim light. She'd placed the concealed knives in one bowl to the side. As the door opened and Falligan entered, he was taken aback by her.

"Forgotten all about you. Well, you're harmless enough. Stay out of the way."

She continued to stack the dishes, more slowly now, lingering likely to learn something of his plans.

Falligan drew close, and Hawk recognized his own dirk as it came near, just nicking the flesh at the base of his throat. He felt the slide of a drop of blood there.

"Kind of you to leave your weaponry in such good condition. My thanks."

Hawk looked at him mildly. "Don't mention it."

"Snaveling thinks you'll try to escape, though I cannot see how. Captain, your crew is compliant in my command and wouldn't mutiny even should you attempt an escape."

Hawk's father had raised no fool. He didn't start a knife fight armed only with wit, and Marley's juggling knives at this point only worried him more. If she dared try anything with Falligan, she would be overpowered and slain before she so much as cut him. Fortunately she seemed to understand that.

So he ignored Falligan's goading. No need to say what they both knew. His crew—skeleton though it was—were already plotting a mutiny, and the rest would likely aid them. Men like Falligan and Snaveling inspired no loyalty.

Hawk dropped his head to his chest in an act of defeat— and a convenient guise for refusing to respond.

"What might the rewards be on the heads of the infamous Hawk and Raven, the colonies' most ruthless privateers? Might this be enough to inspire the Admiralty Court to reinstate me? The pair of you have been a thorn in the side of this navy for a dozen years now."

Hawk was silent. Marley continued to work diligently, as if preoccupied with stacking the dirty plates just so.

When she had collected every plate, bowl, utensil, and tankard back onto the large serving tray, she set it aside and went about cleaning and polishing the table again.

"You must have some redeeming value," Falligan said.

"You know how wealthy my father is. He would pay a king's ransom each for my partner and me."

"Surely you're joking. Your field hand? The African? A ransom. I believe the going rate for such a buck is $250. And I recall your father already owning several hundred on the plantation he inherited from your dead brother."

This host of lies was too much.

But even as Hawk's head jerked up, Marley dropped a tankard to the floor, blessedly distracting both men. As she fell to her hands and knees to wipe up the spill, she caught Hawk's gaze, and the steady encouragement there calmed him.

"You know I will be of much more value to you in helping keep the ship afloat in this storm," Hawk said.

Falligan brought the tip of Hawk's knife lightly across his knee, slicing open his breeches and his skin for several inches. Hawk saw Marley recoil, but when he refused to react to Falligan's bloodletting, she went back to her polishing.

"I'll not free you; I'm not the fool you are. But you are right about the storm. I don't wish to drown dallying here with you. I'll send Snaveling back. Take your tray and go, boy."

She hesitated. Beyond the logistics of making it down the ladder with the heavy tray, she knew her courage was wrapped up in Hawk's strength. She could no more leave him now than she could free him.

"Now, boy." Falligan waited, and she lifted the tray and walked out. She looked back at Hawk. As their eyes met, he saw something in her that made him unable to hold her gaze. She read his dejection and humiliation as the door closed.

Only then did she begin to comprehend his sense of failure. In his mind he'd failed to protect his ship, his men, and his cargo. What he thought of her, she did not know. She was, at best, a stowaway and liability. But she knew him well enough to know he would've given his life for anyone on that ship. Now, she knew they would do the same for him.

She made it to the galley, crestfallen to find another man there in place of Padraig. The old Irishman had become dear to her, and she'd looked forward to sharing solace with him. At least his absence explained the cold fish soup. This fellow, a portly middle-aged man who clearly liked to sample his work, seemed to apply the least amount of effort necessary.

"There you are. I'm going to find a hammock and sleep."

The storm roiled the ship, every man jack aboard frantic to keep her afloat, so he went off for a nap. Naturally.

She remembered Hawk's story for Falligan that she was mute, so she merely nodded at the man. He passed her without comment, heading toward the men's sleeping quarters.

For now, she prayed Padraig was safe on the other ship, where she assumed Raven was as well.

She set the bowl where she'd hidden the knives off to the side while she worked, and began washing the dishes in the cold, dank galley. The stove had never been lit for the meal, and she hoped the men had had something to eat. A single whale oil lantern hung overhead, and as smelly as it was, she was grateful for the dim light.

Her mind continued to turn over ideas for rescuing Hawk, but each seemed futile, and the entire situation, hopeless. She had to get the knives to the men, but so many uncertainties stood in her way.

Would the other ship's men join in a mutiny?

How could she disguise the knives? She noticed the fine linen napkins from the captain's cabin. Unfortunately, there weren't nearly enough to spread out among all the men, or their next food delivery would be the perfect time.

If she carried them in her pocket, she risked easy detection. Large as her pockets were, she doubted she could stuff many dirks into them without the bulges arousing suspicion. And she was certain she couldn't move without their clanging giving her away. And she couldn't leave them here, sitting on the counter.

She grabbed the bulky package of knives wrapped in napkins. She carried them to a lower cabinet, rarely used. On her hands and knees, she shoved the collection to the back wall, where it was unlikely that lazy cook would find it.

Relieved for a moment's respite, she sat back, searching for a way to get the knives to the men.

And as she sat back, she realized she was no longer alone. "What have we here?"

Marley glanced over her shoulder. Percy Snaveling.

She gulped and closed the cabinet without speaking. She didn't need to remind herself she was supposed to be mute.

"Open it."

She obeyed.

"Remove whatever you just hid."

She reached in for the large stewpot beside the knives.

"Don't tempt my patience, halfwit. Whatever you've covered with napkins there."

She withdrew the bowl, and he walked forward to kick it over. The knives clattered across the floor, and she flailed out her arms as if in alarm.

Snaveling grabbed a knife and held it before her face. She went still.

With his other hand, he brought the cudgel across her cheekbone, the edge of it glancing across her nose. She cried out in pain, tasting copper, and tears came to her eyes. All the times in her life she'd flinched against blows that never came, she hadn't realized that real blows came without warning.

She remembered the perverse pleasure Jimmy had found in Nan's weeping, and she swallowed her own tears. When Snaveling raised the cudgel again, she crouched into a ball, her arms over her head.

But no blow came.

She didn't believe his ruse, and she huddled in place.

His voice softened into an oily attempt to soothe her. "Ah, boy, I know 'twas only an act of desperation. I admire that."

His hand came down on her back, patting—then it roved down to her buttocks, shaping and molding.

Her stomach heaved in revulsion. His hand went under the hem of her shirt, grabbing the back of her breeches.

In a moment, she knew he was about to split them in two.

"What are you doing, you disgusting fool?" It was Falligan.

She knew she had no hope of mercy from either man— only different types of suffering. She stayed where she was.

"Boy, stand up."

She scrambled away from Snaveling and came to her feet, shrinking away into a corner.

"She's got a dozen knives there."

"You're in a galley. Do you suppose they don't have knives here? And can you not pull yourself together and set your perverse predilections aside for two days?"

Snaveling squared his shoulders. "Yes, sir."

"Go to the captain's cabin and keep him secured."

"He's knotted from neck to ankle. He's going nowhere."

"Nonetheless. And hide these knives, on your way."

Marley didn't leave the galley that night. The place was small and dark and no one had any interest in being there. With the crash of the storm, the rolling of the ship in steadfast rhythm, and the darkness that descended early, she no longer found a reason to fight.

If a man like Hawk was helpless, what could someone as small and simple as she hope to do?

She closed her eyes, surrendering to the darkness, feeling the tears slip from her eyes. She slipped into a narrow place between the end of a storage cabinet and a wall, where she could hide in peace.

In time, her own body heat warmed the small space. She huddled into the corner, bereft of all hope. If they did not outwit these men, their jokes about hanging would become reality as soon as they reached Boston.

And yet Hawk's stubborn memory persisted. Comforting her, refusing to let her give up hope. Finding her drowning in the sea and breathing life into her; holding her shivering body near and warming her; cradling her under the stars and tutoring her in the amusements of a sailor.

As she sat there, slumped against the wall, she remembered the last private moments they'd shared before he'd captured the ship.

Forgive me for striking you.

She smiled at the memory of his light spanking, as playful as a child's game, and he as surprised as she to discover she enjoyed his play.

Tonight, perhaps, I'll finish what we've started here.

Just for a moment, her tears stopped and she raised her head, dumbstruck by the realization. She wasn't certain when it had happened, but the charming, protective, demanding man had become dear to her.

Marley had never been in love before, so she shouldn't have been expected to recognize it. But she had come to love the impossible captain in all his alluring extremes, a combination of carefree and passionate, brilliant and simple, demanding and generous. A man who ever held her at arm's length but refused to let her go, content to have her there by his side.

No logic or reason could prove it, but she knew in her heart as she sat there with him surrounding her, holding her safe, that up in the captain's cabin, that the thought of her sheltered him, calming him in his worst moments of fear and hopelessness. And together in their separate cold darkness, they lent each other their own courage.

Chapter Seventeen

From the quarterdeck of the *Delight*, Raven watched the *Adventurer* as best he could through the storm. The pouring rain slicked off his oilskin, but the coat did only so much to protect from the biting cold. Snow and sleet mixed with the rain, but the sailors kept the deck salted and so far they could still get around.

His gaze was grim. He had known the exact moment when Falligan had gained the upper hand. It was no mystery.

A seaman had raised the Union Jack.

The *Adventurer* kept an assortment of ensigns, useful for preserving life and limb in tight jams. But Hawk had not raised the British colors since Michael's death.

"What can we do, sir?" This from Deming.

"I don't know yet. What are the options, as you see them?"

"Depends on where the captain is."

"And those options?"

Deming exchanged a tense glance with him, and Raven waved a hand. "It helps me work it out, to hear it aloud."

"The captain could have been taken unawares and tied up. There could have been a gun or knife fight, with the captain injured, seriously or not. Finally, there could have been the same fight, with the captain—"

"Thank you, Deming."

After a moment, Deming added, "Begging your pardon, sir. Not to give you false hope, but it only benefits Falligan to keep the captain alive and well."

Raven looked up at him. "Yes. That's very true, isn't it?"

Deming gave a nod.

"And to board now?"

"Sir, we can't cross in this. We could lose control of this ship and risk lives unnecessarily. Fools commit foolish acts in desperation. A better time will present itself."

"Well it had better do so soon. In no time we'll reach Boston—and a hangman's noose."

"God willing, with better weather ahead."

"Yes. Keep an eye peeled. I'm going below."

He nodded and returned to relieve the man at the wheel.

Anyone could see the ship was heavy-laden in the water, but as Raven raced down to the hold, he began to get an inkling of the ship's load. No wonder Falligan was desperate.

Apparently a herd of cattle and pigs had been slaughtered before the trip, as an entire deck was filled with salted meat and other food stores. This was beyond provisions for their men; these were stores for the starving Navy in Massachusetts Bay. Flour and butter, tea leaves and coffee beans. Salt, sugar, dried peas, oatmeal. Cords of firewood, crammed everywhere.

He hurried back up to the next level, the glorious smells of iron and steel and lead and oil teasing his nostrils. And in a moment he was a boy in the gunsmith's shop back home, pestering his Uncle Jeremiah with a million questions. The sense memories of his uncle's shop nearly overwhelmed him: the warmth greeting him through the open door on the coldest day in February, the pungent aroma of fire and melting ore, and the fearsome hot glow of lead as his uncle poured it into shot molds.

The warmth within him was almost enough to lighten his mood. At the moment, it filled him with melancholy. A man could be homesick within miles of that home with the threat of losing it so real.

Still, the stores soothed him even beyond its magnificent value—especially to the colonials—and he goggled at the artillery. Cannons, carronades, crate upon crate upon crate of pistols, muskets, rifles, bayonets, swords, dirks, and daggers. Scabbards, ramrods, cartridge boxes, and flints. And gunpowder to dwarf their own hidden stores, plus saltpeter for making more.

After several moments, Raven threw back his head and let deep, exultant laughter explode from his chest, and with it a resolute determination. He couldn't wait to show this to Hawk.

This was a prize whose loss would ruin a man—and whose gain, make him a hero.

It was up to Raven to make sure the role of the ruined went to Falligan, and that of the hero to his own captain.

The storm grew merciful in the night, slowing to a quiet rain. Marley had dozed in the galley. The cold made it difficult to sleep, but at least she was left alone. She tried not to think of the occasional rustling in the corner by the cask of oats.

Instead, in those moments of quiet when all the world slept except those who labored longest, she found wonder in the discovery of her love for Hawk. As anyone who's known such wonderment knows, she was certain no one had ever felt this way. She wanted to protect, to safeguard, these strange, unique feelings, that she might always enjoy them. And, as anyone who's loved knows, life's urgent cadence indifferently intruded on her private exploration of life's magic.

So it was early when she built a fire in the hearth, thankful for its luxurious warmth. She'd begun to thaw by the time she started breakfast without the indolent cook's help. She hoisted kettles of water onto the surface to boil and assembled the ingredients for the men's breakfast. The pork that had been so tasty that first morning had grown dull—oh, what she would give for a glass of cold milk, even as freezing as it was—and she couldn't imagine how these men survived on such fare for months at sea.

She prepared a breakfast tray for Hawk and his captors, setting it aside. She slipped the portions of pork into the larger kettle, then as the smaller kettle began to bubble, she salted the water well and added oatmeal, stirring hastily. Cooking on a fire hearth was not the modern gourmet chef experience, she thought as the oatmeal bubbled wildly.

Dear God, how she longed to see Hawk, to touch his face, to try to give him a bit of encouragement. How long would it take to make this food edible?

At last the oatmeal was done, and she took the kettle off the hearth, dumping in a generous glob of butter and even some sugar. Poor guys, they had so little pleasure. Perhaps it would be a treat for them.

She filled the plates with pork and biscuit, the bowls with oatmeal, the cups with hot coffee. Excited to see Hawk, she lifted the monstrous tray and headed for the captain's cabin. If he were still captive, he would need help to eat, and for other morning tasks. She couldn't imagine Falligan freeing him—or feeding him, certainly. The thought of seeing him again, even in a dejected state, filled her with pleasure and with new hope.

"You. Boy."

The hair at the back of her neck went up. Snaveling, behind her in the passageway. She looked at him over her shoulder.

"Give me that."

She ignored him, heading toward the ladder.

Snaveling grabbed the tray from her. "I'll take that *now*."

More interested in at least knowing Hawk was being fed, she abandoned her hope to see him.

When he spoke, his voice was nasal and gravelly. His eyes, narrowed with foul threat, were a rheumy pink. "Mark my words, you'll suffer when we reach dry land. Why, I'll take you so far into the black Carolina woods you'll never see daylight again. And afore it be over, you'll pray for death."

With that, he climbed the ladder.

Marley steadied herself against the wall and headed back to the kitchen, fear buckling her knees. For several blinding moments, she couldn't even think of Hawk, let alone the encouragement she'd memorized by now. She tried to breathe and found she couldn't.

She made it to the corner, lightheaded, and sank onto a small chair. She put her head between her knees and in moments, the lightheadedness passed and her spine stiffened.

Stubbornly now, she focused again on the stove. Two dozen men out there would be hungry. And among them would be men who would jump at the chance to help her free Hawk.

By dawn's first light, Marley had finished serving the men in the mess—with Falligan watching them all. She'd found that along with deep breaths and battle cries, contempt and hatred helped steady her attitude toward the bastards who'd captured Hawk. Perhaps it wasn't the healthiest way to channel adrenaline—but for now, it was a port in the storm.

She stopped to offer him a mug of coffee, and he looked as if she held out a dead snake.

"What is this?"

She bit her lip, her gaze dropping from his.

Shaking his head, he said, "No, by God! Do you not have the sense to bring an Englishman tea?"

She scurried away toward the kitchen. Tea? They had no tea. For heaven's sake, man, it was 1775, and outside Boston. There was likely no tea within 500 miles.

"I'm going to inspect the locked room," Hayworth told Falligan. "If I have to shoot the lock off myself."

He headed down the ladder and off toward the room where the women were hidden. So far, they'd been able to keep the women in hiding. If they were revealed—anger filled her at the prospect of what these three men would do to them.

"Sir!" she called, forgetting her affliction of muteness.

Hayworth turned.

"There's a key to the room, kept in the captain's cabin."

That would distract him for a few minutes. For now, she had the impossible task of finding tea on Hawk's ship.

Think harder, Marley.

Recalling all the minor luxuries Hawk secured on board for himself and his men—good cigars, Tahitian oils—she thought perhaps it wasn't so far-fetched. Perhaps he had some in his cabin? Perhaps Padraig had stashed a precious jar away for honored guests?

She put on a cast iron tea kettle to boil fresh water while she rifled through every cabinet. And at last she found it, forgotten in an unused corner. Stale or no, she thought it might just work. And she lacked the luxury of options.

While she sifted through the galley's storage compartments for tea, she'd come across a handsome and large pewter tankard with a family crest.

Trelawney.

She gasped.

The coincidence of this unusual name, on that mug—the same name gracing the cover of the antique book she treasured back in her own time—was too great. What could it mean? Did Hawk and Raven work for the family who owned the ship? Could one of them—both of them?—*be* Trelawneys?

She blushed at that quantum leap of logic. How could a white man and black man share the same family? Perhaps if one family had owned the other's?

This *must* be why she was here, in this time.

"Where's that *tea*?" came the shout.

She grumbled under her breath and prepared the tray.

While small bubbles formed at the edge of the water in the cast iron teapot, half a dozen freezing men were climbing the ladder to board the *Adventurer*. They had left *Delight* on her far side to avoid detection by Falligan, should he be watching. Each man was heavily armed with knives, and they moved through the icy water silently—and quickly. Such water could kill a man with its embrace.

As he'd swum, Raven glanced at the lookout, but it was their own Cosly, and he reacted as Raven expected. The boy noticed them once, made no remark, then only glanced occasionally, surreptitiously, to chart their progress.

Raven padded up the ladder, his men trailing just behind. His head cleared the edge of the gunwale just enough to see what they were up against.

They were matched man for man, and he assumed the rest were below, eating. Nearby, he recognized a ginger-haired sailor from the *Delight*. Raven sprang over the gunwale, landing on the balls of his feet just behind the seaman, capturing him around the shoulders and holding his knife to his throat.

"Where's Falligan?"

"In the mess. Sir, you'll have no fight from any of us. We'll help as we can."

Raven looked down at the thin, frightened man and released him. "As you were."

With his men close behind, knives drawn, Raven raced toward the captain's cabin. He dropped into the hatch, then turned into the passage.

And there he stopped. For between him and the captain's cabin stood Falligan, holding Marley by the hair, his other hand pressing the tip of a dagger against her chest. Her face was pale, her eyes huge, but she refused him the sadistic pleasure of tears. Her jaw was tight with anger.

Raven took a step backward.

"Careful, gentlemen. I'd hate to slip and cut myself."

He waited, buying time while his mind spun.

"Drop your weapons. There."

He could kill the man in a moment with one throw—but if he missed by a hair, he could also kill Marley.

"All right—of course." Raven raised his hands in submission.

The other men stood behind him, awaiting his direction. He saw Marley swallow—hard.

Raven exhaled, dropping his knife. The others, too, clattered to the deck.

"And in your boot and waist."

The rest of their weaponry fell to the deck.

"Back up above," Falligan shouted.

Raven watched him closely, waiting for the right time. He didn't have much more, he knew. But all the way up the ladder to the quarterdeck, Falligan shoved his knife against Marley's vest.

"Tie each of them to the rigging. Begin with him."

The seaman was one of his own, but still he obeyed reluctantly.

"Get the cat," he directed an *Adventurer* seaman.

"We don't use one."

"Then you'll find one in my confiscated belongings."

Each man tied in turn to the shrouds was occupied in his own thoughts. Raven's thoughts were of his mother, and his sisters, and his father, and his nieces and nephews. And Hawk, whom he'd failed. Could it be that Hawk was already dead?

When the men were either tied or compliant, Falligan released Marley, shoving her to her knees. "Go get my accursed tea, boy."

Then he grew quite casual, as he contemplated Raven and the others with a haughty, aristocratic gaze. He braced one foot on the slide of the carronade running parallel with the gunwale and leaned against the gunwale easily, awaiting the delivery of the whip. Clearly he intended to relish their torture.

And Raven knew in a moment, as he stood there observing the sneering Falligan, that he would not leave this ship alive. He would never again see his father, or his brother, or his sisters—or the woman who had taught him by daily example what this moment called for.

And for her, he would not cry out against a lash he had never felt in his pampered twenty-eight years. He would not beg for mercy, as Falligan wished. He would be strong.

For his mother, he would have courage.

Chapter Eighteen

The top of Marley's head buzzed with rage she didn't know herself capable of as she descended to the kitchen. How could so many good people have tried so hard and failed so badly, only to be conquered by one so evil? Her mind spun desperately for any idea. It had killed her to see the kindhearted, laughing Raven treated like a common criminal—when all he had done was act nobly and without regard for himself.

In the kitchen, she found the tea pot where she'd left it when Falligan had spotted the men boarding and pulled her away. The water boiled crazily, and although the handle was wooden, it, too, was hot. She found a pot holder and grasped the handle, setting it aside. At least half of the water had boiled away, but there was still plenty for tea.

At that moment, Hayworth—returned once more to his quest to enter the forbidden room—strode down the corridor toward the women's room.

She poured the water over the antique pewter tea ball, a disturbing little image: a laughing gargoyle. Or perhaps a demon. Either way, it reminded her of Falligan.

As she splashed the hot water over its face, it gave her a small bit of satisfaction.

And her eyes lit up.

Trying to calm herself, she hurried up the ladder. She had forgone the tray, choosing instead to carry the heavy Trelawney tankard in one hand and the teapot in the other. As she stepped out onto the quarterdeck, her legs trembling, she forced herself to slow down. The last thing she needed was to be so wild with rage that she lost control. She was the last hope of every good man on both ships, and her pulse was hammering.

When you encounter that power, take a deep breath to harness it. And find a battle cry.

She took a deep breath.

Then another.

Then she headed straight for Falligan, leaving him no time to move away from the gunwale. Jem had arrived, miserably, with the whip, but Marley charged ahead of him.

"Something to warm you up, sir."

He glanced at her, surprised at the miracle of the mute boy's speech. A moment later, as he let down his guard to accept the tea, she slung it in his face. She slammed the tankard across his forehead, filled with a power she'd never known.

He erupted in a howl of pain. She swung her other arm hard, following through with full force, colliding directly with his head against the cast iron teapot containing another quart or so of hot water.

The boiling water splashed over him from head to chest, and he flailed in the air, losing his balance, stumbling away in reaction, screams of pain starting deep in his gut. A moment later he tumbled backward over the gunwale from the quarterdeck to the ocean below. The teapot followed him down, but she held tight to the Trelawney tankard, her arm quivering.

"Die, Jimmy—you bastard bully!" she screamed after him, an incoherent explosion of twenty years of frustration. A moment later, she wished she'd thought up a better battle cry.

I seem to be getting quite good at this, she thought as she watched him disappear into the icy waves.

Her body kept dumping adrenaline into her bloodstream, and she spun toward Raven, unable to see him. She could only see Jem, directly in front of her, agog with admiration. For a moment she couldn't even hear the cheers of the men surrounding her, Falligan's men as well as Hawk's, and she screamed wildly with them.

Then her tunnel-vision cleared and she saw Raven and sprang toward him, her shaking fingers working futilely at the knots. The frozen coldness of his skin frightened her. If they didn't get into dry, warm clothes, they'd all die of exposure.

"Knife!" Raven said plainly, laughing. "Can someone help this poor wom—er, poor one?"

But she was already running away to the corner where they'd abandoned their knives and raced back.

"Oh no, you don't," Raven said. "Give that thing to someone with a little steadier hand, if you don't mind."

She passed the knife to Jem.

"Hurry—we have to get Hawk! And—oh, that Hayworth is trying to get into the room where the gu—where the girls are."

"Conrad, take Jenkins and go get Hawk first. Take pistols as well. You can bet Snaveling has one."

The blast of a muzzleloader came from the women's room.

She raced down the ladder and the walkway toward the room. At the open doorway, she stopped, stunned.

Hayworth lay just inside the room, and she looked away. He was dead, and blood stained the deck beneath him. Beyond him, she stared, uncomprehending, at what she saw.

"Mother Barbary?"

The gruff old den mother stood on the other side of Hayworth's body, between him and the women.

"Aye," Barbary said—but no longer a mother. Their protector had been a man in a woman's disguise, and he calmly pulled the dress away, revealing the simple clothing of a seaman. "Just Barbary."

Hawk had placed the gargantuan seaman there in disguise for just such a moment as this. He'd killed Hayworth without hesitating. She felt a little stupid for not figuring it out before.

Hawk! She fled, leaping along the walkway toward the captain's cabin until she caught up with Conrad. He forced her back behind them in the passageway. "If that ass has a pistol, the first to go in will be the first to die."

The door was locked and barred, and Conrad wasted no time. He blew it open with the muzzleloader. The door swung open.

They needn't have feared. Snaveling must have heard the cheering on the quarterdeck, or the muzzle firing in the storage room, and surmised the truth. He cowered before them with his hands raised, dropping his pathetic cudgel.

Beyond Conrad, she caught a glimpse of Hawk, and she shoved the men aside to get to him, dropping to her knees before him, her eyes flashing fire as she smiled up at him.

He had been beaten, his eye blackened—and still was beautiful beyond her memories, his eyes lighting as she entered.

Jenkins jerked Snaveling to his feet, shoving him to walk ahead of him out of the cabin, training his pistol on his back.

Conrad sliced through the ropes and thick knots fastening the captain to the chair from his neck down to his back, and Hawk grabbed Marley close.

Conrad was not confused by his captain hugging his cabin boy. He inched out of their way then sliced through the ropes binding his hips and legs in place.

Then he beat a hasty retreat, closing the door behind him. The blast of the powder had done some damage, but no one would dare bother the captain in this moment.

Marley lay her hand alongside his cheek, lightly touching his jawline. "Did he hurt you much?"

He shook his head. His gaze bore the faintest hint of a smile with delight at seeing her, holding her close, and he relished the vibrant excitement on her face. He sobered as he lightly brushed a fingernail against her bruised cheekbone. "What of you, my dearest love?"

She laughed, throwing her arms in the air. "I'm overjoyed! I'm ecstatic! You're alive and I'm alive and I whacked Falligan over the head with a teakettle! He's gone, scalded, fallen overboard and lost!"

"Ah, I wish I could've seen that." The smile hooked the corner of his lips, but he only watched her tenderly.

"Oh, you would've been so proud! I—what did you call me?" She sat back slightly, scrutinizing his face.

He laughed. "Something akin to 'my dearest love.'" He turned her face this way and that. "Who did this?"

"It doesn't matter. We're all safe."

"Tell me." An edge entered his voice.

"It was Snaveling, but can we think about that tomorrow?"

The anger slowly left him, and he drew her onto his lap, cradling her in his arms, examining her slowly—as if for the first time. His gaze roved her, head to toe.

He tossed away the cap, and he loosened her hair from the braid, enjoying the riotous cascade of her hair over her shoulders. He studied her face, touched her chin, his thumb brushing her lower lip.

She lifted her chin in unconscious invitation.

With a teasing glimmer in his eyes, he lightly pulled away from her touch, savoring what would be their first kiss. He set her hand at her side, his own moving to the vest she'd primly closed to her collar.

His gaze never leaving her face, he opened the vest and removed it from her. And then he did look, his glance traveling downward, savoring the full, lovely breasts revealed faintly in his own soft shirt. His hand rested between them, and he made a sound of pleasure deep in his throat.

"Marley, my love." He drew her close. "My own love."

Then, he set her once more in his loose embrace, his hand resting over her waist. His hand flipped aside the tail of his shirt, moving lightly against the naked flatness of her abdomen. He toyed with the button at the top of the loose breeches, then simply slipped his hand inside, over her belly, his long fingers trailing down toward a place he ached to fill.

A moment later he withdrew his hand, letting it rest along the soft curve of her hips, insane with the thought of the moment he would remove these clothes and love this woman for the first time—his woman, his heart, his love.

And, at last, he lifted her in his other arm, drawing her close to him, breathing deeply the sweetness of her.

"Ah, my darling, how I've longed to kiss you for all these weeks—since that night I first breathed breath into you, as if you were my own, having no life before God had mercy on me and brought you to me."

Her eyes grew darker, the pupils huge with pleasure, and her hand roved from his stubbled cheek to his throat to the place where his shirt opened, revealing his chest. She yanked impatiently at the shirt, and a button came loose.

He was delighted at her hunger as her hand roved over his bared chest.

"Why didn't you?"

He struggled to explain. "In my life, a kiss has come to have great meaning. It wasn't always this way. I kissed many women when I was younger. It grew too confusing, to share something so intimate—so loving. And yet, for it to mean so little. And so I stopped. Until now.

"The only thought that calmed me these past days was the memory of that mouth of yours—smiling at me, laughing at me, jabbering at me. Marley, don't you know what you mean to me?"

As his lips parted, as he cherished the touch of her soft, creamy face under his own clumsy fingers, he lowered his lips until he could taste her breath. So sweet—

And he heard a voice in the passageway a moment before the door opened. "Are you deaf, man? We're in Beverly! I've sent a boat ashore to let Mama know, and she'll have the fatted calf roasting, and you'd best hurry—Oh. Ermph. Well. My fault. So sorry. And all that. We're not at the dock, proper, still have ten minutes or so." He laughed deeply as he turned away back into the passage. "From the state of your brain, though, that may be plenty of time!"

Raven disappeared as quickly as he'd arrived, but Marley's smile held new confidence now, her cheeks pinkened in fetching embarrassment.

Where, before, with other women, Hawk would've been frustrated by the interruption, he found himself instead charmed by the seduction itself. By the teasing lift of her breasts toward him in invitation even as she sighed in disappointment. By the deep rose coloring her cheeks.

Then he noticed, again, her bruise from the abuse she'd endured at his confinement, and a deep shame filled him. He felt the sharp scruffiness of his own beard, the shabby cheapness of the scene before him, with him ready to take her as if she were a common whore, with his broken door gaping.

"No," he said, touching her hand, bringing it to his mouth, lightly brushing her knuckles with his lips as a gentleman kisses his lady. "Not nearly enough time for us."

Chapter Nineteen

The hiss of sleet fell silent early in the second afternoon, replaced by the silent fall of heavy snow blanketing Boston. The woman who stood at the window in the gathering gloom looking down over the harbor in the distance was no longer the young newlywed who'd arrived in Boston nearly three decades before. Her joy now lay not in learning her new husband's likes and dislikes, in finding a deeper purpose than her peers in this city on a hill, achievements that would live on after her, but in all her children and her grandchildren. For they, she had come to understand, were indeed her greatest achievements. And for them, today, she gave thanks.

This day, her baby boy was on his way home. She prayed he would arrive safely. And that, she knew, was the limitation of her influence over him and the inevitable circumstances surrounding him. No matter how much knowledge she might have about the world she now inhabited, she was powerless to protect him. For in the end, she was only a mother.

The first twenty eight years of her life had prepared her for all she had encountered in the last twenty-nine, although she had not known it at the time. Her grandmother had taught her to love history, to reject victimhood and blame, to have unlimited pride in the accomplishments of her people, and humility at her own. And she had been blessed with perfect recall. Even now, coming up on sixty, she remembered dates with dreadful accuracy. It had enabled her to keep her family safer than some—but it had given her many sleepless nights.

And so Camisha Carlyle Adams had lived her life with the curse of prescience, without the power to lift a finger to change a thing. She knew the rules. For more than twenty-nine years she'd observed them, content to participate, rather than attempt to change, this—her flawed history.

"I do not care if your eldest grows up to be Thomas Jefferson's most trusted manservant. You will not influence him in the slightest to change history. For you see, you will fail. And in a moment you will lose all you have come to love. You'll wake up back in the luxurious modern life you once knew, without all the deprivations that in time, you will come to love for their very reminder of your many blessings."

Malcolm Henderson, the man she'd met nearly thirty years before, whom she had come to know as a kindly spirit who manipulated time, had made it clear that were she to lift a finger to influence the major events of history, she would lose all she loved: Ashanti, her children, their children, all her many friends—and, of course, all her other babies. Those infants she'd stolen in the night from the greedy reach of bondage. That much, Malcolm had allowed her: the rescuing of newborns from lives of slavery to the lives God had meant them to lead.

Camisha felt her husband's presence without ever having heard him descend the stairs, sniffing at the appetite-arousing aroma of onions, celery and garlic on the stove. And even though Thanksgiving was still a week or more away, her husband was mad with desire for her cornbread dressing, so she'd relented. Today was a day of giving thanks, too.

The summer and fall had not been the time of bounty her hard-working, hard-loving family was accustomed to. This year, for the first time, they had known hunger. All except the children had sacrificed a meal every day that they would earmark to anonymously share with others in the city. It wasn't much, but it left them with enough extra food to feed two families for two days a week.

"That's all right, I needed to lose that baby weight, anyway!"

That from her eldest, Helen—named after Camisha's mother.

"Something smells good in here," her husband said sleepily, just behind her. "Making me hungry." And then his hands came round her slender waist, pressing his hard strength into her womanly curves as he buried his nose deep in her throat and inhaled. "Ah, now I know what it is."

As he kissed the nape of her neck, she thanked God for the blessedly dull routine of her time-traveling, revolutionary life. For the better part of three decades, each fourth Wednesday of November, as she began preparing their feast, her husband played this game with her. Apparently, she thought with a smile to herself, he had been conditioned to associate the smell of stuffing with ... well, a more carnal stuffing.

Not that she was complaining.

She tilted her head, enjoying the feeling of him. Then, softly, "Ashanti?"

"Mhm." His breath brushed her ear.

"I want to go to Rosalie for Thanksgiving."

His progress came to a halt, but he hugged her hard. "Sure, why not. We've got the entire British Navy tearing up every house on Beacon Hill for firewood. We got a boy up to his ears in treason. And then there's that baby-snatching habit you've developed. Now, my wife wants to take the family on a holiday voyage into Slaver's Paradise. Such a meager request."

When they'd first moved to Boston, this little scolding would've had her slapping his hands away and stomping into the kitchen to sulk for an hour. She had learned more prudent techniques.

She leaned back in his embrace, reaching up to stroke his face. "Let's go back to bed."

His laughter was low and soft. "Don't play that game with me, woman. Why not let's just agree that you're going to win this argument and make it worth my while ... say, tonight behind the woodshed."

"I find nothing seductive about the idea of you pounding me during a blizzard." Yet, with Ashanti, it would be unforgettable.

"Nonetheless, that's the deal you've struck, for me to agree to go back into that den of demons."

She turned in his arms, hugging him hard around his waist. She stroked his back, rubbing her face against the soft flannel of his nightshirt. She couldn't feel them through the nightshirt, but her husband still bore the scars on his back from his first visit to Rosalie, as a young man.

And although they'd been lucky during their few visits since, they were both ever mindful that even as a family of free people visiting a Virginia tobacco farm where no slaves were held, they were in danger every moment they were there. On one side lay their enemy, the British; on the other, their enemy, those who would enslave them.

Forging loyalties these days was a tricky business indeed.

The heavy snow had smoothed the path of wagons and oxen making their way up the slippery hill toward the house where Raven's family was staying—but it didn't warm the men any. Snow frosted Hawk's and Raven's hair and eyebrows, and despite the scarves wound around their necks, their faces were so cold they couldn't form words at times. The trip over land had been neither short nor easy.

The women they'd brought from Bermuda had quickly found entertainment in town—whether they would find husbands might be doubtful, but as long as the harbor was overrun with militia and Navy, they would find work.

As for Marley, she sat in relative comfort surrounded by blankets up to her ears, in a wagon piled high with provisions for the Adamses and their friends. Fresh-milled flour, peas, oatmeal, sugar, salt, salted beef and pork. No one could claim to like the salted meat that kept sailors alive for months at sea, but the men were uncertain what to expect when they returned to the blockaded city, so they had secured a selection of items, marking them as removed from the inventory of their prize. They'd avoided the heart of Boston where now lay only loyalists and soldiers' families—fighting starvation.

In other wagons and on sleds pulled by teamsters they'd hired were firewood stacked on pallets as well as arms, ammunition, and a supply of black powder. They hoarded nothing, taking only what was needed to take care of their own and help those they could. Their mission had been to equip the militia, and they couldn't have returned with a more bountiful prize to meet that need.

Militia from colonies around the area had surrounded the city in April after Lexington and Concord, and no one could enter or leave. Now, their numbers were joined by militia from other colonies, all understanding the importance of this conflict, the vital need to drive the British out of the city—though lacking sufficient firepower to match that of General Gage and Admiral Graves.

In a rare, sane moment, King George had stopped the import of gunpowder years before, claiming the colonies had no need for it, since the English Navy protected them.

In truth, he knew how to keep the American serfs powerless. A lesson Americans would never forget.

Hawk gazed toward the house near the top of the hill where fatwood burned in a cresset. Marley saw the smoke leaving the chimney—and thought she smelled the kind of home-cooked meal old Padraig simply didn't have in his repertoire.

Hunger gnawed at her—at all of them, she knew. Unloading wood from the *Delight*, as well as a small supply of the ammunition and arms for their own defense, had taken the better part of a day, and transporting it to Dorchester Heights, another.

"Smell that?" Raven asked from the other team of oxen.

"Aye. Your mother's cooking."

"Please at least let me get out and walk, to ease the oxen's burden," Marley called.

Hawk spoke. "You are not properly dressed or shod."

"Couldn't have taken horses, could we?" This from Raven, his teeth chattering, craning his head toward the house. "Oh, no. 'A long walk will do us good.'"

Hawk made no further comment.

Marley said, "My shoes are fine. My feet are toasty."

"Do you hear that?" Raven pointed at her, his eyes wide. "That's something my mother would say. Toasty."

"Whose home is this?"

"'Tis a friend of my mother's—and of Michael, whom you might've heard Hawk mention."

She looked at Hawk; she could see the weariness in the grim set of his jaw.

"I can't see a lot of details, but it looks quite lavish, in the darkness."

"We shared in the plunder, and Michael sent most of his back to Toni and their daughter."

The large house looked less like a New England saltbox or farmhouse and more like the grand house of a Jamaican sugar plantation. It was painted a light color—likely white—rather than barn red or slate gray. Storm shutters covered the windows. A deep wrap-around porch enclosed the two-story home, and Marley knew this porch had been created for laughing guests during long summer evenings.

Now, even Raven fell silent as they worked to get up the hill. The oxen, filled with a burst of energy, seemed to sense they were nearing the end of their journey. She went silent, too, watching the two men instead as they made their way across the last hundred yards or so to a stopping place beside the house.

When the oxen came to a halt, Marley threw back the blankets, scrambling out of the wagon and feeling the full force of the cold. Silently she thanked God that Hawk had kept her inside.

She heard the shrill scream of a woman as they turned the corner, and in the gathering darkness a woman came running toward them. The snow, piled deep, turned her run into a high-stepping prance.

"Mama, what are you doing?" Raven's laughter overwhelmed him as he caught the woman up in his arms. "You in your house slippers."

On the porch, he set her down again. The woman tried to speak, then shook her head as tears spilled from her. From beneath her dust cap, she dabbed at her eyes with a deep copper shawl.

Marley stood in the snow at the foot of the steps, watching the exchange in wonder. She saw Hawk's fondness and amusement. She could only guess his thoughts, but of one thing she was certain. This woman was dear to him, and he would kill for either her or her son.

With one arm she hugged her son again, extending her free arm and waving her fingertips at Hawk. He laughed and stepped forward, hugging them both.

At last, she stepped back and looked at the two men. The humor filled her face as she said in a tone both fond and mocking, "The Hawk and the Raven. You *look* like you've been living off of worms these past months."

Hawk tilted his head. "Well, the biscuits—"

"Spare her. We had to live it, but Mother has no need to."

She glanced at Hawk. "How's your father? I've received only one letter from Ruth since I saw him at Christmas."

"As confused as ever a loyal British subject could be in these times."

"Still a loyalist, eh?"

"An Englishman's loyalty for his country dies hard."

"But your father is Welsh!"

"Aye, there's that. Being born in Wales trained him well how to be a good colonist, pay his taxes for nothing in return, and never complain."

A man appeared behind them, filling the doorway. Much like a harsher version of his son, he scowled at the trio clustered before him. Studious and preoccupied with the tragedies of life, he looked as if he rarely laughed on a normal day.

But today was no normal day.

"Group hug?" The innocuous words—startlingly modern— sounded more like an accusation than invitation, and Marley smiled at his gruff affection.

Twin shouts of laughter filled the hallway as the two younger men crowded into the open doorway to grab the older man between them. Then he, too, laughed and went into the family embrace.

At last, Raven's father stepped back. "Son, it does this old heart of mine good to see you both, safe and sound. But who's the little waif you've dragged home?"

Hawk smiled as he took a step down the stairs, then another, his eyes meeting hers as he covered one of her freezing hands in his. "This is Marley."

The Adamses exchanged an uncertain glance, and Mr. Adams rubbed his cheek.

"Marley, this is Mr. and Mrs. Adams, Raven's parents. The kindest, bravest people you'll ever meet."

Mrs. Adams peered at her shrewdly, gesturing. "Well, come on up here. You look like a little icicle standing there shivering."

Hawk escorted her up the stairs as if she were a princess in silk and taffeta rather than a filthy ragamuffin in bedraggled men's clothing.

And then the woman drew her into her embrace and hugged her tight.

"Oh, good grief!" Mrs. Adams grabbed Marley by the shoulders and held her at arm's length, laughter lighting her beautiful face. "Those overgrown boys disguised you! I wondered about the way he was looking at you, but now I *get* it."

Something about the woman unsettled Marley, but she couldn't quite put her finger on it. She seemed familiar—not a close friend, but as if they'd met once, casually. Perhaps, instead, it wasn't her appearance, but her youthful attitude. To have been Raven's mother, she had to be at least in her late forties, but she had the glow of a woman much younger, and when the man beside her burst with sudden laughter at her observation, Marley knew why.

That man closed the gaping door behind them, feeding the fireplace in the entryway. The entryway itself was grand, with double staircases on either side of the hall leading up to meet at a gallery above. And from that gallery appeared a young woman who raced down the stairs, squealing all the way, then barreling into Raven's arms as if he were a rock star.

"I see you still haven't fattened up," Raven said, hugging her.

She only giggled and shook her head. "I eat like the swine, and yet nothing. Mama says I take after Daddy."

"You could do worse," said Mr. Adams.

She threw him a sassy glance. "There are lots of ways I'd rather take after Mama. Like her figure."

"Parks!" Mrs. Adams scolded, amid the laughter echoing in the hall.

"Well, you did get her mouth," Mr. Adams said.

Another young woman descended the stairs now at a more sedate pace, and Marley could tell they were Raven's sisters, but he introduced them: Helen, the eldest after him, and Parks, the baby of the family.

To Helen, he said, "You, too, pretty as a rose bud and slim as its stem." This he said as a compliment, but Marley saw the grim tightness at the corner of his mouth. "What aren't you telling me, Mother? Father?"

His mother gave her husband a quick glance, then smiled at her son. "Tomorrow is soon enough for that. Tonight, we celebrate."

"Where's Eston? And Helen's Taleeb?" Raven asked.

Their father gestured toward the harbor below. "Well, they're where every other able-bodied man is. Down holding the line against the devil Brits."

Hawk and Raven exchanged a glance.

"Perhaps we should join them."

"No, *sir*." This from Mrs. Adams. "You're in much worse shape than they are. Tonight, you scrub and start fattening up those skinny selves of yours. And you," she said, turning to Marley, "I for one would like to see how you look in a dress. And a bath."

Startled at the sudden spotlight, Marley blushed and stammered, ashamed to say these rags were all she owned.

"Marley's wardrobe was lost at sea," Hawk put in smoothly. "And she's dressed as I asked her to, for her safety."

Mrs. Adams gave Hawk an exasperated glance, as if he were a dimwitted dolt. "Well, sweetie pie, the poor child's on dry land now. Do you expect her to drag around like a little boy here, too?"

Hawk took her ribbing in stride and gestured grandly with a half bow toward Marley. "I defer to the judgment of this trio of lovely and entirely fashionable ladies. Outfit my lady as you shall."

Marley's face warmed. In this home of strangers, she felt a comfort and safety she'd not known her entire life. The ladies themselves were dressed modestly and neatly; but, had a stranger inspected, they would've noticed the worn seams at their wrists and the slight fading of the fabric. For so many years, this town had been at war, and the deprivation showed.

But despite that, they presented themselves with the breeding of royalty and the humility of self-respect.

Now, Mrs. Adams' smile was kind. "Between Helen and Parks, they'll fix you right up. Helen, isn't Marley about your size?"

The young woman—perhaps Marley's age—looked her over. "I think she is. Parks, why don't you take her up to my dressing room and help her choose what she needs? I'll get started setting the table for supper. Mind waking the children."

As the younger girl took Marley's hand in her own and hurried up one of the grand staircases, she heard Helen speak to her brother.

"Ray, the children tried to stay awake for you, but they grew overtired and I had to put them to bed. Are you hungry?"

At that, the group dissolved in laughter, with Mrs. Adams responding with a saucy retort she couldn't quite hear.

Chapter Twenty

Marley noticed the bright, airy spaciousness of the gallery they passed through. She found herself wondering if Crispus Attucks had actually spent time here himself; somehow she doubted it. True sailors grew restless as soon as they made port.

"I hope the voyage wasn't too frightening," Parks said. She pointed at one room, her eyes wide in warning as she whispered. "That's the nursery, where my nephews and niece sleep."

"You girls really look like your mother," Marley said as they walked through a spacious sitting room and into an inner bedchamber.

"You mean Helen does. My bosom is as flat as my father's."

Marley almost laughed, but she'd had friends who obsessed over shape, and she knew that for them it was no laughing matter.

"I meant your beautiful faces—the shape, the exotic structure, and the color of your eyes. Like shades of warm caramel."

Parks led her through the bedchamber into a dressing room. Opening a door, she held out her arm to the gowns there.

"Help yourself. Unfortunately Helen has a penchant for the dull and dreary, so you find mostly the colors of nature here. If you were my size, I could dress you in the colors of the skies and our flower garden in Beacon Hill."

"Oh, anything is fine."

Parks produced a golden gown for Marley's inspection. "What about this?"

"That must be your sister's favorite. It's far too fine for such a quiet night at home."

Back it went, followed by another gown, the color of bronze.

"Oh, that's quite beautiful."

"Ugly enough for staying at home?" Parks asked, the corner of her lip hooked in a smirk.

"Just a simple brown or beige is perfect. I'm afraid I might stain or tear one of your sister's favorite gowns."

An impatient breath came sputtering through Parks' half-closed lips, an exasperated noise. She went rifling through the gowns.

"Brown, eh? What about dowager black? Would that be too pretty?"

Marley glanced at her, confused. She and Parks were as unlike as two young women could be, so she had no idea what she'd said to offend her.

"Have I insulted you? Please forgive me. I wouldn't hurt you for anything in the world."

The young woman thawed. "I'm sorry. 'Tis such a dreadfully long time since we've done anything truly gay. All anybody does anymore is pray and fast and figure out 150 ways to cook potatoes and pumpkins."

"Potatoes and—?"

"I'm sorry, please don't tell Mother. She worries so. There's enough food now, but for the last six months—almost the entire time the boys have been gone—life has been so tiresome. No parties, no visitors. And even Sunday dinners! Sunday dinners are always like feasts, but now they're simply awful."

"With the troops here in Boston?"

Parks threw herself on the small couch nearby. "Ugh! The troops! The troops! 'Tis the only topic of conversation! By the time the horrid troops leave, I'll be an old maid!"

Marley began looking through Helen's gowns as if she cared much what she wore. And yet, if she were honest with herself, she thought as she fingered the dainty lace at one prim collar, she *did* care. It would be the first time Hawk saw her as a woman. And despite what they'd been through, despite her tender feelings for him, she didn't know what to do with this sudden interest in appearing beautiful. She hadn't been raised to think it was ever an option.

Perhaps, like Parks said, it was simply the constant *drudgery* of war. Even during their time on the open ocean, they had never lost sight of the fact that in smuggling gunpowder, they could all be hanged for treason.

"You have a beautiful name. Parks. It's unusual."

The girl stood again, pleased by this. "I'm named after a lady my Mama admired. She said my name means that no one can tell me I have to stand, if I'm of a mind to sit."

"Inspiring thought." Even as she said it, she couldn't exactly see anyone holding this young lady down against her will. "So, do you have a beau?"

She giggled at the question even as she produced another dress. "Wear this. 'Tis pretty and plain, too."

A simple warm taupe with a creamy silk ribbon at the wrists and neckline, its coloring and elegant simplicity suited Marley.

Parks withdrew the petticoats and pockets and other accessories she needed to dress. "You can't tell anyone. But yes. My true love is Uncle Hawk."

Marley again concealed her amusement—just in the nick of time. She wasn't too much of a threat if she still referred to him as Uncle Hawk.

"He *is* quite handsome, isn't he?" she said, with a smile.

Parks rolled her eyes dramatically. "Everyone I know loves him. Well, him or my brother. He's funny, and strong, and brave. He's like a knight from days gone by. He would do anything for me."

"I can understand why he's dear to you."

The girl sighed. "Let me show you where the water closet is, so you can wash up."

She escorted Marley to a small room off the dressing room, where she piled all her clothing and a pair of slippers onto a small table.

At that moment, they heard a soft rap on the outer door to the dressing area. "Marley?"

Hawk.

Parks ran to the door, peeking out. "We're almost ready."

Marley closed the door to the water closet, surprised to find a bathroom of lavish elegance, albeit only rudimentary functionality. Quickly, she removed her clothing and although she didn't have the time for a proper bath, she scrubbed until she'd washed away enough grime to form a new person. The water was cold and so the soapy sponge bath went quickly.

When she donned Helen's clothing, the curve of her breasts appeared in the deep plunge of the neckline, and she blushed at the frank display. She lightly tried to coax the flower ornamentation in the midst of the bodice up a little farther for a bit of modesty, but its function was to draw attention, not conceal. The best she could do was flatten the lace; that fourth of an inch didn't hide much.

She looked at her stack of grungy sea clothes, feeling an odd warmth for them. She found a shelf and placed them there so she could collect them later.

"Ready?" Parks called, tapping at the door.

"Do you have a ribbon, so I can pull my hair back?"

With a frown, Parks made a noise of frustration. "Everybody has better bosoms than I do. Even you!"

Faint praise, indeed.

"Sit down there, and I'll fix it up for you."

In only minutes, Parks had tamed and dressed her hair so that it piled in loose, artistic curls above, with just a tendril or two along her temples. Then the girl stepped out of the water closet and stood before a mirror Marley hadn't noticed before. In the dark mirror and the candlelit room, it was difficult to see clearly, but Parks pinched at her cheeks and straightened her own clothing, pouting with comical seduction at her reflection, a silly gesture that silly girls would be making centuries later.

The girl reached into an armoire and produced a lovely shawl, draping it over Marley's shoulders and into the bend of her elbows. "There. Perfect."

She turned away toward the door, and Marley was surprised to catch a glimpse of herself. And for the first time in her life, she saw the woman Nan had described—exotic and beautiful.

The thought of Nan made her melancholy. Back in the twenty-first century, Marley was sure, she would have already reunited with Jimmy. Perhaps without Marley there between them, might he finally be treating her better?

Marley hastily rearranged the shawl modestly and followed Parks into the hallway. The women retraced their steps back through the gallery, and at last, they arrived at the head of the stairs. Raven and Hawk stood with Mr. Adams in the entryway, drinking from snifters of brandy.

The men, too, had scrubbed up. Hawk's hair was damp and shone in the candlelight, and she was taken back to the night aboard the *Adventurer*, watching him play in the basin of water.

Parks cleared her throat, none too subtly.

The men looked up.

"About time!" Raven called, abruptly dismissing interest in them and leaving the room.

His father and Hawk, on the other hand, looked at each other in amusement at his desertion, then waited at the foot of the stairs as the young women descended.

And as Hawk extended his elbow to Marley, an utterly oblivious Parks put her hand there instead.

Marley caught her smile as she met his surprised eyes over Parks' head, and she watched his gaze move over her with fleeting appreciation before he focused on the younger woman.

Mr. Adams bowed and offered her his arm. "May I have the pleasure of escorting you to dinner?"

They followed Hawk and Parks into an elegant dining room glittering with crystal and china and silverware. The room was redolent with heady aromas of dinner, and Marley inhaled deeply in appreciation as she glanced around at the lovely foods. A gigantic, perfectly browned roast served as the table's centerpiece.

Raven, standing behind a chair, noticed the awkward pairing and hastily took his sister's arm, steering her toward a vacant seat beside him. "How I've missed my baby sister on this voyage."

She scowled at his phrasing and when she would've resisted, Mr. Adams took her other arm with courtly grace. "You haven't seen your brother for six months, Parks, and he has missed you. Surely you can take pity on him tonight?"

With the younger lady waylaid, Hawk touched Marley's waist lightly. He guided her toward the other side of the table where he seated her between Helen and himself. Leaning close, he murmured in her ear, "May I take your wrap?"

She lightly ducked away from him, but let the shawl settle just slightly lower.

Parks was displeased with the development, but she seemed to be a well-adjusted young girl, and she was happy to be seated at her doting brother's right hand.

At last everyone was seated except Mr. Adams, and he placed his snifter beside his plate and folded his hands before him. "Shall we pray?"

Marley closed her eyes and folded her hands in her lap, and her face warmed as she felt Hawk's hand cover hers.

He led them in a prayer of thanksgiving and supplication for wisdom and protection for those who fought for the freedom of all men.

At its conclusion, he asked Raven to slice the roast while he opened several bottles of wine and placed them around the table after serving everyone.

Mrs. Adams began passing the dishes, and Marley found herself smiling; she couldn't remember ever appreciating such good food as much as she did in this moment.

Marley drank the wine slowly, reluctant to make a fool of herself in front of Raven's parents.

Mr. Adams asked, "So you captured a prize. Without revealing anything we shouldn't know, what can you tell us?"

Raven, happily chewing, deferred to Hawk—also more interested in the roast beef.

"Well. It would be difficult to imagine any general of the Continental Army, no matter how vivid his imagination, drafting a list of needed supplies more complete than the inventory the men took yesterday."

Raven swallowed and jabbed his fork at Hawk. "Unfortunately, we all know that even with that, it isn't enough to overpower those ships in the harbor—not with their firepower. And they're so well-stocked, we can keep picking off their supply ships and they can *still* last."

Mrs. Adams shook her head, her voice falling almost to a whisper. "No. They're starving, too. I saw a few of them on the road, and they looked downright skeletal."

Helen shook her head. "They *did* look thin. Now they have supplies, *and* they have firewood. They're getting stronger every day, and have already destroyed all our homes in the meantime."

Raven cast a glance from Helen to his father. "What does that mean?"

"Firewood," Mr. Adams said, repeating the word Helen had mentioned as if she'd spoken of gold and silver. The grim soberness in his gaze frightened Raven. "They've dismantled every Patriot's home on Boston peninsula."

"And ours?"

The father of the clan hesitated. No one need say the obvious. "Please, let us think for now on our blessings. Delicious food, a comfortable home, and the love and good health of our loved ones here with us."

With that, Marley looked up to find Hawk's gaze on her. He refilled their wine and rested his hand in easy comfort over hers in her lap. "I take it Toni and Marie are in Jamaica?"

"Since the siege began," Mr. Adams said. "So what will your next move be?"

"Cambridge, tomorrow. To see if we can settle the matter of the *Delight*. It won't be easy. For an organization of leaders still in its infancy, Congress seems especially incompetent to agree on anything, including the time of day." After a sip of wine, he said, "Between us, I am not quite sure Congress has even approved this illegitimate navy of privateers. I've heard our Commander-in-Chief has been outfitting private ships donated to the cause—any seaworthy tub he can get his hands on. I believe him quite brilliant. But in managing this Congress, a group of farmers and fishermen, abolitionists and slave owners, doctors, lawyers, New Englanders, Southerners, ... well, after all, he's a mere mortal."

His hand smoothed down Marley's thigh as he spoke, and she took it between her own hands, interlacing his fingers with hers. The last thing she needed was to become aroused here at the dinner table, and she found just the thought of his warm glance on her arousing. His touch on her was beyond her powers of resisting.

He accepted her rebuff, squeezing her hand and relaxing his hand over hers.

"Marley, what about you?" Mrs. Adams put in, and Marley's cheeks stung with embarrassment, as if she'd been caught in her prurient thoughts. The lady smiled easily at her, though. "Where are you from? How did you wind up on the *Adventurer*?"

"Marley is from Virginia," Hawk put in, possibly the first time he'd ever irritated her.

Mrs. Adams, too, seemed perturbed. "I'm sure she can answer for herself, dear."

He gave a simple nod, then refilled his plate with beef and mashed potatoes.

"Hawk's right," she said. "I'm from the tidewater area. I was separated from my grandmother at sea, and Hawk rescued me from the ocean. He truly saved my life."

"Oh, how *romantic*," Parks said, and as Marley glanced toward her, she realized the young girl had been observing everything between them. She had the most pathetic look on her face—both calf-eyed and miserable.

Mrs. Adams glanced at her younger daughter with a sweet smile. "Dear, could you fetch the pies?"

"Marley, would you like to help me?" Parks beamed at her.

Helen stood, patting Marley's shoulder as she left the table. "I'll help. Clever," she said more quietly to her sister as they left the room.

Raven said, "Oh—you know that cardio pulmonary resuscitation of yours?"

"Yes?"

"It *did* save her life. Her heart wasn't beating when Hawk pulled her out."

Marley's mouth fell open as she looked from Raven to Hawk. "You never told me that."

Chewing, he raised his eyebrows casually—shrugging it off.

"I'm so delighted to hear that. Just that—this dinner, Marley sitting here with us—that makes it all worthwhile."

Then she focused a piercing gaze on Marley. "I was asking about where you were from because I feel like I know you from somewhere. There's something so familiar about you, and yet I can't place you."

"I feel the same way, as if I've seen you somewhere—even as I know it cannot be possible."

"No," Mrs. Adams said. "It couldn't be, could it?"

Raven put in, "Why? You're both from the same place in Virginia. Maybe you grew up with her mother."

"I suppose anything's possible," Mrs. Adams said with a noncommittal laugh. "Would anyone like coffee?"

Everyone did.

"How can I help?" Marley asked.

"Entertain these rogues. A sea shanty might work, if you know any."

Then she, too, patted Marley on the shoulder as she followed her daughters into the kitchen.

"They keep patting me. Is that good?"

Hawk bit his lip as he gazed at her—that utterly innocent, completely seductive expression so peculiar to him. She looked to Raven for answers.

"They like you. Now, if you can win Parks over ... Looks like she's gone a bit spoony on Hawk. Fortunately she has the attention span of a moth, so just give her another hour. Surely Hawk can't be that tough to get over."

Hawk smirked, making a whimsical flourish, a small loop in the air at his forehead—the salute of a jester to his king, perhaps.

"Well, what happens next, about the prize?"

All three turned to Marley, surprised to hear the question from her.

Even as the women began returning, Hawk responded. "Tomorrow, we go to Cambridge." Quickly darting her a quieting glance. "Meaning Raven and I. You'll stay here with the women."

"But—"

"No."

"Cambridge?" Mrs. Adams asked as she placed a tray on the sideboard. Her daughters followed, arranging pies there.

Raven nodded. "We have to arrange for dispensation of the prize. With their impressive inertia, 'tis doubtful Congress has set up anything resembling an admiralty court."

"Lacking, as they do, an admiral," Hawk murmured.

"I beg of you, let me go." None of the men there were surprised that the plea came not from Marley, but from the oldest woman there.

Hawk and Raven deferred to her husband to respond, and they all looked to him.

The patriarch rubbed his chin, perhaps testing whether he needed a shave. Then, as if he'd been daydreaming of butterflies, he abruptly looked up and shook his head. "No. Don't be flighty."

The woman snorted almost comically. "You big, dumb man. When have I *ever* been flighty?"

He smiled at her. "Pie, please."

"Oh, don't tempt me."

"But why can't I go?" Marley interjected. "You have to admit, I helped capture the whole thing."

This, neither man could deny.

"I would so love to meet George Washington."

Hawk tilted his head at her. "I don't recall mentioning Washington."

"You said the Commander-in-Chief."

"Yes, but how would a little girl like you … ah, never mind. I've given up guessing how you know these things."

"Marley, sweetie," Mrs. Adams said, "do you know who William Byrd was?"

"Of course." With that, Marley hesitated. How to describe such a man in the words of an eighteenth-century girl of seemingly humble origins? Ah—truthfully but vaguely. "I recall my father speaking of him when I was a small child. The most polished gentleman in the colony."

"Yes. Well, I lived within a few miles of him near the end of his life, and never once was I allowed to meet him."

"Nonetheless," interjected Hawk with force to end the squabble, "This captain and his partner cannot and will not go down in history as capturing a prize with the good, swift, head-bonking aid of a cabin boy. We will meet General Washington, and we will meet him alone."

"Head bonking?" Mrs. Adams asked, drawing near with the coffee pot, holding it up to Marley with question in her eyes.

"Funny you should ask," Raven said. "Do *not* pass that woman that pot. She's liable to smack a man to kingdom come."

"Ray," his mother exclaimed, confused.

"No, it's true," Marley said, holding up her cup. "I can't be trusted with them."

Mrs. Adams poured coffee all around as her daughters sliced the pies.

Helen asked, "Excuse me, but—we have berry, pumpkin, and chocolate. Who wants what?"

Orders quickly went around, and Raven said, "Perhaps Hawk should tell the story. Although we must swear everyone within this room to secrecy, on pain of death."

"Agreed," Hawk said. "To reveal our humiliation at the hands of a couple of nitwits, and our rescue by a simple maiden with a teapot—'tis almost more than a brave patriot can bear."

Marley turned to look at him. "I'd be careful who I described as simple, considering who was tied up, and who had the teapot."

Hawk gave her a slow smile over his wine glass, which he raised to with a bow of his head. Then he leaned back and told the tale with great relish, as his seamen and Raven had told him. Indeed, it was already the stuff of legend—the gawky young cabin boy disabling their captor with a tankard and teakettle, while the captain sat tied up in his cabin and his quartermaster stood gaping, awaiting the lash. In fact, if anything he embellished on Marley's behalf and at the expense of his own manhood, yet quite without any trace of embarrassment.

Marley flushed with pleasure as he spoke of her with obvious pride.

"Uh-huh." At its conclusion, Mrs. Adams looked from Raven to Hawk. "You two let a little girl rescue you—and you couldn't even bother to put decent clothes on her back?"

All three men laughed.

"That's not the worst of it," Raven said. "He made her *serve* as his cabin boy."

Mrs. Adams pressed her lips together to suppress laughter, but she failed.

"No, *that's* not the worst of it," Hawk said. "The worst was when Deming saw me embracing her, after it was all over."

The dining room shook with laughter. "Oh, come now," Ashanti said. "Deming is a smart man. You can't tell me you fooled him for a second."

"Well ... we did fool you. But the alternative means he and all the rest of my crew failed, and were bested not by a cabin boy—but by a girl. Truly, she was the best part of this trip."

His laughing eyes met hers.

"Well," she added, with practical grace, "except for a ship full of big guns and turnips."

Mr. Adams clinked his fork against his wine glass. "I should like to make an announcement." Having their attention, he went on. "We all know the fourth Thursday of November is perhaps a week off, and we would like to offer thanks for our blessings by visiting our good friends in Williamsburg."

Hawk and Raven cheered. "Fortuitous timing," Hawk said, "given that our next voyage was in that direction to pick up my father for the return to St. George's."

Marley noticed the gaiety in the other women—except for Helen. Even as she noticed, Mrs. Adams also looked at her daughter, but with understanding.

"Helen?"

"I am delighted at the idea of a trip to Williamsburg, but Taleeb is here. How can I leave him, and on such a day?"

Mrs. Adams chose her words thoughtfully. "I can understand how you feel, and if you'd rather stay here, I'm sure the Brownsons will welcome you. Elizabeth's baby is due in another month, and she'll need help preparing for that."

"It isn't that I don't want to go, I do. I'd just like for Taleeb to be able to spend the holiday with the family, all together."

"But Taleeb's family has never celebrated the feast as we do, so how can it be any great loss to him? Plus, the schedule of a soldier is uncertain and is it not unlikely he would be granted leave either way? The city is under siege."

Helen set her glass aside. "But, Mama, since he became a part of our family, he loves Thanksgiving! You know that."

Mrs. Adams, elbows squarely planted on the table, steepled her fingertips above her plate. "Let me understand, then. Even though you're well aware that he may not even be able to attend, the entire family should cancel our plans and hope that the siege—which has dragged on now for seven months— might miraculously resolve itself before then."

Helen said nothing.

"My dear daughter, we would love for you and Taleeb and the children to accompany us to Virginia. But we shall miss you if you cannot."

"Why do you even want to go to that awful place, anyway? They enslave people like us!"

"As does our own colony. Can we *never* depart from this topic?"

"And the awful shacks those people live in! 'Tis a miracle they don't all die of pneumonia."

"Why, my own darling daughter is a snob." Mr. Adams spoke quietly, and his face was neither amused nor teasing. "You're as bad as Boston's worst, and a hypocrite in the mix."

"I am not. I simply dislike the cold."

He rubbed his forehead with the tips of his fingers. "Thus ends this conversation. Our friends there risk their lives to try to improve the lot of those on nearby plantations. They work from sunup until sundown so that their farm might be profitable—the women and children, too, something that you, young lady, have never had to do."

"But Father—"

"Please leave. When you are ready to begin your next sentence with the words *I apologize* rather than *but*, you may rejoin us. You are far too old for this."

Her mouth dropped, and she walked stiffly up the stairs.

When she heard the door above close just firmly enough to register protest—but hopefully not awaken the children—Mrs. Adams smiled and shook her head. "Twenty-six years old and three children, and she still acts like one herself."

The men left to smoke cigars in another room, and she began to clear dishes as Parks and her mother prepared the wash water in the kitchen. After taking a stack of dishes in, she returned to the dining room. Hawk stood in the hallway, leaning back against the wall, his gaze roving over her.

She went to him.

Without speaking, he drew her into his arms, locking his hands behind her back. In a swift motion, he drew away her shawl, a slow glance moving over her. He lowered his lips to her bare shoulder, his open mouth nipping lightly, his tongue lingering. He traveled to her collarbone, her throat, her earlobe.

Then he straightened, his eyes bright with emotion. Finally, he brushed his lips against her temple and released her. She gave him a single, lingering glance and returned to the table. As she hurried with more dishes back to the kitchen, she heard his heels clicking down the hallway.

Later, after the kitchen and dining room were spotless once more, Mrs. Adams led Marley to a guest suite. She'd had a servant light the fire an hour before, and the room was quite comfortable for a house in Boston with no heat at all besides fireplaces.

"I hope you're comfortable. If you need anything in the night, just let me know. Ashanti and I are just down the hall."

"Thank you, Mrs. Adams."

The woman laughed. "Please. Call me Camisha."

Marley smiled, plagued again with a notion of déjà vu. "I know it isn't possible, but I feel as if I know you."

Camisha touched her face, lifting her chin, peering closely at her. She reached for the candelabra nearby and held it up.

Her face drained of expression. "Where did you get that scar?"

Marley touched the corner of her eye self-consciously. "My grandmother told me I was jumping on the bed and hit the headboard, but I don't remember."

Camisha patted her shoulder. "Don't give it a second thought. It's not even noticeable. I once had a dear friend who had a similar scar, and I thought ..." She smiled and leaned forward to hug her. "Goodnight, Marley. Sweet dreams."

When Marley was alone, she quickly slipped out of her clothes, shaking them out and setting them aside neatly. She slid between the sheets, hugging herself. Despite the coffee, she was exhausted, and she soon found herself drifting to sleep.

She didn't hear the door open, didn't hear her fire being stoked, didn't feel the heavy quilt being drawn away from her naked body. Only when she felt the reassuring weight behind her, drawing her close into his embrace, did she know he was there with her.

"I couldn't sleep," Hawk whispered. "I hope you don't mind. You seem to have become an indispensable part of me."

His breath was hot at the nape of her neck, and although he wore a nightshirt, she felt each ripple and thrust of his hard body as he hugged her close.

"Are you all right?" she asked.

After a long moment, he responded. "I've always had insomnia, even when I was a child—until you."

"Why didn't you tell me my heart had stopped?"

"I don't like to remember that. It brings to mind how near I came to losing you."

And a moment later, they both slipped into an exhausted, dreamless sleep.

It wasn't until she awakened alone the next morning, content in the memory of sleeping with him, that another memory of the night before came to her.

That of Camisha Adams' words: *Oh, good grief!*

What kind of eighteenth century woman spoke in this way?

Chapter Twenty-One

The Georgian mansion on King's Highway rose from the gray morning mist as the horsemen approached. The home belonged to John Vassall, Tory and aristocrat, now huddled on the Boston peninsula with the rest of the loyalists. Uniformed men moved about the house, coming and going.

"I do hope they've rid the place of dysentery," Raven said. The house had served a multitude of functions, most recently a hospital.

Hawk didn't reply, nudging his horse onward. They soon dismounted and stamped their feet at the doorway to dislodge the snow, leaving their coats with a footman as they entered.

They were escorted into the office of one Lieutenant Colonel Robert Harrison. He was new to the position, and neither Hawk nor Raven had met him. He was perhaps their own age, but his rank as General Washington's secretary and aide-de-camps gave him a polished authority no common citizen could match.

He gave a nod of acknowledgment as they approached.

"Hawk and Raven to see the Commander-in-Chief, regarding the adjudication of the prize *Delight*."

The man's face lit up, extending his hand to Hawk. "You are welcome indeed, sir. *Delight* is indeed, shall we say, a delight to the general and a boon to our cause, and your accomplishment is nothing short of a miracle from heaven."

After a brief interim where they were announced, an inner door opened wide and none other than Washington himself appeared there. Hawk had met him once in Williamsburg, many years before, but he doubted he would remember him. Washington himself was nearly unrecognizable with his excitement over the prize.

"The infamous Hawk," Washington said. "And how does your father?"

"I wasn't sure you would recall me. A number of years have passed since my father served in the House of Burgesses."

"Ah, but you were the apple of his eye."

He welcomed them into the inner sanctum where several other officers sat, and it was then that both Hawk and Raven grew uneasy about something unspoken in the room. Neither could put their finger on it—until the moment when Harrison offered a single empty chair to Hawk.

Hawk glanced around for another for Raven. Then he met Raven's gaze in the unspoken communication twins are good at.

"If you're short of seating, we'll stand," Hawk said coolly, even as Harrison and Washington himself made to sit.

Washington sent a short glance to Harrison, who held out a hand to the door. "Do forgive me. Your manservant need not trouble himself here. Perhaps he's hungry, the kitchen no doubt will be more comfortable?"

Hawk reined in his emotions, again meeting Raven's shuttered gaze.

Of all the despicable things Hawk had encountered in life—sham aristocrats; contemptuous tidewater landowners whose fat purses bought them into a gentility that none-too-secretly mocked them; thieves; plunderers; turncoats—he detested nothing more than that awkward, meekly obsequious gaze on his dearest friend's face. It said: *I know my place.* In a land where men prided themselves on abolishing the very notion of *place*. The look made him want to race back to the *Delight* and set the entire thing afire.

It took quite a bit to dampen Ray's enthusiasm for life, but these reminders of the world they lived in did the trick. And that enraged Hawk.

Not bothering to veil his contempt, Hawk laughed. It was not a sound of joy, but of mockery.

"*Mister* Harrison," he said, dispensing with the man's military title, "Mr. Adams shall hear your apology now."

"I beg your pardon?"

Raven raised his hand to stop him, but Hawk *was* controlling himself. Had he not, Robert Harrison would've been lying in the corner with a broken nose, in a pool of his own blood.

"You have insulted my partner, Mr. Rashall Adams, of the Boston Adams who are well known on Beacon Hill as brave, upstanding patriots. Mr. Adams has risked his own life countless times over the past five years to serve the cause of freedom—as have his father and mother their entire lives. A freedom, as we all know, his black brethren are not afforded, neither in the colonies of Virginia, nor of Massachusetts, nor in your own Maryland. Mr. Adams is my business partner, and you will apologize *now*."

As he spoke, rather than shouting, his voice grew increasingly quiet—until his last words were a grating whisper.

Harrison was frozen in embarrassment at his blunder.

"For God's sake, Harrison, do it."

This, from their Commander.

This thawed the man's tongue, and he bowed deeply to Raven. "Sir, I do heartily apologize. It was a foolish assumption. I beg your forgiveness."

As he spoke, Hawk's gaze drifted from the officers nearby, staring at their laps, to Washington, watching the scene, his gaze unreadable, to Raven himself, equally inscrutable.

Harrison hastily fetched another chair from the other end of the room and presented it to Raven. At last, the men sat.

Washington leaned back in his chair, looking at them both, aware that their rightful joy had been clumsily dashed. He leaned forward once more, folding his hands on his desk before him. "Gentlemen, you have with your capture of the *Delight* offered the Continental Army both an arsenal that is almost beyond imagining, and the invaluable boost of morale as well. As you said, you have served the cause of liberty well, and I thank you."

Hawk watched the Commander as he rested his hands flat over a ledger on his desk. "I don't have to ascertain the value of the prize, for you, since this is your business. However, as I mentioned in my last letter, Congress continues to be difficult to manage, and they have yet to name a body for adjudicating prizes. Oh, they've assigned two men to the task, but it is a much larger responsibility than they own.

"Only now are we beginning to see fruit from those ships we've outfitted for our fledgling navy. In truth, they have no funds at all to allocate to the operation of this endeavor. And yet, I've men who are willing to serve, and who must be properly outfitted. This will go a long way to arming my men."

He reached for a few papers, and Hawk recognized it as the inventory they'd sent on ahead to him. He looked over the list and again set it aside.

"Sir, may I ask that you simply say what you'd like to say?" Hawk was losing patience with the prevaricating, especially from a man so famous for his directness.

"I cannot yet issue payment for the prize. I do not know when I can."

"Oh." Hawk exchanged a laughing gaze with Raven. "That."

Washington went silent, nonplussed. He cleared his throat, as if to re-establish decorum.

"General, we withheld a number of arms and some supplies for our families' use. We made note of that on the inventory. What's the current crew's cut for a ship full of artillery? A tenth? An eighth?" They both knew the going rate.

Washington humphed, and Hawk guessed it was a point of contention between the general himself and Congress. "Mr. Harrison?"

One of the officers cleared his throat. "The figure was one-third. Congress has raised it to one-half."

"Well, that's quite generous of them, for a body that has no cash on hand," Hawk mused.

"Indeed," Washington said, with a gloomy nod. "I will have the money to pay you, but I do not know when."

Here, Raven leaned forward, speaking with that quiet voice he'd acquired by watching his mother, when she had something important to say to his father.

"Sir, with all humility, we are not impoverished, nor are our families. We will wait until you are comfortable paying us. If your men need coats and uniforms, we beg you deal with those more immediate needs first."

Washington looked at Raven with grim respect and humility. He gave a slight nod of thanks.

Hawk made to rise, but Washington stopped him and turned to the officers nearby. "Gentlemen, if you'll excuse us."

Everyone quit the room except for Washington, Hawk, and Raven. Washington rose, looking out the window on the snow, still falling.

"Boston has been under siege for seven months now. Our militia is strong in spirit. But they know as well as you that, even with the added miracle of *Delight*, we lack the cannonade necessary to repel those ships that refuse to leave.

"I do have a plan underway to secure the heavy guns we need. It may take weeks to accomplish with the poor weather.

"But I need not tell you of our desperate straits, where willing and capable leaders are concerned. Ours is a rich land populated by poor men. Farmers and furriers, bakers and bricklayers. Not warriors.

"I need not tell you the enemy's numbers. They can and do summon troops on a whim numbering more than all our colonies' militia. It is by God's grace that we still live."

He turned away from the window, returning to his desk—but this time, he came to the front and leaned against it.

"You have led many successful expeditions in perilous circumstances. Yet I would ask you now to consider volunteering your ship to serve our new country in our quest for freedom."

"You simply want our ship?"

"No. I merely assume your ship will accompany you. Again, you personally will be reimbursed at some point."

"Sir, I do not understand."

"I wish to offer you a commission in the Continental Navy. At present I command all military forces, but in time I should think you will ably take over the Navy. That is yet to be determined, but I have been greatly disappointed by the results of commanders I have commissioned thus far." He hesitated, then added grimly, "And all of this, of course, assumes that we survive the gallows in the meantime."

Beyond the fact that neither of these men had any patience for government, and despite the flattering offer, Hawk was focused instead on another distraction.

He had noticed—as would any man in his predicament— that Washington had smoothly transitioned from a plural *you* to a singular. That, as the tall man leaned against the desk, he did so not placing himself between the two men seated before him, but solely across from Hawk.

Raven might have left the room, so utterly had Washington dismissed him.

And, even as Hawk had the thought, Raven rose. "General, I can see I'm not needed for this discussion."

"Sit *down*," Hawk said.

With the last of his dwindling reserve of patience, Raven sat.

"So that we are clear," Hawk said. "You offer me a commission."

Washington gave a deep nod.

"And for Mr. Adams, you offer an equal commission on his own ship—perhaps, thanks to him, the newly available *Delight*?"

Washington had the grace to let discomfort cross his face.

"Under the circumstances, you understand I cannot."

"Nay, I do not. What are the circumstances? That I am asked to fight for freedom, while denying it to others? I regret I was not clearer that my partner and I jointly operate a business as equal executors. Watching over each other these past dozen years, it has become a habit."

"You are welcome to take Mr. Adams into your service as a seaman, but he cannot captain a ship. We must be united against the enemy, and a ship with an African at the helm will be divided."

"As I am reminded of the enemy," Raven said, pointing at Washington, "I heard last night that they're offering slaves in Virginia—any old farmhand, mind you—the very same deal you just offered me. How flattered should I be, sir?"

Raven rose and made to leave, then turned back to the general and spoke:

"Proceed, great chief, with virtue on thy side,
Thy ev'ry action let the Goddess guide.
A crown, a mansion, and a throne that shine,
With gold unfading, Washington! Be thine."

With that, he bowed deeply to Washington with the sort of sardonic insolence Hawk had seen only in Ashanti Adams.

"Bronson, you may not be finished with this insulting line of questioning, but I am."

He turned on his heel and left. Hawk was startled into silence; he couldn't remember the last time they'd called each other by their given names.

Washington, visibly shaken, raised a hand even as Hawk rose to follow him. The only reason he stopped was his respect for the grim task facing this embattled man, leading their fledgling country.

"Apparently abuse inspires the muse in my friend."

"I know not how, but he quoted from a poem written by one of his own people, a young lady named Phillis Wheatley. She sent the poem to me, so I'm uncertain how he would know it. But twenty two years ago born in dark Africa, now penning lyrical and undeserved praise to her new country's military leader."

Bronson recognized the name—the Wheatleys lived not far from the Adamses, and Rashall knew her well. He likely had read it long before she'd ever sent it to Washington. "A country that still considers her property. Even in enlightened Boston."

The general gazed at his desk. "Sir, I commend you on your loyalty, and your courage in taking a difficult position. But I am single-minded in my duty to defeat our enemy, the mightiest military power in the world. The role of the African in our country does matter. They must be properly established as free people. Either in this land or back in their own—at the right time. That, I fear, is a battle for another day."

"So you do ask them to fight for a freedom that is not theirs."

"I do not like it any more than you."

Hawk's laughter was mirthless. "Sir, you and I both know you've owned slaves since you were a boy merely dreaming of going to sea, at an age when Raven and I *went*."

"Slavery is a difficult system to dismantle, and one man cannot do it alone. My slaves are accustomed to my protection." He looked at the floor, conflict clear on his face.

Hawk exhaled. "Well. I am accustomed to my good friend's protection, and he, accustomed to mine. We both shall continue to strive for the freedom of these colonies, as we have for these past five years. And might I add, you have turned away the bravest, most noble and clever ally you could have wished for, in Rashall Adams. Not to mention loyal."

He walked to the door and stopped. "And for your own edification, General, Rashall Adams is not an African. His family was working and living free in this land while yours and mine were still bowing to the King. If anyone has earned the right to call himself an American, it is he."

Chapter Twenty-Two

Marley awakened that same morning with the memory of decadent warmth as she slept safe in Hawk's arms. She remembered the evening before, when he caught her in the hallway—she'd been so certain he would kiss her then. And yet, the excitement over prolonging the delay was an excruciating pleasure.

A quiet rap came at the door, and when she answered, a young maid with bright blue eyes and freckles entered, carrying an armful of wood.

"Sorry to wake you, ma'am. You go right back to sleep, I'll have you warmed up in a trice."

Marley threw the covers back, shocked by the cold. Surely she should have listened to the girl, at least until the room warmed up a bit. Instead, she found herself excited at the prospect of spending the day with the Adams women. That was when the memory of Camisha's *good grief* came to her and distracted her—and had her husband actually used the phrase *group hug?* Impressive, the clarity a good night's sleep could bring.

She stopped in the water closet, scrubbed up, and then quickly dressed. How soon she'd lowered her expectations of the eighteenth century—and for that, she had the *Adventurer* to thank. Effectively camping out for a month had taught her to appreciate a bucket of fresh spring water at the ready and servants stoking fires.

She hurried downstairs where Parks was dipping scrambled eggs onto a platter.

"I'm so sorry I'm late. How can I help?"

Parks smiled at her. "Just have a seat. Everything's ready."

The gay laughter of children in the dining room captured Marley's attention, and she followed the sound. Helen carried an infant in a sling contraption against her breast. A tiny pink cap covered the baby's ears. The woman poured steaming black coffee around the table, then placed cream with the sugar in the middle.

"Boys, eat your porridge. That's what your Uncle Ray had for breakfast. Shonny, don't you want to grow up big and strong like Uncle Ray? You're still a tiny thing."

The boy—perhaps five years old—beamed with pleasure. His large dark eyes, as well as his cheeks and forehead, sparkled with his smile, as if his face were lit from inside. He laughed uproariously.

"I'm tiny. Tiny Shonny! Tiny Shonny!"

With no-nonsense grace, Mrs. Adams swung the boy up and into his chair, putting a spoon in his hand. "Eat your oatmeal and hush, Tiny Shonny, Tiny Shonny."

Deep, infectious laughter rumbled in his chest, and Marley covered her own mouth. When Mrs. Adams noticed her, she said, "He does sound like a tiny Raven when he laughs."

"Ray was just like that when he was his size. Looked like him, too."

"Tiny Ray, tiny Ray," the boy sang out.

"Boy oh boy."

Boy oh boy. Another anachronism. A peculiarly twentieth century phrase, she was sure. Could it simply be that the language hadn't in fact changed as much as she'd thought?

No. Of that she was certain. She'd read enough eighteenth-century writing, and listened to the speech patterns of the men on the ship, that she knew something was different about this woman—and she couldn't yet explain it. And she remembered Raven remarking on how her own speech resembled his mother's.

Another boy, perhaps three years old, climbed down out of his chair, squealing in frustration when his grandmother scooped him up, too, and returned him to his chair, beside his brother. "Me wanna johnny cake. Tiny johnny! Tiny johnny!

Helen turned to her older son. "See what you started?"

Shonny grinned at Marley as if she were a secret conspirator.

"No johnny cake today, John. Today we have porridge. Let's try some cinnamon."

This bewitched the child, and with the slight doctoring, he began piling awkward mouthfuls of oatmeal into his mouth. Marley jumped forward and sat beside him. "Would you like me to help?"

He eyed her suspiciously, then nodded and held out his spoon, gummy with oatmeal. Marley quickly fed him, then wiped off his face and served her own plate.

Mr. Adams had left the house before Marley ever awakened, busy with feeding animals and the countless other chores of an ordinary day. She'd learned he also owned a shop in town, but she wasn't certain how the siege had impacted his business.

The women were finishing their breakfast by the hearth when they heard a pounding on the front door, followed by urgent cries.

Parks reached the front door first, and announced over her shoulder, "'Tis Mrs. Brownson's maid, Susan."

Camisha swung the door open wide.

A pale young girl stood there. She trembled in the snow, dressed in no more than a cotton dress and cape and mobcap.

"What's the matter, Susan? Would you like to come in?"

She shook her head wildly. "No, mum. 'Tis milady. Her time's come. Well, no. But she's having her baby now, either way."

Grabbing two woolen cloaks from a nearby closet, she looked at Helen. "Both you girls stay here and pack for the trip. Helen, you need to decide whether you'll be going with us or staying behind. Perhaps you'd be especially useful at Mrs. Brownsons' now. Marley, you come with me."

She handed a cloak to Marley, and they followed the young girl down the snowy path to a farmhouse near the foot of the country road. "How long has she been having pains?"

"It started in the night, maybe four o'clock—she didn't awaken anyone, only got up and sat by the fire," Susan said.

Camisha explained to Marley quietly, "The poor woman has lost a number of babies. They're always born early. One survived—at eight months, this baby should, it just depends on how well she's been taking care of herself. I tell them to eat well to help the baby develop, but they never listen."

As they entered the home, they heard a wail echo through the halls, and they followed the sound upstairs.

The woman in the bed wore a nightdress up to her neck, and a man of perhaps forty sat on the edge of the bed holding her hand between both of his. He ran a hand uncertainly over his rumpled hair.

He gave a sigh of relief when he saw the women. "Mrs. Adams, we are so relieved to see you."

Camisha hung her cloak on a peg, and Marley followed suit. Both women quickly scrubbed their hands at the washstand.

The woman's face was a pasty beige, and Camisha turned to the maid. "Susan, please go down and see if you can find us some frozen spring water, and bring us a glass of ice chips."

The girl raced down the stairs.

"Caleb, if there's any work you need to tend to for a couple of hours, I think I can manage here. Or if you'd like to wait downstairs, it might be simpler for you."

He had tried to hide his worry, but at this offer, the relief quietly filled his eyes.

He leaned toward his wife. "Now you'll call for me, won't you, if you need anything?"

She nodded wearily.

When he left, Camisha drew back the covers and set them aside. "How are the pains?"

"Terrible."

"Have you noted the frequency?"

"Every two minutes, for perhaps a half hour."

"Well, we should see the baby soon. Mind if I have a look?"

Elizabeth shook her head. Marley folded her hands before her and waited.

"Well, I see the head, but you're not quite dilated enough," Camisha said. "It should be soon, though."

Even as she spoke, the woman was wracked with another pang.

Susan entered the room and set the glass of ice chips on the night table beside the bed. Marley offered them to Elizabeth, and she sucked on a small chip, setting the glass aside.

And at last, time enough had passed. "All right, I can see the head crowning," Camisha said with an encouraging smile. "Time to have that baby, Mama!"

And Elizabeth knew what to do.

Marley watched. Knowing full well what she watched, it was still astonishing to witness as the woman pushed. The head emerged, as tiny as a child's doll, followed by wriggling shoulders, torso, hips, and legs. Elizabeth's little girl was delivered, and Marley smiled, filled with wonder.

But even as she opened the blanket prepared for the child, as Camisha quickly fished her finger inside the child's mouth to remove the mucus, they both watched the tiny infant gasping vainly for breath, turning blue, silently struggling to breathe with lungs too small to do the job.

She bit her lip to keep from crying out against what she saw. She prayed for the baby, fearing she was far too small to survive.

"Come on, sweetie, breathe," Camisha cried, turning the baby over, massaging urgently. She turned her over again and puffed gently into her tiny mouth. The baby lay still.

Camisha continued to rub her in different positions, she lay her against her mother's stomach, rubbing her back—dear God, so tiny!—and patting lightly.

Marley glanced at Elizabeth Brownson, but the woman's head was turned aside, silent tears streaming into her pillow.

For another twenty minutes Camisha continued attempting to save the child, puffing into her mouth, until Elizabeth touched her arm.

Camisha looked up at her, her eyes and face bright with tears. "I'm so, so sorry, Lizzy. Her lungs were just too small."

But Marley could only think of modern incubators and how preemies months younger could survive just fine.

"How many, Camisha?" This, from the woman in the bed, a husky whisper.

Camisha didn't respond, as if she knew it was a rhetorical question.

"How many times will God allow me the joy of feeling my child grow within me—only to watch the poor wretch die before my eyes? Nine so far! How many more?"

Camisha washed the infant gently, then wrapped her in a blanket. "Would you like to hold her?"

Elizabeth looked up, considering. "No, not this time. This time, I can't bear it."

Camisha cradled the infant.

"But I want you to take her."

After a moment, Camisha nodded. "Thank you. Did you … What was her name to be?"

"Sunny Abigail." After a moment, she added, "And for a boy, Nathaniel."

"All right, then."

She placed the baby into the bassinet and covered her with another blanket, then moved the bassinet nearer the door. Almost immediately, Susan returned, lifted the bassinet, and silently carried it downstairs.

Returning to the bed, she helped Elizabeth expel the afterbirth, then disposed of that. She washed her hands again, then gently gave the grieving woman a sponge bath, speaking softly all the while.

"Nine so far, you said. Boys and girls, named for the heroes of the Bible, the heroes of our new country. Elizabeth, my dear friend, their spirit lives on in the freedom of others whose own mothers could not grant them that freedom."

Marley listened in bewilderment, trying to understand her words. The mystery of Camisha was beyond her.

Glancing at Marley, she said, "Run downstairs and heat some broth, if you can find any. And send Susan for Caleb, if she hasn't already gone."

As she left, she heard Camisha explaining to the woman that Helen would be staying with her to help for the next few days.

In the kitchen, its hearth cold, Marley looked vainly for broth. The bassinet sat near the back door, a white sheet covering it. Just the sight of it saddened Marley. The door opened, and Susan entered, awkwardly hauling in two large baskets piled with snow.

"Do you know if there's any broth?" she asked the girl.

The girl set down the baskets and nodded. "Yes. Give me just a moment."

Susan hastily drew back the sheet and began filling the bassinet with soft, dry snow.

Marley gasped, shocked.

The girl glanced at her. "Something amiss, milady?"

Marley shook her head hastily. No doubt they were simply preserving the child until a burial could be arranged. But this was a colonial practice she'd never read about, and it was a little unsettling.

Why were these women attempting to preserve this child, as if for some pagan ritual?

Chapter Twenty-Three

Later that afternoon, Marley set the rich mahogany dining table while Parks and Helen finished preparing supper. She heard the noise of horses outside, and she raced to the window, the gloom of the day's events lightened by the shadows of Hawk and Raven returning from Cambridge. But even in that moment, she could tell from their rushed, terse motions that something was wrong. Soon she saw it firsthand, when they entered through the front door.

Raven, cool and distant, gave Marley a curt nod, walked through the kitchen—no doubt a simple check on dinner—then strode straight back outside to help his father finish unloading the wagons.

Hawk had only just arrived, pleased at the sight of Marley, when Raven nearly ran into him headed back out.

Marley looked to Hawk for an explanation, but he silently shook his head, gently raising a hand even as he placed a stack of newspapers on a nearby table. Then he turned to follow Raven back outside in stalwart support.

As they brought load after load of produce and salted meat onto the rear porch, the women left supper warming on the stove and went to work, transferring the foodstuffs to the larder.

It was long after dark when they finished, and the supper they sat down to was hardly the festive affair of last evening.

Parks ladled hot beef and barley stew into bowls, and Helen passed the cornbread. Fortunately, she'd put the children to bed earlier, and Marley was relieved. At least they would be spared their uncle's inexplicably black mood.

She wasn't sure what had happened in Cambridge, but after a few minutes she understood that Hawk was simply upset on Raven's behalf.

Raven gazed into his stew, stirring morosely and occasionally tasting his wine.

After he'd eaten enough to dull his hunger, Mr. Adams cleared his throat and said, "Out with it."

Raven looked at him matter-of-factly. "What?"

"Whatever happened today to turn you into, well, me."

"Oh, it was a fine day. General Washington offered milord over there an admiralship."

Hawk's jaw went hard. "He did no such thing."

"He did exactly that. He said in not so many words that if we all survive the war, you would take over the Navy for him."

"That's wonderful news! Son, why are you so angry? You surely can't begrudge your best friend such an honor."

"In fact I can, when he himself declined it because I was not offered a co-admiral post. Am I so fragile that I must be protected and patronized as if I were a girl?"

Camisha put her spoon down. "Rashall, I will not have this at my supper table. Partly because it's comically childish, partly because in your own perceived injustice you're insulting those of us who happen to be female. But mainly because our time together is so short. So the general offered you no commission at all, is that it?"

Raven sipped from his wine. "No. Of course not. God forbid they put a *Negro* in charge of a ship."

"But you ... thought he might? And you're somehow angry at your good friend because of this?"

"Mother, I know what you've said. Many years will pass before the black man receives the same recognition of an ordinary man for his work—and only when he is no longer seen as a black man. But please understand. At sea, all men are already equal. Every hour I spend on a ship, I am an ordinary man, no different than any other ordinary man on board. I do my work, they do their work, I command men of every color, and they obey. Then later we laugh, we play, we work, we fish. And then I come back home, and …" He shook his head. "Hawk and I captured a ship as big as Boston itself, and what did they offer me as a reward? That hard-won position of seaman."

The table fell silent.

He rushed on. "The same post I hear Dunmore is offering Virginia's slaves. Wait, no! He's in fact more generous, offering them their freedom at the end of their service."

His father refilled their glasses. "You must know this to be a sign of Dunmore's desperation. It isn't as if the governor is a champion of anyone's rights. He owns slaves himself."

"I know that. The obvious difference, sir, being that General Washington is supposed to be better than English aristocracy."

The older man pressed his lips together and fell silent.

"Ray, the general is doing the jobs of three or four men right now. He cannot be expected to also attend to over 150 years of injustice wrought by many men the world over—including men in Africa."

"Mother, that is the *last* reminder I need at this moment."

"It's a reminder you best never forget. Evil and greed and ignorance colluded at a point in history, and it will take many, many years, and the efforts of good *white* men, as well as women, to right those wrongs, to educate the even deeper ignorance. White, red, black, and blue men and women. And I will not have you or anyone else in this family hanging their head over that. I will not have you blaming others for what is not their fault, nor feeling sorry for yourself. You are not a victim. You are a strong, gifted man born in the most exciting period of this country's history, and you will continue to do great things for her."

This only sent him more deeply into himself; what she said, Marley was certain, wasn't anything he hadn't heard before at the family dinner table.

Her gaze darted over each family member there. Helen, whose own husband was garrisoned at the edge of the town on the peninsula. Parks, who cast a sidelong glance at her brother. The matriarch of the family, who more often than not concealed her worry, purely to encourage them. And that lady's husband, who knew better than any of them the ugly truth of what his son said.

The reality sickened her; most of all, that she was helpless to change a thing. She looked up at Hawk and found him gazing at her, as if the sight of her reassured him.

Then he turned to Raven. "Why would you think I would want a post with the Navy? Would *you*, for that matter?" He posed the question with frank honesty.

"This is not a useful line of reasoning. We've both loved the sea for over a decade, and we both want to aid the cause. Why wouldn't I want a commission?"

"Because what we do now is the same thing, except without the stupidity of incompetent leaders, and with greater reward—and, as you said, a sane structure, where men are judged simply by the results of their labor."

"We're pirates! How is a man supposed to court a decent woman, doing what we do?"

He seemed to hear his own insult before Marley did. After an awkward moment, he thumped his forehead and turned to her. "Please forgive me, dear, that had nothing to do with you, and everything to do with me and how I'd like to live my life. I'd like to come home at night to my wife and children and go to the meeting-house on Sunday morning, and live an ordinary life. Just an ordinary man. That's all I want to be."

Hawk spoke lightly. "Ah. Now I see. You want to be a Navy lieutenant who need never weigh anchor. Is that accurate?"

Raven smirked at him, a hint of humor, of his true self, entering his eyes. He broke his cornbread in half and crumbled it into his soup. Dipping his spoon into his bowl, he ate in earnest.

"I know what's wrong," Marley said. "You're tired of the sea, you want a family of your own, and you were reminded today that only at sea is the color of your skin forgotten. And your bad manners are simply a combination of your anger over that and low blood sugar."

The entire table went silent and turned to look at her. Raven jabbed his spoon at her, then at Camisha. "That. Low blood sugar. I've never heard *anyone* say that besides my mother."

Camisha and Marley exchanged a mutually suspicious glance before Marley rushed on. "Nonetheless, the general was just a reminder of a corrupt system."

"No, the general is a *part* of it. But yes, you're correct." Raven had abandoned his curiosity over the secret lingo Marley shared with his mother.

Hawk, too, returned his attention to his food. "Yet it isn't so simple for him to say, 'no, I will not be a part of this atrocity.' He is but one man. Slavery, and the ignorant bigotry that came with it, is an insidious thorn that has embedded itself in the character of our land. If we do not remove it now, it will destroy us."

To that, no one could add anything. Mr. Adams abruptly asked, "My dear wife, may we hope that you have a happier tale from the results of your day?"

Camisha raised her head, her dark eyes large with sadness.

"Oh, no. What happened?

"Mrs. Brownson lost her baby. A little girl."

The men went silent, exchanging an awkward glance and then staring at their plates. Marley found herself surprised at their reaction. It was beyond the discomfort of men discussing something beyond their understanding.

Camisha noticed their reaction. "You know what this means, and it is nothing to be mourned. Just as her child is received into heaven, so there is this. Her child has died that another might know life."

Raven sent his mother a somber glance. "It is not that simple, and you know it."

"Who just got through preaching about the plight of the black man as an ordinary man as if you were Benjamin Rush himself?" She set her jaw in stubborn defiance.

Marley knew better than to ask stupid questions in the middle of this exchange. Even Hawk was lost in his own thoughts, oblivious to her confusion.

Camisha spoke at last. "Can we not break free from this terrible day and instead rejoice? This week we will see our friends at Rosalie. I've missed Ruth these many months, and it will be good to see my boys."

"My Camisha," her husband said, "You know they are not your boys."

She bent her head for a long moment, then raised it again, her eyes bright with emotion. "They will always be my boys."

"Very well. To each of us, there's a time to be born and a time to die. A time to love and a time to hate. A time for war and a time for peace. While we are together, this is a time to give thanks for each other. And the Adamses of Boston will celebrate with the Trelawneys of Williamsburg, and be glad indeed."

With that, he reached to clap his son on the shoulder in solidarity even as he did the same with Hawk. And a shout of gladness arose from everyone at the table.

Marley sat, absorbing everything she heard, watching the joyful exchange in shock. *Rosalie … Ruth …*

The Trelawneys of Williamsburg.

And it all came back to her. The tankard she'd found in the ship's cupboard. The beloved, priceless journals her family had hoarded—now, perhaps, lost to posterity for all time, locked in the trunk of her car. Their exact words escaped her, but the details remained and materialized before her eyes.

I was sad already that my friend Camisha was gone, sailed up to Boston to be with her husband's family. … There was a fire up at the house, and by the time we saw it, we couldn't do nothing but watch it burn. … Mr. Thomas, we none of us know him much. But the first we knew something was wrong, we saw him screaming and crying and running back and forth like a crazy man behind the house, and his little baby screaming and crying and Dan and the other men had to keep him from going in the house. I had to take the baby from him, I was so afraid of what he might do.

And she remembered, unmistakably, a voice whispering forgotten secrets in her ear as she slept. The voice of a man born in Williamsburg nearly three decades before, whose father had held him as he watched the fire that had consumed Rosalie and had taken his eldest son and grandchild. The sound of a voice that had become dearer to her than her own.

"My name is Bronson, my darling."

Chapter Twenty-Four

The *Adventurer* had sailed but two hours south of the Massachusetts Bay's icy waters when the skies cleared and the weather thawed.

Helen had stayed behind in Dorchester with the youngest children, allowing her mother to take Shonny along for the family's traditional holiday.

On the second day of their journey, Camisha put Marley and Parks to work below deck chopping the vegetables and salted pork. These were the oils and acrylics she worked on her culinary palette. She sheer poundage of celery and onions seemed excessive to Marley, but she had no way of knowing the numbers of people awaiting feeding at Rosalie.

At this moment, she had escaped for a break and huddled, stooped in a corner on the quarterdeck, watching Hawk direct the men in the rigging.

Bronson, she reminded herself, already growing fond of his name. It suited him.

They had been sailing nearly two full days and nights, and she had had no time alone with him at all. Occasionally, in stolen moments, she caught him watching her, but she pined for those unending days at sea when she'd had him all to herself, when he tutored her in the simple pleasures of life as a seaman.

Now, he thought her below with the Adams women, and in the sunshine he worked without his shirt, his broad back brown in the noonday sun as he talked to Jem, pointing out some item of interest. She inhaled the salty sea spray as she folded her arms around her knees and rested her chin there, rolled almost into a ball there in the corner. She'd wrapped a woolen shawl around her head and neck to warm herself in the cool autumn breeze, but the sight of him lit a fire within her and she burned for him.

Even as she slipped the shawl from the crown of her head to cool down, he turned, displaying a rippling chest and abdomen, his breeches low on his lean hips. Her lips parted at the utterly sexual sight. She unconsciously touched her tongue to her lips as if in hunger, and then she noticed his gaze on her.

In two strides along the deck and another three across the quarterdeck, he was at her side, crouching before her. One knee rested, then, on the deck, brushing her hip.

"How did you escape your chaperones?"

"I have no need for chaperones. You taught me to take care of myself."

One corner of his mouth turned up. Noticing the loose fall of her shawl, he reached out to bundle her more carefully. "Are you cold?"

Not any more, she thought with a smile. But she only shook her head.

"Well, then." At the warmth in her slow, innocently sensual smile, he lifted his hand and drew away the shawl until it fell into the bend of her elbows, revealing her creamy breasts to his private gaze.

"'Tis only fair," he murmured, his gaze lingering.

"You, sir, are beyond redemption." Even as she said the words, her gaze drifted frankly to his chest, to his rippling arms.

"You smell ... delicious. What is that aroma?"

She laughed at that. "Delicious indeed. Onions, perhaps?"

A robust chuckle burst from him as he considered her. He sobered, the tenderness in his eyes filling with desire even as his lips parted, as he took her face in his hands and dipped his head toward hers.

"Ohhhh, captain!"

She tasted his breath—sweet with anise seed—and felt the heat of his warm, moist mouth, hovering above hers. His eyes closed a brief moment, even as the amused call came again, more prolonged. The soft curve of his lips went tight as he pressed them together.

"Ohhhh, caaap-taaaaain. Oh, captain, oh—"

His eyes were bright with pleasure as he hastily replaced the shawl over her and released her, turning away toward Ray's call.

"For a man who refuses any favor I ask, you certainly require my opinion when I've no interest at all in what you do."

"Hampton is less than 30 minutes off. We'll enter the James there, rather than Norfolk, given Dunmore's antics."

"Aye," he said, rising to his full height, his hands on his hips. "We discussed this ten minutes ago. Why, then, *your* antics?"

Rashall Adams—Ray, as she'd come to think of him, as his family did—arrived on the quarterdeck, his face alight with devilment as he gave Marley a gentlemanly bow. Then he moved closer to the captain.

"I believe you recall the bargain my mother made to ensure your lady's chastity?" He spoke in subdued tones behind a feigned smile, but Marley was able to make it out.

"Ah, yes. That disturbing snatch-me-baldheaded promise she's fond of. And what, pray tell, does the matron believe I can do in three minutes of full daylight with two dozen crew watching that I could not do in three weeks of sheltering my beloved in my own bed?"

Marley's heart sang with pleasure. His beloved.

"What?" Rashall demanded with sharp disbelief.

"You're a clever man, Raven. I said nothing that young Shonny wouldn't have discerned over the past month."

With that, the captain reached for his shirt, where he'd tied it in the shrouds, and donned it.

Despite herself, Marley gave a soft cry of disappointment.

Both men glanced at her—Bronson, in subdued pleasure, and Ray, simply stunned.

"I'm gonna tell my mama," he said as he headed below, shaking his head.

Bronson met her gaze as he buttoned his shirt and slipped the tails inside his breeches, then bowed to her. "Would you like to watch the approach of the shore at my side?"

She placed her hand in his, rising.

With one arm, he drew her close against him, bending to brush his lips against her temple. "How I ache for you, my love. How I yearn for the time you are my own."

She turned her face toward him, and her open mouth brushed his throat.

"Today you shall meet my father," he said. "And tonight you shall be mine."

With the help of a British Navy concentrated on the opposite shore near Norfolk, and a British flag to run up, should they encounter trouble, the *Adventurer* passed through the Chesapeake Bay and into the James River. Although Marley had lived her entire life in this land, over two centuries of change would stamp itself on the land before she was born, and she recognized none of what she saw.

Until they arrived at Rosalie.

And even then, it was not so much the sights, but the smells. The rich, fecund aroma of the river, the unique smell of rotting indigo brush and stout blackberry bushes on the riverbank beneath the thawing snow, and the faint, comforting sting of woodsmoke coming from farther inland. The branches of the elms and ash were bare, their leaves composting in the shadows of the riverbank to shelter their young.

When the captain set Marley on dry ground, she was overcome with a riot of harsh emotions she could not explain. Perhaps it was like returning home after a long journey abroad, to an utterly strange land that she'd only thought she knew.

She had discovered so much while here in this time, and been given so much—and yet she missed so much.

But … what, exactly, she wasn't sure. And it wasn't precisely *missing*, for that matter; merely an anxious fear, an emptiness she could not explain.

She hadn't grown up on Rosalie, and had never lived here—yet the depth of her melancholy was like a homesickness she'd known her entire life, as if she'd discovered an unfathomable answer to a researcher's puzzle of the ages, that a crucial missing fact suddenly righted and aligned itself.

A deep ache opened within her, frightening her in its intensity. In a moment, she grew terrified that it was her own time, calling her home, when *this* had become her home; the man beside her, her love—a love she never could've known in her own time.

She scanned her heart's snapshots, letting the ache open within her as she thought back to the hasty departure she and her grandmother had made, that last afternoon, when she'd wanted to visit Rosalie once more.

But that wasn't it.

It wasn't until the group had disembarked and begun their joyous trek toward the community of the Trelawneys that she recalled the last time she had been on this land.

She stopped, looking back at the *Adventurer*, standing stalwart near the deep bank of the James.

"There she is! Ruth!" Camisha cried, wildly waving her arms. Marley ignored her, desperate to understand what troubled her so.

Her throat ached as she stared at the beautiful ship in its full glory against the autumn sky. Back on that last morning at work, she had knelt in the dig, painstakingly brushing at dirt. But it wasn't until she was back in the office that she'd seen the remains of a man near the captain's cabin of an eighteenth century ship near Norfolk. The dig hadn't occurred here, it was sixty miles from here—and yet fear overwhelmed her.

"Marley."

Hawk's voice was gentle, husky with fondness.

She glanced back, noticing his smile fade as he looked at her. She bit her lip, trying to fight down the emotion in her as he walked back to her, even as the rest of their party began running toward the large group of men and women gathered in the snowy expanse above the river. Those men and women, too, were running toward them.

She could not explain the terrible fear and foreboding that filled her. The researcher she was had no scientific data to corroborate her awful suspicion. And yet, as tears ran down her face, she feared that she had at last discovered the identity of the Lost Sea Captain.

Chapter Twenty-Five

Marley collected herself as she turned to Bronson. "Forgive me. I think I'm just tired."

He drew her cloak more tightly about her. "Shall I carry you? The snow is deep across this meadow, and your shoes, entirely silly."

She gave a choked laugh. "I can walk, thank you."

"That may be true, but I cannot feel your curves against me while you walk."

He hugged her close, brushing his fingertips gently over her wet cheeks—his eyes, those eyes that laughed so often, serious as he watched her. Holding hands, they hurried across the blindingly bright field. The snow was melting into a mire, but the field was thick with vegetation, so it wasn't bad.

Camisha and Ashanti were already across, greeting the people there. Shouts of laughter and soft cries of joy rang across the meadow as they followed Parks and Ray, who carried his nephew on his shoulders.

By the time they arrived at the gathering place, everyone had already moved on and was already hurrying through the woods, chattering loudly all the way. Camisha was the belle of the ball, mobbed by every woman there. The men welcomed Ashanti, and mugs went around to toast their arrival. The clearing between the cabins was wide, and Marley was certain the Trelawneys socialized here. Shaded with ancient live oak overhead, it would be sheltered from the summer sun. A thick covering of pine needles covered the ground, preventing the snow and rain from turning the place into a giant mud pit.

The intoxicating aroma of meat smoking filled the air, and she saw a slow cloud of blue-gray smoke rising from a windowless, stone smokehouse near the end of the cabins.

So these were the Trelawneys of Williamsburg, Marley thought, surveying the crowd. What a striking group to exist at this point in time. An excitement hummed along the surface of her skin—she would know the people she'd read about in their earliest journal.

And in a moment, she knew the worst shame of her career. How her family had hoarded the treasure of this family's tragedy and glory. What if she never made it back to her time? Trapped in the trunk of her car, the priceless antiquity would be lost. She imagined the car towed from the hotel parking lot, left to decay in a junkyard.

Her grandmother keeping it was bad enough, but Marley was a historian. She knew well that the journals deserved to be shared with the world, that stories like those of the Trelawneys could go a long way in healing the strife that would persist three centuries from now.

The dense trees cleared, and before her Marley saw a small village of sorts. Dozens of people—women, children, and a few old men—milled. Perhaps a dozen or more modest cabins stood there. They looked much more substantial than reproductions Marley had seen of slave cabins. Another large area had been cleared of trees and there stood three newer houses, with a fourth under construction.

Behind one of the homes stood a large building that looked like a meeting house.

These homes were not the stately plantation mansions that lined the James River, but more modest homes of equally handsome construction and design—if lacking in luxurious embellishments. By the standards of the "shacks" Helen had derided, however, they might well be mansions. Each home was perhaps five times as large as one of the cabins.

"Bronson Trelawney, you stinking old sea dog!"

The man who arrived was slender and rugged, wearing the simple homespun clothing of a farmhand. His eyes were wide and alert, lit with intelligence and humor, and he grinned broadly as Bronson's gaze rested on him.

"Martin Trelawney, you rotten old landlubber."

The men grabbed each other in a quick hug. "Call me a farmer, if you must, but a landlubber I am not."

"Indeed? Then will you be joining us on our next journey?"

"I've discussed it with my father, and …"

Bronson laughed. "I see. He admires your ambition, but he needs a field hand more."

"He simply needs more persuading. All of my brothers are married now, and their hands are full with their own families."

"Even Hasty?"

"Little Dan, Joe, even Hasty. Pretty little wives, all three of them, and a whole wagon full of children." He smiled at Marley. "Speaking of pretty little wives…"

Marley blushed at his assumption, and Bronson gave a hearty laugh. "No, not quite. This is Marley, and yes, dear to me. So you look out for her, when I'm not around."

He cast Bronson a roguish smile. "Brother, where this lovely lady is concerned, you'd best look out for *me*, when you're not around."

Even as they laughed at their own foolishness, Camisha appeared out of nowhere. "There's my godson Martin," she said as she approached. "Where've you been? I couldn't find you anywhere."

He accepted her hard hug. "Ah, Mother Camisha, what joy to see you!"

She leaned back, inspecting his face. "You look thinner. Older. Are you not eating properly?"

"I'm eating too much. I'm twenty-three now, you know."

She nodded. "Believe me, sweetheart, I know. I mark your birthday every year."

His gaze on her grew tender. "Well, I no longer do. Instead, I mark my day of freedom every year, and I give thanks to God for you."

Once more she gave him an emotional hug. "Have you seen Boots?"

"Oh, he's working. He does his studies in the night, and works long days."

"But the season is over! What could he be working on now? Didn't he know we were coming?"

"Work is never finished on a tobacco farm. He's a grown man, you know Father makes sure we all pull our weight. I think he's patching the curing barns. Shall I fetch him?"

"No, no, I'll see him at supper. Marley, why don't you come with me. There's someone I'd like for you to meet."

Marley glanced back at Hawk, surprised to find his gaze intent on her, a smile playing about his mouth.

"All right, all right, there'll be plenty of time for that later." Camisha grabbed her hand, dragging her off unceremoniously. "Marley, I know that boy's handsome as sin, but don't you let him take advantage of you. God knows I'd be tempted."

Marley laughed. "I won't, but thank you for keeping an eye on me."

They reached the edge of a giant, roaring fire the men had built in a pit, where several women were rocking in chairs, cloaks and shawls drawn about them, laughing and enjoying the sunshine.

"Ruth, this is my friend, Marley. Marley, this is Ruth Freeman Trelawney. We've known each other for nearly thirty years now, and there isn't anything I wouldn't do for her. You were just speaking with one of her youngest sons, Martin."

Marley gaped like a star-struck teenager. Camisha might have introduced her to Abigail Adams, except that Marley knew this woman better, and admired her even more. She was at a loss for a second, until she curtsied. Three cheers for Colonial Williamsburg training, there.

Ruth—as she should've expected—waved a dismissive hand at her. "What're you doing curtsying to me, child?

"I'm just so pleased to meet you."

"I'm just a plain old grandmother and schoolmistress. Nothing to go a-curtsying over." She rose from her rocker and reached out to hug Marley. "Welcome to our home. Would you like some coffee? Rum? Let's go inside for refreshments."

Camisha followed. "Don't tell me you're out of blackberry wine."

Ruth laughed. "Not in this life."

The women walked inside a cabin, and Ruth stuck her head out to call one of the young boys playing in the snow. "Sammy, take this here crate of mugs out to the fire. Then you pass them out to everyone, and tell them libation's on the way. Then check with Little Dan and make sure it is."

"Yes'm," said the boy, perhaps eight or nine years old. He hoisted the wooden box and ran through the door.

Ruth closed the door behind him, reaching into the firebox and feeding the wood stove in the corner.

"What'll you have, young lady?"

"I'd love to try that blackberry wine."

"Excellent choice," Camisha said with her eyebrows raised, to which she and Ruth tittered.

"It sure enough is," Ruth said, uncorking a bottle. She poured three mugs. "Camisha and I have spent years testing it to make sure."

She handed the other mugs to her guests, then took the last and gestured toward the chairs before the stove. "Older I get, the less I love snow," she said, bringing the bottle along for company.

They sat in a cozy semicircle beside the warmth of the stove, and Marley tasted the wine, pleasantly surprised at the smooth, mellow flavor.

Ruth sipped her wine and looked at Marley. "You going with us, tonight?"

She glanced at Camisha, who was shaking her head. "I don't know, Ruth. It's intense. It's dangerous."

"'Tis also the mightiest feeling I ever did have. Oughta let the little girl go along."

"I'm happy to go where I can help. Where are we going?"

Camisha raised her hand. "Just let me think about it some more. Let's enjoy our wine first. Have you been fattening plenty of turkeys?"

Then the two women were off into a discussion of preparation for the Thanksgiving meal. Marley found her attention wandering, and then she noticed it, near the front window: a tiny desk, with a quill and powdered ink.

And the same ledger Marley had grown so fond of during her life.

Without thinking, she rose and moved silently to the desk, reaching for the ledger.

"Marley? You need some more wine, honey?" This from Camisha.

"No, I just wondered … Are you a writer?" she asked, to explain her unseemly curiosity over the journal.

"Well, if writing things down for 30 years makes a person a writer, I guess I am. Camisha tells me I'm a *di-a-rist*," Ruth said, with self-deprecating humor, bobbing her head.

"Oh?"

"I just write down what happens around the Trelawney plantation, and in our families. I don't know if I could make up a story if I had to. But I sure do love reading stories, when I can get my hands on them. And I always need books for my students."

Marley thought of Bronson's library, back on the ship. She knew he loved the books, but perhaps …

"Do you teach all the children on the plantation?"

"Yes, ma'am, I do. Camisha has helped fill in some of the blanks for me over the years, and I do have some books. The hardest part right now for me is when the children outgrow me. There's no place they can go for more education. But Marley, let me tell you this. My children—I mean the children in my school—leave my school with a better education than some poor white folk. Best any of us can do is do the best we can do."

Marley smiled at her straightforward optimism.

A sudden knock came at the door, and Bronson filled the doorway. "Did anyone want to go to Williamsburg with me to say hello to my father?"

Camisha gave him a long look. "Will we be back tonight?"

"Yes."

Camisha, Ashanti, Bronson, Rashall, and Marley went. They borrowed a carriage from the plantation and set out in the mid-afternoon, and were soon in Williamsburg. Marley blinked at how similar the old village was to the place where she would work in another 240 years. All the history that had yet to take place—independence, the trek across the frontier, the Civil War and all its battles, the Depression, and all the many painful struggles blacks had yet to endure in the fight for equality. And yet someday, this place would look almost identical to its appearance today.

The melting snow turned Duke of Gloucester Street into a sludgy mire, and Marley noticed black festooning the windows and door of the Randolph home.

"Peyton Randolph has died," she said.

Her gaze casually passed to Bronson, whose mouth parted in surprise—almost fear. "Just because there's a death at the home need not mean Mr. Randolph was its victim."

What a foolish outburst—what had she been thinking? He had indeed died, she was certain of it, while at the Second Continental Congress in Philadelphia. Any American historian knew this fact well; he had, until then, been considered the prime contender to be the country's first president. Some argued that he had in fact *served* as the first president.

They directed the driver to stop around the corner from the Trelawney home. Bronson led the way, his arm on Marley's as they approached the front door of the Trelawney home.

Bronson opened the door quietly, and Marley, just behind him, peered around his shoulder. A chair facing away from them stood before the fireplace, and in it, she saw the back of a gentleman with thick, white hair.

In his lap was a woman, and they were locked in a passionate embrace.

"Oh, Father!"

Bronson's voice rang with amused disapproval, as if the older man were a child himself, a badly spoiled one.

The man started with a none-too-eloquent "Oh—well!" The woman scrambled off his lap, straightening her skirts as she rose, and Marley blushed. Exactly what had they interrupted?

Bronson reached to light an oil lamp nearby, and then another, and Marley gasped when the woman turned to look at them, at last composed. She blinked more than once, then peered closely at the lady.

It was none other than her own grandmother—Nan.

Chapter Twenty-Six

Camisha and Ashanti laughed softly at the awkwardness. By all indications, Ray's tight-lipped smile reined in a sailor's quip. Bronson ignored it all, walking in and hugging his father.

"I do indeed regret interrupting you, but at least you've answered my question about how you're feeling."

Marley, without an invitation, rushed to her grandmother, whose face paled as she beheld her granddaughter.

"Marley," she cried out, surprised, and the women embraced. "I didn't know what had become of you!"

"This must be the mythical Nan you've mentioned. I had no idea you were acquainted with my family." Bronson came to stand behind her. He bowed low, grasping Nan's hand and lightly kissing it. "Bronson Trelawney, at your service. Marley, this is my father, Thomas Trelawney. Father, this is Marley— good heavens, Marley what?"

"Hastings," she replied, smiling. "Have we never been properly introduced?"

"Hastings? Then you must be kin to Godfrey Hastings," She knew enough of Thomas Trelawney that she placed him in his mid-seventies, but he had the energy and vigor of a young man.

At the reminder of the man Ruth had referenced in her diary, Marley began, "I think perhaps it's only a coinci—"

"Godfrey Hastings is your great-grandfather, dear," Nan said. "You have yet to meet him. Would anyone like coffee?"

Marley's sudden silence came less from surprise than embarrassment at her grandmother's lying. She had come to know her prevarication while growing up, and had come to despise dishonesty as a result. She herself often had that feeling that she didn't quite know the whole story on almost anything, and she wondered if her grandmother had some kind of disorder. She didn't seem to even have a good reason for lying, if there was such a thing.

But this was too much, and she was lying to people Marley had come to love. It was impossible for her to have such a close relationship with a man known in the eighteenth century. She turned to the Adamses, who moved forward into the room and closed the door behind them. Then Camisha got a good look at Nan, with a recognition that stunned Marley.

"Hannah?" she whispered.

The fear that Marley had first known when she realized she truly had traveled in time returned. How had her grandmother done so, as well? And how did she know Camisha? The scientist within her simply refused to accept any of it—although neither could she dispute the physical evidence before her.

Nan moved forward, closer to the lamp, so she could see the others better.

Then life itself became inexplicable.

In the brighter light of the lamp, Marley could see that her grandmother looked twenty years younger—perhaps not even fifty, rather than well into her sixties. And her own face pinkened in embarrassment. She did not appear to be nearly old enough to be Marley's grandmother. Suddenly, the truth itself seemed a lie.

And these two women somehow knew each other. Camisha reached out to her, and Nan drew her close.

"I thought I'd never see you again! Where in the world have you been?" Camisha asked, holding her at arm's length. "You look so good!"

"And look how your handsome young man has grown up! Where are all the rest—your beautiful young girls, your other boys? They looked just like you."

Marley looked on as they inexplicably caught up. Bronson returned to stand behind her, and she unconsciously leaned against him for warmth, for stability against this insanity.

And only then, comforted at his nearness, absorbing his strength, did she notice that her grandmother had never answered Camisha's question.

The women went to the kitchen to make coffee, and Nan asked if they were staying for dinner.

"We can't stay long, I'm afraid," Camisha said. "They'll be holding supper for us at Rosalie. But we do need to talk, just the three of us."

Bronson turned Marley toward him, his gaze searching her face, then he drew her away into an alcove near the front door. He spoke in hushed tones. "You seem troubled. Would you rather stay with me?"

She lay her palm alongside his face, and he turned his head and kissed her hand, then her wrist.

"Aren't you happy to see your Nan?"

She nodded, then ducked her head. "I'll have to explain another time. Now, I must speak with her."

He was not satisfied with this. Clearly, he distrusted poor Nan. Had he sensed her fear just by feeling her heartbeat against his own? "All right. But I shall be right out here."

With that, the women retired to the kitchen, and as Marley sat at the kitchen table, Nan and Camisha went about making the coffee as if they'd done this very thing countless times.

As Camisha ground the beans, she spoke. "Remember the first time we ever met—at the old overseer's home, where your father-in-law lives?"

Nan put water on to heat, quickly building a fire. Marley was impressed with how easily she had grown accustomed to some of the hardships of the eighteenth century. "Yes."

"How is old Hastings? We haven't been out to see him yet—he must be ninety by now."

Nan smiled blithely, removing cups and saucers from the glass-fronted cupboard. She opened the door and called out, "Who wants coffee?"

Over her shoulder, Marley saw Thomas Trelawney smile at her, hoisting a snifter of brandy as if in toast. "We're quite well taken care of." He puffed the cigar. "Ah, what pleasure, to have a son who trafficks in West Indies cigars."

The men laughed.

"Oh—bad news from Philadelphia, son. Peyton Randolph has—"

Disinterested in the talk of menfolk, Hannah closed the door and returned to her busy work, and Camisha and Marley exchanged a frown.

"Hannah, I was a young newlywed and new mother when I met you, and you were scarcely grown, with a child of your own," Camisha said, growing serious as she keenly eyed Nan.

Nan laughed lightly, placing the saucers on the table, then setting cups upon them. She placed the sugar bowl and creamer there, and then looked around anxiously for something to do with her hands.

"Hannah. Sit down."

"Here's the water boiling now." She folded a thick towel around the handle of the kettle and poured the boiling water over the coffee grounds, then replaced the lid and set the silver coffeepot on the table.

"Camisha, have you any more grandchildren?"

"Yes. Helen just had a baby girl. Now tell me what's going on."

Nan sat staring at her hands, folded on the table.

Marley glanced around the room. A unique spirit pervaded this small place—peculiar yet familiar. The home was perhaps forty years old, but it had a distinct character, an aura like that of centuries-old homes in her own time. The collective spirit of love and laughter that lingered long after those who had loved and laughed there had moved on. Still, she felt comforted, as if with their coffee klatsch they, too, would contribute to the secrets shared here over the course of the home's life.

"Well, Camisha, I loved Thomas then, and I love him now. I did not ever expect to see him again, but God has brought us here, and I will not lose him again."

"But you were such a young girl when you met him, young enough to be his daughter, surely not yet—"

"I was one-and-twenty, newly widowed, my husband lost to smallpox, my daughter and I both having recently survived the disease as he did not. And I had a little girl, but four years old, to raise, and no way to provide for her. Dear Will and I lived in that lovely old stone house—and how I loved him. When he passed on, I was devastated. The only thing that kept me hoping, that gave me a reason to get up in the morning, was little Cassie.

"Dear Godfrey told me to come to Rosalie, and he took us in and cared for us. He was broken-hearted at his son's death, but he was kind to me beyond my imagination. He was like a father to me. Marley, you may remember me mentioning him to you, just before we left for our holiday."

Marley nodded, staring at the table. She had noticed one remarkable detail in Nan's speech, and it was not contrived. Her English accent was as strong as if she'd never left the land of her birth—as if all the years of Marley's life were for her merely a gigantic mistake, a do-over.

Nan stopped long enough to pour the coffee into their cups. She offered cream and sugar, but Marley shook her head, silently annoyed at her incessant pretense at normalcy.

"And he truly doted on my Cassie. His heartstrings were wrapped around those tiny fingers. It seemed to soothe the ache within him from losing his son."

Marley looked up at her blankly. Yet another lie—but Marley had been the victim of this falsehood. She had claimed before that Marley's father was her son; now, that story was entirely different, placing her in this era. But how could Camisha know her otherwise?

"Thomas lived in the home at the same time, with little Bronson. He was an austere, forbidding, and yet alluring man. Terribly handsome, as he still is. He, too, was grieving a loss—

that of Bronson's mother. In time, we came to comfort each other, and we fell in love. However, he found that Rosalie bothered him as much as Williamsburg proper did, and he decided he wanted to learn to sail. So he bought a sloop, learned to sail, and asked me to marry him and live out our lives in Bermuda."

Here, she stopped, dabbing at her eyes.

"I could not leave Godfrey. He so loved Cassie, and I was sure it would break his heart. I had to tell him goodbye. He sailed away, and that was the last time I ever saw him."

"But he came back," Camisha said, confused. "Once Ashanti and I began visiting Rosalie—not long after we met—the boys became good friends and we began visiting usually at least once a year. Often, Thomas would sail to Boston for us, to make sure there wasn't ever any problem with our traveling."

"What do you mean?"

Camisha laughed. "Oh, that whole black thing. Some folks south of the Mason-Dixon line tend to capture free black men and sell them as slaves."

"The what?"

Hannah was beginning to embarrass Marley, she was so purposefully obtuse. The woman wasn't stupid—she couldn't quite believe she'd never heard of the Mason-Dixon line—so her inability to sympathize with Camisha irritated her.

After a long moment, Camisha shook her head. "Never mind. So you must have left Rosalie about the same time Thomas first went to Bermuda?"

"Yes. It was simply too painful." This came out an insincere excuse, and Marley and Camisha exchanged a glance.

Nan quickly shook her head. "No, that's not true. It was painful indeed, but I stayed at Rosalie. When visitors came, I went into seclusion with Cassie until they left. I had no interest in meeting anyone else. That *was* indeed too painful."

Camisha's gaze narrowed. "But you haven't been hiding there for ten years, have you?"

"No, eventually I did leave. By then, Cassie had married, and her husband lectured at William and Mary."

The kitchen door opened, and Ray stood there. "We'd better get going. A rider came from Rosalie. Any time now."

Camisha nodded. "Oh. All right, then. We'll be right out." When he left, she went on. "This isn't over, Hannah. I've missed you too much, and I want to hear how Cassie and her husband are doing."

Darkness entered Nan's gaze. "Another time, then."

"Do you suppose we could use your water closet, before we leave?"

"There's one near the back door, and one upstairs, off Thomas's room."

Camisha glanced at Marley. "You're young, you can use the one upstairs."

Marley smiled and climbed the stairs, heavy with the weight of her grandmother's lies. She found the small room off one of the bedrooms and quickly used it. As she left the room, she absently glanced into the bedroom. Two portraits hung on one large wall. One was of the lovely child who, in the folklore of the twenty-first century, was said to haunt the Trelawney home— Emily was her name.

Then her gaze settled on the other portrait. She had no way of knowing, but in her heart she was certain that the young blonde woman, staring soulfully off into the distance, was the woman who'd died giving birth to her only son, Bronson. He had her dreamy eyes.

When they left the home, Marley was torn by any number of conflicting emotions. The most easily identified was betrayal. She had learned growing up that truth was a malleable thing for her grandmother, but now she needed to know the truth.

The anger she had felt toward her had dampened into a silent sadness, but with that came alienation. She didn't know Nan. The laughing, suffering, genteel, and now duplicitous, woman who had raised her was a stranger to her.

Chapter Twenty-Seven

Dinner at Rosalie surprised Marley in its efficient simplicity. Later that night, she would understand that it was not the festive, social affair she had come to expect around the Adams, but simply a meal.

The Adamses ate with the Freeman-Trelawneys, and even Boots, as Camisha had called him, showed up.

After dinner, Ashanti looked at Boots. "What have we heard from Linnondale?"

"The woman's pains began at noon." This from Ruth.

"Very well, then. Who do you think should go?"

Camisha spoke up. "I think—"

"I wasn't asking you," her husband said. "You lead us all about by the nose as it is in this matter. We support you in this Christian effort, but Brother Dan and Sister Ruth must live in this land. They will direct us."

Camisha's mouth snapped shut, her eyebrows lifted at Ashanti's affront.

The large, silent older man who sat beside Ruth spoke. "We take as few as is necessary. I must go to baptize the child who has passed. Camisha must go to be with the woman who labors now. Do we know her name?"

"Keturah."

"Aye, then. We must have watchmen. Bronson, Ray, will you come?"

Each man nodded.

"Ruth must stay behind," Dan said. "She is too important here."

Ruth looked away from him, absently scratching her throat. She clearly wanted to go.

"You matter to the students," he insisted. "You know that."

"I know that. That doesn't mean I have to like it."

"Who else?"

"I would like to go," Marley said.

"No." This from Bronson. "'Tis too dangerous, you don't even know what we're doing, nor do you understand the risk."

"I want to help. I can see you need help."

"She can come with me, Bronson. Being white, she will be in little danger. She has a tidewater accent, she can always claim to be a neighbor trying to do something charitable. She'll be helpful." Camisha nodded at Marley.

They quickly cleared and scrubbed the supper dishes and walked through the woods to the water's edge, then walked up the James River for perhaps three miles. The night was clear but also moonless, and their trek was lit by only the stars. Bronson led the expedition, Marley beside him, Ray on her other side, Camisha near her carrying a basket full of clean towels and several small blankets. Behind them, Dan followed, carrying a small pine box.

Marley still had no idea what they were doing.

Just as they were about to pass over a small stile beside a large boulder, indicating a property line, Bronson held out his hand and hushed them. Ray waited beside him, his eyes focused in the same direction as Bronson's. Marley noticed both of their hands were at their waists, resting on their scabbards.

On the other side of the line of trees along the river stood the figure of a man wearing leather and a long braid—a native, Marley thought. The man watched them, his hands on a line dangling in the water. He raised a hand to them in greeting, then went back to fishing. She shivered as she gazed at him when they passed—witnessing a way of life among people who no longer existed in her time.

They continued over the stile and reached the line of cabins. The owner's house stood off perhaps a quarter mile, and Bronson and Ray took up lookout positions in trees just barely within sight of each other, between the plantation house and the slave cabins.

Dan and the women went on. The sound of a cry helped direct their path, and soon they'd arrived in the meager cabin, lit with a single tallow candle.

A woman sat on a pallet in the corner, braced against both walls, with a blanket spread over her lower body. Another woman knelt at her feet.

Dan placed the small box aside and approached her. "I am Brother Daniel. I shepherd the flock at Rosalie. I am here to baptize the child."

She nodded. He knelt to pray over the woman, blessed her, and left to wait outside the cabin.

"How far along is she?"

"Soon, ma'am."

Camisha knelt at the woman's side, taking her hand. Sweat stood out on her brow, and her lips trembled. "Don't worry. You're doing fine. What will you name a girl child?"

Marley steeled herself against crying at the expression on her face. This young mother had likely never been asked her opinion on much of anything. She seemed at a loss. Finally, she spoke.

"I always liked Esther."

"That's a lovely name. And a boy?"

"Joshua Moses. Moses led his people out of slavery, and Joshua led them into freedom. I expect that be a long journey."

With a kindness that Marley hadn't yet seen so strongly in this woman, Camisha bent to kiss her forehead.

Within another fifteen minutes, the child was born—a healthy, squalling boy. Camisha beamed over him, quickly washing him.

"Don't you dare let her nurse him," the other woman said. "That'll break her poor heart, and that child be lost forever."

"Indeed she must nurse him. It will help her, and help the babe. And she will always remember the look of him in her arms—her son, born in slavery, given up to freedom."

As Camisha wrapped the child in blankets, she glanced at the exhausted mother. "Now you understand what happens next."

The girl's eyes shut tightly, and she wept. "I understand. I want my boy to be free."

"You can never speak of this. Your child was a girl, she was too small, and she died. And you baptized her with the Christian name of Sunny Abigail Esther. Do you understand?"

And at last, in a heartbreaking moment, Marley understood.

She took a deep breath. "Yes. And I can do it. Let me nurse the child, so he won't ever forget me."

Camisha put the wriggling infant into her arms, and he quickly latched onto a nipple, his tiny fingers resting on her breast. Marley did not realize tears were streaming down her own face until she noticed a tear drop from the nursing mother to her son's forehead. She gently wiped it away.

Camisha gave Marley a quick glance, nodding at the door. She stepped outside and nodded to Dan, who silently entered the cabin again.

He took the pine box and sat it on a small table. "Let us praise the Father of mercies, the God of all consolation. Blessed be God forever. For those who trust in God, in the pain of sorrow there is consolation, in the face of despair there is hope, in the midst of death there is life.

"Keturah, as we mourn the death of your child, we place ourselves in the hands of God and ask for strength, for healing, and for love.

"My soul is deprived of peace, I have forgotten what happiness is; I tell myself my future is lost, all that I hope for from the Lord.

"But I will call this to mind, as my reason to have hope. The favors of the Lord are not exhausted, his mercies are not spent; They are renewed each morning, so great is his faithfulness. My portion is the Lord, says my soul; therefore I will hope in him. The word of the Lord.

"Compassionate God, soothe Keturah's heart, and grant that through the prayers of Mary, who grieved by the Cross of her Son, you may enlighten Keturah's faith, give hope to her heart, and peace to her life.

"Lord, grant mercy to all the members of this family and comfort them with the hope that one day we will all live with you, with your Son Jesus Christ, and the Holy Spirit, forever and ever."

He removed the pine box once more. When he returned, the baby boy was sleeping and his mother handed him to Camisha. When she rose and turned to Dan, he began speaking.

"There is one Body and one Spirit; there is one hope in God's call to us; one Lord, one Faith, one Baptism; one God and Father of all. The candidate for Holy Baptism will now be presented."

"I present Joshua Nathaniel Moses Trelawney to receive the Sacrament of Baptism." Camisha's words were soft and clear.

He held a small bowl of water in one hand. "Will you be responsible for seeing that the child you present is brought up in the Christian faith and life?"

Camisha bowed her head. "I will, with the help of God."

Marley didn't know the words to the service by heart, as Camisha did, but she moved to stand beside her in solidarity. She placed one hand on her back and the other over Camisha's, where she held the child.

"I will, with the help of God," she echoed.

"Will you by your prayers and witness help this child to grow into the full stature of Christ?"

"I will, with the help of God," the women responded in unison.

Dan then prayed for the infant and for the family who would be raising him. He gave a prayer of thanksgiving for the woman who had given the child life and sacrificed that he might know the freedom that she had not. And then he dipped his fingers into the water and touched his head lightly. "Joshua Nathaniel Moses Trelawney, I baptize thee in the name of the Father, and of the Son, and of the Holy Spirit. Amen."

They bundled the baby warmly and placed him in the basket Dan had brought, covering all but his face with more blankets to keep him warm during the long walk back to Rosalie. They instructed the midwife attending Keturah to quickly announce the death of Keturah's baby—that she had simply been too small to survive. Although the baby's parents had been white, the child was ruddy-skinned and had thin, black hair, so there would be no disputes about her parentage.

And they left as silently as they'd arrived.

They left behind a woman who mourned the loss of her son, but who celebrated the most powerful moment of her life—when she was able to grant him freedom. Something that was beyond the power of any enslaved woman in this era.

His rebirth as a Trelawney further ensured that neither would he be bound by the chains of ignorance. Keturah's son would work hard, but he would be an intelligent, educated black man born in Virginia in the year 1775. She had no way of knowing precisely what a miracle that was.

Chapter Twenty-Eight

On the trek back to Rosalie, Dan carried the baby, Bronson and Ray walked beside him in silence, alertly scanning the grounds, and Camisha and Marley walked a dozen or so feet ahead.

"I must confess, I had no idea what we were doing there tonight."

"Well, how could you have known?"

"How long have you been doing this?"

Camisha walked without replying for perhaps a minute. "Since my own son, Martin, died of smallpox when he was two. That, too, happened in the winter, and the idea came to me. We rushed to Rosalie and had a few conversations with those at neighboring plantations, and several mothers came forward. We chose the child who looked most like Martin."

"Weren't you afraid of getting caught?"

"I was more afraid of fearful people. The smallpox virus wasn't contagious in my son by the time we got here, but it's a killing disease, so people are naturally cautious. It worked, though. You met my godson Martin today. And my godson Boots, named for my youngest son, Booker, who died when he was born. My babies were the scapegoats so that Martin and Boots might know freedom. So perhaps that helps explain my connection to those young men."

"How many children have you freed?" Marley asked in wonder and admiration.

"Forty-seven, if you just count those children. If you count those children *they'll* have ... then it gets exciting."

Marley could guess, and she was mightily impressed, but she wanted to hear Camisha's take on it.

"This act doesn't free one child. If this baby survives childhood, this action frees an entire family."

"And you've never been caught?"

"I've come close. It's such an unusual act, I doubt anyone who would actively oppose it would believe a black person to be capable of orchestrating it."

"Will you two please shut up? This isn't our front parlor, and we *are* trespassing, along with being the wrong color to be out for a midnight stroll in this part of town."

This came in a loud whisper from Ashanti, walking with Rashall and Bronson.

The women fell silent. Soon, they'd arrived back at the cabins.

Ruth greeted them in her nightgown, and she took in the newborn. She and Daniel and her younger children lived in one of the newer, large homes, and she had arranged for a wet nurse to be waiting for the child. Tomorrow, the baby would be placed with the family best equipped to raise him.

"Is the honeymoon suite available?" Camisha asked with a grin.

Ruth laughed. "Lord, Lord, woman. You still act like you're that 28-year-old woman who jumped the broom here, near thirty years ago."

"That's because I have a husband who still acts like a 17-year-old boy every night."

Ashanti laughed and affectionately patted his wife on the behind. "My ... er, dancing, is slowing down, you know that."

She leaned up and kissed his cheek. "Baby, you're waltzing plenty fast enough for me." Then, to Ruth, "Now what about these three? Do you have enough empty cabins for them, or do we need to double up?"

"Those three on the end right there. I had Boots build fires in the stoves, and with everything you've been through tonight, you should drop right off to sleep."

Marley was dead on her feet when she stumbled into the small cabin, but she still stopped to light a lamp and admire the place while she disrobed down to her shift.

This single-room dwelling likely had housed an entire family thirty years ago, possibly with no furniture at all. Now it had a decent bed as well as a table with two chairs. She stoked the fire before using the chamber pot and putting it away. Then she lowered the brightness of the lamp, turned back the corner of the quilts, and climbed into bed under the layers of down quilts. She sighed with pleasure at the warmth and simple comfort. Still, her sleep was restless.

And in another hour, when she heard the door open and close quietly, she sleepily watched Bronson add more wood to the stove and undress before the lamp. He noticed her watching him and he unbuttoned his trousers, one eyebrow raising in question at her open regard. A small smile tugged at the corner of her mouth. How she loved this man and his playfulness—and how she wanted him.

Then he let the trousers drop.

She gazed at him in the lamplight, aroused at the sight of him, fully erect. What she loved most about Bronson, she realized as her smile fell away, was the feeling of complete safety with him. He would not hurt her, she knew that.

"Couldn't sleep?" she asked lightly.

He laughed and walked to her, throwing back the covers. He gave a sound of mild disappointment. "Far too much linen and far too little of your beautiful flesh. Makes me yearn for the days when you owned no clothing."

He lightly spanked her bottom, taking her in a moment back to their time on the ship. His eyes twinkled as his memory traveled with her. "Scoot."

She wriggled over in the bed—but it was not as large a bed as that in his captain's cabin. He slipped in behind her, his hand cupping her bottom, his fingers spreading over her hip and fitting himself against her. "Ah, my love. Please, I beg of you, take off the shift."

She laughed, a sound low in her throat. "I truly don't think you want that."

"I only want to feel your soft skin against mine as we sleep."

"We will not sleep if I remove this."

He stroked her arm, her head tucked under his chin. Then he reached down to her thighs and caught the edge of the shift, drawing it upward until his bare palm skimmed up along her upper thigh to her hip bone. He settled himself against her naked buttocks, and she gasped in pleasure at the feeling of him hard against her.

He exhaled on a ragged sigh, kissing her shoulder. He turned her onto her back, rising over her, searching her face.

And he kissed her.

Her breath caught at the explosion of sensation, deeper, broader, and stronger for the unexpectedness of his mouth on hers—that mouth she had come to love by watching him speak of his life, of those things he loved.

And he, too, arrested by the flood of pleasure, found his hand floating to rest on her waist lightly as his mouth explored hers.

She raised her hand to touch his face, her fingertips slipping through his hair, moved beyond her own imaginings at the love he conveyed in his kiss.

Marley had, in fact, been kissed before, and for that she was glad. Because now she understood what he'd meant when he'd first explained to her that a kiss meant something to him.

He started to raise his head, then thought better of it, deepening his kiss, and yet with every exploration searching, questioning. This was not a kiss of conquest—it was a kiss of invitation, a promise of more to come.

And then he did raise his head, his blue eyes deep and dark as they moved over her face. "My Marley," he said with gruff wonder, brushing a strand of hair away. "How I love the taste of you. How I should love to kiss every inch of you. Would you enjoy that?"

A girlish blush stained her cheeks at his frankness, and she found herself tongue-tied.

His eyebrows went up in amusement. "I've managed to quieten my Marley. I'm sorry to embarrass you. I wouldn't hurt you for the world."

Gently, he turned her again on her side and curled his body around her. His hand lightly played over her entire body—her breasts, their hardened nipples rising against the shift, eager for his touch; her hips, her flat stomach, and her generous buttocks until she was aching for more of his touch, and she wriggled her hips into the cradle of his body lightly.

"Dear God," he whispered, laying his hand on her hip to still her. He hastily grabbed the edge of the thin shift and pulled it down between them. "Not much of a barrier, but one I badly need at the moment."

Now, he settled comfortably behind her, his arm circling her waist, his hand resting in the valley between her breasts, his lips at her ear. He toyed absently with her pillbox locket, then placed his hand over it. "Good night, my love."

After several minutes passed without sleep, she spoke quietly. "Are you awake?"

"Mhm."

"What do you think about Raven's mother?"

"Ah." He spoke lightly, as if grateful for the topic. "She is a vibrant, magnificent woman, with the face and bearing of an ancient Egyptian queen, a face that bears the marks of a life lived well and happily. More than once, her wisdom and counsel have saved my life. And yet…"

He stroked Marley's arm lightly, as if searching for words.

"And yet there's something about her—as if she's from another world. Raven mentioned to me that he'd seen it in you as well. Perhaps; I've grown too close to you to see you objectively. In any case, I don't remember a time in my life when she wasn't there, doting on me as if I were her own. As if, truly, she was doing it on the behalf of my own mother, perhaps, or a dear friend of hers. I've known many women of all ages, and I've never known anyone like her. Why do you ask?"

"She astounds me—every single day. I barely know her, and I've already been overwhelmed by the reality of her more times than I can remember. Who does such a thing as what we did tonight? Who conceives such a thing, not just for the babe, but understanding its consequence in the world of the future?"

"Pascal said each of us should examine the relationships of our actions to our past, our present, and our future, as well as others affected by our actions. He said it much better than I. But the point being, we all should consider consequence in our own lives and the lives of others when we choose to act. We may be but a ripple in a pond, but the pond of humanity is vast."

"Bronson?" Marley was relaxed by the sound of his voice explaining in the wee hours the philosophy that fascinated and engaged him, and she heard his indulgent chuckle at her soft query.

"Putting you to sleep, am I?"

"Ruth needs more books. Would you loan her some from your library? I mean, the library on your ship?"

"Hm," he said, with stern threat. "I trust you understand the kind of request this is."

"Look how little she has, and how rich we are."

He drew her close, brushed his cheek against hers, and they fell together into a contented sleep.

Chapter Twenty-Nine

Marley awakened early, excited to see Bronson again. She remembered lying in bed, talking with him in that place between sleep and wakefulness, only half aware what she was saying. As she sat up in the room, surprised to find it toasty warm, disappointed to find it otherwise empty, she shook her head, remembering. He had made a comment about someone—Galileo? No, Pascal—that any other time would have had her brain and imagination firing on all cylinders. In another 45 seconds they would've been discussing some early theories on quantum physics. And how had she responded?

She had asked him a question about his books—as if she were a simpleton who wasn't quite acquainted with the things herself. What she'd asked him, she couldn't remember. Then it came to her—the request for a loan on Ruth's behalf.

Instead, she remembered dreamy moments of half awakening in the night, touching him, feeling him turn toward her in his own unconsciousness—and holding her in his sleep, and immediately falling back together into a contented sleep.

So this was love. A resettling, perhaps, of priorities.

The strong, seductive aroma of meat cooking permeated the cabin, and she dressed quickly and hurried outside to make herself useful. Thanksgiving Day had arrived and she would be needed to help prepare the meal for three hundred.

Oh—what a glorious day! The morning crisp, the deep blue skies clear. A long, open pit had been dug in the center of the clearing—perhaps twenty feet or longer—and there, over a slow fire, lay large cuts of beef, pork, and mutton. And still the aroma of smoking meat rose from the smokehouse.

Women and children hurried between the cabins and Ruth's home bearing countless pots, bowls, pans, and dishes containing mysterious delicacies. A boy of perhaps twelve hovered near midpoint at the smoke pit, charged with looking out for anyone who might carelessly stumble too near.

She hurried up the stone path surrounding Ruth's home. Ashanti sat on the porch, watching her approach.

"You enjoying the peace and quiet?"

He smiled. "Take a step inside that door and you'll have your answer. I'm the smokemaster, in charge of everything that's in the smokehouse and on that pit. So I'm the real cook."

She laughed and raised her hand to knock.

"Oh, go on in. They sure won't hear you knocking, the way they're jawing."

When she turned the latch, it opened to a din of female voices laughing and talking.

"Told you," he said as he left the porch, headed for the pit.

Nervously, she found her way inside and to the back of the house, where half a dozen women were busy kneading, chopping, peeling, mincing, crumbling, and measuring, and another half dozen busy assisting and cleaning up after them.

The aromas were enough to make a person's eyes cross, Marley thought, licking her lips.

Camisha stood beside a wooden stove, basting a turkey.

The scene caught Marley off-guard, and she found herself filled with sudden emotion.

You see, Marley was one of three sisters—and the only one to grow up with their grandmother. And yet Marley had no holiday traditions like the rest of us have. She didn't know what it was like when the matron of the family rose before dawn to begin the countless minute tasks of preparation that made a meal like this come together.

These women had the luxury of family, of tradition, of folklore. They had the stories of their disastrous first time to cook a holiday meal on their own—and yet, when you live in an extended family of more than three hundred people, growing every day, there was always the option of tossing out a burned turkey, or a raw turkey, and heading next door to your cousin's home. They knew the strength in numbers, the importance of unshakable loyalty.

Each year at Thanksgiving, Marley and her grandmother and Jimmy ate at a restaurant. Nan wasn't fond of cooking, and Marley had no idea where to begin to prepare a monster meal like Thanksgiving. So she was woefully ignorant about all the most wonderful parts of the day.

Well, today that ended, she told herself.

She walked into the room, smiling politely at the laughing women as she made her way awkwardly through the group until she reached Camisha.

"All's I know is that if I don't have a mince pie for Ashanti, I'm not getting any for a week. And I am *not* talking about pie."

Camisha straightened and turned, seeing Marley, and she burst out laughing, throwing her head back in hilarity at her own silliness. "Well, you got me, little girl. Mrs. Adams has a mind full of smut." The rest of the women laughed. "Speaking of smut, I saw that Bronson creeping out of your cabin before daybreak this morning."

Marley laughed, feeling her cheeks warm. "He has trouble sleeping without me," she said, hearing how ludicrous it sounded even as she spoke.

"Oh, I'll bet he does. And I'll bet he sleeps like a baby after."

"After...? No!" she gasped. "We haven't done that. Only last night, he finally—" She went silent, quickly seeing that confessing her first kiss would only lead to mockery. "Well, I know you were teasing me. But he's been very kind and respectful."

"For all those weeks you were at sea," she said, a smile glimmering at her lips and in her sparkling eyes. "Uh huh."

"Have you been in the blackberry wine already?"

Camisha and Ruth shouted with laughter. Ruth said, "No, but now that you mention it, that's a mighty fine idea! Want some?"

Camisha rolled her eyes at Ruth. "Go sell silly somewhere else. We're all stocked up here."

Marley held out her spread hands. "How can I help?"

An older woman sat at a counter crumbling cornbread and chopping sage, and she said, "Child, you can go down to my place, it's the fourth cabin on the right. Tell Cecil to send up that turkey stock. Now it be hot and heavy, so you tell him he has to carry it himself. And baste the turkey in the oven while you're there. Cecil might already be in the blackberry wine, so don't pay him no mind if he gets sweet with you."

Well, this she couldn't wait to see. "You want all the turkey stock? Not some portion of it?"

"The whole kettle full. We gots lots of dressing to make."

"We have," Ruth corrected her.

"We *have* gots lots of dressing to make," the woman said, making a face at Ruth.

Marley was laughing as she left for her errand. Only as she left the house did she hear Camisha's quip again in her head: *"Go sell silly somewhere else. We're all stocked up here."*

That was almost directly out of a movie; the oddness of the woman using that line sobered Marley. Who *was* she? She tried to dismiss the thought; it was kind of a cliché line, anyway, and there really was nothing new under the sun. It had to be a coincidence.

For the next few hours, she played free agent, filling in here and there where extra help was needed. The weather turned out to be mild for the time of year, so they decided to set up tables and chairs in the clearing. There was plenty of room away from the barbecue pit to place the furniture in a large U-shaped design, to enable everyone to be closer.

Ruth's oldest daughter, Sukey, put her girls, three teenagers, in charge of setting the tables, no small task. All the families would pitch in with the clearing and washing afterward.

Marley's thoughts returned to Bronson. She hadn't seen either him or Ray all morning. Were they at the ship?

When the delectable dishes began to make their way to the tables, she looked around anxiously for the men. Ashanti had enlisted helpers to pile the meats onto platters on serving tables, and now the turkeys sat there as well, waiting to be carved.

And, in that way Bronson had—that she'd come to rely on—he appeared just when she needed him most.

He sat atop a cart stacked with crates. In the back, she saw Ray facing the other direction, sitting beside a silver-haired man. As they arrived just outside the clearing—which by now was not particularly clear—Marley walked to meet them. He saw her, and his face lit up as he raised a hand to her.

She hesitated, unsure how to help. Ashanti hurried forward to meet them. By now, Camisha, too, had arrived, and she watched the men. "Oh, that's Godfrey. You'll love him."

Between Bronson and Rashall, they had already helped the other man down. Marley could see he was perhaps Thomas Trelawney's age—but he was slim and quite spry. He smiled at Ashanti and gave a genteel bow, leaning lightly on a walking stick. Ashanti offered him his arm, and he accepted it.

Bronson drove the cart around the cabins to the meeting house. There, he loosened the horse and tied it at a hitching post near the meeting house. He stopped and washed up at the well, then found Marley again, leading her to the new arrival.

"Mr. Hastings, may I introduce to you Miss Hastings. Hm. Truth to tell, I wasn't anticipating how that would sound until it was almost out."

The fellow had a courtly demeanor that instantly calmed Marley's nerves. He bent over her hand, lightly taking it in both of his before releasing it. "What a pleasure to meet you, dear. Please, call me Hastings."

"I'm Marley."

He straightened, his pale eyes keen on her. He leaned forward, taking her chin firmly and tilting her face, peering, his other hand pushing away the hair that always dangled at her cheekbone. His thumb brushed at the crescent-shaped scar at the corner of her eye, and he blinked, his eyes dampening. He let the tear fall unheeded as he spoke, his voice a whisper. "Marley? Are you my lost Merrilea? You ran away from me that day, and I could not catch you quick enough."

"That's my given name," she said, confused at his cryptic words. "But I ..."

She remembered her grandmother's lie. *Godfrey Hastings is your great-grandfather, dear.*

It could not be. It was simply a coincidence.

"You're *Merrilea?*"

The booming voice beside her came from Camisha. She turned to look at her in surprise, and she nodded.

"Rachel's sister? Juliana's sister?"

Marley and Camisha stared at each other in disbelief—Camisha, from observing the truth, Marley, from her knowing it.

"Your name is not Hastings, Merrilea. Who told you it was?" This came from Hastings.

She turned back to him. "My grandmother, Hannah Hastings."

His lips pressed tightly together. "I see." He reached to grasp her hand once more and kissed it. "Let us give this some time, my dear, and enjoy the festivities. After all, I am old and at the moment quite hungry for Ashanti's delectable meats. And Ruth's delicious blackberry wine."

Marley smiled at the thought. "It's good, isn't it?"

Camisha waited, lightly rubbing her back with affection. "All right, you're off the hook for now, but we are going to talk."

He laughed. "Come, child. May I have the pleasure of your escort for this gracious bounty which we are about to receive?"

Again came that fearful emptiness that had troubled her when she first suspected the identity of the Lost Sea Captain.

And she felt the smallest piece of the inexplicable slip comfortingly into place. Who was she to say what could not be, what was not possible? She had before her the evidence otherwise.

Chapter Thirty

Marley sat at Hastings' right hand, and Bronson sat at hers. Open bottles of wine stood on every table, and Bronson filled Hastings' glass, then hers, then Ray's—on his right—then, finally, his own.

Marley had not yet had children, so she did not know that it was possible to fall in love at first sight with one's own flesh and blood. But if indeed this old gentleman were any relation to her, she now knew the feeling. From his first finicky request for a finger bowl before tackling the ribs, to his dry quips at the endless jokes of *Ray shell*, as he called him, he kept her laughing so steadily that she only sipped her wine when she could see his mouth was full, for fear of spitting it all over. He ate with the impeccable grace of the well-bred Englishman he had clearly once been, from his regal accent, but he enthusiastically enjoyed the uniquely American dishes—ribs, collard greens, candied sweet potatoes, oyster stuffing, green beans seasoned with onions and Virginia ham, crabcakes—and finally sweet potato pie.

Bronson continued to refill their glasses, but she sipped slowly, wanting to savor and remember every moment of this day. He refilled Ray's glass. "Here you are, Ray-shell."

Hastings laughed lightly. "Well it is his name, after all."

"It's Ruh-shawl," Marley said.

"He was named after Rachel." After he sipped his wine, he hiccupped. Then he nodded sagely at Marley. "Your sister."

She glanced at Bronson and Rashall, and they all giggled together.

Ray took the remaining bottle and placed it beside him. "I'll keep this safe. I think you've had plenty, Sir Talks-a-lot."

"Shonny! Shonny!" The cry came from Parks, who sat near the other end of the table with her mother. "Ray, do you have Shonny?"

"No, I thought he was with you."

In a moment, Camisha was on her feet, and the rest joined them.

Marley looked about. After several minutes of searching, she glanced out at the old Rosalie ruins. Was there someone there? Much more of the old plantation home still stood than would remain in the twenty-first century. Three of the four walls still rose three stories high, and the place was a death trap. She was sure that each time a good windy storm came through, a little more of the old girl gave up the ghost; that's how these old treasures, left to their own devices, slowly reverted back to the soil.

She hurried toward the ruins to check. She didn't mention seeing anything—it could've simply been a bobcat, or her eyes playing tricks on her.

When she was only a few dozen feet away, she saw the child, playing near the entryway, dancing up and down happily. She picked up her skirts and ran, calling Camisha as she ran. "I see him! I've got him! Shonny!"

The boy looked back at her, his face beaming with delight. "Look, Marley! A little girl, just my own size!"

"Stop him, Marley—hold onto him! Don't let him go in there." This from Ruth, a shrill shriek.

Just as the child was about to totter through the arched entryway, Marley grabbed his shirt.

"See?"

"Shonny, there's no little girl—"

And she stopped, her breath leaving her. For just inside the house, waving gaily at Shonny, was the transparent silhouette of a little girl that grew more easy to see, the longer Marley looked. A cold winter breeze passed across her, cutting through the warm sunshine and making her shiver.

She stood still, staring at the child, and she began to see details around her, but what she saw was the child standing in the same place where they stood—outside the ruins, looking in. What was this place where they stood?

And the longer she stared, the better she saw her.

At last she recognized the little girl, because she'd seen her portrait in Thomas Trelawney's bedroom in Williamsburg. His beloved granddaughter, Emily.

But … no. She strongly resembled her, but it wasn't quite her. She wore modern clothing; her hair was darker. Marley smiled at the apparition and waved at her.

The child waved back.

Camisha arrived behind them. "What—" She caught her own breath as she, too, saw the little girl.

Marley whispered. "Could she be a ghost?"

Camisha grabbed her grandson, pulling him back against her, and Marley drew closer to the boy.

The little girl jumped up and down, waving her arms. So did Shonny. The little girl, dressed in jeans and a frilly shirt, curtsied. Shonny giggled and bowed deeply. He held out his hand as if to ask her to dance.

"Emily?" Camisha said, her voice tremulous with emotion.

The child beamed back at her and shook her head. She looked over her shoulder, calling someone.

A young, blonde woman, perhaps in her early thirties, arrived behind the little girl, grabbing her. The child pointed to Shonny. The young woman nervously moved away from the arched entryway, as suspicious of it as Camisha.

The young woman peered at Camisha. Carefully, she mouthed a word, her eyebrows knit.

"*Cammie?*"

Camisha nodded with a smile.

The woman was overcome with emotion, and she touched her chest. "I'm Emily."

Camisha laughed joyfully. "Child, you've grown into a beautiful young woman. I know your daddy must be proud of you and your family."

Marley wasn't sure how much the young woman understood; they could only see each other, not hear. Shonny wasn't happy with any of these developments, and he waved his arms gleefully again, making the little girl laugh.

Then, on the woman's other side, another woman arrived. She was older, perhaps Camisha's age. She frowned as she stared into the entryway, then her mouth dropped open as she, too, realized who she was seeing.

"Oh, dear God!" Camisha cried, her voice catching. Her hand covered her own mouth, as she tried to control her own emotion.

The woman who stood with one slender hand on her daughter, and the other on her granddaughter, was older, much older, than she had been the last time Camisha had seen her. Within the riot of black curls—in her usual French twist— were threads of gray, and she wore tailored slacks and a turtleneck and blazer.

The two women stared at each other, tears filling their eyes as they gazed at each other for the first time in nearly thirty years.

Marley could not have known this, but Camisha knew it in a single glance: In the first twenty-eight years of her life, this woman had known more horror, more pain than most people ever knew. But in the years since then, joy had become her companion, and it had been kind to her, finding its place in the few lines on her face. Now, the delight of seeing her dearest friend—lost to her for all time—filled her face with equal joy and pain.

How badly each woman yearned to hold the other in her arms. *Just once more, please?*

And each woman knew she dare not pass that threshold, or all she had come to hold dear might be lost.

Silently Camisha passed Shonny's hand into Marley's, and Marley scooped him up silently. Curiously, the boy watched his grandmother playing with her friend as he had with his.

"Rachel!" Camisha cried out, that same joy they both had known in their different lives spilling out in her tears. "How I want to hug you!"

The other woman nodded, touching her own heart as tears overcame her.

Still they neither heard anything, but they both laughed in their tears.

And Camisha took the smallest step forward.

Rachel did the same.

Camisha reached out, her hand trembling, to the midway point in the entryway.

Rachel as well.

They both pressed their hands forward until they touched—their hands clearly visible to all there, the pale skin gripping the black skin in the solidarity of unshakable friendship.

And at that moment, all the sounds, all the colors, all the richness of the other worlds where they both had once lived came to life, as real as the place where they lived now. Marley and Camisha saw the early autumn leaves and an overcast day in the Rosalie where Rachel lived, and Rachel saw the shades of brown and the setting sun in Camisha's world.

"I miss you, my dearest friend," Camisha cried out.

"I miss you so much. I'll always love you, Camisha."

"I love you, too, Rae."

Marley heard their voices echoing softly through time, as if in her own memory.

"Rachel, this is your sister, Merrilea," Camisha said, still holding her friend's hand.

Rachel's gaze swept her in astonishment. "Merri?" she cried. "I must see you, talk to you. Honey, I just want so much to hug you."

But Marley knew, even as she stared at the graceful sister she'd missed for so many years, that there was something about this time portal that made such a thing impossible. Why was Rachel so much older than she? She was farther along into the future, now.

They were looking into the time portal of Rachel's life. She was looking into the time portal of Camisha's, where Marley had lived only a few weeks.

The inevitable consequences and progression of each person's distinct timeline must explain why Nan suddenly looked so much younger, Marley thought.

Nan must have been born in this time! And she had aged in another—but when she returned to her rightful time period, she returned to her actual age.

All of it became possible in this new reality only because Rachel and her family had come to visit Rosalie, and her granddaughter happened to stand still before the portal, at the exact same moment that Camisha's grandson happened to stand still before the portal. Both had stood there long enough to see its images materialize; at first, Marley had seen nothing. The longer Marley and Camisha had stood before the portal, the clearer the images grew.

But it was the innocence of children, dawdling and staring off into space, able to believe the impossible, that opened the portal and enabled their loved ones to see.

"Look, Merri—do you remember this? Show her the locket, Em."

Marley carefully leaned close as the young woman withdrew the heart-shaped locket from so many years ago, and Marley couldn't speak. The piece was exactly as she remembered it. Emily turned over the locket, and Marley blinked to clear her eyes of tears, and the words came into focus. *As time is, so beats our hearts—tender, immortal, forever.*

"Here's one of the portraits!" Marley removed the portrait from the pillbox and showed her. "This is the only one I have—but I'm so thankful I do."

Then, as she watched, another person appeared behind Rachel—a man, taller even than she, with curling, graying black hair. His hand rested on Rachel's shoulder in easy familiarity.

Despite his age, he was handsome and serious, and Marley needed no introduction. She'd met his father in Williamsburg, a man he resembled strikingly. He stood there in expectant confusion as his own vision cleared and he saw into the portal, and a surprised smile burst over his face. "Camisha Carlyle!"

"Grey Trelawney, you're still as handsome as sin. And it's Camisha Adams now, you'll recall."

Rachel waved at Marley. "Please, Merri! Try to find a way. Malcolm Henderson must know a way. He would not have allowed you to go back in time, were it not possible. What did he tell you? Did you go through this portal?"

"I don't know anyone by that name. I was lost in a shipwreck in the Caribbean. I woke up in Bronson Trelawney's ship."

"Then you came here for a reason that has to do with Bronson—he's my husband's younger brother. My friend Jennie died giving birth to him. Thomas's wife. Merri, take care. We all know such things are nonsense, but some there believe he was born under a curse. The men all die before the age of thirty."

Marley felt the blood drain from her face.

"What?" Rachel asked, alarmed.

"Do you remember his birthday?"

"Ask him. It was near the beginning of July. It was just before we traveled back to the twenty-first century."

And then she remembered Ruth's diary. *It was still here.* Bronson's fate wasn't yet written. She tried in vain to remember the exact dates of what she'd read. None of them came to her; when she'd read them, she was captured by the story, not the dates. *Some historian you turned out to be!*

"Merri, where have you been? Where did you grow up?"

"With our—Shonny, no!" The child broke free, and in a moment, Camisha released Rachel to stop her grandson from falling into another time. She fell to her knees, catching the boy who howled with frustration.

And when she and Marley looked up again, everyone in the portal had vanished. Her complete focus on the child she loved had broken the supernatural connection.

Camisha soothed the boy. Marley continued to stare into the ruins of Rosalie—the archaeologist in her wanting more than anything to investigate further. There was still so much left of the grand plantation home that would decay over the next two and a half centuries. Through the entryway, she saw a pile of materials, many rotted away over the past thirty years. She had no way of knowing that those materials were the same roof that had collapsed on Grey, Rachel, and Emily in the moments they escaped this time and traveled headlong into the twenty-first century.

Then, farther along the wall, where the upper level had collapsed and broken through the ruins, she noted a peculiar artifact. It looked almost like a newspaper section. She moved toward the opening in the wall.

"Marley, don't!"

"No, I won't go in. I just want to see ..."

She cast a glance about her and found a sturdy section of fallen limb. Bracing her foot on the limb, she broke off a branch and used it to shove at the stone concealing the rest of the artifact. These stones, these bricks, would have fallen from the level directly above—where bedrooms could have looked out on the woods at the rear entry of the house.

With some leverage, she pushed the stone away, and the artifact fell out onto the leaves gathered at the base of the ruins.

"Oh, Marley, it's the newspaper."

Confused at Camisha's astonishment, Marley bent to grasp the fragile section of newspaper. Only the heavy stones had protected it from the destruction of nature.

Then she understood Camisha's disbelief. This was no colonial artifact; it was a section of a modern newspaper from the year 1994. And in the center of it was this headline:

Three girls found living in squalor

Just below the story—even larger than the story—was an arresting photograph. Three children, looking exactly like they were—hungry, terrified orphans, their faces smudged with dirt. They looked like the poor rural children Marley had gone to school with while growing up: clothing worn, bodies thin with hunger, faces as apt as not to be dirty, their parents more focused on finding their next fix than caring for their children.

Except Juliana's. Rachel had kept her as polished and neat as a new penny, neglecting herself to care for her sisters.

Tears overwhelmed Marley at the memories of those days—when Rachel had sheltered them both, just as she was doing in the photograph, holding Baby Juliana tightly with one arm, holding Marley with the other, her body awkwardly bent around her as if to shield her from the threat of the strangers surrounding them.

"Don't you worry, you little sweeties. Mama and Daddy will come for us, soon." Rachel had said this how many times, during those terrifying days and frightening nights of endless darkness. Nothing was darker than an abandoned farmhouse in the country at night. Darkness had come to terrify Marley in those days.

The tears that ran silently down her cheeks came from a source she couldn't identify. She thought she'd mourned those days of unending loss. Her stern, bookish father, her whimsical fairy of a mother, murdered in an unspeakable act that only Rachel had witnessed, about which Marley still didn't know all the details. As always, she had taken care of her sisters, stopping Marley from venturing into the room when she was afraid of the dark in the closet where she'd huddled, holding little Julie in her lap.

Then, returning to tell them they were going camping, that Mama and Daddy were hurt and their girls had to go away so they could get better.

She would not see Stonefield again, until she returned to the home with Nan. Alone. Her sisters, gone—and where, she did not know.

And then, the rest followed. She quickly read the article. Nothing she didn't already know.

"Do you remember your childhood, Marley? Because Rachel didn't. For years, she blocked out every single bit of her life before she was adopted by Max Sheppard."

And Marley was so consumed by the memory of her grief that the name Max Sheppard didn't register in her memory. At least, not yet.

She nodded, trying to swallow down the tears as Camisha stroked her with her free arm. Shonny grew quiet, reaching over to pat her face, his usually joyful face serious with sadness for her weeping. She smiled at him and kissed his cheek. "I'm okay, Shonny," she said, but could not even then stop her tears.

"I remember everything except *that* day. When my parents were ... you know. And there are details about being separated from Rachel and Juliana that I can't get straight. I've forgotten most of them. I just still don't understand how they wouldn't let Nan keep us all together. You know how those systems are. They'll do almost anything to keep siblings together. Nan's always told me it was because she couldn't afford to ..."

Abruptly, they looked at each other. "That woman was lying," Camisha said.

Now, anger overtook Marley's tears. The rage boiled up within her grief, and, noticing Shonny, she bit her lip and turned away, trying to force it all down.

"Mother?"

Marley looked over her shoulder. Parks was headed their way, and Camisha waved at her.

Hastily, she wiped at her tears, but it was hopeless, and she walked a few feet away, staring at the faded photograph of her and her sisters.

Camisha sent Shonny off with Parks, calling, "We'll be there in a moment, dear. Keep an eye on him and make sure he eats something. He's going to be cranky soon if he doesn't."

A few moments later, Camisha touched her shoulders, embracing her as if to impart her own steely inner strength.

"I believe you were angry?" she prompted her, and Marley gave a listless chuckle.

"What's the point of anger, now? It's all gone. Rachel and Juliana have already grown up with other families, and our parents are still dead."

"Marley, we don't know the whole truth yet. I knew Hannah when she was a young girl. I don't know anything about her before I met her, but I can guarantee you she was born in this century. How did she wind up raising you in the twenty-first?"

"I don't care. I never want to see her again."

"We don't know her reasons for doing what she did, or even if she did anything wrong. Most people do the best they can—they just don't know they can do better."

Marley turned to her and hugged her, wearied by her grief.

"Where did this newspaper come from, anyway?" she asked when she leaned back.

"I found it in the bedroom of the man who adopted Rachel, after the tragedy. It's a long story. I found it with a locket—the locket was empty, though; it had no portraits in it."

Marley reached again for the necklace. She withdrew the pillbox and snapped it open, letting the small portrait fall out into her hand. She again showed it to Camisha. "Can you guess who this is?"

"I don't need to guess. It's Rachel. I knew her from ... well, Marley, I knew her from the time you lost her, until the time I lost her."

The tears shone in Marley's eyes as she closed the locket. "Then if I had to lose her, I'm glad she found you."

"You know, I've learned that grief does pass, and in it one can find the seeds of joy. And now, the joy I find is that, finally, I have a friend, a dear friend, who knows the truth! I can tell you everything. I can explain it all. I've told Ashanti, but still at times I wonder if he thinks I'm crazy. Then I tell him something I know will happen in the next year, and that shuts him up for a while."

The women laughed, and something about Camisha's utter joy at life crystallized in Marley's memory. And she knew why Camisha had been familiar to her. She had seen her, that last day she'd spent in Williamsburg; walking along the street, laughing with Rachel.

And she remembered looking into the other woman's eyes and seeing her own sister—and the woman looking away without recognition.

"Now I know why I've had a feeling I knew you, since I first met you."

"Because of the amount of Rachel I have in me?"

"Perhaps. But I saw you in Williamsburg—with Rachel. You were with an older couple. Rachel looked right at me, but then she didn't remember she even *had* a sister."

Camisha gave a sound of exasperation, then laughed.

"What?"

"I started to ask you why you didn't say hello. Or at least, see you later."

Together, the women laughed and Camisha turned away from the shared past of her friendship with Marley's sister, and into the new joy of knowing Marley.

Chapter Thirty-One

As they walked back toward the others, Camisha spoke, with a gravity Marley had never seen in her. Not even when the woman had discussed the deaths of her children. "You know you can't discuss this with anyone."

"Not even Bronson? I don't think I can't *not* speak of it with him. He'll ask me where you and I have been, for one thing, and I would have to lie even to answer that."

Camisha hesitated. "Ashanti knows the truth, but he would never admit it to anyone, including you. He's too fearful of the truth. I should not be in this time—neither should you. But fate—or, as I believe, God—has allowed it for reasons beyond our understanding. I choose to do small acts of good that can't change the tides of history, but that might help the lives of ordinary people. I never thought about it, but I guess it's the same kind of thing I used to do as a pro bono lawyer. Just try to help brighten one corner of the world. Sure helped prepare me for the life I live now.

"I should never, for example, attempt to persuade Thomas Jefferson that he *must* include the famed slavery clause in the Declaration of Independence. If he did do that, as much as I might like it as a modern woman, perhaps the very disagreements that make our country so unique would destroy us before we ever started. And these colonies would remain under British rule forever. And, yes, it is more important that this country be born than that its pedigree be unimpeachable."

"But—I can't tell Bronson?" she asked again. "He could keep the secret as well as Ashanti. They're secret agents for George Washington, for Pete's sake."

"It isn't a matter of his trustworthiness, it's a matter of his allegiances. First of all, you have to remember how you felt when you first realized the truth."

"I thought I was crazy. Or maybe in a coma."

"Exactly. And Bronson's only confidant, as far as I can tell, for his entire life, has been Rashall. By the way, I heard the boys mocking Hastings, but Ray *was* named after Rachel, like I was named after my father. His name was actually Cameron."

"Are you like him?"

"I don't know. He was a police officer, and he died when I was just a little girl—I don't remember him. Anyway, that's why I named him Rashall. Most all the time, I called *her* Rae. And those boys have the sort of friendship Rachel and I had."

"So you don't think I should trust him with the truth?"

"Marley—why do you suppose your grandmother called you that, by the way? Rachel told me the family called you Merri. Well, no matter. If you and Bronson marry, you can swear him to secrecy. That may be sticky, though. He and Ray are joined at the ear. You tell one, you're telling the other. We know Ray can be trusted, but you have to learn to deal with that relationship, and that's what I mean by allegiances. Their brotherhood—it's rare in men. No doubt the result of saving each other's necks on multiple occasions. Always understand that if he's forced to choose between you, he will choose you, as I chose Ashanti when I remained in this time. But, as Ashanti can tell you, there will always be a Rachel-sized hole in me. And if you can avoid that with our boys, that will be God's handiwork."

Then she remembered the old article she'd read, her last day at work in Williamsburg—of three people disappearing through this very entryway, and a black woman named Ruth screaming and running away. She explained it to Camisha.

"If that's a time portal, I think Ruth might have seen someone travel in time. Has she never mentioned it?"

"No. I think she might be too afraid of it—you know, superstitiously."

"Let's face it, you couldn't blame anyone for being skeptical here. But who did she see, I wonder? I forget the date of the article, but it was long after the fire."

They mused over this. By the time they had begun walking back toward the group, Marley knew the secrets of Rachel's life, and her own, that had eluded her for so long. She knew where her scar had come from, she knew about her sisters, her own past, and how Rachel had grown up. There were still many questions, many missing pieces. But many, too, had been filled in.

"Camisha, don't you miss the conveniences of modern life?"

"Don't you?" A moment later, she held up a finger. "Think of being with Bronson before you answer. Perhaps on the ship, where I know conveniences are at a minimum."

Marley nodded. "I see what you mean. A price I would gladly pay, if I were given the choice. But the surprising truth is, there are many—*many*—aspects of modern life I don't miss. The constant distractions of technology stopping us from living in the moment, the needless and endless 'improvements' of that same technology that only further serve to distance us from one another."

"Amen, sister. You tell me, when I see my rear end get just a little bit softer, whether I wish my husband had a smartphone where he'd be in there every day looking for Kim Kardashian's fake butt, or some little twinkie in the next town where he could … ugh." She shuddered.

Marley laughed out loud. "Fake, really? You think so?"

Camisha smirked at her. "Child, we don't care! We don't have to worry about that! Look at that Bronson of yours. That face of his? Him young enough to be my son, and I've had to shut down shameful thoughts of that boy. In the twentieth century, he'd be doing something stupid like designing web pages, and he'd have silly women throwing their silly selves at him every day, thinking that makes them *empowered*. He'd be useless as a human being."

She shook her head and went on.

"No, ma'am. There are things I miss. Not a day passes that I don't miss my best girlfriend and pray for her and her family. And seeing her, seeing her girls—it did this old heart good, I tell you that.

"Not a day passes that I don't miss the conveniences, the inventions, most definitely the medicine. When ... when my little Martin died of smallpox, I took that opportunity to inoculate the other children, the way I'd read about when I was in school. Abigail Adams will be doing the same to her own children in the coming months; I was fortunate to know about that twenty years ago. Ashanti was terrified—he doted on our children, and he didn't want to lose another. He'd survived it as a child, but he lost his mother and his sister to it.

"But our time runs short, Marley, and we must continue later. I will tell, you, though, even with all of that—living with ignorance in a world where the lie of race was created to control those who can't stand up to the powerful—all of it is the price I pay to enjoy the life God meant me to live, and do the work he meant for me to do. I do not change the world, I just try to improve life where I believe I can."

They returned to the table, where Godfrey Hastings was now sitting alone, being entertained by one of the children. The little girl found his embroidered waistcoat endlessly fascinating, her tiny fingers patting a bird here, following the braided cuff there.

Marley sat beside him, and Camisha, across from him. "You will never believe who Marley just met. Shonny, too, but he's always meeting imaginary people." Her face went comically serious. "Maybe I better take that kid a little more seriously. Well, maybe if he brings up his imaginary friend Kanye."

Hastings gazed back at her. "I take it Mr. Kanye is a luminary of the distant future? One who can glide through the air on the power of his mental acumen or his dashing demeanor?"

Camisha made a face. "Well. I don't know about that. Maybe on the power of his ego."

The women laughed.

"Marley met Rachel!"

He nodded, responding as if she'd named the mistress of a neighboring plantation. "I see. And how is she?"

"Happy. Still as trim and pretty as she was thirty years ago. She was with Emily, who has a little girl of her own."

"And did she call Merrilea by that detestable sobriquet?"

"Of course not. She knows her as Merri."

"And who do you think garbled the young lady's name beyond recognition?"

Camisha and Marley exchanged a glance. "Hannah."

"The same person who chose to call her Hastings, rather than Miller, her given name. As proud as I am of my family's name, I despise it being associated with whatever nefarious activity she cloaked."

"My last name is Miller?"

"Your father's name was Miller. Your mother was Cassandra Hastings. Hannah used the name to conceal the truth from you. Had you known this, I presume you could have found Rachel quite easily."

Marley absorbed this. So at least part of the story Nan had told in Thomas Trelawney's kitchen was true. Her father was Robert Miller, not Robert Hastings.

"No wonder I never could find anything about him on any basic web search."

"I've no idea what constitutes a web nor a spider in the twentieth century, but I gather it has to do with the spinning of all of mankind's knowledge."

"That's actually right," Marley said. "The only thing I still don't understand is why Nan couldn't take on Rachel and Juliana, as well as me. And I wish I knew where Juliana was."

Hastings straightened. "Yes. Well, perhaps our dear Camisha here has stored in her eidetic memory the recipe for a truth libation of some sort. The amount of knowledge stuffed in that head makes me wonder if she ate of forbidden fruit."

Camisha pointed. "Now how'd you know that word?"

"Fruit? Oh, truth libation? I fabricated it. It runs in the family, you know."

"No, *eidetic*. In the twentieth century, we refer to *photographic* memory to mean essentially the same thing."

"And when did *eidetic* enter the collective vocabulary?"

She looked to the side, thinking. "Not sure."

"I see. Well, as soon as the dictionary is invented, perhaps you can get back to me."

Marley laughed out loud, loving this little man. He looked at her with a merry smile that she suspected was rare. It held a bit of a guilty look to it, as if he himself knew that smiling at his own wit spoiled it. Or as if he were still a schoolboy, one who'd been scolded for that wit many decades before.

"For now, all this unthinkably luxurious feast, including the turkey, has made me sleepy. I dare not conjecture why for fear of blurting an anachronism and being branded a time jockey myself."

Camisha threw back her head, laughing. "You know good and well I told you about tryptophan, that time we visited back twenty-five years ago. It was the first time we had Thanksgiving dinner down here—and it was when I met Hannah. That was when I first told you about the time portal in the ruins—"

She stopped, remembering. "That's how Hannah knew about it. She overheard me telling you. She was in the house that day—in fact, when I walked out of your office, she was loitering in the hallway. She pretended to be dusting. I knew I couldn't trust that woman."

Hastings sighed, then patted Marley's knee. "My dear, could you fetch your young man, so he might accompany me home? I believe he and the Adams men lurk near the wooded line over there, watching us, smoking those dreadful cigars."

Marley glanced in the direction he pointed, and even as she looked over, Bronson raised his hand.

With that, the trio headed back. Soon Rashall and Ashanti stood at the table across from Marley—not sitting, simply watching her as if she were about to perform a party trick.

"What?"

Camisha suddenly started screaming. "Ruth—Sukey—Dan—Little Dan—Hattie—get over here *now*."

Then she stood by her husband and caught Marley's gaze, her eyes widening as she gestured toward Marley with her head. *Look behind you.*

Marley turned, finding Bronson on one knee in the pine needles, holding out a hand to her. Expectant joy sprang up within her, and she placed her hand in his.

"Merrilea Cassandra Miller—my Marley—the night I met you I had grown hopeless with loneliness. I had sailed the world, not even knowing I was searching for you, and had met many who only made my yearning for you grow. When God dropped you into the water outside my ship, I swam out to find my prayers answered. Except for one."

His chuckle was small and nervous under his breath as he brushed his fingers against the tears slipping from Marley's eyes.

"Please don't cry, my darling, for someone will laugh when I do as well, and I would hate to have to thrash poor Raven for that."

The men and women and children crowded nearby laughed softly.

His voice falling to a whisper, his eyes bright with love for her, he went on. "Answer my only prayer now, my Merri Marley. Tell me you love me, and that you'll be my wife, my helpmate, my love."

Overwhelmed, Marley felt Hastings' gaze keen on her, his eyes filled with warmth and wisdom. "He's already asked my blessing, Merrilea, and you have it."

"Yes," she whispered. "Yes, I'll marry you."

Chapter Thirty-Two

The entire gathering shouted with celebration, and they were quickly surrounded by well-wishers and by loved ones. And just as quickly, bottles and jugs were passed for a celebratory toast.

Only then, as Camisha offered the toast, and everyone gathered in wishing the couple happiness, did the glorious reality strike Marley. Today, she realized that her destiny, too, was to become one of these people with whom she'd felt so intertwined throughout her life—the next bride of the Trelawneys of Williamsburg.

"Walk with me?"

She looked up into Bronson's eyes, dark with happiness in the cooling afternoon. She gathered her cloak more closely around her as he led her across the field, past the ruins of Rosalie, to a copse of huge, old live oaks.

"Do you like this place?"

"I love it. And I love the people."

"Enough to live here?"

The question took her by surprise, and he laughed. Sitting on an old stump, he went on. "Well, not right away. But I've been speaking with Silas, one of the master carpenters who has built Dan and Ruth's home, and he and Hasty can get started on one for us right away, if you like. We should be able to move in by perhaps the summer."

"When's your birthday?"

He frowned in amusement. "Well, I suppose they might make it by then. 'Tis July fourth."

"Your thirtieth?"

He nodded, drawing her between his parted thighs. His lids half closed in sensuous contentment as he lowered her to sit on one thigh, and one arm wrapped around her, his hand resting low on her waist.

"We need not live here all the time. I have a lovely home in St. George's that you might prefer."

"Bermuda, you mean? I've never been there, but I've heard it's lovely."

"It is. It's quite English, though, and life grows more uncertain by the day. And since you're from Williamsburg, I thought this might please you."

He arranged her cloak around her, then slipped his hand inside to rest at her waist.

She laughed at the coldness of his hand, and he smiled easily. "You've had quite a bit of blackberry wine," he said. "Am I perhaps taking advantage, asking your hand?"

"I was just worried about you being cold."

She pulled the cloak around his arm, and he laughed, drawing her still closer. His hand at her waist rested just underneath the heavy curve of her breast.

Her breath grew shallow as she glanced at the crowd laughing and dancing in the distance. With some effort, he slowly looked away from her, removing his hand from within her cloak.

Then he turned back, catching the ties at the neck and pulling her into his kiss. She framed his face with her hands, her palms spread over his cold cheeks as she kissed him—and he let her. She explored, tentatively, then with bold demand, her thumbs at the corners of his mouth as she opened her own, tasting the cigars and rum on his breath. She gave a sigh of satisfaction as she wrapped her arms around his head, and he held her, enjoying her leisured exploration.

She raised her head only enough to look into his eyes. When they opened, the pupils were large with arousal, and he gazed at her lips.

"Would you have me tonight?" he murmured.

"You mean …?"

He laughed. "Well, that, too, certainly. But our kith and kin are all here. An officiant is here. I sent someone into town to fetch my father and your Nan."

Her gaze fell away from his.

"Marley, I understand you're upset with her—"

"You don't know the half of it."

"Then tell me."

"I will, another time. If she's coming, I'll just get over it."

"I don't understand. What does that mean?"

"Well, that tomorrow, I'll thank you for fetching her."

"Just to be clear—Daniel isn't properly licensed to marry us."

"He need not be."

His mouth curved with the hint of a smile. "It isn't a concern. This will always be our wedding day—a day to give thanks. And we'll build our home here. In the new, grand style, with the columns of ancient civilizations governed by the people. Two stories, with plenty of bedrooms for all the children you should want—and looking out on the river road and on the old Rosalie ruins. Speaking of which—what were you and Camisha and Shonny doing out there today?"

But her attention was distracted on the home he described to her—their home. Two hundred forty years from now, it would still stand on Rosalie—where one of the last surviving Trelawneys still lived.

"I'll tell you that, also, later. But you know that curious way Camisha has about her?"

"Yes."

"Rashall was right. We are alike in that way, she and I."

"Ah, a riddle."

She smiled at him, reaching out to lightly stroke his curved lower lip with her fingertip. He captured it between his lips, suckling lightly.

"Do you like riddles?"

"What do you think?"

She raised an eyebrow. "All right, then. Let me think. Well. Camisha and I come from the same place, and we were born in the same place. Yet she is thirty years older than I because she left one day earlier."

His eyes sparkled with concentration as he glanced from her toward Camisha, who was dancing with her husband. Drummers and strummers had materialized as the darkness drew close.

"Give up?"

"Don't tell me. Let me figure it out."

She laughed. "You never will. Oh, there's your father's carriage. Let's go get married. Wait, where's he going?"

"Shh. Stop worrying."

As they returned to the gathering, Ruth captured Bronson. "Did you set up all those books in my schoolroom? And in those beautiful bookshelves?"

"They were just some shelves Hastings had sitting around," he said. "I'm glad you like them. Marley suggested you might."

At that, the older woman caught the younger in her arms. "Aren't you just an angel. Now you go on up to my bedroom, where you'll see Camisha working on your wedding gown. You," she said to Bronson, "You go make your preparations for your marriage bed."

Stirred, Marley cast a look over her shoulder at him to catch his reaction to that—an understated, erotic smile directly at her. She hurried on to Ruth and Dan's house.

The noise of the celebration continued as the sun began to sink toward the horizon. A few hundred feet away, on the other side of the James River, three men stood observing with a shared spyglass.

"Told you it was them," said the smaller, the doughier of the three. "Ripe for the plucking."

"How was I to know? They were supposed to be in Boston." This from a man with an eye-patch and bandages wrapped around half his face. Not yet fully recovered from his injuries, Stephen Falligan threw the man a contemptuous glare. How he despised this paederast. How he would enjoy killing him. If only he wasn't such a clever ferret at unearthing useful information.

"Shut up, both of you." The third man gazed through the spy glass at the group celebrating, his lean jaw tight with rage at those he saw through the glass.

He was older now, his black hair peppered with white, his clothing far finer than it had been the last time he'd seen Rosalie, that night he'd visited with a torch and a kettle of whale oil. A lifetime had passed since then; he was far richer, he had powerful friends who'd never heard of James Manning, the Rosalie overseer, and he certainly had no need for anything from any of these people laughing and dancing across the way—but for the hatred and rage that had driven him for the past three decades.

And the loss of his two boys.

"You call that ripe for the plucking, you halfwit? I call that a countryside full of slave risings in the making. But I don't care about them. Thirty years ago I might have. Now, there's only two I want gone, and it's that tall, black bitch and her buck, and anyone who gets in the way. I want them dead, and I want them to suffer to the point that they beg for death."

The man with the eyepatch listened to the bilious rage in the old man. He'd known this man since childhood. He'd once watched him beat a slave child to death for simply touching the stock of the whip that he'd left hanging on a peg. Falligan had felt that lash himself when he sailed with him, after he was driven out of the Royal Navy. The old man was propelled by hatred and imaginary slights the way fools were driven by dreams.

Falligan was a much simpler man, as was his motivation: money. He would gladly take the old bastard's gold to kill anyone in the group they surveyed; but he would not do so without destroying those who had nearly killed him, and then left him for dead.

"Begging your pardon, sir. In my experience in inflicting pain—and it is indeed extensive—suffering is most elegant when it occurs in the anguish over others."

"What are you prattling on about?"

"Their eldest, the Raven, and his contemptible partner, Hawk. Their deaths—even better, their suffering to the point of death—would deliver them to the place you wish."

"Now you begin to make sense. You have a mind like my own boy, Shep."

"Thank you, sir. I should enjoy making his acquaintance."

"He's been gone ten years now."

"I'm sorry to hear that, sir."

"He ain't dead. He just lives in another place—another time."

Falligan exchanged a glance with Snaveling. Unfortunately, the other man noted it.

"Don't look at me like I'm mad. I know what I speak of." With that, he placed the spyglass in Falligan's open palm with a brisk slap.

The men walked through the woods downriver perhaps a mile to the location where the coxswain and two oarsmen awaited their return.

Falligan and Snaveling boarded after the other man, allowing him to choose his seat first. Of all those on the luckless end of this man's hatred, none were more hapless than black men like those guiding the boat. Always safer to allow him a wide berth.

With long, broad strokes, the men drew them down the James. The wind picked up, the twilight grew colder, and the tide turned as they neared Norfolk, and the oarsmen labored harder.

It was pitch black when they reached the harbor, filled with Royal Navy warships. The men made for a frigate near the shore, and when they arrived, a seaman called, "Who goes there?"

"Stephen Falligan and guests, servants of his royal majesty."

The men climbed the ladder. A young officer with a log book greeted them. "Your names and your business." The disdain in the gaze raking them made the question seem beside the point.

"Deepest apologies for our appearance, sir. We were both lost at sea, not so many miles from here. We have yet to replace our clothing."

In point of fact, this was only half true at best. It could be said that Falligan himself had been lost at sea until a whale boat had come upon him treading water in Massachusetts Bay. And not a moment too soon. The deadly combination of his wounds, his exhaustion, and the unbearable cold had come close to killing him.

Percy Snaveling, on the other hand, had merely overpowered his jailer and gone missing in the night. All three men had turned up at the same shabby public house in Marblehead where they'd met a dozen years before: two, looking for opportunities; the third, his purse fat with opportunity.

The officer sniffed, his gaze on them unimproved with charity for their plight.

"Your business, then?"

"We are here with information that may be of interest to your commander. We wish to see Lord Dunmore."

"And your names."

"James Falligan and Percival Snaveling, both of London. And this gentleman is a native of this colony, a respectable merchant, and a Loyalist: Mr. Lucian Caine."

Chapter Thirty-Three

In the end, there was no better day to wed than the day on which Marley and those she loved celebrated their blessings.

In Ruth's house, she and Camisha hastily worked an eighteenth century makeover miracle on the bride.

"You really don't have to go to all this trouble," Marley said, alarmed at the sudden pile of clothing that appeared on the bed in Ruth's bedroom.

"Now you're about my Sukey's size, so what do you think about this peach-flowered dress, with the ivory quilted petticoat underneath? I think it suits your coloring."

"It's gorgeous, but I hate to take Sukey's clothing!"

The lively animation left Camisha as she straightened and folded her arms across her chest. "Girl, you are making me tired. This is your wedding day. We'll make Sukey new dresses to replace whatever you take. And that child has way too many clothes already. She's a grown woman, and that husband of hers dresses her like she's a little doll."

Marley gave into their fussing and allowed herself to be scrubbed and rubbed with oils and dressed in finery and, in the end, she glowed with sensual excitement. For the first time in her life, she felt utterly beautiful.

At the end, Ruth opened a small chest with reverential care. She removed a delicate old scarf; once it might have been dyed with yellow bark of the black oak and red berries grown in a mysterious land that would be known as the Dark Continent. Now it held only the memory of those colors, along with a rich heritage of love.

Ruth was filled with sudden emotion as she held the cloth out to Camisha. Camisha hugged her, then accepted the cloth and began to dress Marley's hair as Ruth spoke, trying to swallow her tears.

"My mother, last time I ever saw her, gave me this down in Caroline, before Lord Windmere bought me and then set me free. One day, she said, we'll be back together in Glory with our loved ones. I didn't know it then, but she was saying a Bible verse. 'And God shall wipe away all tears from their eyes; and there shall be no more death, neither sorrow, nor crying, neither shall there be any more pain: for the former things are passed away.'

"Miss Marley, I hope you don't mind, but Camisha told me who you are. I met your beautiful sister Rachel, years ago. She was a kind lady with a good heart, and if it weren't for your sister and the good she did with Lord Windmere, I'd still be a slave. We all would. My Dan, he might've been sold away years ago, instead of watching his children grow up, and being able to ransom the freedom of others with the loss of our own.

"I'm saying, you don't know what tides you turn when you toss a pebble in a river. I see that same kindness in you, that same sight she had, and that Miss Camisha, here, has. I wish you and Bronson every delight in this life. Someday, I promise you, honey, you'll see your sister again, same as I'll see my mama and my brothers and sisters again."

Camisha finished her hair and hugged her. "Honey, don't cry. Nothing sadder in this world than a puffy-eyed bride."

After she collected herself and patted cold water on her face, she touched the scarf. Camisha had fashioned her hair into an elegant chignon at the back of her neck, her head and hair all covered with the lovely scarf.

"Now take this," Ruth said, removing several slender volumes from it, placing them in a drawer, and holding the box out to her. "You put the scarf in this tonight, and send a boy back with it tomorrow."

Only when Ruth put the carved box with its hinged top into her hands did she recognize it. This was the same beautiful box that one day would hold *The Trelawneys of Williamsburg*.

Marley held the box to her breast, bending her head to deeply inhale its comforting, familiar cedar. She nodded, unable to speak.

A short tap at the door came, and Sukey entered. "Everybody's down there," she said.

The women descended the staircase, but both the house and the clearing were empty. Except for the Trelawney carriage with a brightly dressed footman. He bowed low when they approached and handed the four women inside with elegant formality.

"Where—"

Camisha smirked. "Really? You think we're going to tell you?"

Marley laughed. "My blackberry wine's wearing off."

"Well, we'll fix that right up before you know it. You definitely want to be able to remember marrying the man *you're* marrying."

They arrived at the river and in the waning twilight, with the ship festooned with evergreen garlands and lit with torches and lamps, the people standing in every inch of space and spilling out onto the dry land, it looked like a welcome from heaven itself. At the base of the boarding steps placed at the side of the ship, her groom stood in a black suit—coat and breeches, silver waistcoat, pale silk stockings and snowy white shirt with a stock tied at his throat—that lent him a startling sexuality, credit he scarcely needed.

At his side stood Godfrey Hastings, the great-grandfather she already loved.

"I do not know how you expect me not to cry," she said.

Camisha smiled, her own gaze shining.

The footman helped the older women down first, and then Marley. Camisha and Ruth took her arms and escorted her the short distance to the *Adventurer* and to Hastings. Camisha carried the storage chest in her other arm. She released Marley near the steps and handed the box to Bronson.

And then she saw Nan, standing to the side with Thomas Trelawney. She hesitated, her anger at her grandmother a discordant note in an otherwise harmonious day.

Nan walked forward. As Camisha and Ruth released her, her grandmother took both her hands in hers.

"My darling Merrilea. I cannot yet explain to you why I did the things I did. But I ask you to forgive me, not for my sake, but for your own. Anger in one's heart is a seed of bitterness that will poison the rest of your life."

"Of course, Nan. I forgive you." Marley hugged her grandmother. "I'm so sorry."

"Darling, you've never been anything to me but a joy. Do you truly not remember why I called you Marley?"

She shook her head, pressing her lips to fight the tears.

"You met your great-grandfather, many, many years ago."

Shocked, Marley glanced at Hastings, standing nearby, watching the proceedings with a mixture of affection for Marley and suspicion for the woman speaking. She went on.

"Not long after—well, a long time ago. You had never been called anything but Merri, but he called you Merrilea, your given name. And you repeated it, trying to reproduce his accent in your own adorable tidewater tongue, and it came out *Marley*. You seemed bewitched by the sound of it—it was the only thing that would comfort you in those long, dark nights of grief. And so I started making up songs with it, and soon I was calling you that as well. Marley, it was how *you* said the name your mother gave you."

Nan held her by the shoulders, smiling brightly. "I wish you every joy and happiness with your young man, Merrilea."

With that, she turned toward Hastings, who moved forward with his elegant walking stick, offered her his arm, and escorted her back to the boarding steps.

Then a voice came from the ship. "Who giveth this woman to be married unto this man?"

Marley glanced up, surprised to find Raven there, also in a suit. His club of hair had been plaited down the nape of his neck rather than over his shoulder.

"Her great-grandfather," Hastings said, giving a slight bow. He then walked forward and placed her hand in Bronson's.

Hastings' eyes shone as he smiled at her. "God bless you and your new family, *Marley*."

She then turned to Bronson, who walked close behind her up the steps, whispering low in her hair. "Are you surprised?"

She whispered back. "With Ray? He can't legally marry us, even if he *is* a captain. That's a myth."

"Oh, he'll be devastated. Let's humor him, shall we?"

When they reached the gunwale, Ray grasped her by the waist and hoisted her over the side. Then came Bronson, Hastings, Thomas and Nan, Camisha and Ruth.

She was surprised when Ray picked up a Book of Common Prayer from a table and began the ceremony. This was not a ship captain's ceremony. The somber piety with which he began the ceremony made him seem a different man—one much older, and certainly not the jester she'd come to love.

More shock came when Bronson recited his vows—legitimate wedding vows.

"I, Bronson Ambrosia Trelawney take thee, Merrilea Cassandra Miller, to my wedded wife, to have and to hold from this day forward, for better, for worse, for richer, for poorer, in sickness, and in health, to love and to cherish, till death us depart; according to God's holy ordinance, and thereto I plight thee my troth."

He looked at Marley with sober devotion—and a hint of expectation.

Marley looked at him for an endless, awkward moment, then she looked to Rashall desperately.

"Oh, of course!" He jumped, Raven once more as he turned the book toward her, laying his fingertip alongside her vows—nearly unrecognizable in their 16th-century form.

Marley was surprised; the words were virtually identical. In such an old, traditional ceremony, she would have expected something more subservient for her vows.

As she returned the book to Rashall, Bronson placed there three rings. One, a traditional band, the others stunning keeper rings, encircled with diamonds. Then he once more joined hands with Marley. In the flame from a torch, Marley saw an engraving inside the band that she could not read.

Rashall took the rings and looped them in order onto the tip of his index finger, then held it out to Bronson. Bronson grasped the stack of rings, and Rashall gave him a small nod.

"With this ring, I thee wed. With my body, I thee worship; and with all my worldly goods, I thee endow. In the name of the Father, and of the Son, and of the Holy Ghost. Amen."

Rashall then offered a prayer, and said solemnly, "Those whom God hath joined together, let no man put asunder."

The ceremony continued with blessings and prayers, and even a celebration of communion using a common cup.

At its conclusion, Rashall himself hugged them both, Bronson first with a stiff pat on the back, and Marley exactly as she'd seen him hug his own sisters.

"You be good to each other."

With that, they led the procession off the ship, his arm around her, his hand stroking her back. He lowered his head to murmur in her hair. "Can this thing in your hair come off?"

"Patience, my husband. I look forward to unwrapping you as well."

Purely sexual pleasure flooded his face at her words, and he chuckled. "Unless you have no wish to partake in your reception, put those thoughts aside."

"You started it."

His hand lowered to the firm, full swell of her backside and caressed her openly. She swatted at his hand when she heard the indulgent laughter behind them.

Being the married couple, they were given the carriage, but Bronson helpfully offered rides to their respective parents, all of whom declined.

And as soon as the carriage departed, he caught her in his arms and drew her across his lap. He held her immobile for a long moment, his free hand upturned in the air as if in wonder as he examined her. That hand opened and closed in anticipation, and his fingertips lightly touched her cheek, her throat, then hovered above her body as if unsure where to start.

At last, he cupped her rounded buttock, pressing the fabric tight between her upper thighs, his fingers tracing there as his mouth lowered to hers.

"Dear God in heaven! I cannot do this or I shall have you naked as we reach the cake table."

He pushed her back, his gaze hungry on the ample soft flesh displayed above her stays. "'Tis far too dark in here," he whispered. "Just one touch … one kiss—"

With that, his mouth lowered to her breasts, his tongue flickering into the deep valley between them. He raised his mouth to her ear. "How I love your womanly charms. And now, you must sit over there, and keep your hands to yourself."

With that, he brought her alongside him on the seat, his hand slipping with swift, sure knowledge into the fabric between her dress and her petticoat.

"Dear God, you wore no shift on your wedding day!"

His hand was between her thighs, his chest rising and falling. In a moment, he withdrew his hands from her, moving away. He looked toward the other window, where the shades were pulled to keep out the cold. Then, slowly, he began to laugh.

"What?" she asked, trembling with desire.

"This will be the shortest time any bride has spent at her reception."

She laughed, and their amusement went a long way in softening the edge of their hunger for each other. Looking at her warily, he reached out and took her hand in his, pressing his lips against her knuckles.

Chapter Thirty-Four

Every liquor known to man had been brought to the wedding, and the bride and groom took part in toasts and well-wishing and, at last, cutting the cake—a traditional orange cake that Marley herself had baked for Thanksgiving, but had then saved for their reception.

Bronson lowered his mouth to his wife's ear. "And now, to bed."

A ripple of excitement ran through her veins and down the back of her spine as he kissed her cheek, his hand sliding down her waist to her hips.

"Now."

With that, he caught her up in his arms and strode to the carriage.

"We didn't even talk to your father!"

"I cannot hear you. There's a buzzing in my ears that will not go away until you're naked in my bed."

She gasped and waved at Camisha, who stood laughing with Ruth and Nan.

On this trip, the carriage rushed straightaway through the cold night to the ship. Bronson again carried her, and he took the boarding steps quickly, alighting on deck with graceful ease.

Then, down the corridor to the hatch, where he lowered her before dropping down himself. Half a dozen more steps and they saw Jem, waiting in dress clothes, a towel folded over his arm. He bowed slightly to his captain.

"Congratulations, sir. Madam," he said, with a twinkle in his eye at his old peer.

Marley wondered if Bronson himself had set up the room, as perfectly outfitted as it was. Food stood in covered dishes on a trolley, along with an opened bottle of wine. She glanced at Bronson. "Oh! Is it—"

With an intimate smile, he nodded. "Blackberry, of course."

"Sir, I hope the room is to your liking."

"Yes, Jem. Well done indeed," he said. "Now begone."

Marley stifled her laughter and flashed him a look.

"My apologies, Jem. Please join the rest of the group on shore. They're having a party never to be forgotten—or perhaps that *will* be forgotten, if it gets any better. Look for Raven's mother. She can show you where to sleep for the night."

"But you don't need—"

"You've fulfilled your duties so well, we'll manage. Truly, you'll have much more fun on shore. Enjoy yourself. 'Tis the best part of being a seaman."

The boy nodded and made his escape, closing the door behind him.

Bronson looked around the room, inspecting. The room itself was warm, with a hot fire in the stove. The copper tub, filled with steaming water. A supper they had no need for—though perhaps they might need sustenance later in the night. And there by the long bank of windows, a single hammock, beside a table filled with cigars, an ashtray, glasses, a bottle of rum, and another opened bottle of wine.

Presently he heard the sound overhead of Jem walking down the steps, and as he looked at her, a shyness seemed to enter him. His hesitation filled her with a potent arousal—and a provocative sense of power.

"What first?" she asked.

"A cigar under the stars?"

She nodded, and he held out his hand in invitation. She put hers there, and he led her to the hammock, pouring a glass of wine and one of rum. He held it out to her, raising his own glass. "To a lifetime together, spent in the arms of my love."

Their eyes met as they sipped. Marveling at a man who could be flirtatious on his honeymoon, she crossed with a mysterious smile to the windows and looked into the winter sky.

"Never have I seen so many stars as on those nights I've watched them with you. I wish it were warm enough to lie on the deck."

"Before you know it, we'll be back in Bermuda. We've millions of stars to see."

"In the world I once lived in, we've all but blotted out the stars, looking at ourselves."

Then she lowered her head, noting the empty bookshelves. She turned to him. "Thank you so much for loaning Ruth your books."

"I don't loan books. They're too precious if lost. I'll replace them. It was a small thing to do."

She noticed Ruth's box on the table, and she set the wine aside and raised her arms to work with the scarf.

"Let me."

His voice was gruff as he set the cigars in the ashtray. He walked behind her, his hands gentle in her hair, quickly loosening it from the scarf. She accepted the scarf from him and folded it, placing it in the box.

"I would know about this world you speak of."

"Which one?"

"The one you speak of from time to time. The world you once lived in, as if it were on another planet."

Marley found a cigar and puffed it with leisured ease. She followed it with a mouthful of his rum, pleased with the tastes.

"Tonight I will tell you. Undress."

His eyes lit with amusement at her direction, and he gave a courtly bow. "As you wish, madam."

She rested her hips against the table, tasting the cigar and the rum as he crossed to the dressing area. He removed his coat and his waistcoat, hanging them on pegs inside his closet. His back was to her, and she enjoyed the freedom of watching him, seeing the strong flex of his back through his shirt as he moved to slip out of his shoes and put them away as well. Unselfconsciously, he loosened the pin at the back of his stock, then folded it and placed both the stock and the pin in a drawer.

He turned, his gaze narrowing as he caught her watching him disrobe. He walked toward her, a crooked smile at his mouth. "If you'd like to see the stars, perhaps I'll stop here."

She only smiled at the obvious line to follow.

"Indeed?" he asked. "I kindly hand you a double entendre of that caliber and you merely smirk at me?"

"I dare not try to best such keen wordplay," she said dryly. "However ..." She set the glass aside, held out the cigar to him, and reached up to unbutton three buttons of his shirt. After a moment's consideration, she unbuttoned the rest.

He let her arrange his clothing to suit her, tasting the cigar and the rum. "Well?"

"You seem a little shy. Just thought I'd help."

She saw a flash of gold within his shirt, and she reached for it to tease him about his pirate's plunder.

The items on the chain slid into her palm, and he watched her, a half-smile playing about his lips, as she held her hand up to examine his trinkets. She stared, not quite able to make them out in the light. Then she brought her lips to his chest and kissed him, and he gave a light sound of pleasure. She looked again at the ornamentation.

A cross and a dove.

She gave a soft cry and dropped them. She handled them again, remembering the coroner she'd met at the dig that day, carrying the personal effects of the man he deduced to be a sea captain—including a cross and dove necklace identical to this.

"They're quite harmless." When she met his gaze, she was surprised to find a gaze as innocent as a boy's. "'Tis but an effort by my father to protect me."

Filled with affection both for him and the father who had worried over him, she forced the terror within her away from her. Later, she would deal with it. She brought them to her lips, then returned them gently to his chest. He started to remove the necklace, and she touched his hand, stopping him. "No. Don't take it off, ever again. Wear it always. Even when we sleep."

"My thanks." He walked to the hammock and refilled the rum. "I admit I'm a bit intimidated tonight. My vows echo in my memory. I must have heard those words a dozen times in my life, but they meant nothing until I spoke them to you. *With my body, I thee worship.* Doesn't that strike you as ... striking?"

"Almost erotic."

"Yes." His gaze on her was heavy lidded. The corner of his mouth hooked into a half smile. With practiced grace, he settled into the hammock with his cigar and rum still in hand. Jem had covered the knotty ropes of the hammock with a thick, red velvet spread, and Bronson looked like some exotic blond sultan, leaning on an arm, legs spread casually, one bent.

"Should I get my own rum? I'd rather have that for now."

"What's mine is yours, my love."

"And mine, yours." With a flourish, she gestured at the length of her body. "Your preference? 'Tis only fair."

The fire lit his eyes, and the cigar smoke wreathed his head. "Very well. Remove the dress."

The rum had stirred a warmth that began deep within her, and she unhooked the dress with some effort and let it fall.

"And that quilted ... thing."

Rather than stepping out of the lovely ivory petticoat, she pulled it over her head. She folded both garments and lay them in an empty drawer, placing Ruth's wooden chest with them.

He bit his lip thoughtfully, gesturing at the stays. "That contraption must go."

At last, she stood gazing at him in stockings and a gauzy short shift.

"Perfect. Come, my love, and lay with me." He set the cigar and the rum on the table.

This time, the arrangement came easily, gracefully. She thought sharing a hammock must be like marriage; tricky in the beginning, but a much more relaxing rhythm when each realizes what the other brings to the balance.

Bronson settled her hips easily within the cradle of his own, his hands lingering on her hips. She wasn't aware when she gave a soft sigh at his caressing as he melded against her in intimate precision.

Inhaling the sweetness of his cigar—for she had learned that far more often, the aroma of better cigars was not at all unpleasant—she lightly pressed her hips against him in response and turned her upper body to gaze up at the stars. She lay within his embrace, unaware of his scrutiny on her.

"Is this how you ever imagined spending your wedding night?" he asked.

"Hm. I don't think I ever imagined it. I wasn't sure I'd ever get married. What would you rather be doing?"

She puffed the cigar and handed his to him, then shared a sip of wine.

"I wish life allowed us the pleasure of multiple experiences in the same time. For I would already be—well, worshipping you with my body. And we would be discussing the last books each of us read. And we would be attempting to reason through a solution to Ray's completely justified frustration over this world. And we would be dancing with the rest of the Trelawneys. Forgive me, my love, for my selfishness. I couldn't bear sharing another moment of your company with anyone."

"Is that all? I mean, things you want to do tonight?"

"No, in fact. I would love to have a bath with you, but neither of us is dirty."

She laughed to herself at his logic.

"I would also enjoy weighing anchor and leaving this strife-riddled colony behind. But at this moment, in truth, there is nothing I would rather do than be lying here with your lovely round arse against me. It is the sharpest masochistic pleasure to know I need only unbutton a button or two and lift your shift to thrust myself deeply inside you."

His voice was a low, hypnotic murmur at her ear, and he lightly kissed her there, his mouth warm and open.

"And the longer I hold off, the greater the thrill. And also, come to think of it, I look forward to going to sleep, as I will likely wake up with my mouth on some lovely part of you."

She puffed her cigar, noting by the timbre of his voice that he wasn't through daydreaming.

"Or we could be over at the table, sketching out our home. It should be done soon, so they can get started."

She looked up at her husband—and then she saw how he watched her. He lightly kissed her forehead, then brushed her lips with his. "How dear you are to me. You are my life."

Then he leaned back, his eyes narrowing as he inserted the cigar between his teeth and glanced at her with purely sexual desire. His free hand slipped underneath her shift, skimming upward over her curves a deep sigh escaped him. Then he closed his lips around the cigar and puffed, and as swiftly his roving hand left her.

"I could not have fashioned a woman more perfectly suited to me, to my every need, were I sitting at God's footstool with a list—as at times I suppose I did. I love your heart, your shyness, your boldness, your adventure, and your woman's voluptuous body that makes me mad with pure lust. I love your brain perhaps most of all—your quickness, your wit, your curiosity about everything you encounter. So it leaves us here: what the hell is the meaning of that riddle?"

She laughed aloud, delighted at the ode he had just written on her heart in that soft, husky voice. "I will tell you, but first you must copy down what you just said, so I can look at it when we're apart."

"I shall write you no letters, because you'll never leave my side. Now. Tell me the meaning."

"I thought you wanted to figure it out. It hasn't even been, what, fifteen minutes?"

"You'll find I am not a patient man when you in particular are teasing me. It enflames my desire for you—that I've done well to contain, today. I'll make no promises if you continue."

"You know, smoking isn't safe for you, even if you don't inhale, but you are just unforgivably sexy with a cigar."

He dismissed that, distracted with the riddle. "You said that you and Mrs. Adams were both born in the same town, but she's thirty years older because you left town a day later?"

"No. We're from the same place. Think spatially."

His eyebrows drew together. "You're not speaking of geography."

She sipped her rum and gazed at the stars.

"One more clue."

"The answer is in the rest of it."

"Thirty years older, a day later ... Time."

Her eyes widened as she touched the tip of her nose.

"What does your nose have to do with it?"

She laughed softly at the petulant distrust in his expression.

"All right. But you have to promise me that you trust me. And you also have to promise you won't tell anyone. And if you think we should tell Rashall, just let me know first."

"Out with it!"

"I was born in 1991. My sister, Rachel, was born in 1988. Camisha is my sister's age. They visited Colonial Williamsburg one day. They traveled back in time to 1746. My grandmother and I took a day cruise in the Bahamas, but a storm came up and I was washed overboard. And you know what happened after that. I also have a younger sister, but I don't know where she is. Ah. I should stop now. You're doubting my sanity."

He was staring out the window, and he quickly shook his head. "Perhaps your sobriety."

"Speaking of, we're almost out of rum. Should I refill?"

"Most definitely."

She reached for the bottle, and he took over the task for her, putting out his cigar in the ashtray.

"*How?*"

"I don't know."

"And why?"

"Maybe Camisha can explain why Rachel came. Knowing Camisha, knowing the modern world we left behind, I believe she came so she could make minor improvements in the world. Like the things she does with the babies who die. I do know Rachel fell in love with your brother, Grey, and returned with him to the twenty-first century. And his traveling to another time enabled him to free his slaves."

"So he's actually alive in another time?"

"As far as I know."

"How do you know all these things?"

"Ruth doesn't know I know it, but she keeps a journal. When she was still enslaved, she could neither read nor write—but Hastings taught her how, and over time, she opened the school. Back in my old life, Nan had a magnificent book called *The Trelawneys of Williamsburg*. It's a collection of all the journals in a leather-bound box, to appear like a grand old family Bible.

"The only problem is that one journal is missing. From this time period, for the next six years."

"What happens during that time period—that is, historically?"

She hesitated. "First of all, I'll always tell you the truth. If I can't tell you something, for a good reason, I'll tell you that, and I know you'll trust me. But I will tell you that in the next year, Thomas Jefferson will write a document declaring this country's independence from England, and that all men are created equal. Congress will sign it—each man—and a war will be fought. We *will* win our independence."

He sipped from the rum and passed it to her, and she drank.

Excitement gleamed in his eyes as he considered her words. "To think, all men at last declared equal. The madness of human beings owning one another, over."

"No."

"You said—"

"Bronson, my darling, please promise me you'll say nothing, do nothing to try to change this. It may mean I have to go back to my old time."

He shook his head. "Just explain. You know I'll do nothing without our agreement."

"Do you know Thomas Jefferson?"

"I do. Tom and I were quite close as boys. We attended William and Mary together. I attended at a younger age, having been a voracious reader for many years. We studied philosophy together."

Marley felt a shiver steal over her.

"Are you chilled?" he asked, tucking her close against him.

"No. It's simply intriguing. Your ideas and beliefs were formed by the same men who informed those of possibly the United States' most important founder—"

"Whose most important founder?"

"That's what our country will be named. He'll write the Declaration of Independence in the coming months, and in it he will include a clause attacking slavery. He will assign blame to the King for blocking every attempt to halt or impede slavery, and he'll address Dunmore's proclamation freeing slaves who fight for the British. It's a strong stance against slavery."

He didn't attempt to fill her silence.

"His stance will fail. South Carolina and Georgia, as well as those in the north who have ties to the slave trade itself, will refuse to sign the measure unless he strikes the offending passage."

"And he'll strike it."

"Bronson, this is exactly what Camisha mentioned to me earlier as something that she would never attempt to influence. If Jefferson sticks to his guns and leaves it in, we may well never become the great country that I assure you we *will* become."

Watching him struggle with this impossible truth made her ache for him. He drained the rest of the rum and carefully made his way out of the hammock, leaving her ensconced in the velvet. Without him cradling her in his arms, she quickly felt how cool the room had grown.

He crossed the room and, after a trip to his water closet, he returned to the room and refilled the wood stove. She came to her feet unsteadily—way too much rum—and made her way to the water closet.

Ah. No arguments here about seat up or seat down, she thought, remembering Jimmy and Nan bickering over the topic. The seat was simple, wooden, with a hole in it. Form following function, if she ever saw it.

She returned, and a smile came to her lips at the sight of Bronson on one knee beside the copper tub. He'd placed a host of candles on the table near the tub, and even now swirled a hand in the water, inhaling the aroma of jasmine filling the air. His hair was wet and curled like flowing gold in the candlelight. His shirt hung open, and she leisurely enjoyed surveying him. The basin held the water where he'd bathed.

"I missed watching you wash. It's become one of my favorite pastimes."

"Come." He held a hand out to her, his gaze on her tender. "Let me instruct you of others."

Chapter Thirty-Five

Marley joined Bronson at the tub, resting her hands on his shoulders, loving the face looking up at her. She traced her fingertips along his cheekbones, his strong jawline, and the curve of his lips. Then she slid her fingertips into his curling, wet hair, drawing him near. He lowered his head against her abdomen and inhaled deeply. Self-consciously, she shrank away from his seeking mouth, his frank enjoyment of her.

He laughed, a deeply sexual sound as he looked up at her. "My shy Merrilea. I will know every inch of you tonight. As you will know me."

The warmth of his innocent examination filled her, and he leaned away, his hands rising between her thighs to roll down first one stocking, then the other.

An awkward, inexplicable embarrassment filled her over her near nakedness. He had seen her body more than once. It was scarcely concealed now. The first time she had ever seen him, she had lain very nearly naked in his bed.

His large, strong hands skimmed underneath the hem of her shift and upward, lightly tracing a path that left her aching for more of his touch, even as he lifted the shift entirely off her and threw it toward the closet.

"What about this?" he asked, lifting a hand toward the pillbox around her neck.

"Oh, yes." She removed it and placed it on his dresser.

His eyes sparkled with arousal and even a lighthearted amusement. "How I shall enjoy this night," he murmured, holding out a hand for her above the tub.

She smiled mysteriously, hesitating, and grasped his shirt at the collar, easily pushing it away. He complied with her request, and his shirt drifted atop her discarded shift.

She lay her hand in his, enjoying the sight of him in the candlelight—still sun-browned in late autumn. She stepped into the water, lowering herself there, loving him for the utter, sweeping luxury. The jasmine oil filled the air, and she breathed in its romantic aroma.

"It's heavenly. I've never known such a luxurious bath."

He gently steered her shoulders backward so she relaxed against the lip of the tub where his own body leaned, leaving a most comfortable pillow.

She luxuriously rubbed her head there, turning her face to the side against his trousers, feeling the rise of him hard and long against her cheek. Without thinking, she opened her mouth and dropped kisses along his length with a sigh.

His hands rose from her shoulders to her face, his fingertips thrusting into her hair, as he almost imperceptibly pressed himself closer to her mouth.

Then, he turned her head away and reached for a small cloth on the lip of the tub. Dipping it in the perfumed water, he moved it lightly over her cheeks, down her throat, over her shoulders and down her arms to her fingertips. He caressed each part of her body; the lightest touch of his strong hands on her shoulders licked the arousal in the center of her body.

She noticed the slight tremble in his hands as he released her and drew the cloth back to her collarbone and down, into the deep valley between her breasts. He lifted the cloth above her breasts and squeezed out the water, watching the drops of water lazily course along her nipples. She arched her back toward his hand, but he merely continued to tease her—first with the falling water, then by trailing the cloth across one hardening nipple, then the other. Her nipples were fully erect, aching for his mouth.

"Are you cold, my darling?"

His whisper was low in her ear – and then his warm breath blew down, caressing her nipples.

"Oh … good gosh … no, not cold," she murmured.

He laughed, then lowered his mouth to her shoulder and nibbled lightly, drawing kisses along a line to her ear. "I should so love to suckle at your lovely breasts."

His words enflamed her, and she looked toward him, capturing his mouth in hers, kissing him with hungry seduction.

"Is it wrong to feel such decadent pleasure? I did not know such feelings were possible."

"Merrilea. I merely worship thee with my body."

He reached for a bottle from the table and let a single drop fall into his wet hand. Silently, he rubbed his hands together; the smell was different—a sharp mint.

Encircling her with his arms, he lay his hands flat over her upper chest then slowly drew the lightly tingling oil down to her breasts. She lifted her breasts free of the water, offering them up to his touch, her own hand reaching back to fondle him through his breeches. She fumbled at the buttons—there weren't many—but then his hands were on her breasts, and she cried out as he knowingly, exquisitely, spread the oil to the tips of her breasts. Her erect nipples grew even stiffer, standing out for his mouth, and she gasped with the sensation.

"Oh, God, it's so hot!"

"Does it burn?" he murmured teasingly, deep in her ear.

"Yes."

"Here?" Lightly, he pinched her nipples, then caressed her breasts, hefting their weight in his hands.

She gasped. "Mhm. Oh, yes."

One hand left her breasts and she cried out in disappointment until she felt it gliding downward across her stomach. The slight tremble she'd noticed earlier in him was gone, and he was making love to her with the deft knowledge of an experienced lover.

With an expert hand, he parted her thighs, placing one gently against one side of the tub and the other against the other side. His touch light, he used the cloth to lightly stroke both her legs, even as his other hand continued touching her breasts.

Then he casually abandoned the cloth, his lean, strong hand caressing her thighs. The fire of the peppermint oil cooled, and his hand slipped along her inner thigh until he reached the place that radiated heat.

She heard his long, low sound of appreciation as his fingers lightly played there. All at once he crushed her against him, his mouth kissing her ear, one hand encircling her waist, the other closing over her rounded hip.

A moment later he gentled, forcing himself to release her as he moved to the other end of the tub. She was moved as he took another drop of peppermint oil and massaged her feet in the humblest of ministrations.

He put her feet back in the water, placing his hands on his hips. She lazily licked her lips as she investigated his chest—perhaps his most beautiful physical feature, she thought.

He reached for a towel as he stood, and held out a hand to her. Rising to her feet, she stepped over the side of the tub onto a small towel he'd placed there. Holding out her hand for the towel, she was surprised to find a wicked smirk on his face. "You're joking?"

"Very well, then." She held out her arms, her elbows bent and her hands lifted in a queenly flourish, presenting herself for his attendance.

He quickly patted her arms, her back, her breasts, then knelt to dry her legs.

And then he lay the towel aside and would have lifted her in his arms.

"No," she said. "Kiss me."

She saw that he heard the imperious note in her tone, and with a lift of an eyebrow, he gave a deferential bow. What made a kiss from Bronson remarkable was as much the anticipation as the kiss itself, and she was pretty certain he knew that. Despite playing along with her game of ordering him about, he took his time; even for a true queen, she knew, he would savor each moment.

Meeting her gaze, he raised his hand to cup her face and lowered his mouth to hers, tasting lightly, then returning and delving more deeply. His fingers slid into her hair, tilting her head up as he drew her body full-length against his, as his hands slipped from her hair down her back, cupping her hips even as she impulsively lifted her thigh, twining her leg around one of his.

He lifted his head. "Aye, I will kiss you, and well. You might prefer to lie comfortably in our bed."

A smile tugged at the corner of her mouth at the phrase.

"*Kiss* me."

He bent to taste her breasts, his lips and teeth lightly nipping. Then he suckled, dividing his attention between them.

She gave soft sighs at the intensity of sensation, certain he was not doing it to pleasure her, but because he enjoyed it.

And then he dropped kisses along her flat waist, her lightly rounded belly, and lower. He easily slipped his hand to the back of her knee, throwing her thigh over his shoulders, and dipping his mouth between her thighs. She heard—she *felt*—his soft groan as his lips and tongue played along the outer flesh there, and she went weak in the knees.

He caught her just in time, and she fell into his arms.

"As you wish, milady," he said, gazing into her eyes with an arousing combination of conquest and surrender.

He hastily tossed back the quilts and lowered her into his bed. Quickly, he walked around his quarters snuffing candles and lamps, then returned to stoke the stove. He left a candelabra burning beside the bed.

She stretched out in luxuriant happiness, watching him unbutton his breeches and hang them in his closet. As he moved, she weighed again her earlier opinion of his chest being his best physical feature. She'd never had as clear a look at his naked body as now. It was a tough call; he had so many alluring features.

He climbed into bed beside her and let his eyes drift over her as if enjoying the candlelight on her flesh.

Kissing her lips with tender grace, he pushed back the hair from her face. He hesitated, then kissed the crescent-shaped scar at the corner of her eye. "Who did this?"

"Nan said I hit my face on the bed. But Camisha told me it happened the night my parents were killed. I don't remember."

He petted her gently, his kisses slowly trailing from her face to her breasts, and then—her excitement soared—lower. A blush stained her cheeks as he clutched her buttocks in his large hands, cupping her to his mouth as if her womanhood were a fount and he a man dying in the desert.

She gasped, then cried out in pure joy, her hands playing lightly in his hair. But then he teased her, drawing back each time she felt an overwhelming pressure tightening her abdomen. With an intimacy that sent an electric current pulsing between her thighs, he casually placed one of her thighs, then the other, over his shoulders.

She stroked his hair, whispering his name, then begging him for something she had only imagined before now. Then his mouth closed directly over her most sensitive center, suckling lightly, then harder.

His name came from her in a cry of need as waves of ecstasy washed over her. As the spasms slowly passed, she felt him rising over her, her thighs still over his shoulders. He smoothed his hand along one thigh, then the other, as if he simply enjoyed the feeling of her. His hand moved between her thighs, lightly exploring, knowing her keen sensitivity. He slipped a finger, then two, within her, and the mild discomfort was eased when he finally brushed his thumb against her, setting her trembling again.

Adrift in sensation, she was surprised when she looked up to find his gaze on her with quiet affection, even as one hand extended her thigh into the air and the other played between her thighs.

"Bronson." Her hands roved the breadth of his chest.

"Yes, my love."

"I feel it again."

His mouth went tight as he watched her. At last, he gave her a rakish smile. "And so shall you, again, and again."

"But I want to … um, kiss you. I mean, the way you kissed me." She lowered her hands from her chest toward his torso, but in his current position, he was too far away even to touch.

His face grew solemn at her words. "Then I'll dream of that until you do. But for now—"

He lowered himself between her thighs, and her skin tingled when she felt the smooth round tip, the hard length of him seeking there. He slid lightly along the outer flesh, his tongue at the corner of his mouth, as he watched her response. He rested on an elbow, the other hand caressing and teasing her breasts. He dipped his mouth to suckle her breasts even as he sought entry between her thighs with slow, knowing thrusts that teased at her, then slipped inward into her wetness.

"Dear God, Marley. You'll be the death of me. You're the most sexual creature I've ever been with. You seem to genuinely enjoy my touch."

Breathless laughter came from her at his phrasing. *Well, there's a big fat duh.* She marveled at him, at his athletic strength and grace, the ease with which he held his body above hers, taut, while he made love to her with his mouth, his hands, his entire body. Truly, he worshipped her with his body, as if he had been created for her alone.

"Kiss me." She raised her parted lips to him, and he lowered his mouth to hers, his body more insistent as he pressed himself more deeply into her.

He drew back, raising himself so that he could watch her face as he breached the fine barrier once and for all. He sank deeply within her, filling her. Her eyes closed at their joining, and then opened again, finding his gaze roving over her.

"All well?" he asked.

"You're very—large."

"Too much?" he asked, and made as if to withdraw.

She quickly curled her thigh around his back and held him close. At her frank acceptance, he lowered a hand between her thighs, caressing her swollen flesh even as he thrust within her.

Then he drew both her thighs up around his waist, and she gasped at the sharpness of the sensation within her. He grasped her round hips in his palms as he thrust, tilting her pelvis ever so slightly to deepen the sensation. The orgasm built within her, and his fingers dug into the soft flesh of her hips. She looked up at him and was lost in his gaze.

She saw the urgency in him even as he held himself back, the frank sexuality and the breathless wonder at the electricity joining their bodies.

Again his fingers returned to play lightly, then with the practiced expertise of a man who had already come to know her body as well as his own. And he felt her own arousal under his hand, and as she whispered his name, as he felt the first pulsing of her around him, he lowered his long body over hers, kissing her throat, his love for her pouring deeply within her as his adoration spilled into her ear.

His arm curved around her head, his hand playing through her hair, then drawing her even closer to him as she felt his heart beating within her.

They lay that way for some minutes, unwilling to part. At last, he shifted to one side, thrusting a pillow under his head and gazing at her.

"I do truly adore you. I will cherish and protect you the rest of my life."

He lightly twined her fingers in his and rested his head above hers. She took that hand and kissed his fingers, pressing her face against it.

He rose and walked to his closet, and she relished the decadent pleasure of observing him naked. "Are you sleepy?"

She shook her head, unsurprised by his abrupt change of subject. "I am utterly content."

He retrieved a dressing gown and a thick flannel shirt from his closet and slipped on the gown. "Are you hungry?"

"Not particularly. What is there?"

He lit a candle beside the cart and removed the silver covers from the dishes. "Ah! A loaf of bread, sliced turkey, cranberry sauce, potatoes, yams, that 'green bean casserole' thing she makes, slices of pie, and—how I worship that woman! Her home-rolled pasta and cheese."

"Home-rolled pasta and cheese?"

"Yes, she makes these tiny noodles and mixes them with cheese and bakes it all until it's rich and toothsome and chewy and... you must ask her for the recipe. No one else in the entire American colonies knows of this. I might never need visit Boston again if you learn how to make it."

"It's macaroni and cheese! Thomas Jefferson invented it."

"I beg your pardon, Mrs. Adams invented it. And she would never have named it after those pretentious fops."

She laughed. "Different macaroni. And the Italians invented it, but you're right, since Jefferson hasn't even visited Europe yet, to my knowledge."

He stabbed a forkful and ate it. "'Tis delicious even cold."

"Well, let me heat it on the stove." Marley donned the flannel shirt he'd left for her—it made for a cozy robe.

She placed the gravy and casserole and yams on the small stove to warm. She couldn't get the mac and cheese away from him to heat. The loaf had been sliced in thick, aromatic slabs— *thank you, Camisha*—and she set slices out on a plate, spreading one slice with cranberry sauce, then topping that with slices of turkey and dressing.

While she waited for the gravy to heat, she peered at the mac and cheese. He held it out, offering to share.

"No, I was just looking at it. It's all handmade." She marveled at what must have taken Camisha hours. She had known the hardships of women in the eighteenth century, had spoken of it in tours of the old town, back in her old life. But it was striking to see firsthand. "What a demonstration of love."

A small smile went over her face as she observed his bliss. "How often do you eat that?"

"Two, three times a year, if I'm lucky. Why?"

"Do you love it that much?"

"This is perhaps my favorite food."

She laughed in delight.

"What? 'Tis quite good, you know."

"It's just that in my time, children love it, and there's so much about you that's boyish. Adults do, too. I was just thinking … where I grew up, you can buy a box of the stuff at the store for a couple of dollars and have it ready for eight people in ten minutes. The pasta, I mean. You have to add the cheese and bake it, still. It had to have taken her hours to make just the pasta."

He searched her face, attempting to understand as she went on. "In my life, we had so many conveniences. You can buy a meal entirely prepared and frozen at the grocery store, and heat it up and be eating five minutes later. Our entire world is disposable."

"How tasty is that kind of meal? Is it like a seaman's food?"

She laughed. "Oh, about as tasty as it sounds—although it's generally worm-free. We are in such a rush to do the meaningless that we gladly relinquish the moments, the experiences, that matter. We spend an hour in a car getting to work. An hour at night, getting home from work. And after fifty years of this kind of living, we look around and wonder what happened."

"What's a car?"

"Oh, no no no. Another time. Tonight … do you really have to wear that robe?"

He looked down at himself, then at the elegantly set cart, bemused. "I'm not an animal."

She laughed at his sense of decorum.

The corner of his mouth hooked as his eyes sparkled at her. "Do you realize how ludicrous I would look, sitting here at my table eating, entirely disrobed?"

"Ludicrous is the wrong word. Luscious, you mean."

He poked his fork toward her with an eyebrow raised. "For such a shy and retiring lass, you have a tiny streak of the libertine."

"How my grandmother would howl at that."

"Why so?"

The gravy was warm, and she considered her answer as she made his sandwich.

"She only meant well, she merely found the idea of my having any other dimension beyond that of an historian and a bookworm, well, downright comical."

She dribbled gravy over the turkey and dressing, topped it with the other slice of bread, and sliced it in two. Scooping out some vegetables, she placed it before him and poured herself a glass of wine.

She walked to the dresser, slipping the pillbox and its chain back over her head. "Almost forgot."

"I'm quite sure your grandmother must be a delightful matron to have raised you—not to mention charming my own father. But ... I do not yet see it. What is this, by the way?"

"It's a Thanksgiving sandwich."

He smiled patiently. "Yes, and delicious indeed. I've never tasted anything finer."

"Oh, you mean—" she held up her pillbox. "This, sir, is a silver repousse pillbox. Don't ask me what it means."

"I can tell you. A jeweler—or a talented smith—works on the back side of a piece, hammering out the tiny details of a design in relief. But what's inside it?"

She opened it and showed him the miniature. "This is my sister, Rachel. It was done the last year we were together. My grandmother gave it to me, not long before the storm."

"She has hair like you, though darker."

"I saw her today."

"What? Here at Rosalie?"

She recounted to him the events of the day, skipping Rachel's mention of the death of Bronson's mother. He was intent on her, his face showing a skepticism she still couldn't blame him for—even when she described seeing his own brother.

"You don't believe me."

He briefly searched for words. "It is not that I don't believe you. 'Tis you, someone I trust completely, telling me something I've always known—or thought—to be impossible.

If you told me men can indeed sprout natural wings and fly, and have always been able to, it could not be stranger."

"The Fourth of July. Your thirtieth birthday. You will see this country declare its independence then. I will be with you to celebrate. If you wish to see it firsthand, we need to be in Philadelphia, at Carpenter's Hall."

A distance entered his gaze briefly, until he refocused his attention on his sandwich. Then he set it back in the silver plate, covering it. "That's a goodly portion of food. I'm saving the rest for later."

He drank from his wineglass. After a moment, she realized he was uneasy, and her mention of his birthday had brought it on.

Not tonight. And let him be the one to mention it.

She touched the back of his hand lightly. When his eyes met hers, she sent him a look of reassurance. Then she rose, slipped out of his shirt, then removed his dressing gown and put it away.

As he stoked the fire, she crossed to hang the garments in his closet. She turned and caught him watching her, and she smiled. "Has Camisha told you about tryptophan?"

He laughed, walking to her in easy confidence. "I'll let you rest, but I can't imagine myself sleeping tonight." He kissed her forehead and cupped her hips, drawing her full-length against his nakedness. "Come and lie with me."

He snuffed the candle at the table then crossed to the bed and lay down first, then drew her down into his arms. They found a comfortable position, and she rubbed her face against his chest, just below his collarbone.

"Would you rather I didn't tell you such things? Perhaps it's better that way. Earlier, I was only attempting to show you it's true. I can't explain it, but it's true."

"Tell me all you wish. I am a man full grown, I need no protection. I wish for nothing to ever be between us. You are my wife, my heart. The truth is, I can't imagine a more awful, fearsome burden to bear than yours. What if I ask you a question each night about the future, and you answer it? And other than that, you tell me what you need to, when you want to. And in exchange, I shall tell you something I've learned, in this time."

She nodded. Several minutes passed as he caressed her—lightly, tenderly, still learning the curves and hollows of her body.

"Ah. So as not to surprise you, tomorrow we must travel into Williamsburg."

"Why?"

He chuckled at her whine. "I don't wish to leave our sanctuary, either. But I'll not have my wife outfitted in Rashall's mother's old clothes, or dear God traipsing about my ship in my baggy old breeches. And we'll be back here by tomorrow evening."

"But I can't move around on this ship in all those silly skirts women wear today."

He hesitated, and she knew what he was about to say.

"No," she said, with resolute force. "I will not stay behind. You told me you would never leave my side. And you need me to help. If you don't let me go, I'll stow away."

For a time, he declined to respond. He lay, still stroking her absently, as if neither of them had spoken.

"I shall bring along my tankard. An added incentive."

He exhaled in a comical snort. "Well. Then the argument is at an end."

Something in his voice gave her pause. "Do you resent me doing what I did with Falligan?"

He looked off at his closet. "I resent your having had to. You get in the way of that resentment at times. 'Twas not your fault, and in truth I owe you my life."

"Yes, you do." She lightly kissed the base of his throat, where she felt his pulse.

"Very well." He sighed in resignation. "A sailing we shall go."

She beamed with pleasure, inhaling in excitement, hugging him hard.

"Bronson?"

"Aye."

"What does the posy say? In my ring?"

After a moment, he murmured with odd stiffness, "Ah. Providence divine hath made me thine."

She looked up at him. "Doesn't that old posy go the other way? 'hath made thee mine'?"

"That, only you can say. That I am thine, I know to be true." This, he said with his usual inflection.

For another long moment, she gazed at him, until he looked down from his random perusal of the ceiling to meet her eyes.

"All right, 'tis a falsehood. Dear God, I tremble at how well you know me. I cannot even tell you the whitest of lies."

"Well, the second part didn't sound like a lie."

"That's because I did come quite close to using that exact engraving, and for that reason. I am thine indeed, and God wrought that."

His words moved her, and she tried to find a way to explain to him all that he had come to mean to her. But he went on.

"However, I did not. Instead I used one that's perhaps less romantic, but the dearest truth in my heart. 'Memento mori.'"

"Remember ... death?"

He nodded silently.

For perhaps a minute she didn't speak. What a grim motto to consider one's dearest truth.

"What on earth does that mean?"

"'Tis how I live this life. It means each moment we share—all of us here—is stolen from the grave. None of us is immortal."

And if his earlier reaction to her mention of his thirtieth birthday weren't enough proof, then she knew now that he took seriously the so-called curse. She held her tongue, uncertain yet the most polite way to attempt to tell the brilliant man she loved that his long-held superstitions were rubbish. For now, it did not matter.

***"I have loved you more since the moment I saw you, plummeting into the depths of the ocean below me, than many men love in a lifetime. I have seen the same joy for life in you. We are not promised tomorrow, Merrilea. And so, today, we live. We *live*. This moment for me is the warmth and softness of you in my arms, the river rustling outside, the smell of the hickory fire keeping us warm, the faint aroma of that dismal whale oil that never leaves this ship, the smell of the turkey gravy, the memory of that sandwich—savory, tart, sweet, all the flavors of all foods in a few bites—and the enflaming memory of the flavor of you. The fulsome joy within me to love a woman so singular and unique, with a smile to break my heart—and to be loved by you. And, yes, the warmth of your tears on my chest now.

"My beloved. Only by remembering that our lifeblood drains away as we speak can we truly wring life dry. Never forget that death awaits us all. For only then can we live."

She lay with her head near his heart, absently rubbing the gold symbols on his necklace, and she vowed that she would rid him of his fear of death. And she vowed that she would let him teach her how to live.

They lay awake that night, their first night together as husband and wife, and told their secrets. They laughed over silly exploits, and they talked of disappointment. They made love again, they napped and woke up making love, and they ate once more before she rolled the cart into the hallway, telling him he was going to die of food poisoning if he didn't desist eating day-old stuffing.

That night, that was the question he asked about the future. What did tomorrow's wise men know about illnesses and injuries and how to prevent death? The poignant question made her wonder where his curiosity lay—was it merely scientific, or did he worry about his own fate?

She explained germs and bacteria and viruses. She explained vaccinations and antibiotics that had been invented and overused to a nearly catastrophic point, within less than a century. She explained the smallpox inoculation process that Camisha had used. And she explained, with deliberate purpose, that science had abandoned many of its superstitions, such as evil spirits causing disease. She didn't consider using the word *curse*. She knew she didn't have to. Perhaps it was a start.

He thought long and hard about what he'd learned that was worthy of first sharing on this night where memories had come to be celebrated and made. At last, he took her hand in his and said, "You can push yourself much further—and much farther—than you think you can. Long after others have given up, you see, you in fact can go on. Try it tomorrow and see."

"For example?"

"Anything. Treading water. Swimming. Running. Solving a puzzle. Achieving truly anything you seek to achieve, whether it be physical, mental, emotional, or spiritual."

"Holding your breath."

"Exactly."

"Bronson?" she whispered sleepily.

"Mhm?"

"I know I was dying when you rescued me. My parents had come to take me on. I'm certain of that."

He knew that too well. Silently, slowly, he crushed her to him, kissing the top of her head.

Thank God, he thought, *that they did not*.

At length, she whispered, "Say it to me again, so I don't forget."

"You can push yourself much further than you think you can."

And when they finally went to sleep, deep in the night, they still held one another—refusing, even in slumber, to leave a single moment unlived.

Chapter Thirty-Six

In the end, their Indian summer interlude passed, as do all best-loved moments in time. As does all time, loved and fondly remembered—or despised, its passing celebrated. It ended, not with a fall of snow, but with a call from Big Dan for a family meeting in the meeting house.

They met on the last evening before the *Adventurer* was to sail for Bermuda for more gunpowder, and it was only a fluke that Bronson and Marley were at Rosalie. They had planned to head to Williamsburg to determine whether Thomas, now completely smitten with his newly found old love, had any interest in returning to the loyalist island. Bronson himself had begun to wonder whether even the fortune he'd left buried behind was worthy of returning for. He was certain he had the contacts to eke out another hold full of gunpowder for the patriot cause, but that required only a few hours there. With all the faults and sins of the bastard republic to which they were about to give birth, he was certain defending the patriots' cause was the right course.

They left the wagon outside the meeting house as they entered, and when Marley saw an unfamiliar frontier man standing at the front of the group, her heart sank. This was no ordinary frontier man. Instinctively, she clutched Bronson's elbow, holding him back.

The grim, ruddy-faced, ginger-haired stranger stood ramrod stiff beside Dan, holding a long rifle, its butt planted squarely on the plank floor. He wore ankle-length trousers and a light brown hunting shirt emblazoned with the words LIBERTY OR DEATH. In his free hand he carried a leather hat.

This man, she knew, was a member of the famous Culpeper Minutemen, the Virginia company of the colonial militia that would soon dissolve into the Continental Army. They were much feared for their fierceness.

Bronson instinctively headed forward, but Marley dug her fingernails into his arm, and he stopped, glancing at her meaningfully. He bowed low and extended his hand as if it were simply a matter of gentlemanly manners. *You forward or me forward, we go forward together.*

Reluctantly, she found the seat she knew he would've chosen, near the front. Rashall soon joined them there, followed by Camisha and Ashanti. Parks no doubt had stayed behind to keep Shonny entertained.

Presently, Dan called the meeting to order with a prayer, then continued. "Most of us have heard of the British forces at Great Bridge. Tonight we are joined by Captain Nathaniel James, whose company travels through Rosalie tonight on their way to the battle. Captain James asks us for our support as we are moved by Providence. Captain James?"

"Aye, I thank you kindly. As you all know, my own wretched former countryman, the thief and knave John Murray, Lord Dunmore, purloined from our colony last April the gunpowder rightfully belonging to us. He has akin to a small fleet in Norfolk, and 'twas there, after the gunpowder incident, that he fled like the coward he is.

"Now, he's done the very thing he knows will cause chaos, with his proclamation of martial law, and the freeing of any slave willing to join him."

At this point, the burly man inhaled deeply and chose his words to the almost entirely black audience with care. "In freeing the Americans who were held enslaved, he inflamed the countryside. Everyone, certainly everyone in this room, knows this man has no interest in the freedom of anyone in the American colonies. England will do what it can to keep us all in chains."

The crowd was restless but attentive.

"We need your help, with whatever you have. If you can join us in our fight, God bless you. As you likely know, we are most in need of ammunition and anything to defend our land. I believe most of you are farmers, but then, so are we. If you hunt to feed your family, if you own a rifle or a musket and know to use it, we ask you to consider joining us."

He looked around at the room. No one responded.

"We have heard back from the lines that Dunmore's forces are now perhaps a thousand. Including the Culpeper Minutemen and Colonel Woodford's Second Virginia Regiment of the Continental Army, we have less than half that. We are hoping for help from other militias, but we yet have no promises. North Carolina is expected to join us soon."

Marley noticed Bronson and Rashall conferring, and she met Camisha's worried eyes behind their heads.

The two men stood together. "We and our ship's crew will join you," Ray said. "We can also transport men, if that helps."

Bronson said, "We have a dozen new rifles we can donate to the cause, if you have the men trained to use them. Our own men are adequately armed. There are between two and three dozen men available."

"Thank you, sir. We expect to be there in less than two days' time."

"I'll join the boys," Ashanti said, raising his hand briefly but remaining seated by his wife, holding her hand. At this point, her head was lowered, her eyes closed, her lips pressed tightly together.

Rashall and Bronson returned to their seats, and the floodgates opened. Marley watched the drama in the meeting-house as loved ones reacted to stoic volunteers. Although lighting from the lamps and candles was poor, she could not have missed the same tight-lipped worry from each wife, each mother, as she'd seen in Camisha.

In these women seemingly always left behind, she saw the same silent forbearance that their mothers and grandmothers had learned over the past century and a half. For herself, she felt nauseated with fear, and yet she knew the only acceptable response was silence and, perhaps, faith.

She scarcely heard when Bronson gave the departure time for all those who would travel with them. The ship was still comfortably laden with stores from the last trip, and no one expected the battle to last long—for good or ill.

Dan led the assembly in a closing hymn, and then in a prayer.

At the door of the meeting house, Bronson and Rashall were besieged by volunteers, and Marley had no choice but to go with Camisha. As she left Bronson's side, he gave her an encouraging smile.

The older woman put her arm around her as they walked, and they joined Ruth back at her home. Dan, as the spiritual leader of the Trelawney clan, was expected to watch over those left behind while the men were gone, but that responsibility didn't make it easier for him.

"I should be with them," he said, from the bottom of the steps. "At least I can help them load any necessary supplies."

Ruth spoke sharply to him. "Promise me you don't get on that boat. How are two hundred women and children going to take care of themselves with not one single man to protect us?"

He sighed and gave a slow nod. "I promise."

And then he, too, was gone.

As the women entered the kitchen and began to slice bread to make baskets and baskets of sandwiches, Ruth spoke, pointing toward the parlor across the way. "Marley, I forgot all about it, but the dressmaker delivered your wardrobe this afternoon. He said Captain Hawk expedited the order, and they've had seamstresses working day and night the whole week."

She looked across the hall, where dozens of boxes were stacked. She opened one, and her heart ached.

The buckskin was soft underneath her fingers, and she withdrew it, placing it across the back of the chesterfield. It was the sort of outfit she'd always dreamed of, something that suited her and probably no other woman alive. It was just as practical as it was cute. The milliner had even included a bit of fringe at the edge of the short dress.

In a smaller box next to it were the moccasins Bronson had made for her, which they'd used as a pattern, and two other, sturdier pairs, with soles. Also in the box was a leather hat made according to her requirements. It resembled the hat their speaker that night had carried—similar to a cowboy hat, but without any molding. A detachable wool lining made it workable in any weather. And in the back were two features she expected to find handy: a small snood, fastened securely to contain her hair, and just below that, a concealed hole, underneath a flap that buttoned closed, should she prefer to let a ponytail out in warmer weather.

Before she could stop herself, she closed the parlor door and dressed in the buckskin dress that ended at her knees and trousers that went to her ankles. She rifled through the boxes until she found a pair of warm socks, slipped them on, then put on her old moccasins. Impulsively, she brought the newer moccasins as well, slipping them into a handbag that would make a decent possibles bag. It might be helpful if she had to walk far. She folded the hat and placed it in the bag as well.

A knock came at the door just as she was folding her other clothes and placing them into the empty box.

She opened the door, and Camisha inhaled with a grim smirk. "Well, hello there, Sacajawea."

She gulped. "I'm going with them."

"Like hell you are. You'll only be in the way."

"Camisha, I can't stay behind. I know something about Bronson."

"Don't tell me you believe that ridiculous curse nonsense?"

"You know the only thing that matters is that he believes it. Wait—you know about that, too?"

"I met the crazy bitch who raised his mother—Jennie, you know? You remember Rachel talking about her? Well, the woman who raised Jennie used to visit Williamsburg after Jennie died. She happened to be here one time we visited. She turned Thomas into a raving lunatic. He'd thought she didn't believe in the curse, but then she started giving him more details about it, and with everything he'd seen happen—Grey's death, Emily's death, and Jennie's death—he soon came to believe in it. She claimed to be wracked with guilt because she'd never told Jennie about the curse."

"How old was Jennie?"

"Somewhere in her mid-twenties."

"Camisha, you know how stupid this is. Hell, people die young all the time anyway. Between the smallpox and the oil lamps giving off God knows what toxins, it's a miracle anyone lives to adulthood. And I'll find a way—when he's ready—to make sure he understands that it isn't any imaginary curse, but just a self-fulfilling prophecy. But for now, I need to be with him, no matter what."

For the moment, she realized, she wasn't ready to share the story of the Lost Sea Captain, not even with Camisha.

The older woman rubbed her neck, her mouth tight. "All right," she said at last, with reluctant acceptance. "I'm not going to stop you anyway, I guess. But you have to listen to what he says, and do what he tells you to do."

"Do you suppose Dan might have a powder horn and a measure he'd loan me?"

Camisha gave her an exasperated look. "Child, you are running right out of favors. We can't ask him, he'd never let you. Let me see if Ruth would know."

They found these items—but it was tougher work to find spares. She couldn't leave him without the tools to load his gun. But eventually she found what she needed and slipped it into her possibles bag, then secured that at her waist.

She got to work. Soon they were loading a spare wagon with the baskets of food, and Little Dan's eldest son volunteered to take her to the ship.

He started to help her climb into the wagon, but she shook her head. "Better get used to getting around on my own!"

As they started off, she asked him his name.

"Dan, ma'am, like my father and his father."

"So if they're Big Dan and Little Dan, what does that make you?" she teased.

He laughed. "I know they're both big, but my mama says I'm going to be bigger than both of them. So maybe I'll be Bigger Dan."

They laughed together. When she reminded him of the importance of his job taking care of the women, his mouth went tight. "Oh, you want to go, too. How old are you?"

"I'll be thirteen, come February."

Her eyes went wide. "Then I can see why they chose you to stay behind."

He shot her a skeptical glance.

"You don't look your age. You look much older. You'll be a good protector, a leader with your father of those left behind. Why do you think you were chosen to take me to the ship? I'm the wife of the ship's captain, and we're delivering important provisions for the battle. Can you think of a more important job anybody back at home could be doing right now?"

He looked at her with new respect. "Thank you, ma'am. I'm doing my best to keep you safe."

"I know you will. When you pass out these sandwiches, I want you to tell the men to eat heartily, and be strengthened for their battle. This will help build their courage when they face the enemy. Can you do that, Daniel?"

With this new, more manly assignment, he sat up even straighter in the seat and clicked the horses to a trot. "Yes, ma'am, and I will."

As they approached the ship, Marley withdrew the hat from her bag. She hastily wound her hair into a knot and hid it within the snood, then pulled the hat down firmly, settling its brim to a place where it comfortably concealed her face. Daniel (as he henceforth referred to himself) checked himself when he otherwise would've handed her down. Instead, he followed her directions and took charge of the contents of the wagon. He opened up the wagon to distribute the baskets of sandwiches.

"Eat up, men! Eat hearty, and be strengthened for your battle." He soundly patted each man on the shoulder in turn.

Marley jumped down from the wagon, glancing around for Bronson, but he was nowhere to be seen.

She hastened up the gangway and over the gunwale, where she was promptly arrested.

"Why, good evening."

Her starched spine wilted. She tilted her head back and looked into Bronson's unamused gaze. For talking with this guy, this hat was no better than that ridiculous cap she'd had to wear as a cabin boy.

He bowed with all due respect, then pulled her so far up into the bow, she thought he might mount her as a figurehead. And then she recalled the purpose served by this part of the ship. She screwed up her face in distaste at the smell of the head. "*Sir!*" she protested.

"Madam," he retorted. "You are no less desirable in that outfit than you are in a shift."

"I am fully covered and entirely modest and I am not having this argument right now."

"On that much we are agreed, because you're going back to the Adamses, who will have charge of you until I return."

"But you promised."

"I doubt for a second you thought that meant I would allow you to go with me into battle."

She hesitated. "All right, then. Please make me a promise."

"If I can. I will not lie to comfort you."

"Stay out of your cabin."

"Why?"

"I can't tell you."

He waved a hand distractedly. "I would not be *in* my cabin as a matter of course, during battle. But, yes. This promise I will keep."

"Bronson, please let me come. I can shoot a musket, I can shoot out a squirrel's eye from 200 yards with a rifle."

She did not admit that this was true only of a paper squirrel. She had never killed even a pesky animal—let alone a human being.

His voice lowered. "I do not know the kind of muskets and rifles they have in your pampered time, but these require mastery."

"These are exactly what I learned to shoot with—it was part of my job. I've shot with actual antique rifles from this time. And 200 yards is *twice* as far as the most accomplished athlete of my time can run with a stupid football and be a millionaire!"

His face went slack with confusion as she overwhelmed him with the trivial measure of a man in the twenty-first century, but he was unmoved.

"If you don't have enough guns, I can load for others. I can even make paper cartridges, if you have the paper."

"How do you even know about paper—why do I ask. No. Take these mysterious talents and go home and protect Mrs. Adams, that I may remove you from the cares of my mind."

The sweeping condescension, his utter dismissal of the idea that she might be useful to him in battle, angered her.

"Oh, all right!"

She stomped away from him and down the gangway, then disappeared into the crowd surrounding the wagon. She moved to the other side of the wagon and sank down to watch Bronson until he finally turned away, responding to a question from another man. Both headed abaft.

She hesitated only a moment, pondering what she was about to do. She respected him and knew the last thing he needed was a distraction. But he had no way of knowing her competence with a firearm. She understood what it was like to work under pressure. Jimmy had certainly taught her psychological warfare.

Still, she thought how little he had asked of her, and how much she yearned for his trust. How much he would need to rely on it—whether he understood it or not.

Reluctantly, she turned away and began to walk back toward the cabins.

"Good sir!"

The call came when she'd walked perhaps thirty yards away, and she turned.

It was Captain James, calling her.

"Yes, sir?" she asked, turning back.

"You shall not desert, this early in the game. Board with the rest."

"But, sir, you don't understand. I—"

"Nor do I care. Go on now."

"Yes, sir."

With that, she raced along the gangway and boarded, then immediately slipped down a hatch. She caught the ladder almost in afterthought as she hurried down, then a few steps on the next deck, then down again, and again, and again, into the hold.

She prayed her husband would forgive her. In the end, she had no choice.

She would help him, as best she could.

Chapter Thirty-Seven

The ship was underway only a few minutes later, slicing through the cold waters of the James, downriver toward Norfolk. Even with her eyes closed, Marley could hear rats rustling and squealing. The place was dank and musty and very nearly lightless. In thin strips of lantern light coming from the hatch, she saw a selection of casks, no doubt some containing foodstuffs, should their battle drag on, and some containing gunpowder.

She crossed to one, tried to move it, and failed. Some kind of salted meat, or perhaps rum. She tried several others before she was able to budge a cask without hearing any internal liquid. She withdrew her knife, and carefully pried open the lid.

Rich, faintly aromatic powder filled the cask.

She located a scoop and carefully filled the powder horn, then closed it and settled it at her waist. She saw a long, more narrow crate and pried it open, sighing loudly when she spotted three rifles. She knew that most of the men at Rosalie—indeed, any colonial family—likely owned their own guns for shooting food for their families, so perhaps Bronson's offer of firearms had been unnecessary. She withdrew the rifle from the crate and carried it closer to the hatch, admiring its beauty and its craftsmanship. Then she returned to the long crate and closed it, laying the rifle atop it.

From another box she was able to find balls, and settled a generous supply of these in her bag. Finally, she was able to find a cloth that she cut into small squares for patches, using her knife and the muzzle of the rifle to get the size right.

When she was certain she had a supply to last her through the night—no soldier could carry an unlimited amount of ammunition—she found a dry corner away from the food and took a quick nap. When she awakened she thought she'd slept only a few minutes, but she regretted the nap, because she wasn't sure. She could've been asleep for ten minutes or for two hours. At least, the ship was still moving.

Why was everything so quiet?

She loaded her rifle and crept up the stairs nervously. The next deck contained cables, and was deserted, illuminated by only a single whale oil lamp.

Men were positioned at the next deck, behind cannons. And as she hesitated, peering around, someone grabbed her from behind, covering her mouth with one hand and divesting her of her rifle with the other.

"Why are you here?"

The angry whisper in her ear filled her with relief and terror. As he removed his hand from her mouth to grab her waist, he pointed her back to the hatch.

"Be careful, it's loaded," she whispered.

"Down."

She skipped down to the cable tier in four steps. He took it in two. She backed away from him instinctively, tripping over a gigantic cable and landing against a wall.

"I sent you to Rosalie. Why are you here?"

"I was leaving, and Captain James stopped and accused me of desertion. I had no choice."

He continued moving toward her. Only faint light showed, lighting his cheekbones and the curve of his jaw. His eyes and his mouth were in shadow. "Can you in fact hit a target at 200 yards?"

"Yes."

He moved closer. "Are you sure James had no idea you're a woman?"

Now, feeling his heat within inches of her, her fear melted away into hunger. Still, his anger at her left her uncertain. She could not bear his rejection.

"Yes."

"Is he blind?"

He lowered his head, his mouth hovering over hers—she tasted his breath, felt his urgent need. He skimmed his hand lightly along the lacings on her dress, then cupped her breast—the soft leather was far too thick. She lifted her breasts in supplication to him, lifted her lips in invitation—and he drew back.

"Are you quite aware of what you're feeling right now?"

"I need you—very much."

"Excellent. *That* is what I feel when I see you in this. I need my wits about me in battle—not occupied in imagining ways to have you on the cables."

Her hands rose to his chest, lightly scratching. "It would only take a minute, I promise."

He stepped away from her. With the butt of the rifle firmly on the deck, he leaned the muzzle toward her.

She was stung, and she took the rifle dejectedly as he made for the ladder. Then he walked the few steps back and pressed his lips hard to hers. "But know that you *will* be punished for that, most emphatically. Next time, consider what you're doing before you toy with a live round."

He rubbed her bottom, then lightly patted it before he strode away.

The *Adventurer* sailed down the James and into the Elizabeth River. They followed the river nearly to Great Bridge, anchoring offshore. The number of men who'd traveled with them filled the landing boat several times, but soon they were all safely ashore.

Marley looked back at the ship, filled with a sense of foreboding. The land and its terrain was different in these days, and even lacking simple landmarks, it was difficult to get her bearings. She had traveled this area frequently all her life—both as a child with her parents and in her experience with the *Adventurer* dig.

This Elizabeth River was astonishing in its newness and purity. And yet, she knew, as they had passed through the harbor town, that already the estuary was beginning a pattern of decline that within 240 years would leave its toxic floor entirely lifeless.

Still, she knew by its simple location in the river that this was the location where this ship would be destroyed. Whether today or another day, this was where the *Adventurer* met its end.

She had no idea how any of them would find their way home—but she was relieved when the ship was empty and the last of them had made it to shore. The Great Bridge Battle, after all, had no major patriot casualties; for that, she was blessedly thankful.

The *Adventurer*, however, originally had. She would have been unsettled at the idea that she was changing history—except that history was far better off with Bronson around.

She glanced about, noticing on the far shore another ship. In the dark night, little was visible but the stars—and a few lamps flickering on the warship. The Royal Navy.

"Marley."

At Bronson's urgent whisper she turned, hurrying to catch up to him. He'd gone perhaps just ten feet without her while she gazed at the ship, but his face, drawn and tense, anchored her in the present. They weren't exactly on a church picnic.

So what if American fatalities hadn't appeared in history's reports of the Great Bridge battle that she'd grown up with? she thought, sobering. Neither had she appeared in that time.

Focus, for heaven's sake. Memento mori. Not a bad motto to live by, after all.

Her breath escaped her in the cold, and she was grateful for the long-sleeved, lined flannel shirt Bronson had retrieved from his cabin and placed over her. His purpose had been to disguise an outfit he found arousing, despite its long hem and trousers. But it gave her an added insulation as well as warming her with his faint scent. There were some perks to a place where doing laundry was so inconvenient.

The surreal scenery around her captured her attention. The sulfurous smell of the salt marshes lingered in the humid December morning. The sweeping silence was unnerving as the hundred men trudged away from the river and through the weeds. She knew that up ahead lay a battle scene plotted out by the opposing military leaders: on their side, one Colonel William Woodford; on the other, Captains Leslie and Fordyce.

They reached the camp in another hour and joined the ranks. In the distance, she heard the orders being given in an English accent, and her blood stirred with adrenaline and pride at the reminder of where she stood. The first battle of the American revolution on Virginia soil was the Battle at Great Bridge. Virginia, the mother of presidents, the birthplace of a nation.

By the time the sun began to rise over the Chesapeake Bay, the men of Virginia had been engaged without result by the British Army's grenadiers. The Brits had retreated back over the bridge, and Virginia had lined up behind its entrenchments. Several cannons were lined up there.

Finally, when visibility improved, the musket fire began. Marley walked to the edge of the camp, then peeked out for a better view.

A cannon boomed from the other side, and Bronson rushed out to grab her back behind him.

"Stay here."

"Like hell."

"I'll return posthaste."

She snorted. "You can't shoot and fight me, and you might as well realize that now. I *will help*."

He shot her an angry glance.

They joined Rashall at the entrenchment, and he made room for them in the line of men along the dirt barricade.

"We'll never reach them with musket fire at this distance," Marley said.

"Well, thank you, General Pocahontas."

"Must everyone make fun of my outfit?"

Bronson glanced at the line of big guns. "Why aren't we firing our cannons? Where are the carriages—Ah. The smoke clears."

"Some blockhead left both mountings and carriages behind. The guns are there to intimidate."

"Hope they remembered shot for the muskets."

After perhaps another five minutes, Woodford directed the riflemen off to the left. Marley followed in that direction, and Bronson grabbed her.

"Can you tell me why we're here, if not to help?" she asked.

Rashall glanced at him. When Bronson merely glared back at him, he shrugged and returned to reloading his musket. "'Tis a fair question, is it not?"

Bronson sighed and headed in the direction of the Culpeper men, knowing he need not direct her to follow.

They crouched into position, and Marley aimed her rifle, hesitating a moment. She had never once fired a gun toward a human being. She knew that if it hit true, the ball inside this rifle was likely to kill a man.

While she struggled with herself, a cannon fired, and a ball whooshed directly above Bronson's head. They all crouched, and the ball fell far behind them.

Marley came back to her knees, aimed at the gunner controlling one of the cannons, and fired. The gunner went down. She spun the chambers, quickly scanned the cannons for their progress, and fired again. Another casualty.

"Holy—" Bronson's exclamation echoed those of the men who spared her a startled glance.

Trembling, she scrambled out of the line to allow another rifleman to move into position while she reloaded. Her gaze strayed toward the men she'd shot. One was on the ground, cradling his arm. Another lay still on the ground beside him.

The minutemen had brought a good supply of paper

cartridges, and so the balls she'd brought remained merely a weight in her bag.

She reloaded, returned to the line, aimed at another gunner, and fired. She aimed for hands, but people rarely stood still during a battle. More than once someone stepped into the line of fire, and once she watched, sickhearted, as she hit a man square in the chest.

After her second time at the line, other men began offering their rifles for her use and reloading for her instead while she shot.

Surprised at their humility, she continued shooting, taking down one gunner after another.

Presently, a ball came whistling past her ear, and Bronson threw her to the ground, his eyes wild as he landed atop her.

"Get the shirt off. You're as vivid a target as those lobster-backs." He quickly pulled the maroon flannel shirt over her head and threw it to the bottom of the entrenchment.

She pulled her hat back in place and crawled into a crouch, lower now, her gun even with the top of the entrenchment. She aimed, she relaxed, and she fired.

Aim. Relax. Fire. Aim. Relax. Fire. Aim …

Marley's hand shook. She tried to steady herself, then aimed again. More shaking. Relaxing was impossible. She moved away from the entrenchment to allow another man to take her place.

She felt lightheaded, nauseated.

She scrambled behind a tree and vomited. She glanced back at the line, noticing Bronson eyeing her. She gave a short wave and nod, reassuring him she was fine. She collapsed against the tree, trying to catch her breath. Then she quickly crawled back to his side.

"All well?"

"I don't think I can shoot for a bit."

"Stay at my side. Look! They're spiking their guns," he shouted.

Marley peeked over the entrenchment. Sure enough, the gunners were hammering spikes into the touch holes, disabling the guns—at least temporarily.

Surrender. The battle was over. A loud cheer went up.

Rashall arrived with laughing glee. "Scarcely enough time to finish shaving and breakfast." He looked down at Marley. "You look green. Too much for you?"

She gave him a pale smile.

"Quiet." This from Bronson.

Rashall glanced back at him. Then he walked away after a simple pat of encouragement on her back. "See all of you back at the ship. I'll begin boarding and preparing to weigh anchor."

Bronson casually sank to sit in the dirt beside her, now holding her rifle as well as his.

"You're a better shot than I am," he said at last, with a small chuckle. "Not sure how I feel about that."

She smiled. "I got to learn how to do it at my old job. Then I got to teach people how to."

"What else did you do?"

"I'm an archaeologist. And a historian. I divided my time between digs and the duties related to them, and spent most of the rest of my time lecturing about how people lived in the past."

"And by the past, you mean *now*."

"Yes, I suppose."

Ashanti approached them, his handsome face grim. He stooped beside them, bracing his musket across his bent leg. He lay his hand on Marley's moccasin. "Merrilea, I know who you are."

She nodded, knowing Camisha would've allowed no secrets between them. "Of course."

He looked across at the British, then back at her. "As someone who has watched a woman with modern sensibilities living in these rude days, I can tell you it will be hard for you. If you have the choice, choose the way of your sister."

"Mr. Adams, my wife belongs with me." This from Bronson with quiet assertion. "We are together until death."

He nodded. "Your brother recognized he could do more through his own death than through staying here."

"Grey did not die," she said. "He was only thought to die."

Ashanti looked at his musket. "That I do not know."

"I saw him. I saw him through the portal in Rosalie, a man as old as you and Camisha, there with my sister. He looked exactly like Thomas Trelawney looked in portraits done of him at the same age."

"I'm not here to argue. I am here to tell you that my Camisha is ten times as strong as any woman I've ever known, and this time is hard for her. Were it my choice, I would in a moment take her to a better time. This is an awful time for anyone."

"And yet the men and women who fight these wars will be remembered, some day, that they began a fight that would eventually afford freedom and equality to all."

Marley glanced at Bronson, startled at his clarity. He knew firsthand how his best friend was treated; he knew that a better country lay in the future; and he knew the many battles necessary to reach that place.

Ashanti reached to touch Marley's upper arm, then grip it with bracing encouragement. "I mean to strengthen you, child. To prepare you for the life you will lead here. I never even lived the life of ease Camisha describes to me—turn a faucet, clean water is delivered; press a button, your home is warmed; press another, your home is cooled. It is beyond my frail understanding. You will miss it."

"Mr. Adams, I do appreciate that. But I grow used to this life. No minor convenience compares to the warmth of my husband's love."

He nodded. "Yes. And when you see your first child die because you can't fight an invisible enemy in his bloodstream, your husband will be the target of your anger and your sorrow."

"Then if I am ..." Bronson caught her hand in his. "I shall bear that anger and that sorrow for her, and I will do so gladly."

Ashanti sat back, contemplating them. "Then I shall pray for you both every day of my life, and I pray that my son finds in time the love that you share."

She came to her knees and gave him an impulsive hug. "Thank you, sir. We share that prayer for Rashall as well."

Ashanti nodded and rose.

"All well?"

She stood. "I think so."

The men were beginning to pack up their belongings, and as she followed Bronson and Ashanti toward the ship, she looked back at their morning's handiwork. The field was cluttered with dozens of British soldiers who lay dead or dying. On the bridge, the commanders were discussing terms of a truce to allow the British to remove their dead.

The nausea had transformed itself into a dark shadow abiding within her, and she didn't know how to rid herself of it. She remembered the ball flying just over Bronson's head, the shot whistling just over her own—yet that shadow remained.

When she looked back at Bronson, he watched her with steady, sober calm. He held out his hand to her and she put her hand there and followed him and Ashanti.

Captain James walked beside them.

"Sir, that laddie of yours is quite a shot."

In the early morning sunlight, his eyes sparkled with amusement.

"Captain, that's no laddie. That's my wife."

The redhead stopped in his tracks, shocked. The rest continued walking, and he gave up attempting to reply as he walked after them, his sensibilities shocked into silence. But the men nearby, including others from the Culpeper minutemen, cast her admiring looks.

Just as they reached the shore, a tremendous fireball rocked the ship. Seconds later, a second, terrible explosion followed. A noise arose from the men, and Bronson stared, dumbstruck.

Marley scanned the ship at the other shore.

But Ashanti screamed in a horrible sound. "Ray! *Rashall!*"

Then she saw. Nearing the other shore was their own boat, and thrown across a seat in that boat was Rashall, bound, gagged, and limp.

Ashanti dove into the water, and Bronson set his rifle aside and dove after him, stopping him.

Marley was more direct—aided by that unwelcome shadow that had materialized within her. She raised her rifle—which still contained an unspent round.

Even as she prepared to fire at the other man in the boat, he dragged Rashall's unresisting form across him. She had no clear shot. He climbed out of the boat, stumbling on the ground, and drug him toward the warship.

"Shoot out a window in the captain's cabin." Bronson said from his vantage point in the river. "Quickly, before he's inside."

She obeyed, unsure of his purpose.

Marley could not see the person within the bowels of the warship who had fired the deadly cannonade that had ignited the gunpowder on the *Adventurer*. But they all saw, clearly, the man who had abducted Rashall. He wore no uniform—simply the outfit of a farmer. He was large, with a powerful build; thick, white hair and a beard, both elegantly trimmed.

This man was no farmer.

Big Dan materialized to aid Bronson in pulling Ashanti out of the river.

They pulled him to shore, where he stood shaking with anger and fear and likely cold.

"What ship is that?" Dan asked.

"I know not. But you see the British ensign, and where that goes, the Ethiopian Regiment follows."

Marley shuddered.

"What is that?"

Ashanti answered Dan, choking out, "'Tis hundreds of men so desperate for freedom they'll believe the lies of those who enslaved them to begin with."

He shook the river water away, adding in tired resignation, "And I know the man who stole my son. The very dastard who tried to kill Camisha thirty years ago and who did in fact destroy Rosalie. James Manning. He may no longer be called by that name, but he is one and the same."

Chapter Thirty-Eight

Bronson cursed himself for the dozenth time for allowing Marley to come on this ill-fated trip. This was precisely the sort of complication he had feared.

Once they had wrapped Ashanti in a blanket to warm him from his icy dunking in the Elizabeth, and once he was collected enough to see reason, he, Bronson, and Dan consulted on their next steps. No one would leave this place without Rashall. They determined that Dan would lead the others on the long walk back to Rosalie; there simply were not enough horses to be found nearby to offer a better alternative. The sooner they headed northwest and reached Rosalie, the greater their chances of avoiding exposure.

Bronson was torn over which route for Marley might be less treacherous—trudging sixty miles with dozens of men, or staying here with him in the midst of warships. He didn't consider it long; he had no doubt she could take care of herself, but he could no more let her go than he could leap across this river to rescue Rashall.

Staying behind would be Ashanti, Marley, Bronson, and all of his men. Beyond having just watched their home and livelihood explode in front of them, their leader and brother had been taken captive, and not one of them would've obeyed an order sending him away.

"Cap'n Hawk, have ye forgot?"

Bronson, deeply distracted by Rashall's abduction, only stared blankly at the man who'd spoken.

Benjamin Crowell was his oldest sailor and still one of the best. In his fifties, he was wiry and wizened and wise. His earliest memories included this man, and he wouldn't trade him for a dozen younger sailors. And yet, Crowell hadn't sailed with him for years now. He had remained behind at Rosalie, paid by that sentimental old Hastings, keeping his charge, a nearly forgotten ship, scraped and oiled every day, just as if he was ready for his old captain to call "All hands on deck."

On her last ocean voyage, nearly thirty years before, she would have crossed many oceans to carry human souls into bondage in a strange land.

The old man seemed to read his misgivings. He bowed his head, cleared his throat, then looked up. "The demons of her past have been exorcised, sir. That, your brother had done before you were ever born. Along with the ongoing cleaning and sanding and scraping, we've had clergymen come and bless the ship, so she might be useful again." Again he bobbed his head, and when he looked up, Bronson saw the good heart that his own brother must have loved at one time. "We all want to feel useful, sir, even when we're old. Don't we owe old Cap'n Grey that much, for the good he did?"

The other men standing near him exchanged a look, and Bronson raised his eyebrows. "Well, Mr. Crowell, that we do. And in the end, we don't have much choice, do we?"

Excitedly, the man said with earnest conviction, "Sir, I make my vow, she's as seaworthy today as she was that awful day we lost the captain. Fact, she's more seaworthy. She's shiny and strong as a new snow."

He knew this ship better than anyone except the man who had built her, more than thirty-five years before. But that man had been gone nearly 30 years now. And during all those years, Crowell had cared for her like a doting swain.

"Very well, Mr. Crowell. Take your crew, and those riflemen. Deming, you lead the floating effort as well as the return. I expect you back within two days. If we aren't here, look for Dunmore's so-called Ethiopian Regiment.

"Beware, these channels are filled with British artillery. Brother Dan, if you could spare enough men to help support Crowell, I would be in your debt. Mr. Adams, will you be able to be calm here, or should you prefer to accompany Brother Dan and Mr. Crowell?"

This he disliked adding, but it was imperative that all the men here understand the challenges facing them and how it would go. Their lives depended on the chain of command, and in any other situation, Ashanti Adams was always in control.

"I'll stay." He gave Bronson a somber bow.

Their path made straight, the Rosalie men strode off, filled with the purpose of rescuing Rashall.

Bronson noticed Marley staring in puzzlement at the smoking hulk of the *Adventurer*.

"Mrs. Trelawney, will you be able to focus on our efforts here, or should you prefer to accompany Brother Dan as well?"

She met his gaze with quick submission and a curtsy, and in a moment he regretted his harshness. Her eyes in the noonday sun were sunken with darkness that would not soon leave her—this he knew from his own life.

The circumstances of killing a man mattered not to the dark stain it left on one's soul. The only reason that justified it— defending oneself—comforted a man not a whit. For a woman, he dared not guess the damage it had done.

"Gentlemen," he said. "We shall try the most direct route possible to retrieving our brother. We shall begin by asking the British Navy for him. We have little hope of success, but we'll try."

He had left with him perhaps two dozen men; he knew he very well might need each and every one of them before it was over with.

He and Ashanti, with Marley walking just behind them for protection, returned to the battle site. The weary British soldiers were now carrying away those who had died in the battle, and Marley's gaze was drawn to them.

When an officer noticed their approach, he told them to halt. "Leave your marksman behind."

Bronson turned to Marley, taking her rifle and handing it to another man. The officer moved forward and he met them there on the bridge. Bronson introduced himself. The officer, weary and drawn, made no offer to return the courtesy.

"Captain, we just witnessed someone in one of your ships destroy our ship as well as abducting my partner, a free black man and resident of Boston named Rashall Adams. There has been a grave misunderstanding."

"We have given no orders to fire at any ships in the harbor. Nor would we abduct a free man. Good day."

"Begging your pardon, sir, I do not believe that either of the acts were committed by your men. The ship itself appeared to be deserted when we passed it earlier this morning. And we saw an older man by the name of Manning dragging Mr. Adams onto the ship. He may go by a different name."

"How do you know this Manning?"

Bronson turned to Ashanti. "He and I had a serious disagreement when we were both young."

"What kind of disagreement?"

Ashanti glanced at Bronson, knowing full well how this man would respond to the facts.

"My wife humiliated him in court and proved him guilty of perjury."

The officer gave a snort of derision. "In court, sir? No slave may testify against a white man."

Bronson saw the fire flash in Ashanti's gaze with the abundance of ignorance in the man's words, and he quickly spoke. "Captain, the gentleman you address is Mr. Ashanti Adams, a free man of several generations as well as the father of the kidnaped man. We believe the kidnaping to have been done as an act of revenge."

"What do you want from me? As you can see, I'm quite busy removing my men who were lost."

"We want the return of our kinsman. We believe he may be destined for the Ethiopian Regiment as if he were a slave."

"That regiment is not here, sir, and I say again that we do not do such things."

"Well, somebody sure—" Marley cut herself off even before she saw Bronson's silencing glance.

The fact of the matter was, press gangs *still* kidnapped all manner of Englishmen and boys, forcing them to serve with the Navy. But this man was of no mind to aid the enemy in the least.

"Can you tell me, Captain, whose ship that is?"

"Sir, I have told you all I can. Good day." The captain turned and left.

They returned to the place where they'd anchored the *Adventurer*, and Bronson directed four men to find a place for them to camp and gather wood. Four others, he sent to gather food while they still had light.

Those remaining scouted and found a clearing suitable for a camp along with a nearby spring. No man there would have suggested camping on the battleground—the deaths had rendered the grounds hallowed.

At the camp, they gathered firewood. Soon, the others returned with turkeys and grouse, which they quickly dressed and placed over spits. They ate silently in the cold night, disinterested in conversation or each other.

Ashanti sat on a fallen trunk, gazing out over the water toward the British ship. They had seen little activity from it since Rashall disappeared within it.

Darkness came early, and Bronson had the first watch. Marley buried her possibles bag under a pile of leaves and curled up there. He watched as she tried to sleep, but—whether due to the cold or the day's events—she eventually gave up.

She rose, grasped her rifle, and walked to him.

"Need another watchman?"

He held up his hand to her as she lowered herself beside him. His arm went around her shoulders, and she leaned into his warmth.

"Can't sleep?" He removed her hat to lightly kiss her head, then replaced it.

"I thought I had a healthy attitude about times such as these. I understand wars, I understood this battle better than anyone else here today."

"Marley, you're a—"

"Please don't tell me I'm a woman."

"You're a *novice*. The first time I killed a man, I knew I was no warrior."

"You've killed a man before today?"

"I've lived the past decade and more on the high seas. The world's most cutthroat men live there. There is much I have done to survive that I will never tell you—shameful as it is to admit even to myself."

He scanned the woods, up to where Ashanti sat staring.

"Killing is not the same as shooting. The first time sickens you. It casts the blackest blot upon your soul. You entreat God in heaven day and sleepless night for forgiveness, for him to remove that blot. But weeks pass and it only remains."

He rose and added another large log to the fire. When he returned, he sat beside her, leaning forward, gazing down at his intertwined fingertips.

"Until one day you realize that God has, indeed, removed the blot. And you rejoice, until the time comes again that you must kill or be killed yourself.

"And the blot returns, so impossible to bear that you grow certain God has at last sent his vengeance on you. But then! What wonder—in only a day or two the blot lifts itself.

"Over time, each blot makes a fainter impression. Each time grows shorter between the killing and the forgetting. Until one time, when you are obliged to kill a man to avoid death yourself, it means no more to you than throwing a blow back at a man in a public house brawl."

He touched her chin, lifting her face, and her eyes glittered with tears.

"'Tis bad enough that any man must do this to survive in this world. I would prefer my own wife's heart remain soft, her compassion intact to teach our children the meaning of loving one's fellow man when I have come to see that so few of us deserve it."

Her hands closed tightly around his arm, pressing her face against his sleeve. Her voice had fallen to a whisper. "You love your fellow man. You can't convince me otherwise."

"It took me years to understand that this is God's own gift to protect us, just as a coat or scarf might. Now I am able to distance myself before the pain descends. That no doubt strikes you as impossibly cruel."

She shook her head. "I'm only grateful you learned to protect yourself."

"In any case, I don't want you developing a callused conscience. For now, you're sounding sleepy. Why not stretch out here beside me, where you're warmer?"

She curled up at his side, and in moments, with the heat from the fire and his body radiating around her, she was asleep.

Early the next morning, the ship across the way sailed back down the Elizabeth River toward the James and, ultimately, Norfolk.

Marley awakened to find Bronson standing at the edge of the camp, watching the ship sail away. He looked pale and haggard.

"Didn't you sleep at all?"

"I cannot."

"Where do you suppose they're going?"

"I'm told there are many ships of the Royal Navy cluttering Norfolk harbor, and my guess is as I said. To deliver him as a slave to the Ethiopian Regiment."

"I'm so sorry about your ship."

"I'm grateful no one was hurt. As shipwrecks go, this one may have been spectacular, but at least its destruction hurt no one."

Late that afternoon, as the sun's rays were long and golden, they saw the approach of another, square-sailed ship.

Marley sighed in relief as the ship anchored and a coxswain rowed out to gather up the remaining seamen. Two short trips later, they were aboard the ship.

"Well done indeed, Mr. Crowell," Bronson said, clapping him on the back. "I haven't seen her in many years, but I imagine she's more beautiful than the day she first set sail."

"Sir, there's just one thing. Years ago, when we were scraping her down to nothing, then replacing the worn bits, and having her blessed, well, sir, we had her christened again. We thought it best be done by that same clergy, just to play it safe. Sir, some awful things went on, on this ship, back in the day."

"I understand, Crowell."

"No, sir, you don't, not yet. The clergyman, he was a pushy fellow, even insisted on baptizing all of us who wasn't already. Then he'd only stand for one name, and so we hope it meets with your approval. 'Tis out of Corinthians, Cap'n, case ye want to look it up: 'For this perishable must put on the imperishable, and this mortal must put on immortality.'

"To wash out all the evil done in her time as the *Swallow*, sir, she be named *Immortal*."

Chapter Thirty-Nine

The *Immortal* sailed into Norfolk disguised in British colors. She anchored across the harbor from the warship with the cabin window Marley had shot out, and Bronson, Deming, Ashanti, and Marley rowed across in the darkness to see what they could learn.

The visit was short, the ship empty. Bronson hastily inspected each level of the ship without result, and they rowed back silently.

They climbed the ladder and retreated to the captain's cabin, which was lit dimly by a single lamp.

Marley looked around the room, wondering how much of this was original to the ship and how much had been added to accommodate her husband's tastes. She knew nothing of her husband's older brother except what she had learned from Ruth's journals. Once he had been a slave trader, but in his will had freed everyone on his plantation and supplied them with the means to carry on their lives there as free men. He had built the magnificent mansion at Rosalie, its opulence a tribute to his life's work—the place that now lay in ruins.

Most of the ship, she suspected, was original; she matched the look of a ship that had been commissioned thirty-five years ago but that had spent much of that time in dry dock and freshwater.

"She's in better shape than the *Adventurer*," Bronson said. "And she was but a few years old."

As she walked to the windows and glanced up, a smile curved her lips as she recognized an update. A bank of windows had been added at the end of the ceiling, as in the *Adventurer*. Perhaps Grey Trelawney had been a more practical sort than Bronson, less apt to pass his evenings stargazing and smoking cigars.

What a detail for Crowell to have recognized as important to Bronson.

"What is her state with armament?"

"Sir, we added cannons on the lower decks, but for flexibility we stayed with carronades above—18, 24, and 32 lbs. She's stocked to protect near or far, but she's still fast."

In other words, while she was no warship, she could hold her own.

When, Marley wondered, had she become the sort of person who referred to ships with a gender? For good or ill, she had become a sailor.

"Marley?"

She turned at the sound of Bronson's voice. He held a chair for her at the table, and she joined the men. Jem poured freshly brewed coffee into mugs and served them.

"Without wasting time, let's make some deductions. Rashall has been taken by a known killer, with assistance from unknown sources. The kidnaper could not have fired the guns that destroyed *Adventurer* while in that rowboat. At least four men would have been required to do the firing."

"Two can operate a carronade," Deming put in.

"True. And we believe here that the kidnaper did so out of revenge."

"But why after so long?"

The table went silent. Marley spoke up.

"Crimes fall into the categories of passion, premeditation, or opportunity. Perhaps here, the three converge."

The men glanced at her.

"Say Manning pondered long on how to get his revenge—years, decades even—until an opportunity presented itself. What if the destruction of the *Adventurer* was an act of passion, not premeditation, recognized by one of his partners?"

"And we've certainly had no such threats during the time we were away from Norfolk—a place swarming not only with the Navy, but with loyalists."

"Sir, who are the two most obviously wanting you dead?" Deming asked.

"Yes," Marley said. "Falligan and Snaveling."

"I thought you killed Falligan," Bronson said.

"I scalded him, then hit him over the head with a teapot. He was screaming as he fell over the gunwale. Can I help it if he can swim?"

"You just took out half of the British army at Great Bridge, and this cur, you let get away?" he asked with a smirk.

"With a *teapot*. Had there been a spot of gunpowder at hand in your cabin, the outcome might have been different."

"Indeed. Well, Falligan has fallen in with seedy characters over the past ten years. It's not inconceivable he and this Manning fellow know each other. The man who had Rashall, however, looked more like a nobleman than an overseer."

"He's had thirty years to earn a fortune by hook or by crook," Ashanti said. "Nonetheless, I assure you he is without honor. A rapist, a sadist, and a murderer. I pity his sons."

"Sons?"

Ashanti nodded at Bronson. "I remember at least two boys—nearly young men, that is—joining him in the fields at times. Let me think. Their names escape me."

"All right. So he may have at least four people working with him. Phil, you and I shall scour the docks with the story that we're looking for a runaway slave. We meet back here every half hour for a report. Mr. Adams, I hope you understand that the risk is too great for you, and I need you here too much, looking after Marley."

"I do understand, although Marley has proven conclusively she can look after herself." With that, he gave her a nod.

"Nonetheless. Can I count on you both to look after the ship against our enemies?"

They agreed, and within minutes the men spread out. No sooner had they departed than they both returned with the location of the ship where escaped slaves were signing up for Dunmore's Ethiopian Regiment.

"Smallpox is aboard the ship, and many of the newly freed are dying," Deming said. "I'll go. I had it as a boy."

"We've all been inoculated, including Rashall," Ashanti said.

Marley glanced at Bronson, who said instead, "I'll go, of course."

"Have you been inoculated?"

"I am going."

"I thought you were inoculated when we were?" Ashanti asked.

"I was in Bermuda then. But I am hale and hearty and we all know that no one shall stop me from going. And you? Have you had the disease?"

She ducked her head. In point of fact, she had been born nearly twenty years after it had been eradicated in the U.S. In her time, the only concern for smallpox was bioterrorism.

"I see. Then *you'll* stay in this cabin, with the rifle, until Rashall is aboard and quarantined."

With that, the men were gone.

She looked around the great cabin, curious about what she found. The captain's quarters felt exactly as she would have imagined. No amount of refurbishing or priest's blessings could have scrubbed away the troubled soul of the man who had once carried hundreds of human beings into bondage—the man her sister had fallen in love with.

Carrying the lamp with her, she opened the closet, startled to find clothing there. The style of the middle century men's clothing being similar to that later in the century, it was dated only by the length of coats and waistcoats and the detail of the trim. Fashioned from rich silks and velvets and intricately embroidered, they reflected a wealthy man of taste.

Tellingly, someone had kept these garments free of cobwebs and dust. Occasional evidence of a moth was the only proof that the items weren't new clothing.

She grew curious about Grey Trelawney: who he was, where he had attended school, why he had chosen such an abhorrent livelihood. One thing she knew from the most casual examination of these clothes and this ship: He had been loved and respected.

She inspected the cabin, as best she could without lighting another candle or lamp. At last, she came to the table and sat at the captain's chair behind it. Turning, she saw the ships of the harbor behind the *Immortal*, and she imagined the brother of Bronson Trelawney sitting there, gazing out as the South Atlantic—and the port villages of Africa—receded behind him.

Shifting in the chair, she felt her thigh connect with a drawer, and she opened it. Several ship's logs lay there with a quill, a tiny dish, and a small box of powdered ink. She brightened the lamp, then withdrew the log on the top and opened it.

The notations on the left took the same format as they had in Bronson's log, but contained nothing particularly interesting. The series of columns, left to right, indicated hour, speed in knots, water depth in fathoms, the course in which the ship was steering, the wind direction, and remarks.

She read the remarks simply for something to do, beginning with the most recent entry.

Remarks for Tuesday September 19, 1775
  This day begins with mild and pleasant weather. 12:30 left Rosalie.
  NNW breeze, making our work light. 4:45 arrive Stonefield. Mr. H and Miss J debark to remain behind as we prepare to return to R. Weather continues mild.
  The trees grow colorful. Lovely day to be alive and on the James.

Was the canny old Crowell such a philosopher?

She scanned through, detecting a pattern. Every month or so, Crowell and a small crew took the ship out for a pleasure cruise, generally to Richmond, sometimes—though not recently, and not as often—to Norfolk. To preserve her hull, she presumed, they kept to the freshwater.

She turned a page, noticing a different handwriting.

Remarks for Saturday February 18, 1774
The day is cold but pleasant. Mr. Crowell abed with a fever. 12:15 left Rosalie.
Winds right blustery NNE. 5:00 arrive Stonefield. Left Mr. Hastings here for a visit with Miss Julie Anna. The old couple who took her in all them years back were in right good spirits. That old man doesn't seem to get any older. He's looked the same for ten years.
2:30 left Stonefield, 6:30 arrive Rosalie.

Marley gaped. Julie Anna? Could it be the person after whom her own sister, Juliana, had been named—perhaps even an ancestor, since Hastings himself was?

She continued to scan the ship's log, but Crowell's notes resumed. They referred frequently to *H* and *J*, but gave no more personal details, simply the presence of the two. Because the ship sailed rarely and only for short trips—most with few remarks—each spread easily contained a year's worth of entries.

And then several blank pages appeared before another entry, also by Crowell. But his handwriting was much faded by time. Indeed, a few years had passed between his last, later entry, and the earlier years when the ship had sailed.

Of course. He thought his captain had died in the fire at Rosalie. The ship had been entirely in dry dock, then.

Crowell remarked on only two more voyages.

Remarks for Tuesday, July 6, 1746
Red sky this morning. 6:30 we left Rosalie and a storm behind us but we are still on guard.
An unusual voyage and short, to Boston. We are today a ship without our captain. He trained and taught us well and any one of us could lead the ship and mark the log—but my heart is heavy with a sense of foreboding, I know not why. We have aboard as an honored guest the lady

who saved our captain's life in court this week, and her husband, Boston bound.

Remarks for Tuesday, July 13, 1746

12:00 Depart Massachusetts Bay. As foul a storm I haven't seen in ages, as we return to Rosalie.

Captain Grey alerted us all before we left for Boston that he has given up the triangle trade. We are free to find other ships or remain behind at Rosalie, but most of the men are sailors brokenhearted at the idea of dry land.

I am loyal to my captain and will seek a post with Mr. H. I know that blaggard lying Manning left a welcome hole, so perhaps I can serve as his overseer. His boys Sheppard and Jack did most of his work, anyway. He was a sorry lot, but his boys was good. That Sheppard, he doesn't look nothing like him—Manning burly and black-haired, Shep pale with those cold blue eyes, like an iceberg. Still waters, my mum would say.

Sheppard. Finally the name Camisha had mentioned rang with familiarity in Marley's memory—so long ago, back at the hotel registration desk as they prepared to leave Williamsburg. The tall, icy man of whom Nan had been so terrified.

But it made no sense—after all, Sheppard was a common name, wasn't it? Surely it was a coincidence.

She returned to the ship's log, turning the page. There followed an entirely different, faded handwriting, and a new author. This man had made full use of the remarks column, expanding about the concerns of his life.

Remarks for Friday April 21, N.S. 1746

This day begins as have the past seven, in clouds and foul weather. 12:30 arrive at Rosalie after but four hours in the Chesapeake Bay.

God save us all, 45 have died of the original 184. Two others gravely ill. A fever afflicted the ship, its first victim the winsome wee one from the S.L. village. Her sunny smile haunts my nightmares.

Mr. Gideon Miller leaves my employ this day after being with me since this ship's start. He reminds me a slave ship is no home for a family, no place for small children to grow, as I know too well. Hastings has promised him employment and protection working for his son Wm. and wife at Stonefield. Gideon is not fond of that area for that curse business involving his family, but his circumstances are precarious.

I truly fear for him; for his son, Robt.; and other children they may have. His wife Sarita is striking and beautiful; with riotous black curls that take on red fire at night, and skin like burnished gold. She does not look like a woman from her region but she is indeed a Negro. A free woman, also, her freedom paid dearly by Mr. Miller across the years. They are welcome to abide at Rosalie—but I know not how safe they would be there, either. The other bondsmen would fear him and resent her.

Apart from all this, I am plagued by anger, by discontent. Their source, I cannot tell. Their target, I do not know. I know but that the memory of the little girl—my own Emily's age—brings me to tears in my bed. Now, when I would already be itching to leave the shore—dear God in Heaven, help me. I dare not contemplate another voyage like this one.

As she read the confession of the slaver, pieces of the confusion that had plagued Marley for all of her life began to work toward each other, pushed so by this lost absolution. Her father, the son of a sailor; her father's mother, according to Nan, *a beauty from a faraway land … in your lovely dark eyes are her laughter and her tears.*

Nan had been born in this time. Was it so far-fetched that Marley's own father—and perhaps her mother—had as well? Her own birth certificate placed her birth in a hospital in Richmond, Virginia, in 1991, but she had never come across a similar document for either of her parents.

She continued paging back through the ship's log, and then into those below it, aware that she was reading the innermost thoughts of Grey Trelawney, the brother of Bronson who was presumed to have died at Rosalie in 1746, not long after Bronson had been born. And that if she understood correctly, she and her sisters had ties to the Trelawneys that went back nearly three centuries.

Chapter Forty

Deep in the dead of night, Norfolk harbor lay cold and silent except for the creak of wood, the occasional lap of water against the quay, and the stroll of a watchman along the waterfront. In the distance, faint laughter and conversation echoed from behind closed doors, where sailors made merry between voyages.

A small boat drew alongside the ship where the Royal Navy housed the most recent recruits of the Ethiopian Regiment. Six men waited in the boat. Five would go aboard and seek Rashall; the sixth would remain with a rifle for unforeseen complications.

Bronson's gaze moved over the harbor, crowded with Royal Navy ships, looking for any previously unrecognized threat. He found none.

God had favored them this night with an overcast sky, darkening the harbor and their likelihood of discovery. The Royal Navy had favored them by anchoring apart from the other ships.

Deming, the man among them most adept in hand-to-hand combat, led them up the rope ladder left there to welcome any escaped slave. He was a tough, scrappy little man they'd stumbled across in a tavern in Shanghai, astounded to discover he'd been born in Surry. He'd joined on that moment. He was a lieutenant without parallel; intelligent, loyal, trustworthy, and hard-working. His unquestioning courage outmatched that of the fiercest hunting dog. Above that, he had a gift for strategy beyond that of any ordinary sailor, and he could have easily captained his own ship. Bronson was glad he had no desire to.

He hesitated, his head level with the gunwale of the Royal Navy ship, as he sized up the threat on deck. He waited, one hand held out flat to the men below, for perhaps a minute. Then he leapt silently over the gunwale, and even as Bronson hurried into his slot, he overtook the sailor on watch, silently choking him into submission.

As he passed out, the men hastened over with athletic grace and spread out across the deck as they'd planned. They had little time before he'd come around. Bronson headed straight for the captain's cabin, his knife drawn, Deming perhaps ten feet behind—far enough to provide a second volley, if need be.

He opened the door silently.

"Drop it, Hawk."

Across from them, sitting behind an elaborate table, was Stephen Falligan, a pistol trained directly on the door.

"I'd listen to him, if I were you."

This from none other than Percy Snaveling, perhaps 15 feet across, sitting leisurely in a chair, with another pistol. This weapon was focused on Rashall, who lay tied up on the deck.

"Ah," Bronson said, as if caught off-guard.

The angle wasn't ideal. He hesitated, even as he casually brought his free hand behind him, signaling to Deming with four fingers.

Then three. Two.

When his index finger closed, he hurled his knife at Snaveling's chest and dove toward Rashall. The knife flashed with the gold of the lamplight in a half spin and hit its target true.

Before Falligan could so much as cock his pistol, Deming's knife sank into his heart.

Neither man made a sound as they went down.

Bronson pulled the pistol away from Snaveling as he withdrew his throwing knife, wiped it, and replaced it in its scabbard. He placed his fingers firm against Snaveling's fleshy throat, feeling for a pulse. Then he turned to Deming, who was already at the table, retrieving his blade and Falligan's pistol.

"Be certain the bloody bastard is *dead*."

"My pleasure."

He hesitated a moment, glancing at the handkerchief stuffed in Rashall's mouth.

"Never again shall we know such a moment's peace."

Rashall's eyes went dark with threat.

Bronson hastily pulled out the handkerchief and tossed it aside, then withdrew a knife and swiftly sliced the ropes binding him.

"Can't feel anything at all below my waist, and do not say it." Rashall struggled with numb limbs, moving awkwardly, and Bronson jerked him to his feet.

The three hurried up the hatch and Bronson gave a three-note whistle as they raced back to the quarterdeck. The men assembled there just as the sailor on night watch began to come around. Deming slugged him squarely, catching his rising form and gently lowering it to the deck.

"Master?"

Disoriented at the word, Bronson found his attention drawn by the whisper from a young boy—hard to tell his age, Bronson thought, but perhaps as young as nine or ten, or as old as twelve or thirteen. Not much more than skin and bones, with utter terror in his eyes as he looked toward the captain's cabin. Of whom was he so fearful?

"Can I come with you?"

Rashall and Bronson assented in unison. "Can you go down the rope?"

The boy nodded. "I think so. I came up it."

They allowed him over before them, with the other men hurrying down beside him, watching their step so as not to upset his progress. Rashall went over after them, lowering himself alongside the boy, allowing him to make his own progress.

Bronson went last, keeping watch over the ship for any threat.

Mr. Adams leaned up to hug his son around the shoulders, and Rashall patted his father's forearm. "Father, I'm fine."

With a strong hand, Bronson gave Mr. Adams a bracing slap on the shoulder blade. "All's well, sir," he said.

The man nodded silently, coughed, and stared out toward the *Immortal*.

Bronson and Ray took a place on either side of the boy, who shivered without complaining in only a thin linen shirt and breeches—no shoes or socks at all.

Bronson removed his coat and wrapped it around the boy, and Rashall patted him on the back. "Better now?"

He nodded.

"What's your name, son?"

"Master, I be George."

"Well, George. My name is Rashall Adams. You can call me Raven. Call no man *Master*, son. Show respect to your elders and to ladies with *sir* or *madam*, and to the man who employs you, but from this day forward, you are a free man."

The boy's nervous features relaxed into a smile. "I like that, sir. I be a *free man*."

"How did you end up on that ship?"

"I hear tell they was offering freedom to slaves, for joining. I'm only—well, I'm young, but I'm strong. The man that took me on told me he had a job for me, but..." He went silent abruptly for several seconds. "Sir, I did not like the work. I was hoping I could maybe clean or carry things. Maybe even learn a trade like the men I see in town."

"How old are you, George?"

The boy hesitated.

"It's all right. You're safe with us."

"Nine years old, sir. Least that's what I think. My mama and daddy both gone. Daddy got sold, Mama died of the smallpox."

"When was that?"

"Last year. I been getting by all right, I suppose. I wished I'd never left Yorktown, sir. I just thought it might be right nice, to go to sea. I hear tell, ships is one place you can be the same as a white man."

Rashall met Bronson's gaze with a raised eyebrow. "Well, son, that depends on the white man. Sometimes, if he works real hard you can."

Bronson shook his head with a smile.

"I can work hard, sir. I'll be happy to show you." He turned his face up toward Bronson.

"I'll wager you can, George. You think you'd do well as a cabin boy?" Bronson asked the child.

"I reckon I can. I'll try my hardest."

Rashall spoke. "George, meet your new employer: Mr. Bronson Trelawney. You can call him Cap'n Hawk."

The boy held up his tiny hand toward Bronson, and the big man caught it in a light, firm grip, giving him a respectable shake. "And my co-captain, you'll call Cap'n Raven."

At the *Immortal*, he again let the boy go first along the ladder, and he hurried up more confidently now, with Bronson and Rashall on either side of him.

As they crossed the gunwale, Bronson gestured around the deck. "Welcome home, son. Tonight, you can bunk with Raven."

His dark eyes flickered uncertainly toward Raven as he took an instinctive step away from him—even though he'd just been relaxed and easy with both men.

Bile rose within Bronson, filling his throat until he could not speak.

Raven exchanged a grim look with Bronson, thanking God that Percy Snaveling no longer walked this earth.

Bronson dropped to one knee, now level with the boy. "Tell you what. Would you feel better bunking with Jem, the other cabin boy? He's a truepenny, as fine as you."

The boy laughed, relieved, and the sound stung Bronson, somehow. "That be just fine, mast—*sir*."

"Rosalie, sir?" Deming asked.

"And quick, while the wind is with us."

Deming gestured to the waiting seamen, who quickly surrounded the capstan and began to push, raising the anchor.

Bronson sent one of the men to escort George along to Jem's small room off the captain's quarters, and he and Rashall watched the boy hurry after the sailor, the tails of Bronson's coat flapping after him against the deck.

Rashall shook his head. "Poor lad's probably never been off the plantation until this. Pity the first creature he mistakes for a human being is in fact a snake."

Bronson looked at him, and after a moment Rashall met his gaze with an awkward smile. "Thanks. For coming after me."

"Only for the countless times you've done the same. My worry is the man who remains out there—who your father knew. Manning, was it?"

Ashanti Adams leaned against the gunwale nearby, but at this he joined them. "Yes. James Manning. He and I went several rounds, the first time I ever visited Rosalie. Also, the first—and only—time I was ever beaten."

Rashall gaped at him. "Why didn't I know this?"

"Why would I tell you such a thing?"

No response.

"And what about the smallpox? Did you see it aboard?"

"I heard it was below deck, but fortunately I had yet to reach that destination. When I was brought on board, the captain was absent and Falligan gave the quartermaster a story about my having escaped from their Regiment."

"How many men did he have with him? Falligan, I mean."

"Just Snaveling. They were the only two I saw from the time I was taken."

"No, you were taken by Manning," Ashanti said. "That, we saw."

"Well, I was knocked out, so I saw nothing until I awakened on the Navy ship." He rubbed his neck, yawning.

"Let's just try to get some sleep."

Since none of the three had slept since before Great Bridge, they said their goodnights. Bronson opened the hatch and slipped down into the corridor to the captain's quarters.

A candelabra burned near the bed, and he found Marley sleeping there, turned toward the windows. A pang came as he considered their marriage bed, gone forever, destroyed, lying at the bottom of the Elizabeth River.

And he thought of his beloved library, grateful the books had found a better home, in the Trelawney schoolhouse. It seemed a peculiar distraction, but how odd it was, that Marley had made the request—just before the ship was destroyed.

In that moment, with a fortune in Bermuda and a fortune here in this land he loved, his true home, he gazed on all he stood to lose in the world, lying trusting in his bed. Tenderness for her overwhelmed him; and for her otherworldly wisdom, the simple suggestion he loan his books to Ruth.

And her startling—and prescient—statement about Peyton Randolph's death, when she had no means of knowing that.

And then: her demand that he stay out of his cabin.

The deadly temptation to ask her his own fate plagued him now; had she known of the ship's destruction? Was he to have been on the ship, but for some minor change she might have made in the past two months?

And again, he dismissed the temptation as he would the temptation of a pox-plagued whore, with this woman waiting in his bed.

He leaned down to brush the hair from her temple, to kiss the tiny, moon-shaped scar there. He whispered, "Today, I learned I can never thank God enough for you."

He stoked the stove quietly, washed and brushed his teeth, undressed, and slipped in behind her. Unconsciously, she wriggled into the cradle of his thighs. The invitation was tempting—yet at the same time, there was something wholesome and solemn about the moment, and he a man who hadn't slept for three days. After a night spent fearing for Rashall's fate, staring down the muzzle of a pistol, then stumbling across the young runaway, holding his wife was a pleasure simple and sublime.

He smoothed her hair back, kissing her throat lightly, then her shoulder. She stirred.

"Shh. Go back to sleep. I didn't mean to awaken you. I only missed you. We have Ray, and all is well."

"How long have you been gone?"

"Time matters naught."

She turned her face toward him, finding his mouth with hers. Her body followed, and he surrendered to her soft demand on his weary but willing body. Her hands slid through his hair, and with a graceful, deft motion, she drew him underneath her, straddling his lap.

She rose over him, meeting his eyes as she lifted her breasts to his mouth. He accepted them in turn, calming her urgent passion, her awkward movements, with his hands at her waist.

But her hunger would not be calmed. The sensation of his mouth, his tongue, on her breasts, her nipples, enflamed her, and anxiously she drew away to kiss his ear, his throat, his collarbone, his chest and nipples, her mouth swiftly lowering to him as she knelt beside him.

He watched her in fascination as she opened her mouth, tasting his ready length, her tongue flickering out over him. His hands slid into her hair, lightly encouraging her as lightning shot through him, and her innocent explorations soon left him near the edge.

He shifted in the bed, slipping his head beneath, then between, her parted thighs, sighing at what he found there. She truly enjoyed tasting his body as much as he did hers. She cried out, her cry captured on his willing flesh as he opened his mouth and suckled and tasted between her thighs, his hands gripping her buttocks and drawing her closer into his kiss.

He lost himself in sensation—the taste of her, the feel of her—even as her tongue played over him, then she let him slip deeply into her mouth while her hand cupped him with instinctive, exquisite lightness—he was taut, ready.

Then the need to be deep within her outstripped even this pleasure, and even as he would've done so himself, she shifted again, slipping away from tasting him only long enough to straddle him. He gasped at this; she was a continual surprise and joy to him, ever unfolding.

His gaze devoured the sight of that womanly body, glistening golden alabaster with a faint sheen of sweat, in the candlelight. Her intimate kiss had left him on the precipice of climax, and in another moment she captured him within, and he clutched her against him even as she moved in rhythm, as she learned the motions that pleased them both. With utter restraint, he resisted—as long as he could—the urge to take over, to thrust within her, to claim her as his.

For this moment, he was hers to take.

Her eyes rose to meet his, and his gaze was intent on her body, her face, watching her make love to him. His gaze was transfixed by her hips, undulating with sensuous, rhythmic grace, with building pleasure as she rocked against him.

His hands cupped her breasts, his palms, then his fingers, teasing her nipples. Then one hand slipped between their bodies, finding the center of her pleasure swollen and aching for him. She cried out softly at his touch, her motions more forceful but less certain, and the sound was his undoing.

He pulled her down to him tenderly, burying his face in her hair and whispering dark endearments, and he held her to him even as he rolled her onto her back, then resuming his leisurely fondling as he drove roughly within her. His need for her was maddening, and even as he felt her convulsing around him, he sank his face against her neck, his mouth and teeth closing hard over her throat. He gave a deep growl of pleasure as he continued thrusting, at last reaching his own climax.

Minutes later, as he collapsed beside her, as he pulled her again within the cradle of his body, he kissed her throat, her ear, her temple—as they had begun. The world's weight had been lifted from him, and he was floating toward sleep.

"You are my life," he whispered. "My love. My own."

She brought his hand, resting between her breasts, to her lips.

"Bronson?"

"Aye."

"Do you know where Stonefield is?"

"Yes. Hastings' old home."

"It's where I grew up." The cooling sweat on their bodies was evaporating, and she drew the quilt over them.

"Do you know who lives there now?"

He held tight to the place of sleep beckoning even as he considered the question, surprised at the answer. "You know, I don't. I'm not sure anyone does, anymore."

"They do. Aside from Norfolk, it's the only place *Immortal* has visited in years. Hastings goes each time."

"Then we'll go tomorrow. Perhaps take the old boy along with us?"

She hugged his arm, and he drew her hard against him, inhaling the aroma of her. "I think we have to take Nan with us as well."

"Aye, my Marley."

He moved again toward sleep, gratefully.

"Bronson?"

"Aye."

"What would you do if my other grandmother were black?"

He rubbed his face against her hair. "I believe the proper etiquette would be never to remind you that I first suggested it."

A minute passed after his easygoing jibe. "Good night, my love," she whispered.

But this time, Bronson heard her voice only in his dreams.

Chapter Forty-One

The *Immortal* sailed upriver, her passage watched by the trees of the James—the dogwood, the elm, the mulberry, ash, maple, and countless varieties of oaks and live oaks, only the last still bearing their greenery as Christmas neared.

The ship's captain eyed the sky with skeptic ill humor as they departed Rosalie. Within his ship were his father; that man's new lady love; his own best friend, and that man's parents; a gentleman who had managed Rosalie since it had come to be; and that man's great granddaughter.

And it was that young lady who watched her husband look for any storm that might threaten his passengers.

"I tell you, it's a superstition."

"And I tell you, 'tis simple weather. The sky was as red this morning as a lobsterback's finery."

Marley knew he spoke the truth, but she couldn't bear his worry. She raised an eyebrow at him.

"Yes. I saw it as you were tending to my morning hunger for you, with that lovely mouth of yours."

At this, his gaze shifted to her even as he stood stock still. An echo of a smile curved his lips, and that old habit of biting his lower lip returned.

Dear God! She thought, marveling how a woman learned her husband. How had she not noticed before? His nervous tic was a sign of sexual desire. Oh, it was too tempting, to tell him. But with God's own grace, they would have many years together, and many times that she could read this and know how to calm him. That was worth far more than any laughter they might share at this moment. Besides, laughter was a bottomless fount.

"You are insatiable and shameless."

She tilted her head, her mouth breaking into a wide grin as she joined him at the rail, her hand lightly brushing the back of his. "For you, yes."

"Do not talk this way. I cannot retire with you to my cabin in the midst of a sunny day." Even as he scolded her, he reached out and drew her against his hard body, casually scanning the deck. But for Deming behind the wheel, facing forward, the deck was empty.

"Especially with such a dark storm on the horizon, somewhere out there in that blue sky."

"I like this gown," he said, for all the world hugging her with a husband's lighthearted affection.

"You can't even see it, you profligate."

"But I can feel it."

Before she was aware his intention, he slipped his hand inside her cloak and cupped her breast, his thumb brushing aside the fabric to tease her hard nipple. He flicked the wool aside, baring her breast to the morning sun and lowering his head to suckle until her knees went weak.

In afterthought, she hastily focused on Deming, who still gazed off into the river ahead of them.

Then he drew himself upright with a satyr's smile, straightened her clothing with prim precision, and returned his attention to the sky—leaving her to grab the rail to steady herself.

"That was cruel." Her voice was low, husky, revealing her arousal.

"Remember that, my beloved, should you think to tempt my patience again. For when you do it, I shall make you hungry for my plowing."

The teasing crudeness in his words only worsened her arousal. "Perhaps I shall go below and take care of this myself."

His eyes flashed at her threat. "I tell you, do not test me. Next will come a spanking, my love, and I won't care if Deming does watch. And since I know how you enjoy it, I'll make it a joy to dread." Then, more loudly, he said, "Good morning, Mrs. Adams."

Marley turned to find Camisha poking her head through the hatch.

"Would you care for coffee? I'm making a pot."

"Indeed I would. We were just discussing going below," he said, his eyes meeting Marley's with lighthearted amusement.

She gave him an exasperated glare.

"Oh, you two," Camisha said, shaking her head as she closed the hatch.

"That woman is a seer beyond, in truth, knowing the future," he said, as he hugged her to his side and soundly kissed her forehead.

They joined Camisha in the kitchen, where Ashanti sat on a counter, chatting with his wife.

"So what's the purpose behind this day trip?" Ashanti asked.

"I told you—"

"Yes, yes, I know. Celebration of family."

Bronson hesitated. "Marley read the old *Swallow* ship's logs, and learned that someone lives there."

"I'm surprised, given all poor old Crowell did to exorcise the ship's demons, they didn't destroy those logs in a fire."

"No seaman would ever do such a thing. Sailors may be accursed with sin and wrongdoing, but ship's logs are sacred. For exactly this reason, I might add."

"Then I propose we sit down and discuss what she learned. Rashall must not be privy to this information."

"Why?"

"With each person who knows the truth, the risk of our living here grows. Rashall himself is an anachronism by extension."

Once Camisha had intimidated Marley, but knowing Bronson had changed her, and now she shook her head. "No, he isn't. He was born here and raised here and knows nothing about any other time—nor could he."

"I mean, he's not even meant to exist, but for my presence here. None of my children are. I don't wish to risk it."

"'Tis too late."

Camisha's head swung around to Bronson, and her lips went tight. "What have you done now?" Then she glanced at Marley. "Didn't I tell you he couldn't keep his mouth shut?"

"He knows all my important secrets, as I do his. Were it Rachel, would you forbid her? Or would you not instead insist on her being there for you?"

Ashanti laughed, glancing at his wife. "Ray's his Cammie."

"You shut up. I wish I'd never told you, either."

His laughter continued. "Uh huh. You thought you were just dropping in to ye oldie timey for some fine Ashanti loving, then heading back to your modern condomodium."

"Condo*min*ium," she muttered, again glancing at Marley. "That's his idea of wit. Didn't I tell you you'd be sorry for telling him?"

"Sorry for telling who what?" Rashall appeared from the corridor behind Marley.

Camisha sighed, her head dropping in resignation. "All right. We all gather, all our secrets just as naked as jaybirds—is the officer's mess still available, Bronson?"

He shrugged. "The captain's cabin is large enough for all of us."

"If we're going to get to the bottom of it, we need Hannah and Hastings—if he'll even have anything to do with us. Bronson, what about your father? Or will he want to have us all thrown in the Public Hospital?"

He hesitated, clearly torn. "Obviously he'll betray no one. I'm truly worried about the strain it may place on his heart—his spirit."

"Well, it's your call, son." This from Ashanti, abruptly taking the reins from his wife.

"Perhaps we try without him, first. But he's a stubborn man, he likely won't accept being left out." This from Bronson.

"Yeah. God forbid we have a stubborn man there," she said, looking from Bronson to Ashanti to their son. "We'll go collect him and Hannah and meet you there."

Jem arrived to put the coffee trolley together and wheeled the service into the cabin.

Bronson, Marley, and Rashall joined the old man who sat at the bank of windows, gazing out into the river receding behind him.

"Seems a pleasant day indeed. What was the morning like?"

Bronson threw Marley a knowing glance. "Red sky, sir."

"Oh, dear. Well, at least you're not out at sea, where the greater problems would occur from it. In any case, I thank you for inviting me along. I've been going over the books with Little Dan, and I'd developed quite a headache. This is a welcome reprieve."

"Problems?"

"The opposite. The young man no longer needs me at all. The weaker my eyes grow, the sharper grow his figures. 'Tis a challenge indeed to find any error in his work."

"Then perhaps it's time you train his surrogate," Bronson said. "Or perhaps, if he's a competent bookkeeper, he's—"

"Correct you are. He's already training several young men, just so that they might have the knowledge. We effectively have a college of accounting at the Trelawney university. Wise young men—knowing this farm won't support everyone indefinitely."

Watching this old man, separated from his entire family so many years ago, having found an adopted family in the freed men and women of Rosalie, working long after most men would have retired, Marley was filled with a sudden surge of warmth and pride that she was a part of his family. Despite his prickly exterior, he had a huge heart.

He was in jovial spirits for what he'd been told was a river cruise without destination, something for which the family could join together for lunch and return to Rosalie by nightfall.

Marley's guilt over deceiving the old man—he didn't even know the others were aboard, besides Camisha and Ashanti, both of whom he loved—was tempered by a stubborn need to resolve this, if such a thing was possible.

She poured coffee in the cups while they waited for the others to arrive. From the small pot Camisha had made, she poured tea for Hastings, adding a dollop of fresh cream and passing it to him.

His eyes twinkled merrily. "Thank you, child."

She gave a nervous nod, uneasy at the conflict soon to follow. A moment later, by habit, she took a deep, steadying breath, as Bronson had taught her. In her old life, her stomach would have been in knots for their entire meeting. Now, she focused herself to live in this moment. She placed Bronson's coffee in front of him, relishing the simple task, the look of encouragement he gave her. Without saying a word, he knew how fearful she was.

This moment alone was worth everything, no matter what happened.

Only then did the fear descend en masse despite her preparations. For what she feared, she realized, was that waiting at Stonefield would be an unwanted and unavoidable portal to her old life. It wouldn't be the oddest thing that had happened lately.

As she released the saucer, he placed his hand over hers and squeezed.

Then a soft tap came at the open door, and Ashanti pushed the door wide. His wife followed, her gaze cautious on Hastings as she escorted in Hannah. Thomas followed her, glancing around the room. "Godfrey! Had no idea you were even on the ship."

"Nor I you, sir. So good to see you again. If you'll forgive me for not rising, my gout troubles me."

Thomas crossed the room and shook his hand. "You remember Hannah, of course?"

Hastings inclined his head graciously as Hannah curtsied to him. "I could never forget my own William's wife."

Thomas bowed his head at the reminder. "Yes—about that, Hastings. Hannah and I are to be married this week at Bruton Church. I hope you'll consider blessing us with your attendance."

"Congratulations to the both of you—happy news indeed."

"Son—have you any champagne?"

For the first time she could remember, Bronson stammered, startled by his father's news. "I—I don't know."

Marley jumped to her feet, touching his shoulder blade in gentle reassurance. "I'll take care of it."

She stepped outside the cabin and found Jem at his post, sending him on a quest for champagne and glasses.

While they waited, Thomas said, "'Twas your own nuptials that inspired me, son. I hope that you and Marley are as happy as Hannah and I. And I only wish that your brother could have known the same happiness."

Camisha and Marley exchanged a glance. The older woman spoke. "Interesting that you mention that, sir. In point of fact, there's something you should know, and I believe it will give you peace."

Hastings went into a coughing fit, then cleared his throat. "Forgive me," he said, his eyes warning Camisha. "I have no idea what brought that on."

At that moment, Jem entered, carrying a tray full of glasses with several bottles. He placed it on the table. He held out a bottle to Bronson in question, and the captain gave a nod, dismissing him.

Bronson uncorked two bottles of the champagne and quickly poured, and Marley passed out the glasses. When everyone had a glass, he looked to Hastings to toast the bride-to-be.

The old man gazed into the bubbling wine, as silence lurched through the room. Marley had the sudden fear he might decline. He was a man of principle, and for reasons she did not fully know, he disliked Hannah.

He grasped the stem of his glass. "Hannah, I have known you for most of your life, and you have indeed been like a daughter to me. I wish for you in life that you be granted everything you so richly deserve. Thomas, I especially wish you happiness and peace."

He bowed his head even as he raised his glass toward her, and everyone hear-heared and huzzahed the bride. Hastings drank down the champagne in one gulp.

Marley sipped, her gaze meeting Bronson's. He, too, had noticed that the man had managed to walk a fine line between decorum and honesty.

She refilled their glasses, and Bronson faced his father.

"Father, you have been blessed with a long and prosperous life, and I strive to be a blessing to you in your old age. I have looked up to you as any son would, but never have I seen in you the happiness I see when you are with Hannah. Instead I have seen pain and heartbreak, and I have seen you overcome that pain and heartbreak by accepting new challenges, by learning new skills. Were it not for you, I would never have developed the love for sailing that's one of my greatest joys, and I will ever be grateful for your influence in my life.

"Raise your glasses to my father and his new love as they look forward to their life together. And may we all be ever mindful of each moment of our own lives, and how swiftly they flow away. To Thomas and Hannah!"

The group cheered and drank, and again Hastings drained his glass. He held out his glass toward Marley, making a face requesting more. She quickly refilled everyone's glass, but the toasting was finished, and Bronson deftly guided the conversation back to Camisha.

"Mrs. Adams, I believe you were saying…?"

She gave a thoughtful nod. "Yes. Well. I believe—that is, I'm certain …"

Marley was stunned at what she was hearing, from a normally poised woman. Hadn't she been an attorney, at one time? She stopped, steepled her fingertips, and began again. "Thomas, in this room today is one person, as far as I can tell, who knows the full truth. There are six more who know some part of the truth. And then there's you. As far as I can guess, you may know nothing."

"I don't understand."

"No, sir, you couldn't."

Hannah rose abruptly. "If you'll excuse me, I am suddenly beset by a sick headache. Thomas, would you join me?"

And with that, they were gone and the attempt at truth ended.

Hastings glanced at Marley. "I could have predicted that, you know. I expect you could have, as well."

She pressed her lips together and sighed.

"Guess that clears up who knows the most," Camisha said, rubbing her chin with the back of a finger.

Marley shut down, angry and ashamed that this liar was her grandmother.

"Land ho!" The cry reached them from far above.

"Of course land ho," Rashall muttered. "There's land ho, either side of us, for hundreds of miles. Why can't we ever just say, 'we're here'?"

Marley looked up, surprised at tears stinging her eyes as he made her laugh. She gave a choked gulp, then noticed Bronson's gaze gentle on her.

"Come on," he said. "Let's go ashore. Learn what your grandmother prefers we not know."

She leaned to kiss his cheekbone and nodded.

As they all rose, a tap came from the door, and a seaman entered. "Sir?" he asked Hastings.

The old man gave a nod and allowed the burly young fellow to place him over his shoulder; then cover him with his blanket. Marley followed after with his walking stick.

When they had placed the gangway, the group from Rosalie—with the noteworthy exception of Hannah Hastings and her fiancé—debarked.

They didn't have to walk far, just *up*. The bank's steep incline continued thirty yards, and emotion filled Marley as she recognized her family's ancestral home. Startling, how much it looked the same, and she glanced back at the *Immortal* to reassure herself that she was still where she belonged.

The stony foundation where her family had built the home at the turn of the last century—still the same. The stone exterior—identical. The shutters, the only part of the exterior made of wood—still black. A pale gray tendril of smoke emerged from the chimney, along with a delicious aroma.

On the stoop, the seaman set Hastings down. The old man raised a hand at the rest of the group, and leaned against the doorjamb with the other. "Just Merrilea."

She stepped forward and placed his walking stick in his hand. He opened the door for her with a merry smile. "I trust you remember your own home."

She crossed the threshold nervously—only then wishing she'd insisted on having Bronson along. Just to be safe. She looked back at him uncertainly—startled to find him equally anxious.

"He'll be waiting for you." Hastings held out a courtly hand toward the living room.

A shiver moved through Marley as she moved inside. The living room had a welcoming hominess it had not had since her parents had died. The walls were painted a pale peach, and a fire crackled in the hearth. She'd forgotten how gigantic it had been—large enough for she and Rachel to play within, during the summer. A hooked rug of maroon, burnt orange, antique gold, umber, and mahogany ran the length of the room under the furniture—like a carpet of autumn leaves.

A rich brown leather chesterfield faced the hearth, with two high-backed armchairs across from it—on either side of the fireplace—both much older than the sofa. They might go back as far as the turn of the century. In a corner stood a newer piece—the same cradle in which, one day, her parents would swaddle their daughters in turn.

On the far wall remained her favorite spot, and she found emotion rising into her throat. The heavy drapery—different now from that last fearful morning she'd been here, a rich flowered pattern of dark gold and wine—was closed.

She remembered the nervous young woman she'd been, and only now recognized how much she'd changed.

Hastings entered and closed the door, then called, "My dear, you have a visitor. A young lady."

Excitement filled Marley; she wasn't sure of the correct etiquette for meeting one's presumed ancestor.

The drapes slowly slid back as Hastings led her forward, First she saw dainty black shoes with brass buckles; then heavy black skirts, falling to her ankles as she lowered her feet to the floor. The drapes slid all the way to the wall, allowing the bright sunshine to flood the room, and a young lady perhaps even younger than Marley stood there.

Marley schooled her features as she stepped forward; she'd expected a much older woman—an ancestor never seemed young—and to find a girl her own age was a surprise. She grew cautiously hopeful, her intimidation fading.

Suddenly Marley grew aware of her own heartbeat racing, even a bit of perspiration between her shoulder blades. She'd always been a loner, had never had girlfriends the way other girls in school had. And she wanted this woman to like her. She wanted more than that. She wanted her friendship and her love. Then Marley knew why. The window seat. Marley felt an instant kinship with anyone who could remain hidden in the window seat rather than greeting guests she heard arriving.

The girl set her book on the window seat, then withdrew a pistol hidden in her skirts, startling Marley. This, too, she set aside with the book.

She turned to Marley, gazing at her with wide, hazel-green eyes. Wildly curly, blue-black hair was fashioned into a neat bun at the back of her head.

Marley's mouth parted in surprise. She knew this girl—but she couldn't have. She certainly had never met her. She just seemed eerily familiar, but she couldn't think of anyone she resembled. And then she placed her.

She looked similar to the woman Marley saw each morning in the mirror.

"Dear, this is Merrilea. I've told you about her."

The girl stepped forward and curtsied with a demure smile, then moved closer to her, taking both Marley's hands in hers as she searched her face.

"Merrilea, this young lady is Juliana Miller—your sister."

Chapter Forty-Two

In the cozy warmth of her family's ancestral home, Marley could do no more than stare back at the young woman holding her hands.

"I have been told so much about you," the girl said, tears springing to her eyes. "I have hoped for this day all of my life."

Despite everything—despite where and when she was, despite her marriage to a man born in 1746, despite all the miraculous events she had seen—Marley hesitated.

How could it be?

She reached out and pushed back the wispy tendrils of hair at her temple. Marley's gaze focused, then went cloudy, as her thumb brushed the thin white crescent at the corner of her eye.

"You're my own little Juli," Marley whispered. Without the least hint of awkwardness, she embraced her sister, fearing that she might break her bones. She laughed. "It's just as when you were a baby. Rachel would give you to me to hold, and I'd stay frozen in that same position, equally terrified of dropping you and breaking your tiny bones."

"Fret not—I am strong and sturdy."

The women held each other until they were sure their tears were spent, then each took an arm of their great-grandfather and led him to the chesterfield.

"You look just like me," Marley said in wonder.

Hastings raised his hand as if to forestall an argument that he had already settled. "In truth, she looks like both you and Rachel, and none of you look exactly like the other. I see your grandmother, Sarita, in the two of you. The most stunning, beautiful woman I ever had the pleasure of knowing. An Amazon, kind, true, the most perfect chocolate skin, who adored her modest English husband—a sailor who ransomed her from bondage. He was outmatched in beauty," he said with a chuckle. "But Merrilea—in you, I see my own dear William."

Juliana's skin was a shade or two darker than Marley's, confirming in a moment that all three sisters at least had a darker ancestor. She was equally as exotic as Marley and as classically beautiful as their eldest sister.

"And—our mother? Do you see her in any of us?"

Marley instantly regretted the words. Her sister remembered nothing of their mother; but for Hastings, she could see that he remembered too well.

"My own darling Cassie, so lovely like her mother, but so good and true, like my William. I saw my Cassandra in Rachel."

It was true—Rachel had looked like their mother.

"But how—how can any of this be?"

Hastings, too, laughed at Marley's skepticism. "After all you've seen, child, you doubt?"

A smile blossomed over her face at a striking moment in her life: the convergence of awareness of her place in time, in this time, this moment—and utter joy at the complete goodness of God's generosity. Perhaps life was dreadful and difficult, but it did have its moments—and this was one.

"Then—Juliana, do you know everything? All of our history?"

"Do you?"

The young woman's response was innocent, even hopeful, not confrontational. And yet, it gave Marley pause.

"No, I don't."

Hastings grasped their joined hands. "There is much we may never know, and much I believe we should leave unspoken."

"Why? Truth can never harm."

"Indeed it can." Hastings' expression was grim. "We already are far into the supernatural. We are certain of nothing. I would hope that everyone would be content with what they have been given. My old heart has been broken too many times to count over the past thirty years."

Then Marley remembered. "You knew. You knew about Juli, you knew about Rachel, and you told me nothing. For all these months, I might have known my own dear sister. What else haven't you told me?"

He pursed his lips. "If I have been less than forthcoming, I have had good reason."

"But—"

The back door opened, and she heard the footsteps of someone entering the kitchen. "Juliana, 'tis us."

Marley remembered the pistol the young woman had hidden in her skirts, realizing she had been home completely alone in these woods. How did the poor girl live?

"We have company." Juliana rose and walked toward the new arrivals.

"Oh, how wonderful!" This from an elderly woman who entered, removing her cloak. She crossed the room and placed it on a peg near from the fireplace, patting stray hairs into place. "Godfrey! How good to see you."

She had a youthful sparkle in her blue eyes and a similar energy in her step, and Marley found it difficult to tell her age as she approached them.

A man entered with similar exuberance; his hair was a wild froth of white about his head. He carried large packages wrapped in brown paper, and he grinned broadly as he set them on a table and came to place his hand on the woman's shoulder.

"Godfrey Hastings, you genteel old thing."

"You speak as if it's a felonious trait," Hastings said, raising an eyebrow.

The man threw back his head and laughed. "Oh, I've missed you, my good man. We always seem to be away when you come and go."

"Well, I did bring a ship full of other guests with me, but they shall wait outside while we finish our chat. Merrilea, this is Malcolm Henderson, a—er, a good friend of mine. And this is Mary Van Kirk."

Something about these two was disturbingly familiar—but only faintly so.

"Malcolm, Mary, this is my great granddaughter, as well as Juliana's sister—Merrilea Miller."

"Merrilea *Trelawney*," she said with a smile.

"Dear, forgive me. Merrilea has recently wed the young brother of Lord Windmere, Bronson."

Both of the convivial couple went abruptly silent. Their mouths fell open in inelegant unison.

"I see," Mary said. She slowly smiled at her companion. "Have we been keeping up with our messages?"

Silently, he looked down at her. "Why is that always my job?"

"I didn't decide that. It just *is*."

His mouth worked awkwardly, until at last he sighed. "Then no. I have not."

Mary stepped forward and extended her hand. "Congratulations on your marriage, Merrilea. We were indeed expecting you, but not today. Consequently our supper fare is meager indeed."

"We knew your sister, Rachel," Malcolm said.

Now it was her turn to be stunned.

"Aunt Mary and Uncle Malcolm are from another land, far away," Juliana put in. "From the way they describe it, it sounds quite like a fairy tale."

She looked to Hastings, attempting to cloak her confusion.

"Mary and Malcolm are brother and sister," he explained. "They travel about quite similarly to the way you have, and they aid others in their travel."

"You mean like a ... travel agent?" *In time?*

"You might say that. We are empowered to enable crossings through different *lands* that otherwise would, er, be impractical. I believe we're more properly defined as border control." This from Malcolm, who glanced at Mary as if for her thoughts on the matter.

Then, as she stared, she finally placed them. These two were the elderly couple she'd seen that day so long ago in Williamsburg, when she'd first seen Camisha with Rachel. Rachel had mentioned them when they spoke through the portal at Rosalie.

The couple were indeed travel agents—of a sort.

She sighed. "I need Bronson with me. Juliana must know the plain truth."

"And she will, dear. In time."

"She will know now. Today."

She turned for the door, but at that moment Bronson opened it. He walked the short distance to Marley and grasped her hand. "All well?"

She nodded, then introduced the others, beginning with the elderly couple and ending with Juliana. "And this is my baby sister."

He took her hand and bent deeply over it, then straightened, his gaze meeting Marley's in confusion.

She raised her hands and shook her head.

"Perhaps I know the answers."

The voice at the open door drew their attention, and they turned to find Hannah Hastings standing beside her fiancé, her face drawn with an emotion Marley could not define. Perhaps shame.

"*You.*" The voice was thick with contempt. However, it came not from Hastings—but from the kindly old Mary Van Kirk. How could she know Nan?

"Yes, me. May I be condemned by you all, but I will not live another hour with the lies I've known for twenty-five years now." Without waiting for permission, she turned to the Adamses, waiting patiently outside. "Come in and get comfortable. This will take a while, and none of you are likely to speak with me afterward. So I suggest we enjoy our last time together. If you'll excuse me, I'll make tea so we might behave as civilized folk."

With that, she disappeared into the kitchen as if it were still her own. Bronson walked to the fireplace and stoked the afternoon fire. He and Rashall fetched chairs from the kitchen so that everyone might sit, but he, instead, walked to the window and stared out. Marley joined him there, watching the steel-gray clouds moving in behind the trees.

He drew her against his chest lightly. "Red sky at morning," he reminded her in a quiet murmur, kissing her temple.

She nodded with dismal resignation.

Nan returned with a pewter tea service on a tray and set it in the midst of the table. "Marley, if you would serve, it would be a great help to me."

Marley nodded and poured the tea. And as Nan began to speak, the storm broke over the tidewater, pelting Stonefield with heavy rain and hail. As Nan continued, so did the storm, far into the night.

"There is not a single person in this room whom I have not wronged, one way or another. My tale will explain. Although I do not deserve your forgiveness, I ask it anyway.

"Thomas, Merrilea, Juliana—Rachel, though she is not here to hear my confession, nor to dispense forgiveness—Camisha, Ashanti, and, by extension of my betraying those you love, Bronson and Rashall.

"Godfrey, you gave me the love of a father and I betrayed you, as you know. I hope, not for my sake, but for your own, that you can someday—the sooner, the better—release your anger toward me. Forgive me not for my sake, but for your own.

"My story is long, and none of you have ever heard it. Feel as you wish toward me. Hate me, despise me, refuse me your forgiveness. I ask only that you not pity me, and it shames me to know that because you are all good-hearted, that is likely all that you *will* feel. And of that, even, I am undeserving. Bronson, sit down and listen to the tale. It will break your wife's heart."

Chapter Forty-Three

I know nothing of my parents. I was born in London, in 1729, and abandoned at an orphanage. From the age of four, I worked at a mill six days a week. The older I got, the longer my days grew. I worked 60-70 hours each week until I was 9, when a man, supposedly my uncle, came to claim me.

Almost immediately, he sold me into indentured servitude to pay for my passage to the colony of Virginia. In Virginia, the ship's master sold my papers to a family from the old country. I grew excited, certain that life could only be better. At least I had a small pallet in the kitchen, near the hearth, and my prospects seemed more promising. Indeed, the grandfather of this family was kindly to me, petting me with more love and gentleness than I had known until then.

One day when I went into his room to clean, he brought me onto his lap and read to me, and even now I remember how much this delighted me—that he could open this small item—this *book*—and draw forth from it a tale of brave knights, pretty ladies, and fearsome pirates. I was quite agog with wonder at what next awaited.

Then as he held me he began to touch me in a way that was shameful. Even now, I as a grown woman of many years cannot tell what he did.

Affrighted, I made as if to stand, and he hit me across the face with a stiff hard hand, making my ears ring and my eyes sting with tears. At this he repented and patted my shoulder as if nothing had happened and I went on to finish my chores, musing at these strange occurrences.

The next time I had necessity to enter his room, similar events occurred. Always he began with the kind embrace of a good man; always he roamed into that which I did not understand and which gave me the darkest, most unspeakable kind of sadness; always when I struggled, he struck me.

Always, this happened when the rest of the family was out. After this, I attempted to avoid his company except when others were present. He found me, though, regardless, and this went on for a long and dreadsome time.

In time, I came not to protest the abuse, for perhaps in his way, I thought, the old grandfather loved me.

Only now do I know that my dark sadness was shame and that my hunger for any scrap of love made me submit to this mistreatment—even to the point of being beaten, I cared not. I had never known love, and I came to believe this *was* love.

He did things to me that no grown woman should have to endure, and I a child not yet ten. Later I would be grateful that he did not do worse.

The children in the home were cruel to me, beating me, taunting me. As I grew older, the grandfather died, and I was bereft to know I would miss the morsels of counterfeit kindness this despicable man fed me.

And then the master of the household began to take notice of me—and his wife took notice of that.

When I was fourteen, at the insistence of his wife, the master sold my papers to another family, the family of a wealthy merchant sea captain. I was to serve as a companion to their elderly aunt, who was of poor health and confined to her quarters. They were quite good to me, and gave me a lovely, small room. I learned many skills from the house staff there— how to sew and mend, how to cook, how to clean. I was treated well, and soon it came time for my labor to be completed, and I began to seek paying positions using the skills I had acquired.

In Norfolk with my mistress to shop for groceries, I asked after work, and was given the name of a lady nearby who sought a maid. The happiest hour in my ill-begotten life so far came when I knocked on the door, and a young man answered.

He was a plain young man, but he smiled with the joy of life itself, and my finest moment was that hour he fell in love with me on sight.

The young man was William Hastings, visiting the son of that lady.

I spoke with her about the job, and when I left with my mistress, we had not walked far when we ran into William again. Later I learned he had been waiting for me. He asked the lady who held my papers if he could court me—perhaps believing she was my mother. God forgive me, I never corrected him.

We soon married and I moved into Stonefield. In another year, our daughter Cassandra was born. Later that year, a couple came to work for us, sent by Godfrey to help us, with a young son named Robert.

They were a godsend and, I soon learned, a curse—he being a sailor but willing to work, she being a former slave. Alone they were accepted, but the two of them caused much anger to some when they were obliged to travel into the town for provisions. Still, we kept them safe here at Stonefield, and little Robert adored Cassandra as if she were his own soulmate, she even just a babe.

I was content, but I had an uneasy feeling that something in my marriage was lacking—in point of fact, I doubted I loved William as he deserved because William was never less than the most loving, kind man a wife could hope for. I worked hard to be a good wife and mother to make up for whatever unknown lack this might be.

And before I knew it, it was over. William died of smallpox when Cassie was four, and I had no idea how to take care of our little daughter, let alone the house with servants, on my own. So I wrote Hastings and asked him if he could possibly take us in.

Of course, I didn't know firsthand of the tragedies that the Trelawneys had recently suffered—first, Thomas losing his wife, then losing his son and granddaughter. And if all that weren't terrible enough, that fine mansion at Rosalie had been burned down, and both Godfrey and Thomas were living in the former overseer's home. It's quite a lovely, comfortable, and spacious home, of course, but nothing to compare with Rosalie.

Now, as for the Millers, a curious thing occurred. Although I had loved them and wanted them to stay there at Rosalie with us—and despite Godfrey's reassurance that they were welcome, they soon moved away. Godfrey did not explain to me where they went, although I learned soon enough. This was the first time I had ever known him to be less than perfectly honest with me. He is a scrupulously good man, and as one who had become accustomed to lying, I recognized the signs of honesty in him.

However, I soon was captured with other concerns. When I met Thomas, I thought I'd never seen a more forbidding, austere, and frightening man, and I was powerfully drawn to him. I cared, too, for his son Bronson, who was my Cassandra's own age. The children grew quite close during this time.

Thomas, to my delight, developed an affection for me, and when I knew him better, I realized there was little to be afraid of in Thomas, and that he would never raise a hand against me. Despite his dangerous aura, he was as kind and gentle as my own William.

During these same years, Camisha and Ashanti came to visit Ruth and the others, and I found Camisha refreshing and she became much like an older sister to me.

Thomas had begun sailing for amusement and enjoyed it, and then, because he has a head for commerce, he soon made a business of it. The only commodity he refused to traffic in were human beings, and it was to his credit, because traders made a pretty penny buying those slaves who survived their masters' death—and then selling them at a profit. Thomas's heart had been changed by the life—and by the death—of his oldest son.

When my young Cassie was seven, Thomas invited us along on a visit he had planned to Norfolk, and Ruth Trelawney accompanied us as my chaperone.

I cannot explain the unwholesome hunger that ate at me, and while we stopped in at a store for supplies Ruth needed to purchase, I wandered out and walked along the quay, admiring the ships in the harbor and trying to imagine the adventure that occurred on these ships.

From a smaller ship docked at the quay, I noticed a dark brute of a man, black-bearded and handsome, looking as I imagined the pirates looked that the old grandfather had told me about.

He watched me from the ship, his gaze insolent on me. My initial reaction to him was rightly fear, and yet in that same instinct I was drawn to him. He invited me aboard for a tour.

Although I had not known what I sought as I had left the store, I found it in the man Lucian Caine. He showed me around his ship, including his cabin, and when he seduced me, he brutalized me. I told him who I was—the daughter-in-law of Godfrey Hastings, and he was delighted. I knew not why at the time.

I fell in love with him that day.

I had made my way back to the group before Thomas returned. On his return, he delighted me with gifts—a lovely silver hairbrush, and a silver repousse pillbox. He knew how I suffered from headaches and thought this an elegant way to have my opium tablets handy. I rarely took them, but they were the only relief to be found for my sick headaches. I tried to decline the gifts, but he insisted.

When we returned to Rosalie, Thomas surprised me by proposing to me. I still remember the moment, with little Bronson sitting on my lap, playing with the pillbox. Such a brilliant little boy—his father had explained to him that day the function of the box, though I doubt he remembers it at all.

However, he no doubt remembers his father's heartbreak that day, or in the days that passed. It gave me no pleasure to break Thomas's kind heart, and when I did, he left Rosalie for Bermuda, where he remained with Bronson for a long while, visiting Rosalie only infrequently, avoiding me when he did so.

Just as I began to pine for my Lucian, he arrived at the plantation to visit me. A young man came to the door one day, posing as a peddler, and invited me to see the wares in his wagon. When I ventured down the path, I found Lucian waiting at the wagon, with another youth, and I learned these were his sons, called Shep and Jack.

He sent the boys with the wagon on up to Rosalie to peddle their wares to the Trelawneys. He explained to me that the boys were his sons, his wife passed away. Our hunger for one another was great, and we satisfied it there in the mossy forest bed. He promised he would visit again soon, he swore his undying love for me.

And then the years began to pass. Any parent knows this moment, when the days of the week blur with the activities of the growing child. Cassie was a brilliant young girl, and Hastings engaged a tutor to teach her and to help Ruth with her school.

By this time, my Cassie had grown into a truly stunning young woman, far more beautiful than I. This would have worried me, because my beauty had been nothing but a curse my entire life, drawing terrible men as well as good. I was pleased that despite her beauty, she had but one flaw. An unmistakable birthmark on her cheekbone in the shape of a crescent moon. Indeed, it did seem quite enough to put off some suitors, and for that I was relieved. I knew that a man who would love her true and well would not care about the mark. And my own daughter had been raised with love, with men who loved her, and whose heart had not been so cruelly tortured at such an early age that she knew the difference between love and its poison twin.

Jack, as it turned out, was quite taken with her. She wanted nothing to do with him, however; she found something not quite right about him. I did not see it and thought that the son of a successful merchant like Lucian would be a good match for her.

The Adamses arrived for a visit during this, and all were delighted to see them. Camisha was thrilled to see Cassie growing into a young woman, and I find it noteworthy now to recall how tenderly she treated her. I believed it to be love for me that made her adore Cassie; it was not. Whether Camisha knew it or not, it was love for Cassie's firstborn. I did not know it then, but it's so simple now. Camisha had grown up with Rachel and loved her—Rachel had already by then come to that time, while I was yet at Stonefield, her mother growing within me.

Back then I was, as always, concerned with my own problems rather than anyone else's, and my chief concern was that of my daughter making a good marriage. I was certain young Jack would be a loving husband who would provide comfortably for her.

I asked Godfrey his thoughts, and told him Cassie's own concerns. Godfrey, knowing how I had treated Thomas, had come to have nothing but contempt for me—but he doted on my daughter as if the mark on her cheek were the true moon, and her eyes the stars. He said he would ponder it. *I once knew a young woman,* he said, *who suffered much as a child, and perhaps we can avoid it with our own dear Cassie.*

It was near the end of the Adamses' visit that I overheard a conversation between them, Godfrey, and a man who came to visit—a merry, white-haired gentleman named Malcolm. I heard a story I thought almost impossible to know—that not only was it possible for people to travel in time, but that Camisha had done so herself, and that our own Millers had indeed traveled in time—to an era when it was much safer for a white man and his black wife and their children.

Although Camisha had known that time travel was possible, she had had no control over the experience herself—only her fervent connection to the time to which she traveled. Had she not requested from Malcolm to remain permanently in this time, she would have soon returned to her own time. But it was apparent that she fell in love with Ashanti and had no desire to return to her old life.

I learned that a time portal existed on Rosalie in the entryway to the brick mansion. It had been left there for those who were meant to travel in time, I understood many years later. But that day, I learned that all one needed to travel through it, with intention, was to stand still long enough to see into the other time. Most people, Malcolm said, were unable to detect time portals because their focus was always elsewhere, never in the moment. Such are the miracles we miss each day.

This fellow also explained that a person could control his own time travel, by way of possessing a talisman from the desired period in time while crossing the portal. I could not conceive of this! According to this madman's claims, if I had a small relic from the years before Christ walked this earth, I could travel to that time—knowing as I did about the time portal at Rosalie.

At that point, he told them, the person had just twenty-four hours to experience that era and return to the portal with a talisman from their own period—only enough time for the calendar not to move—before they return through the portal. Otherwise, they remain in that time for the rest of their natural lives.

This was all far beyond my ability to understand, and I stored it away, finding it an interesting story. Just when the Adamses kissed us all goodbye, Lucian arrived from a long voyage. I had not seen Lucian's other son visit since that first night, and was told he was attending university to further his knowledge of keeping books.

It was that night that I, wishing to entertain him with any bit of knowledge I might have, told him what I had learned from the strange conversation between the old man and visitors we had had in the past. I told him that Camisha was a woman of the future, having traveled in time just this way—yet later I would remember that my fatal phrasing made it sound as if she had perhaps traveled *to* the future—not *from* the future.

This story, he found strangely compelling—especially when I mentioned her name. He was like a man obsessed. He told me that he loved me, that he would be back, and for me to wait for him. And he left that moment. He did continue to visit, but he was a merchant sea captain and the visits were sporadic. I understood by now that he had no interest in marrying me. I still loved him, still hungered for him, but I realized the foolishness of my actions too late.

One day, some weeks later, a young man visited Rosalie. I did not know him, but Godfrey acted as if he were an old friend. He introduced him to Cassie with great fanfare—I remember his emotion as he told them to always care for one another and always tell the truth.

He was a professor at William & Mary, he told us, and he had come to study important events in our area, to mold the young minds learning there. He would not be there much longer, and when he left, he said, he wanted to take my Cassie with him—as his bride.

Godfrey is not the romantic that I am, and he saw it differently and blessed their marriage. As the oldest man in the family, of course, this was his say, and my daughter was married immediately.

Only then did I learn enough about him to realize that this young man was the same Robert Miller whose parents had traveled in time. I also perceived that there was yet another way to travel in time for a period longer than twenty-four hours, where there is a connection between the person and the time, and their intentional usage of a talisman. Robert was born here; his connection was real, and he spoke of the many maps he had in his possession, any one of which I suspect was his talisman. Even so, he could not remain here indefinitely, and it would destroy me to lose my daughter forever.

During this, Lucian came to visit, and I told him of the events. I told him that Jack would be a much better match.

You see, I would never be able to see Robert as anything more than the son of the servants who had once worked for William and me. One would think I would recall those days when I myself was mere chattel—wouldn't one? But William had been so good to me, I had forgotten my own humble roots.

Robert invited us all to join him in Williamsburg for a lecture he was giving. By now young Bronson was studying at William and Mary as well, and so we made an outing of it.

Who should be sitting in that lecture than Jack! I grew confused when Robert referred to him as "Mr. Manning," believing as I did that Lucian's last name was Caine.

I was quite embarrassed to see Jack's heartbreak as he watched Robert tending to Cassie. As far as I was concerned, we could not leave quickly enough.

When we returned the next day, Godfrey's home had been ransacked, particularly Robert's room. Fortunately, nothing was missing except a small memento belonging to Robert— something he called a Phi Beta Kappa key. Although he was fond of it for its sentimental value to him—it was not his talisman, nor did it interfere with his time-traveling to the period he wished to visit. In fact, its date was 1976, of no import that we understood. Robert had traveled from the 1980s, and it was to that time that he would of course be returning.

I persisted in my stubborn desire for Cassie to marry Jack. While professors were admired well enough, he certainly could not provide my daughter the sort of comfort that the son of a merchant could. Nor could he love Cassie as Jack did, with the pure white passion of a thousand suns.

Perhaps a week passed when Lucian visited me again, and I was quite delighted, since his visits were not normally so close to one another.

However, his visit was not like his usual social calls. *My boys are gone*, he said. You see, he himself had stolen Robert's memento as a way to travel back in time. At the last moment— after the boys had gone through the portal but before he himself had—he saw Camisha visiting with Ruth there at the cabins, not far from the ruins. He quickly stepped away from the portal and allowed the opening to close.

He had expected his boys to return the next day—not realizing the degree of latitude and freedom they would have from him in another time. Perhaps they chose to stay, or they might have simply lost the talisman. We'll never know.

I attempted to comfort him. I would ask Camisha if she had any ideas on how to get them back to this time. I still had no idea how much he loathed Camisha.

His savagery was so painful I could not respond at first. Then I cried out that we would always love each other, that we could perhaps even have a child of our own.

At that, he mocked me, mercilessly. I remember his words as clearly as if it were yesterday.

You fool! Do you not wonder why you have never conceived? Have I once given you any opportunity to be with child? How stupid are you? I am a married man, and my name is James Manning. I sent my sons to kill the nigger, her friend, and Grey Trelawney. Now I learn I've sent them on a wild goose chase in time!

And for the first time, truly, I saw him as he really was. I was nothing more to him than that small child once had been to the old man who had abused me, and I with no more sense than that child.

He beat me for what felt like hours, demanding to know where Camisha was. And at that, at last, I realized I could in fact do something noble, for perhaps the first time in my life. He did not know they lived in Boston. He did not know that in 1976 she had yet to be born. And now, his sons were trapped in that time. They could not hurt Camisha there. I had no idea how short-sighted this was.

By the time Cassie and Robert married, I had recovered well enough to attend.

Cassie told me she and Robert would be leaving for distant places, and she was uncertain when they might return. Still, no one had trusted me with the truth, and I surmised on my own that their destination would be another time entirely.

I begged them not to go, and I told them—and Godfrey—what had happened with Manning's sons. Neither Cassie nor Robert were concerned, since the time frame was entirely different. They were traveling to a period years later, and in later years, cities were so busy with the many inhabitants that people could go a lifetime without ever meeting others who lived in the city.

On the day they planned to leave, we traveled to the Trelawney slave cabins. By then twenty years had passed since their liberation, and they had remarkably improved on their belongings and on themselves. Some were better educated than I, perhaps hungry for education in a way I was not. The cabins had all been improved, with glass windows and wood stoves added for warmth and cooking.

In fact, Robert knew and remembered some of the slaves who had been brought here by Grey Trelawney. I don't know how he knew them, but he did. And then they moved to what I knew to be the time portal—and although it hurt me to know my own daughter would be happily rid of me, I was willing to let her go.

Remember, Robert said, *Hold on and never let go.*

Until the last second, I was resolute—and then I could not bear it. As they walked through the portal with whatever talisman Robert had brought with him, I lunged to grab hold of their joined arms. But rather than pulling them backward or breaking their progress forward at all, I followed them into their new time, the exact moment Robert had originally left.

When I awakened, we were all back in Williamsburg—but in the year 1986. Robert had always been a well-respected history professor there, working on a project about the importance of education. And in the course of that project, he had been desperately hungry to know Thomas Jefferson, to endow him with the ideas that had informed the revolution, and to witness the conception of the new nation with the tyranny of the Stamp Act.

I soon met a man my own age who was as true as the day was long—Spencer Lewis, an older, retired widower who fell madly in love with me. We married, and I learned that my daughter no longer trusted me, so we lived at Spencer's home and I tried not to plague my daughter and her husband. My life was as comfortable as I had once hoped—and utterly empty, although I did learn to love Spencer.

Robert and Cassie lived in a small historic home in Williamsburg, where their first daughter was born, beautiful Rachel, and then my own beloved Merrilea. Fortunately, once Rachel was born, my daughter and her husband were happy to have me know their children.

Spencer doted on the girls as if he were their own grandfather—and that was the name they gave him. I was always Nan, of course.

And then Robert planned a long overdue sabbatical, during which he planned to write a book about the timeless quality of freedom and the fundamental philosophies that made the American revolution possible, and their importance in the founding of free nations throughout the world. The writing went exceptionally well, and they soon learned my Cassie was expecting their third child.

By the time of the sabbatical, they had learned that old Stonefield was for sale again. They were dismayed at the changes that had occurred in the past centuries, and they hired a contractor, who reversed these changes, restoring the old stone home to her former glory—or at least something close to it.

Then, I received word that my Cassie's little Juliana was born, and Spencer and I made plans to visit, to help out. But before we could, Spencer had a heart attack and tests were run, determining that surgery was required.

And later that week, Spencer died during that operation. I was prostrate with grief, and it took a week before I could pull myself together enough to come to Stonefield. Even as I prepared to leave, I received a phone call from the police in Richmond. They urged me to come as soon as possible, that my daughter's family had been attacked, and my granddaughters were missing.

They neglected to mention that Cassie and Robert had both been killed in the attack. However, the nature of the attack was so brutal that it made the national news, and I heard on my way to Stonefield.

By the time I reached the house, the crime scene investigators were finished, but I was shocked to realize that the house still held all the evidence that hadn't been removed. I was left to clean that up myself. I could have hired a company to do it, but I was distraught and embraced it as penance. My poor, innocent daughter and her brilliant young husband—and where were my granddaughters?

I began trying to look, myself. In the alleyway behind Stonefield, I found two tiny, heart-shaped miniatures—one of Rachel, and one of Merrilea. I remembered the Christmas gift that Robert had given Cassie the previous year, but this was the first time I had seen the miniatures they eventually had painted.

I called the detective and he rushed out and retrieved the evidence, then returned it to me after Forensics had attempted to find any fingerprints. Only a child's fingerprints were there, and I knew the girls had to have dropped them accidentally.

While visiting the police department to meet with the detective running the investigation, I met another kind man— or so he seemed—my own age. He calmed and reassured me and fell in love with me. For my part, I knew I would never love another man, but I was entirely without hope, without desire to reason. And when he arrived at Stonefield with his belongings, I did not stop him from moving in.

That man was Jim Bainbridge. His friends called him Jimmy. He was charming and vain, but he seemed kind.

Then came the day when fate softened its abject judgment against me: my granddaughters were found. My grief was softened, and I went outside in my daughter's automobile to claim the girls from the police station.

And in my driveway, I saw a black limousine pulling in behind me. At first I thought I was quite insane; the man who stepped out looked exactly like the eldest son of Lucian—that is, James Manning.

You're Shep Manning, I said. You *killed my daughter.*

He corrected my misconception. Both he and his brother had been afraid of their father and had feared him finding them in time. To help avoid this, he had dropped their old last name and adopted his middle name as their last name. Their first names were the same, his own being Maxwell.

He assured me he had no interest in harming anyone, that in fact he had recently lost his wife and his own daughter—a lie, of course, as I deserved. He told me he was in a position to make my life easier. He offered me the kind of cash that I'd never known, enough for me to comfortably raise Merrilea and Juliana.

I refused, bade him goodbye, and moved to get into my car.

He grabbed me and spun me around.

Let me say it plainly. While I do not wish to harm you, I will, should you be foolish enough to decline again. My lunatic brother Jack killed your daughter and her husband, and his tendency to go off his meds might suddenly resurface. In any case, you and all three of your grandchildren will most certainly die.

I was heartbroken and hopeless. I had no choice. Not only had I brought on the brutal murder of Cassie and her husband—I had now enabled this monster who had complete control over all of us.

He told me never to contact Rachel, nor to allow either of her sisters to contact her. He was as good as his word, and I signed over my parental rights. I never saw Rachel again. The money was delivered in cash the next day.

Jimmy soon revealed himself to be the sort of cad that I had always chosen, and as I tried to cope with the children, he began to spend the fortune I had hoped to use to raise my granddaughters.

When Jimmy began to abuse me as the others had, I no longer cared. I no longer wanted to live. I knew that the children were in fact much better off with a stranger than with me—but now I came to a place where I could neither eat nor sleep, terrified that Max Sheppard would follow through on the rest of his promise.

I wished I could somehow go back to the day before I met James Manning, a time when Thomas still loved me. In the same moment, I knew that for me, too much time had passed. I was as broken as a person ever could be, and I knew in my heart that I could never undo all the events that had made the person I had become.

At last, a solution came to me. The appropriate talisman lay in the gifts Thomas had given me the day I met Manning. That day was the last happy day in my life, and the safest time I could imagine for the girls—before Manning had existed in my life.

I filled the pillbox with painkillers and left it at home, intending to return home and swallow them all. But I did bring the silver hairbrush that Thomas had given me that day. I drove the girls down to Rosalie. I walked them to the portal, and I hugged them both close to my breast and kissed them and whispered my fondest hopes for them in their lives.

Then I lay the hairbrush across Juliana, her arms holding it in place. I placed one portrait in each of their hands, in case they were separated—Rachel's portrait into Merrilea's, and Merrilea's portrait into Juliana's tiny fist.

At last, there was no more putting off to be done. I stood still and waited to see clearly into the portal. Eventually, it did appear, as Godfrey's friend Malcolm had indicated it would.

Then I held Juliana in one arm and Merrilea's hand with my free hand. Staying firmly on this side of the portal, I knelt and placed Juliana on the ground where the Trelawneys would quickly find her, and I gently nudged Merrilea, telling her to be a big girl and take care of her sister.

As bad timing went, who should be there besides Godfrey Hastings? He would've been perfect, had he not seen me—but see me he did, and he angrily called out to me. Until that moment, I had believed that Godfrey was incapable of such passion.

You would abandon two young children in a field?

Godfrey, it's my grandchildren, Juliana and Merrilea. Take them and raise them as your own.

Merrilea, come here! he said.

And I rushed away from the portal and ran toward my car. Only when I was perhaps twenty yards away and stopped to look back did I hear the tiny voice.

Nan! Nanny-nan! Don't forget Marley!

Oh, dear God—my little Merrilea had stepped back through the portal, holding her arms out to me as she began crying and toddling after me.

What had I done?

I rushed back to gather her in my arms, my tears pouring freely, wetting her cheeks as I held her close. And I hurried back to see if I could snatch back little Juliana—but the portal was closed. As long as I stood there, it would not open again, and my Juliana was lost from me for all time.

Chapter Forty-Four

The storm had continued to rage through the afternoon, and now the rain drummed against the stones with quiet persistence as Hannah fell silent.

Marley was numb. She glanced without expression at her husband, who sat in the chair at her side—his elbows propped on either knee, his fingertips touching, his own gaze on the floor—and then at her sister, sitting on the couch. Juliana had paled, looking as if she might faint—or vomit.

Beside her, Mary held her hand and sat as stoically as Malcolm, on Juliana's other side.

Camisha and Ashanti sat near the fire—much the same as Bronson, regarding the floor in grim silence.

Standing beside his mother, Rashall focused on Juliana. The sight was a welcome distraction—he was fascinated, and the thought pleased Marley. Then she realized she knew nothing about her sister. For all she knew, she might be engaged to be married. She might *be* married.

Godfrey Hastings sat in a chair alone, grimly staring at his walking stick.

Thomas, at the window, watched the rain without expression, as if unaware that his fiancée had been speaking for the better part of an hour.

In the end, the person who broke the silence was the one who had begun it when she finished her soliloquy. She still stood near the tea service. "Malcolm, why was I allowed to travel back to my natural time again? I expected to spend the rest of my life where I was."

He tugged at his ear, then rubbed his chin, selecting his words. "You know the answer to that. You have explained it in the past hour."

"I truly don't. I thought it might be a second chance to love Thomas."

"You are a dangerous actor and cannot be trusted with such knowledge, to the point that we must take action to remove this threat."

This startled everyone in the room except Mary, who went on, "Tomorrow you will awaken in your bed with all memory of those events related to the time travel wiped away."

Malcolm continued. "Everyone you know, as far as you are concerned, has always lived in the eighteenth century."

"But—my daughter, Cassandra. Those memories? And … Marley's childhood?"

"Listen to me. You will remember nothing of the twentieth or twenty-first centuries. You lived here, gave birth to your daughter, she married Robert Miller, a neighbor boy; both died in a way you do not remember but have no native curiosity over. Even if someone were to ask you how they died, you will deftly change the subject without realizing it."

Then Mary spoke. "Look at the people in this room. Look at the suffering you caused. To overcome your own suffering as a child, you came to be a person who felt no sympathy toward anyone else. Through your recklessness, you caused the death of your own daughter and her husband. You sold your granddaughter to a man you knew would abuse her, and you abandoned your other granddaughters—mere days after all the trauma these little girls had already undergone! When you were forced to deal with poor little Merrilea, so confused at that abandonment, you raised her in a home where she grew as fearful as a mouse, and you allowed a man without honor to waste the resources that could have been used to improve her life. You left Juliana unattended in a field, and her barely two months old. And has it not occurred to you even yet that you yourself and Cassandra were still living in 1753, the year you left your granddaughter? Did that not occur to you as a catastrophic anomaly in time?"

One glance made it clear that it never had—not even during the decades that had passed.

"Godfrey was running a plantation, and as much as he would have loved to raise the child, he recognized the potential for disaster. You would have had no idea who these foundling girls were, and God knows what you might have done with them. Godfrey dislikes this time travel business already. For all your rude eavesdropping, you might have understood that. Fortunately, he knew a couple ideally equipped for rearing a foundling, or a wild animal may have otherwise slain our beloved Juliana. You betrayed Thomas—"

"Stop it." From the window, Thomas turned, grimly surveying the room. "This endless haranguing helps no one."

At this Hannah rushed to him, grasping his free hand between hers and bringing it to her lips. "Oh, Thomas! Can you then forgive me?"

He looked down at her, his silver gaze sad. "Today, no." After a long moment in which she peered at him with naked humility, he sighed. "I no longer know what to believe from you; even this seems affected. But now I am angry and later that will pass. I have wronged others and know that God can work miracles of forgiveness in a person's heart. I have known forgiveness when I did not deserve it. Who can say. If what I have heard today is possible, perhaps this is. Mayhap along with the time-travel in your memory will go those terrible things that were done to you, that left you incapable of accepting love from an honorable man. In the meantime I will pray for us all, and I suggest you do the same."

He disentangled his hand from hers, placed it on his walking stick with the other, and returned his attention to the rain, which was beginning to slow.

"Very well, then. I understand your anger and for now merely hope that all of you can forgive me in time. I love each of you as much as I know how. Juliana, may I impose on you that I might retire to a spare room? If not, I understand. I am ready to put this day behind me."

"Of course." Juliana, the one with the fewest memories of this woman, rose from the couch and led her down the hall.

When she returned to the room, she hesitated at the doorway. "Forgive me for my poor hostessing. I know all of you must be hungry. Allow me to make some bread and reheat our stew, and we will have supper."

Marley and Camisha joined her in the kitchen. Camisha retrieved dishes even as Marley opened the silverware drawer, oddly comforted to find that 240 years before, forks and knives were kept in the same place.

They worked silently to set the table, then returned to the kitchen, where Juliana was mixing cornbread. She passed another large bowl to Marley. "Perhaps you could mix up some pan bread or biscuits, so they have a choice?"

Marley mixed up a simple quick bread, and they placed the skillets into the oven.

When she straightened, Camisha touched her shoulders. "Juliana, I am—or was—very good friends with your sister, Rachel. We were quite close, thirty years ago."

"What happened to her?"

"She has a family with Grey Trelawney, in the future."

"Ah! This very thought is beyond my imagination."

"You'll understand, in time."

They joined the others in the front room. They were speaking as men ever did—the weather and what the travel going home might be like.

As they spoke, Marley stood next to the desk on the wall opposite the fireplace. The men discussed what Dunmore's next trick might be, after the spectacular loss at Great Bridge.

She glanced down at the desk idly, noticing the silver hairbrush that had delivered Juliana to this time. Beside it, she saw a tiny framed portrait. "Oh, my!"

Bronson rose and walked to her, resting his arm on the wall above her head as he bent to see what she held. "My Marley. You've found your other half."

"One of my other thirds, perhaps. I'll never stop missing Rachel. I don't believe in harboring anger, but it flabbergasts me that I could have known her at any time, but for my own grandmother being dishonest with me about my own name— or Rachel's adopted name. And all those years, spent with that awful, abusive Jimmy."

He kissed her temple. "I know. It is not fair. Did you get nothing from the relationship?"

"I learned to sail."

"That, you would have learned anyway, although perhaps it did make my way easier. I am selfish to say it, but I am glad you're here with me. And if what Hannah said earlier is true, in doing it, she saved your life."

She leaned against him, comforted by his smell. Then she joined Juliana on the couch, holding out the framed miniature to her. "Yes, it's you. Aunt Mary told me about you, some years ago. I had no idea you lived in another time."

Silently, Marley opened the pillbox, showing her its twin. "This is our oldest sister, Rachel. They were kept in a locket our mother owned. On the back, it was engraved. It said, *As time is, so beats our hearts—tender, immortal, forever.* I stole it from our mother's jewelry box to give to Rachel for her birthday. Rachel was so angry with me—she always looked out for me. Mama was so amused, she insisted that Rachel keep it. It was a gift from our father, you see. It was before you were born, or you can bet he would've made sure there was room for three."

"What were they like—our parents?"

"I was three when they passed away, but I remember them so well. Twenty years later, my heart still hurts for them. Mama was beautiful—she looked like Nan, except that she had a beauty mark on her cheek. She had the faintest English accent, also like Nan. She was kind, and intelligent, and generous.

"Our father was—as you just heard—a professor at William and Mary and an historian. Nan mentioned once to me that our other grandmother was beautiful and exotic looking. I think that you and I probably look more like our father's side of the family than of Nan's."

"And the scars we share … do you know where those come from?"

"The man who killed our parents did it."

"Our poor Papa and Mama. Do you suppose they suffered much?"

And in one of those rare moments of her life, Marley lied without a single regret. "I think not. I believe it ended quickly."

Anxious to turn the topic of conversation in another direction, Marley called out to Rashall, who stood chatting with Bronson and Thomas and Ashanti.

"I'd love for you to meet someone. He's the funniest, most charming man I've ever met—aside from my husband."

His eyes flashed suspiciously toward her, and she impatiently gestured him over.

"Rashall, have you met my baby sister?"

He scratched his neck suddenly, then shook his head silently. She had the strongest urge to ask him if he'd been drinking.

"Well, Juliana, this is Rashall Adams, my husband's partner on the *Immortal*, their ship. Rashall, this is my sister, Juliana Miller."

He bent low over her hand, bringing it to his mouth in a shy gesture.

"Hello, Mr. Adams. Are you enjoying yourself?"

"No. I mean, yes, I am enjoying myself. I mean, no, this is all terribly sad. I mean—please, call me Rashall."

She gave him a wide smile in genuine pleasure at his halting words, her lips parting and revealing even, white teeth. Like her sister, her mouth was shaped so it seemed each corner held a small dimple, and her smile deepened her beauty.

Rashall fidgeted, staring at her uneasily.

"All right, then. Merrilea tells me you're a ship's captain."

"No. Bronson's the captain, I'm just, well, not a captain. I'm more of a, well, no captain. I'm actually an ordained—well, as ordained as I can be—but I'm not a priest, I can, you know—I'm, well, yes I am ordained."

Marley watched, mystified as he stammered like a child. And, abruptly, he pressed his lips together as if to staunch the babbling flood of syllables. She glanced back at Juliana, who met her gaze with an innocent smile, as if nothing at all were amiss.

"Soup's on," Camisha called from the kitchen.

"I'll go help," Rashall and Marley said in unison.

Marley swallowed down laughter, but she couldn't keep herself from smiling broadly at him, then lay her hand alongside his forearm as she rose. "Ray, why don't you see if Malcolm can direct you to any wine that might be available? Or would you rather help Juliana—"

By then he was already ducking his head in a hasty bow, then heading off on the quest for vino.

The women exchanged a smile. "I'm not sure, but either he's sweet on you, or he's having some sort of nerve fit." Marley patted Juliana, and together they joined Camisha in the kitchen.

Chapter Forty-Five

As Bronson gazed out over the Sargasso Sea, he filled his lungs with the warming sea air. With each tick of the rising mercury, his spirits had lightened. Now, he squinted for any sight of the British island on the horizon. It had been a long winter, and he was ready for April's sunshine on his back.

On New Year's Day, John Murray, the Fourth Earl of Dunmore, had ordered the burning of Norfolk. Although the town had been infested with loyalists, they—like Boston's Tories—had deserted their homes for the Royal Navy ships in the harbor. The British Navy began bombarding the town, but then came ashore to selectively destroy patriot homes. Likely the good Tories stood at the gunner's elbow wringing their hands and imploring them to "aim it that other way." At that point, the patriots had taken it upon themselves to loot and destroy what was left.

Dunmore remained floating in the Chesapeake Bay for the time being, but Bronson was certain his days as an American governor were numbered.

In February, the Virginia Gazette had published excerpts of a small book—a pamphlet, no more. Bronson had secured the entire work since and read it to his wife, the Adamses, and a goodly group of Trelawneys at Rosalie, over lunch.

Naturally, Marley already knew all about the book and its author—an English defender of American freedom, named Thomas Paine. She had called it America's clarion call to equality.

The winter grew miserable and by January Bronson, Rashall, and all of their men were mad with the cold and the deprivation of war.

They had returned to Boston in March to collect Helen and the smaller children for their journey to St. George's. As a reward for some good deed certainly performed in another life, he had arrived to the majestic sight of the entire blockaded British fleet evacuating the harbor.

They had waited just offshore to watch the spectacle, but they were close enough to hear the cheers and the laughter. Bronson had grown close enough to many of the citizenry to feel their tears of relief.

"I hear tell me patron saint drove the snakes out of Ireland, but I be ready to ask the Pope to name a St. George Washington!"

Padraig, of all people, had appeared that day to witness the promenade of warships. The old Irish cook rarely made an appearance above deck. That the British chose to leave the city on the seventeenth of March was something for those who had grown up there, like Padraig, to celebrate always.

Now, with his passengers aboard the ship his brother had once commanded, he oddly found himself anticipating his thirtieth birthday. Still a few months off, but this was the first year in many that he looked forward to it, just when he had the most to lose, if that infernal curse were true.

The benefit of turning down history-making commissions from a wartime general was the freedom to arbitrarily declare holidays, and his crew was drunk with excitement over an entire week on the island to do as they wished. After that, they would get to work. As tempted as he might be to remain on the island until he quietly passed his thirtieth birthday with Marley at his side, a new country he loved was being born, and she needed every man capable of fighting for her.

Rashall sat off a dozen feet with young George. "Now here we'll make a bosun whistle knot. Some people call it the Chinese button knot. You've got your carrick knot, there—"

"Desist!"

Rashall looked up. "Excuse me?"

Bronson gave him an incredulous look. "The boy just made a carrick, and you're taking him directly into the bosun whistle? Why not send him off with Conrad for a while to learn navigating?"

"Aye aye, Cap'n!" The cheerful young boy, ever eager for life's next moment, raced off toward the wheel.

Bronson gazed after him. "'Twas a jest, but with his exuberance, perhaps he'll be running the whole ship in another month and I can lie about all day."

Joining Bronson at the rail, Ray raised his spyglass. "I think you do already with that wife of yours."

"Every chance I get. The island should show in the next few hours. Have you recuperated yet?"

"From?"

"If my wife is correct, you're either pining or heartbroken."

"Your wife is incorrect. I am fine and looking forward to finding suitable company on the island."

"Suitable. We know what that means. Be sure to bring a sheath along."

"How crass you are, my domesticated friend."

"Indeed. And I'm sure you meant a proper chess partner."

"Speaking of chess, what's your strategy with the powder?"

"We are on a pleasure cruise, celebrating my honeymoon, albeit five months late. At the end of that, we'll take care of business. If things continue, this might well be our last voyage here. The heat will grow too hot, the territory too hostile."

"And our … deposits?"

Bronson hesitated. It wasn't the first time he'd thought of the gold buried under the Bermudian Trelawney home. "I'd like to take it on this trip."

Rashall nodded, and for a time they were silent. Then, suddenly: "I'm thinking of adopting the boy."

This surprised Bronson. "Young George? Why? He'll be like Jem, son to us all."

"Exactly that. A boy needs a man for a father, not a crew."

"Are you implying something about Jem?"

Ray leaned back against the rail and, closing his eyes, tilted his head up to the sun's warmth. "Absolutely not. The boy is Kit's, not yours, and 'twas kind of you to bring him on. But I am not you. I grow hungry to put down roots."

"Then why did you sail right out of the life of the young lady at Stonefield?"

With rare foul humor, Ray cast him a dark look. "Does nothing about my courting her strike you as a predicament?"

"Clearly there is black blood in my wife's family. Do you think *I* saw that as a predicament?"

"Yes. And your wife looks quite as white as her sister does. And, notably, as white as you."

"What do you think your mother would say to you about that? You, who she named after a white woman."

Ray ignored that. "My mother knows things I do not, things that are apparently upsetting enough that she wasn't at all surprised that General Washington declined to offer me any kind of commission."

"Still here we are at Cambridge, long after General Washington has decamped."

"I am trying to help you see the truth. What world should we choose to live in, my wife and I? Where our children are not allowed to attend school? Where I become a field worker? In what world, sir, could a love like that live?"

Bronson giggled. "Sir?"

Ray's lips went tight.

"Tell me this. How different will this world you bemoan be without Juliana in it? Will losing her change the world?"

Ray gave him a quick look; Bronson had gotten through. Still, he hesitated.

"My friend, you forget no one is a greater champion for your happiness than I. I have seen you know many women. And I saw the way you looked at that woman—the way you look at your mother's cooking after you've been eating hardtack for a year."

"She's a beautiful woman, I'll give you that. Did you see—green eyes? And when she smiles, it's as if the sun has risen."

"Oh, my. Yes, she's as gorgeous as my Marley. Now shut up. I've seen how you feel about her. And I say that if you don't act on that—and soon—you will regret it the rest of your days. And that new son of yours as well. Think how delighted he might be to find himself suddenly in possession of a mother as lovely as Juliana."

"Land ho!"

Rashall harrumphed. "Well. There you have it. Two experienced sea captains, so knotted up by mere women that in sunny daylight we miss an entire island."

"Mere women. Perhaps those you've known in the past. Not the young lady we met in December. Not my wife. And if your mother gets wind of that phrase, well, God help you."

"Good day, sir."

Bronson laughed as Rashall strode toward the hatch. These seamen had sailed into St. George's so frequently, they could manage blindfolded. As they neared the island, he watched the Union Jack slide up the line. A troublesome unease gnawed at him for their *Appeal to Heaven* flag. And only then did it strike him.

Somewhere between their departure last October and their arrival today, he had—without any awareness of when it had occurred—lost his identity as a man born in the British Empire but roaming the seas, subject to no man. Now, he was an American.

Glancing around the deck, he noticed his wife emerging from the hatch, and the warmth that lit his shoulders stole into his heart.

She'd brought with her the buckskin outfit she'd fashioned just for such trips, but she was out of it now, and perfectly a woman. Today in a white frock studded with caramel-colored roses—nearly matching her eyes. Those eyes roved over the shrouds, smiling and waving as she saw Jem far above. Jem surely must have waved back. For his part, he couldn't take his eyes away from her. The salt breeze caught a few loose strands of hair that whirled around her head.

How he loved her.

When she saw him, a look entered her visage that he had come to love. There was something about his person that she found pleasing. He knew not what. He simply stood leaning to one side on the rail, bent slightly, one elbow on the rail, the other hand casually tossing and flipping his spyglass.

Her step hastened, and his own desire for her grew even as he attempted to control it. He stopped flipping the spyglass, fearful that in his excitement he might well drop it.

She reached him and lay her soft, cool hands against his forearm. Her fingertips slid beneath the cuff in a surprisingly intimate gesture, and she tiptoed to kiss his cheek lightly.

"Did I hear we're there?"

"Still a bit left. 'Tis true, the crew knows these waters. But the island is surrounded by coral reefs and is a graveyard for many ships. Still, we should be off the ship in another hour."

"Then … do we have time to …?" Her tongue touched the corner of her mouth as she lowered her gaze, then looked up at him imploringly.

"I would love nothing more. But it shouldn't be very enjoyable for you, my darling."

"I should find it quite enjoyable right now to kneel in front of you and—"

He kissed her with quick, silencing passion. Her dark eyes lit up with seductive fire, and her fingers curled around his bicep with hungry insistence. "Please?"

The quiet urgency of her plea reached him. He was but a man, after all. "Two minutes. Go."

As she vanished down the hatch, he busied himself with leisurely glances at the island. *Yes*, he thought. There was the place.

On the way to his cabin, he directed Deming to set them down off a remote beach of which he was fond. It would take them longer to row ashore now, but that was the least of his concerns at the moment. Deming would place them off a pink beach, he and Marley would return, and he would do some serious body-worshipping for an entire week.

And with that in mind, he retired to his cabin. As he entered, he noted her sitting demurely on the bed, and he closed and barred the door behind him, leaning back against the door. Leisurely biting his lip, he contemplated her with a glimmer of a smile.

She flew into his arms. When he would've been gentle with her, she would have none of it. She tiptoed to kiss his jawline, then his ear, biting lightly. He caught her hands in his, and she grabbed them and shoved him against the door, catching him off-guard.

He was aflame with arousal, but he forced himself to relax, allowing his wife to pace her seduction.

Releasing his hands, she hastily unbuttoned his shirt and pulled it open, covering his chest with open-mouthed kisses as if he were a feast—licking, lightly biting his nipples. Her hand lowered to the buttons at his breeches and made quick work of those as well, then let the front drop away.

She gave a sound of hungry satisfaction as she lightly grasped and stroked him. *My, but the lass was a quick study.*

His breath caught as she knelt before him, taking him between her lips, tasting him, her hands cupping and stroking him, even the sound of her enjoyment bringing him pleasure.

Surprised at how quickly she'd left him fully hard, needing her, he forced himself to wait. What kind of woman had he married, as full of lust for life as he himself?

And then he brought her to her feet, hastily seeking her mouth with his, cupping her breasts, impatiently pushing aside her dress—dear God, no stays, just soft, full woman. He pulled his mouth away from hers and suckled at her breasts.

"Bed," he directed, straightening.

"No. Here. Now." Her gaze was smoky with pure lust.

In a smooth, swift motion, he cupped her buttocks, lifted her against him, and turned, bracing her against the door with his body. Clutching her skirt and petticoats in one fist, he lifted them, displaying her long thighs to his seeking gaze. She raised one leg around him, seeking him, but the position was awkward.

As if she were no heavier than a bird, he slid his large hands underneath her, parted her thighs, lifted her, and planted himself within her in one stroke. His mind was wild with her frantic seduction, and his thrusts were hard, without nuance, almost violent. Even so, she dug her heels into his back as if he were a stallion, giving his forceful motion new need. As close as he was, he suddenly realized he was slamming her against the door.

He gasped out, "Am I hurting—"

She interrupted him with a stark direction, and he endeavored to oblige.

A sudden knock. "Hey, it's me—"

"Go-a-way!" he ground out, even as Marley's pleasure overcame her, followed by his own.

They both heard Rashall snickering as he climbed the hatch.

He lowered his head to lightly kiss her mouth, his nose brushing against hers. He felt her breath mingle with his own, and he found himself marveling over the many miracles that had taken place so that their breath might be one.

"I no longer know where I end and you begin. You are with me in my waking moments, and in my most blessed dreams. You are in my heart now—and when we are miles apart. I am lost without the sight of your face, the sound of your laughter. My heart and yours are one."

Chapter Forty-Six

Although Marley knew nothing of it, there were two Thomas Trelawneys. The first was fearless and curious, an adventurer; the second was cowed and chastened, a penitent.

The first was born the son of Grey Davies in 1699, on an island in Wales, to a family of wanderers and adventurers. Gypsies were said to be in their distant heritage, and Thomas's hair was as black as a Sardinian's. His eyes, a piercing gray so bright as to be silver, made one cautious without knowing why.

His father had wandered to the village of Anglesey as a youth and taken up fishing, and the sea air had agreed with him. Thomas, a curious lad, had wondered before wandering, and it was a man of letters who had come to their town to live out his last years who awakened in Thomas the yen for far-off lands.

The man, a fascinating law professor originally from Cornwall, recently of Oxford, had spoken with a calming, understated accent that gave Thomas an instinctive shame over his own provincial, lyrical tones. In the moment he met him, the boy of 12 began to emulate him. Thomas's own father did not begrudge the boy his book learning, and Thomas learned early on the importance of a father looking out properly for his son.

By the time the man died four years later, he had taught the young man all he knew. He had learned Latin and Greek, he had read the classics, he had learned every detail of English law. And he had learned that much of this would be of no use to him unless he had a formal claim to such knowledge. He advised the boy to go to London for this, and he even gave him the funds and the name of a man who would admit him to Oxford based on his own recommendation.

Thomas traveled to London and there in a shop met a well-born young lady named Lucy Huntington. He spoke and behaved like the gentleman he had appeared to be, and when he introduced himself to her, he made a distinct break from the island boy he'd once been and became the son of a barrister who had taught at Oxford and recently passed away. *Thomas Trelawney, at your service.*

He had awakened the morning after their elopement in southern Scotland with fierce regret—for the wanderer in Thomas had been awakened in the past year, and he would not be denied.

He left like a scoundrel in the night, leaving her a stack of notes to pay her way home—instructing her to seek an annulment. Not for decades would he allow himself to think of her again—while he sailed on to Virginia and then through his formal education at William & Mary; married a woman he soon learned was barren; met a young man claiming to be his son; watched his wife die of a fever; and then married a young woman he cherished, Jennie.

And in that time his eyes were opened and he came to accept that the young man who'd laid claim to his name was in fact his son. It had taken almost a decade before the young man—Grey—had forgiven him for his rejection, and Thomas was granted the joy of knowing his granddaughter, Emily.

One might think that the second Thomas Trelawney had been born when he rejected his family name, but no. That had occurred at the age of 47, when Thomas watched his most beloved wife die giving birth; followed two days later by the fire at Rosalie, the death of his son, his precious granddaughter, and Rachel, the woman who had loved them.

With these events, the spirited adventurer had been broken and became obsessed with signs and seers. It had taken the young woman, Rachel, telling him in plain terms of the suffering his little wife Lucy and her son had endured at his hand before he came to understand the consequences of his adventuring. The old midwife at Rosalie had seen death in Jennie, and he had ignored her warning.

And so in 1746 Thomas Trelawney the fearless adventurer became a chastened poltroon. He resigned from his place as a burgess in Williamsburg, he spent his days raising his son, and, when his mourning began to heal, he yearned for the ocean he'd known as a boy. He fed this by learning to sail, and the sea became an elixir, a tonic for his spirit and his heart.

And then Hannah Hastings had come into his life.

Thomas, still a romantic, now a coward, had loved her in a moment but had kept the beautiful young widow at arm's length. He had learned his lessons about consequence, and about reaping what one had sown—about his own tendency to destroy the people he loved the most.

He came to believe that this daughter-in-law of his own son's good friend Godfrey Hastings was as good as Godfrey himself, and he endeavored to love her.

We know how that turned out.

On his honeymoon with Jennie, they had visited an island due east of Virginia, and they both had loved it. She had loved its exotic character, with its grape-scented sea mulberry and its pink beaches. He had loved it for St. Peter's, an Anglican church that had endured amid hurricanes for over a century. Thomas was drawn to that which survived the unendurable.

And so, when he lost Jennie, it was in the shadow of that citadel that he sought protection for his young son and built a new home, one where his son could grow strong and faithful and true in the warmth of the Bermuda sun.

His home lay in the heart of St. George's. The home looked more like the offspring of a sugar plantation house and his straitlaced colonial home back in Williamsburg. Not quite as large as a plantation mansion yet spacious, it had a broad porch running along its entire front—and plenty of room for guests. The home itself was elevated to protect it from flooding during tropical storms, its lowest level unused.

Marley stood on the walkway watching Thomas as he approached his home.

He had slowly thawed in the face of Nan's contrition and invited her along when Bronson returned him to St. George's. She had undergone a mental and emotional transition so traumatic she had rushed to the rector at Bruton Church for absolution.

Marley could tell she didn't yet have Thomas's forgiveness, however—but likely he, too, would forget in time. Bitterness and hatred took more energy than most people had.

When they arrived at the house, a crisply uniformed man welcomed them, surprising Marley with a broad Gullah accent. Indeed, she would find it an unusual sound on the British isle.

"Ah, Mr. Bronson! How good to see you back so soon. I see you escorting a pretty young lady today."

"Mesu, this is my wife, Merrilea. Marley, this is Mesu. He's been here as long as I remember. Mesu keeps the place in one piece, whether it's a cloudless day, or whether there's a hurricane blowing."

"Please, call me Marley," she said, extending her hand.

He bowed deeply to her and kissed her hand. "I am honored to make your acquaintance, Madame Marley."

Within the home, they might have been at any colonial plantation, with its tastefully appointed decor. Everyone was shown to a guest room to relax after their long journey while their belongings arrived from the ship. With this chore complete, all the men of the *Immortal* were dismissed for holiday—save a handful who would serve as crew for the newlyweds' belated honeymoon.

Bronson's exhaustion from the voyage caught up with him, and he napped while Marley read on the verandah outside their room, their door open. She had learned early on that her husband, who'd taken his first step on sea legs, slept soundest to the pounding of the surf.

From their suite, she could look out on the Atlantic ocean and the thick, verdant foliage below the verandah. She sat there with her book open, enjoying the distant crash of waves against the rocks. An hour passed as she inhaled the strange scents—a combination of the salt air and the unique flora of the island. At last she understood why so many people loved beach vacations.

She heard another door open down the way and looked up, happy at the thought of a chat with Camisha.

Nan emerged from her room.

Marley looked back down at her book.

"Oh—I'm sorry, I didn't realize you were out here reading. I'll leave you to it."

After a moment, Marley said. "It's all right. You're welcome to join me, or I can go inside—"

Nan shook her head, her eyes wide. "Don't be silly, Merrilea."

"Come and sit with me, if you like."

"They're serving tea soon. Imagine. Tea to a gaggle of Americans. Some Brits don't learn. I asked that they add coffee for the colonials."

Marley smiled, concealing the anger simmering within her.

Her grandmother sat in the chair beside hers and rocked quietly back and forth, gazing at the horizon.

"I have a question."

Nan glanced at her.

"*Can* you understand the extent of the damage you did not only to Mom, to Dad—but to your own granddaughters, every single day of our lives?"

"Merrilea, I'm afraid I don't know what you're speaking of. But when one makes a decision, they make it once. Not every single day."

"That's not true. Every day when I woke up, you chose again to look me in the face and lie to me. When I got old enough to wonder why I had the same name as your married name—rather than my mother's married name—you lied again. My father suddenly became your son, rather than your

407

son-in-law. And to do this lie, you denied you'd ever said otherwise, as if I were too stupid or absentminded to remember what you had told me. All the years, the countless lies, the mockery you made of me because I was my father's daughter, loving the past. Nan, I loved the past because I was a part of it! My parents were born there! I deserved to know the truth! Instead, you created an awkward, fearful, broken bird of a human being who didn't know her own name."

"Marley—"

"Don't call me that! If not for Bronson I would still be living in a darkened library, studying ancient manuscripts and imagining the people who lived in those times, feeling guilty for the old book that belonged to me rightfully.

"No, actually—if not for Bronson, I'd be dead. He saved me, he breathed life into me, and he restored me to the full person my mother and father and Rachel created, full of bravery and laughter. Nan, I am sorry for the suffering you've known in life, but much of it, you've brought on yourself. And I earnestly hope Thomas Trelawney can forgive you, because I don't know that I ever can."

She rose from her chair, tears spilling from her eyes as she returned to the room.

Bronson sat in an armchair, leaning forward, his gaze on her pained. He'd clearly awakened during her tirade and waited. Now he rose, closing the door behind her and drawing the drapes.

She rushed into his arms, and he held her silently as she wept.

At last, he handed her his handkerchief, and she wiped her face and blew her nose.

"Would you prefer I call you Merrilea?"

"Call me what you like. One of my greatest joys is when you call me your Marley. The name on your lips only brings me happiness. As for Nan—this may change, but today I want nothing more to do with her."

He held her to him, stroking her hair and massaging her back. "Do you remember what Malcolm said? It's been removed from her memory. Truly she has no knowledge of what you speak of."

The reminder somehow made it more difficult. In that moment, Marley wasn't sure which was worse—living a dishonorable life and remembering how your misdeeds had made others suffer—or to exist without apparent consequence, to an empty world without knowing why.

"Except you have to live with the fallout."

He kissed the nape of her neck lightly. "That's why I'm here." After a moment, he added, "You do know that I have a grossly unpleasant chore ahead of me?"

"What's that?"

He hesitated, his gaze grim. "I shall have to kill this Manning fellow. He's proven he will leave us no peace, no matter where we go. And I do not live my life looking over my shoulder. Or knowing that my loved ones must."

"Just let me know how I can help."

He stopped in his father's room long enough to tell him goodbye—they would return for him next week, if he was of a mind to return to Virginia. As they left the house with the few belongings they'd brought, they found Rashall, too, leaving, carrying the bag a servant had just brought up.

The two men stood on the porch regarding one another. Marley walked to a nearby cedar tree, leaning back and holding her hat as she gazed up idly.

Bronson smiled grimly, gesturing at the bag. "You're not coming along on our honeymoon, you know."

"I would show you up."

"Never make that joke again."

Rashall laughed, then slowly sobered. "I'm going to visit the parish church. See who's there now. See if I can stay a few days."

"Ah. Should be a nice visit. It *will* be just a visit, won't it?"

A pained smile came to Rashall's face. "I don't know."

"You say this to wreck my honeymoon, out of jealousy."

"Truly, what kind of man waits five months to take his bride on a honeymoon, and then cuts it short after a mere week? Most come back from a honeymoon with a newborn."

"What kind of man goes off on holiday while his country is at war?"

"One who's fetching gunpowder. Need I remind you?"

"What brought this on?"

Rashall considered that. "Two men had to die in December, that I might live."

"As I recall it, two men tried to kill you. They were no sacrificial lambs, as well you know."

"The killing grows old."

"We do not kill unless a life is at stake."

"I need this time, my friend. I hope it will be enough to remind me of the job we have."

Bronson clapped Rashall on the shoulder. "Shall we walk you to the church?"

"No. I still need to tell Mother and Father."

With that, they descended the steep porch steps to Marley.

"You take care of this boy while I'm gone. He's not used to being without his quartermaster. Deming's capable, but you'll have to step up to keep him amused."

Naturally, she had to have an explanation, and so he gave it. When he saw her surprise, he laughed. "You didn't think I would put my dearest friend's marriage on the hook by pretending to be an Anglican vicar, did you? I was ordained here one year, while I skipped a voyage to Polynesia."

"I had no idea. Is there any way we can help, Rashall?"

After a long moment, he hugged her. "You can pray for me, Marley, as I always pray for you both. Some wisdom on my part would be especially useful. Not all of us are blessed with the clarity of a burning bush."

"We will."

And with that, he turned back to the house. Climbing the steps, he disappeared inside.

Marley hugged her husband's waist. "He'll be all right. He just needs some time to himself."

He turned, thoughtful as he gazed up St. Peter's. The place that had always reassured his father left Bronson troubled. "This time, I think it's more than that."

Chapter Forty-Seven

Marley descended the mahogany staircase with stubborn cheer, noticing her husband gazing gloomily at his pocket watch. For the past ten days—even while they were lounging naked on his quarterdeck, stargazing—he had been distracted. He'd sent a message to Rashall on their expected departure time after he and Deming had secured and stored the gunpowder. The boy had returned with the simple message of thanks.

Only with Rashall gone had she realized what a hole he left behind. She had come to love him as a brother as her husband did. Interestingly, the idea of him contemplating moving on as a man of God did not surprise her terribly. He was as good-hearted as they came. She had briefly entertained fond fantasies of him marrying her sister, and the four of them roaming the seas for the rest of their days—but apparently that was not to be.

And if he was weary of life on the sea, this would perhaps be a good option. The main downside she knew was the American Revolution. Inevitably, Bermuda would become hostile to the new country and visiting might be difficult—if not impossible—for Bronson and her.

"All well?" she asked, a phrase she'd come to fondly associate with him.

He smiled absently. "Of course."

"An utterly fake smile."

"We lack the time for me to slice open a vein."

She gazed up at him, and he softened, taking her arm and escorting her from the home.

As they exited, she saw Thomas ascending with his walking stick, no longer wearing the frock coat and hat he would've worn as a barrister in Williamsburg. Today, merely a white lawn shirt, buff breeches, and black boots.

He was alone. Marley had no idea where her grandmother was, and she didn't much care. Although she wasn't yet aware, Bronson had said his goodbyes to Hannah earlier in the day, thanking her for raising a woman like his wife—and politely asking her to absent herself from their departure.

He regarded his son with alert gravity, his lips tight. Neither said anything. Both knew the risk that each ran. Thomas, at nearly 77 years of age in a year when he had long outlived the odds. Bronson, less than three months from a birthday that a curse had determined he would never celebrate. Neither man apt to care much for superstition on this day. And nothing they could say this day would be new to the other man.

They were not a pair who left things unsaid. Unlike many men, certainly unlike those of his day, Thomas had showered his son freely with affection, and the boy knew well he was loved. Unlike some well-born sons, Bronson revered his father and returned that affection openly. So on this day, they truly knew what was in each other's heart: that this, more so than ever, may be their last goodbye.

Bronson hugged his father hard, and Marley saw the awareness move over him as he gentled his touch, knowing his father's frailty had increased since he'd last left him here.

When Thomas leaned back, he briskly tugged at his son's shirt collar as if he were once again a four-year-old lad, and he was teaching him how to dress. Bronson knew better, and he produced the cross and dove he'd worn his entire life.

"They're here," he reassured him. "I never take them off."

Thomas gave a slight nod. "God be with you, my son."

"And with you, my father."

Thomas turned to Marley and held out a hand to her. "I learned late in my life how dear forgiveness is and how destructive it can be not only to those who seek it, but particularly to those who harbor bitterness and resentment. It is a cancer of the heart. I have forgiven Hannah for her misdeeds, as terrible as they were for all of us. I hope you, my dear daughter, can as well."

Marley was surprised to find herself in tears at his unexpected admonition. She tiptoed to kiss his rugged jawline, and he hugged her with sudden affection and strength. "I love you, dear Marley, and pray for you and my son each day and each night."

"I love you, Thomas. God be with you, kindest father."

And with that, the son returned to his wife and escorted her to the quay.

Marley gazed around the harbor, taking in the moment before her. There, off perhaps a hundred yards or so, waited the *Immortal*, her white sails slack and golden in the afternoon sunlight, the sky perhaps the richest blue she'd ever seen. For a moment she wondered if it were only that way because it *was* this singular moment. The scent of sea mulberry filled her head, the unique aroma she had learned from her husband.

The boarding party waited in the boat. Jem and George were excited to have been chosen to row—not a child's job, after all—and Camisha and Ashanti waited with them, both withdrawn and silent, Camisha twisting a handkerchief. Bronson handed Marley in, and she sat beside the older woman, covering her hands lightly with her own pale, cool fingers. Sitting beside her, she could see the tear stains, could feel the heat of her hands. She disentangled one from the twisting and lightly held it in her own lap, stroking her forearm, soothing her.

The wind rose, and as Bronson boarded, he gave Jem a nod.

They were ten yards from shore when they heard: "Yo! Need another man to help you row, lads?"

413

There stood Rashall, bag in hand.

The boys shouted, "Aye, sir!"

Camisha burst out in tears as the rest collapsed in relieved laughter. The boys quickly reversed course, bringing the boat back for their quartermaster.

Rashall joined them, taking a spot on the bench beside Bronson and grabbing an oar as Bronson grabbed the other.

"Just remembered I have one last job," Rashall said, his old sparkle tempered with a new somberness.

Camisha wagged her finger at him. "Uh uh—you do not *ever* say that 'one last job' nonsense."

"Wh—" He frowned at his mother, his lips pursed in question. Then he shook his head. "Never mind. I'm sure I do not want to know."

"No, you do not." She leaned back, and Marley smiled as the older woman glanced over at her, shaking her head with wide-eyed emphasis. "No, he does not."

The *Immortal* arrived in Norfolk at midday at the beginning of May and slipped past the cowed British Navy undisturbed. Her captain had determined that indeed discretion was the better part of valor and had once again—the last time, he swore to himself—worn that navy's colors. By dusk, she anchored across from Hog Island and sent ashore a party to alert the militia in Williamsburg of their arrival. In all due haste wagons returned to convey the gunpowder to the magazine.

Camisha had insisted that Parks and Helen remain onboard, and the young women were happy to do so, looking forward to the time they could return to their home in Boston. Although Rashall had attempted to force his mother to remain as well, she had important letters to deliver and refused to obey. Ashanti and Bronson knew their wives better than to even attempt to influence them, and the landing party followed a safe distance behind the gunpowder convoy.

The tidewater woodlands intoxicated Marley with their aroma. In one of those oddly distant moments—as if she were watching herself from slightly outside her own body—she again perceived that she walked beside her husband through virgin forest of this land, over two centuries before she had been born. A finger stole along her spine, filling her with sudden fear.

She clutched at his arm convulsively, and he glanced down at her. "Not to worry, my darling. We are quite safe here. The few natives left are friendly."

"It's not that. It's … " She couldn't describe the preternatural stirring within her—as if she had been completely wrong about her theory with the *Adventurer* being the ship that would be unearthed in another 240 years with a man's skeleton and a cross and dove necklace identical to his in the captain's cabin.

As if fate itself would not deny Bronson the inevitable conclusion of the fear that had been visited on his family in the form of an ignorant superstition.

He stopped, waving the others on, and cupped her face in his hands, lightly kissing her in that mesmerizing way of his for his simplest of kisses—always casual yet entirely erotic, his lips parted as they brushed and held hers.

He gazed at her in the fading twilight. "I have much to live for, my darling. I will never leave you, and God has reassured me that I will live to teach our grandchildren how to tack a sail. If I had ever been destined to die young, I am certain that God's delivery of you into my life has erased that event."

She smiled, soothed by his certainty. She had no way of knowing that he spoke more out of his own desire to reassure her than any divine message he'd received. They continued on their way into Williamsburg.

No matter how many times Marley saw this town during so-called Publick Times, she never found it less than stirring. Market Square was still lively with merchants selling the last of the day's fowl and livestock, and harried housewives and enslaved women hurried home to finish dinner.

Marley and Camisha waited in the kitchen at Thomas's home while the men went on with the group. They made tea simply for something to do, but still Camisha seemed distracted. She bustled about the kitchen, looking through the drawers. Then she moved into the living room, lighting a lamp and opening Thomas's desk drawers.

"Ah. Now you're talking."

She withdrew a leather portfolio, a small container of black paint, and a paintbrush. She sat at the desk, neatly painting in large letters: *18.1.3.8.5.12.*

"What does that mean?"

Camisha hesitated. "All right, I suppose it won't hurt to tell you. It's a not-so-secret code for your sister's name. Eighteen equals R. One equals A. And so on. I'm leaving her a letter that in another 240 years from now, with another small miracle and a large favor from God, she might receive. And a letter for my mother."

"But how—"

"She'll be visiting this house someday, believe me. It's one of the homes that survives untouched into the twenty-first century—because it's a Trelawney home. And Malcolm has promised to leave it here for me—for her—attached to an artifact that was meaningful to me and her."

"What kind of artifact?"

"You'll find out soon enough."

"Do we have time for me to write her?"

Camisha gave her a somber look. "You cannot. You grew up with your crazy grandmother, and Malcolm doesn't trust you yet—he's still nervous about what you might do or say."

Marley's lip trembled. She was stung at the thought. "No one's ever respected or safeguarded history more than I," she said, appalled to hear her throat choke with tears. "I would only tell her that I love her and hope to see her again someday. It's not as if I'm freaking Mary Smith Cranch."

"Who?"

"Ha. I thought you were the big History PhD."

"No, baby, I'm a lawyer."

"She was Abigail Adams's sister," she said, dissolving again in tears.

Camisha laughed and pulled her into her arms. "Oh, honey, look at the mess you are." Grabbing her upper arms, she pushed her away from her. "Oh, good gravy. Are your nipples sensitive?"

Marley wiped her nose, blushing. "Isn't that kind of personal?"

"No, you knucklehead. I think you might be pregnant. Boy, you Miller girls are just kind of clueless about men sometimes. Have you had a period recently?"

"No," Marley said, wonderstruck. "I haven't. Not since before we left for Bermuda. Do you think?" she asked with a giggle.

"Now what do you think? I know that husband of yours and how he looks at you—hell, how he acts even with people around you two. 'Hm, my dear bride, let us retire to my cabin that I might discuss with you an important matter.' I'm sure that boy's been doing you twice a day since you were married."

"Camisha!" Marley laughed.

"Well? Am I lying?"

"No," she said sullenly. "Probably more often, though."

She sighed. "Help me find a dust cap. That might not be easy. Maybe Thomas still has some of Jennie's stuff upstairs."

"What do you need a dust cap for?"

"And an apron. Much as I love this old town, I just can't see them letting an uppity black woman wander around in the Raleigh Tavern without a proper servant's uniform."

"Why the Raleigh Tavern?"

"Will you stop asking me questions and find me an apron? Go look in the kitchen. No doubt he has servants."

"I'm not going anywhere until you tell me what's going on."

"Well, the fifth Virginia convention is about to convene at the capitol, and even though I'm not sure where Thomas Jefferson is—he's due in Philadelphia in just a couple of weeks—I know for a fact Bronson Trelawney is in town tonight."

"Camisha?" Marley asked, growing tired of the mystery of her prescience.

"So I think there's a good chance Thomas Jefferson and Patrick Henry will be as well—and they're likely as not to meet up at the Raleigh Tavern's Apollo Room."

"Seriously?" Every nerve ending in her skin prickled with excitement.

"As a heart attack." Camisha pushed the swinging door into the kitchen and emerged perhaps half a minute later with the wardrobe items she'd sought. "Got one for you, too. Put it on, just to be safe."

Marley hastily shoved the cap on her head, pushing her hair out of the way, and tied the apron around her waist. "Do you think Malcolm would mind if we met them?"

She laughed. "Girl, like I *told you*. Thirty years ago I lived within maybe five miles of William Byrd—for *months*—and never once got to meet that man. Even though he'd have just told me to empty his chamber pots, I'd have made him talk to me about law. Hell, your sister got to party with him every night, and she didn't know him from Adam. Did I ever tell you that my son, Eston, is named after one of Sally Hemings' children? Or that she's my ancestor? Honey, after all these months, we've *still* got a lot to talk about. And *yes*, I am going to meet my melancholy great granddaddy Tom."

Chapter Forty-Eight

Camisha led Marley through the busy town—filled with people laughing, on their way home to dinner, or out to meet old chums and bump the gums over a pint. Presently they reached the Raleigh Tavern, and they hurried onto the porch, under the lead bust of Sir Walter Raleigh, and inside.

The older woman looked around; no matter how old she grew, she would never have her fill of this place in this time—so much a part of her, she felt its aches and pains in the morning. It gave her a prescient nostalgia to know the old girl was entering her last days—that in only another four years, Williamsburg would begin her decline and the cup of liberty would pass on to her children.

The spring night was beginning to cool, but the place was packed with men there for the convention, and those men were eating, drinking, and laughing boisterously. Fires blazed in the fireplaces, almost unnecessarily. Even with the door frequently opening for those bustling in and out, the tavern was quite warm.

They passed into the Apollo Room, and she glanced at the corner where she and Rachel had taken the selfie with the Jefferson painting behind them. Of course, now the painting didn't yet exist. After tonight, it would.

As delighted as she always was to see her son and Bronson, she remembered that day so long ago now—truly, that had yet to occur—and her heart swelled with that age-old ache. Not a day passed that she didn't mourn Rachel.

Just inside the room, they passed an artist with sketch sheets. Even as she noticed the man finish a charcoal sketch of a couple in the corner, Malcolm Henderson approached the artist. "Mind if I have a go at it?" he asked. "I'm working on my figures, and it isn't often I get to see so many."

"I was just finishing up." The gentleman collected his materials and bowed to Malcolm before departing.

Malcolm ignored Camisha and Marley, and she noticed Marley's confusion. Quickly, she shook her head.

Boisterous laughter rang from the table in the corner, and she stared at the back of Thomas Jefferson's head, growing tongue-tied. She and Marley stood there, quite like a couple of groupies at an after party.

Bronson glanced at them, then did a double-take, a confused smile crossing his face. "Marley?"

She ducked her head, still unable to speak. Camisha couldn't judge; she couldn't open her mouth, and that was saying something.

All the men at the table rose, and the two nearest her turned, towering in historic stature over both of the tall, mute women.

"Tom, Pat, the lovely woman hiding behind Marley is Mrs. Camisha Adams, Rashall's mother. And this shy young woman is my own wife, Merrilea."

Both women curtsied, both men bowed.

"Don't tell me this young lady is the one who made mincemeat of those at Great Bridge?" Jefferson asked. "I'd heard that your new bride was quite an expert with a rifle."

"Much as I would love to be a legend," she put in before her husband could brag otherwise, "'Twasn't me, sir. He knew I was terrified to be left behind and so he allowed me to come to the camp, but the victory belonged to the Continental Army."

He tilted his head, conceding in a manner that indicated he believed nothing she said. "I see."

"'Twould break my heart, seeing credit not go to the proper historic characters."

Bronson watched her, a small smile quirking his mouth as she continued her colonial folderol.

"Please join us," Henry said. He glanced around and found two chairs against the wall, drawing them to the table.

"Here, you sit over there, beside the other men," Camisha said. "I believe the man there is planning a painting of you."

They followed her directions and as all four men smiled at Malcolm, who was busy sketching lightly, he gave them a gracious nod.

"Where's Mr. Adams? We sent him after you two."

"We didn't see him. We just came on our own."

"Ah. Well, he's only been gone a few moments—I'm sure he'll arrive shortly. We were just discussing the Second Continental Congress," Bronson said, glancing meaningfully from Marley to Camisha.

At this, she sat in delight next to Jefferson, and Marley joined her at an angle so as not to block Malcolm's view.

He nodded to Bronson. "Yes, but do you recall the first Virginia convention? Old Dunmore thought to dissolve the House of Burgesses, so we adjourned to meet here."

"That should have been our first sign that the romance was over." This from Rashall.

"More so that we should have known our father is a brute who abuses his children. Now if you want a tragic romance, that would be my pining over my Belinda."

Bronson gave an impolite laugh. "Oh, Tom, I don't mean to be—well, mean, but you truly were besotted."

The soulful dreamer and architect of the nation stared into his wine glass. "That I was. In this very room, dancing the night away while she set her heart on a less studious sort. Poor wretch, and she married another only a few months later."

"I warned you to study more French and less Latin. And then this gentleman, on fire like an Attic orator at St. John's, with his 'liberty or death' alternatives. It's a wonder any fun at all was had, with the ongoing quest for liberty."

Jefferson spared Bronson a smile. "But we did have fun, didn't we? Do you recall that visiting professor we had—you were but a lad, your father had you stuffed so full of learning you were but—what, eight or nine?"

"I was thirteen. And his name was Miller," he said, glancing at Marley. "Robert Miller."

"The man's love for the colonies was like the cleric George Whitefield's for salvation—he spoke of the unborn country as if he were a prognosticator of philosophy and rhetoric."

"Perhaps he was. He's been right so far. But look who we have here—your tutor in the Enlightenment, Mr. Wythe."

The man who appeared across from Jefferson was not as tall as the others, but in stature considered a giant. He was older, with more wrinkles and less hair, than when Camisha had known him. He looked around the group, his gaze resting on her. "I beg your pardon, but we know one another, do we not?"

She stood and curtsied deeply. "What a mind you have, sir. Yes, thirty years ago you let me help you defend Grey Trelawney when he was on trial for his wife's murder."

"Ah, yes! I recall as if it were yesterday. I don't know that I had ever met anyone so naturally gifted for defending those who were innocent yet for whom circumstance made innocence seem highly improbable."

"Mr. Wythe, it's such a pleasure to see you again. The trial of Grey Trelawney was truly one of my crowning achievements in life—and here is another, my son Rashall Adams."

Rashall rose to shake his hand. "Will you join us, sir?"

"I am afraid I cannot. I have one more matter to attend to this evening before we convene in the morning, and I spied you all here and contrived to say hello. Tom, are we still riding together to Philadelphia?"

"With pleasure, sir, and at your leisure."

And with that, Wythe bowed to the table and left the tavern.

"I don't mind saying, I would have enjoyed seeing that trial," Jefferson said. "What an intriguing sight it must have been, a comely young African woman debating the likes of Peyton Randolph."

His words surprised her, although they shouldn't have. He might instead have marveled at watching a mule do a minuet. Everything she had ever read as a young woman told her that Jefferson was indeed a racist, believing blacks to be as helpless as children.

"Begging your pardon, sir, but I was never an African. I and my ancestors are American—as American as ... well, sir, as American as you and your own children."

She noticed Marley's suppressed smile at her words, but she knew Jefferson could never guess what she had just said.

Oh, but he had—at least as much as a man who had no idea that his seed would someday result in the woman—still comely, thirty years later—sitting before him. "I humbly beg your forgiveness, Mrs. Adams. I meant only to compliment you. Truly any lover of law and justice would have loved to watch such a match."

Because Camisha did indeed love this man, the historic document he would finish penning in the next two months, and the country whose birth it would effect, she lay her hand on his ruffled wrist. "Sir, I do have one question of you."

He gave a simple nod.

She selected her words thoughtfully. "If—as is quite likely—the subject of slavery arises in Philadelphia, how will you respond?"

"Freedom is not a political right, or a national right. Freedom is the basic right of all mankind. And for that I will fight."

"Sir," she pressed on, "we are adults here. We know the importance of enslaved men and women to the southern economy."

Bronson added, "Let us be honest—not simply to the south, or to this land, but to the entire world. The north relies on the work of the southern slave as much as the southern planter does. We are hypocrites if we claim otherwise."

She nodded. "True. Then, Mr. Jefferson, you can expect that your countrymen will resist any effort you make to insist on the inclusion of enslaved Americans in any petition for freedom. What say you then?"

"I shall stand on the rock of the principles that must form the new country."

"I see. What do you do if they flatly refuse to support any provision for the freedom of slaves?"

At last, perhaps, she'd gotten her question across to him. He raised his eyebrows briefly and gave an exasperated laugh. "Another prognosticator, I see. Well, the fact is, I do believe in the prudence of your question. And I have an alternative plan. First, we abolish the trade itself. Second, we ameliorate conditions for those who currently are enslaved. Third, we establish an end date, after which any slave born is automatically free."

"And after the slaves are freed—what then?"

"They should be returned to the place of their ancestry."

Camisha gazed at him expressionlessly. "Sir, many of these people and their ancestors have lived here longer than some whites. They speak English. They know nothing of life in Africa, or the West Indies. Why not integrate them into American society through education?"

"We have seen the result of slave uprisings, where the loosed negro is—"

"Mr. Jefferson, you speak of my people as if we are animals. We are not. Race is no more a fact of science than unicorns. It was a lie created by those who would control and subjugate others."

He smiled and nodded at Bronson. "Now this is the woman who debated Mr. Randolph, God rest his soul."

Camisha closed her mouth, conceding an argument she had not expected to win. Indeed, as she gave up the fight, she happened to catch Malcolm's gaze—and found him frowning at her, deeply disturbed.

Her argument with Jefferson had been the most verboten act she had undertaken in thirty years. Never once had

Malcolm been obliged to correct her; she simply knew better. Meeting Thomas Jefferson two months before the signing of the Declaration of Independence had offered too great a temptation. She told herself she only wanted to know *why*.

"In any case, in whatever circumstances, it is imperative that slavery be ended—that our children's children may not suffer God's wrath."

"Speaking of children," Camisha said, glancing at Bronson as she abruptly changed the subject, "I believe your young bride has news for you."

His eyes darkened in pleasure and expectation.

"I'm not positive," Marley said, raising her gaze to his. "But I do think I might be—um, with child."

The corner table rang with delight and good cheer, and he leaned over to kiss his wife's cheek, then brought her hand to his lips in a sudden, fiercely happy gesture. Rashall proposed a toast, and Camisha rose and looked on as her son gave the toast.

And it was this moment of joy and celebration that Malcolm captured on his canvas for posterity, of the men around the table. The painting that had captured a festive Jefferson so unlike the studious philosopher history recorded had simply been rejoicing in a friend's celebration of his first child.

The celebration went on into the night, with Marley sipping tea as the men drank ale. Ashanti rejoined them there, and they passed the night before the Fifth Virginia Convention in pleasant diversion.

And so it was amid the exciting bustle of the Raleigh Tavern—as it teemed with men there from all over the colony for the convention—that a man appeared, just as Camisha had released her earlier, pointless frustration and decided to enjoy herself. She was having the kind of fun she hadn't had for— well, perhaps ever. At least, since the last time she'd made merry with a signer of the Declaration of Independence.

And then she noticed a tavern wench pointing toward them. She spoke to a dark-haired, clean-shaven man she didn't recognize until it was too late. He appeared there as if straight from her nightmares, as he'd looked thirty years before, disguised to all except the woman who had been at the root of his humiliation in Williamsburg.

James Manning swept into the Apollo Room as if on demonic power, appearing only a blink after she saw him, straightening his arm toward their table. She did not know his target. Even as she dove toward Rashall, and Ashanti toward Rashall, Rashall toward Bronson (or perhaps her, as she would later assume—although she didn't have a curse hanging over her head), Bronson toward his wife—everyone shoving loved ones out of the way—Manning raised his arm and fired a pistol.

Jefferson bent over to retrieve a dropped napkin in an astonishingly random act of tidiness that saved his life, and the blast went through the window and straightaway toward the King's Arms Tavern across the street, where Jane Vobe would the next day be obliged to replace a shutter shattered by the blast.

Camisha stared at the tavern across the street, shaken. *I can't believe, of all the people sitting at this table, the only one we didn't think to protect was the guy who really needed to stick around.*

Rashall, nearest the door, reacted most swiftly, following Manning a moment later. Bronson leapt after him before the crowd reacted, and Camisha leaned out the window to watch. Manning raced out into the street.

Before Bronson had time to draw his pistol, Rashall raised his arm and fired. Manning jerked and collapsed into Duke of Gloucester Street.

Bronson reached them and held out his loaded gun to Rashall. Without speaking, they traded guns. No one in the street had been paying close enough attention to say for sure who had done the shooting. By the time the crowds in the taverns spilled out into the street, Bronson was kneeling beside Manning with an empty pistol beside him, searching vainly for a pulse.

The idea of a black man killing a fleeing white man, regardless of the heroic nature of the act, might have caused a sheriff and a grand jury some degree of heartburn.

Inside, Jefferson and Henry were already pressing outside with the crowds. Camisha, Ashanti, and Marley stared at one another in shock. "Holy Cow, I nearly got Thomas Jefferson killed. Malcolm would not have liked that."

She, too, followed the crowds outside. They found their way to Bronson, where he knelt over the prone form of James Manning.

A moment later, the sheriff—Robert Bolling, his name—appeared beside Bronson. "What happened?"

"I'm not sure. I was with friends celebrating at the Raleigh Tavern, and he shot at our table. As he ran, I shot him. I believe he had an old grievance against my brother, Grey. He has attacked my partner and me numerous times and in fact destroyed my last ship at Great Bridge."

Camisha's glance strayed to Rashall. His hands were on his hips, his breathing erratic, his face ashen. He bent over at the waist—and she realized he was controlling nausea. She knew her son had lived a dangerous life on the seas, and so his reaction now assured her that he, in fact, had shot Manning.

And then the truth struck her.

She had heard Marley's suspicions about the shipwreck of the *Adventurer*, but she was certain she knew the complete truth in this moment. If not for her son—someone who was not even supposed to have existed in this time—Bronson Trelawney would have died tonight, just two months before his thirtieth birthday.

One last job, indeed.

Chapter Forty-Nine

Marley sat on the chesterfield in the Adamses living room, in Boston. The city was in her June finery, and on a leisurely day in the twenty-first century, this would be the finest time to visit.

On this day in the eighteenth, it was a time of heartbreak. Without twenty-first century technology that offered the illusion of uninterrupted closeness, thousands of miles apart, goodbyes had meaning and people couldn't deceive themselves otherwise.

The woman sitting across from her, soundless tears streaming unheeded down her face, had become something of a sister, something of a mother, to Marley. She was the most solid tie Marley had ever had to Rachel. She did not know what life held in store, or whether they would ever meet again.

She could not imagine the sadness this woman knew, aware the same was true of her relationship with her eldest son.

They had returned to Boston to hear the good news that both Eston and Helen's husband Taleeb had a short leave. This had comforted them and certainly delighted the children—and then, last night, finally, Rashall had taken them aside and given them the heartbreaking news.

He was joining St. Peter's in Bermuda to serve the Anglican church as a vicar. Perhaps in time he would be able to return—ideally to a church in Boston. But for now, he felt certain this was the way forward.

Camisha's heart was breaking. She knew—as she'd told Marley—that Rashall was a grown man. He was certainly in better hands serving God than he had been smuggling gunpowder. But she didn't like him living in Bermuda's nest of Englishmen, all of them no doubt by now enflamed against the colonials. And being black certainly never helped—especially in a small island nation, where island nations had become synonymous with slave-trading. Where ships came and went every day, as likely as not to be trading in slaves.

And so, again, they were headed out to Bermuda on *Immortal*. So, again, whether they liked it or not, they were saying goodbye to loved ones.

Even as she thought it, the front door opened with all the young men and women except Marley. They'd been down to the ship, collecting delicacies sent by the Trelawneys at Rosalie. Pies and jellies, frocks and new shoes. In exchange, they sent the Trelawneys books. Always books.

Rashall's young charge, George, had taken the Adams grandchildren under his wing, and the dynamic offered him a childhood that perhaps he'd never known. He and little Ashanti—Shonny —had been in constant company during the entire time the family was here.

Helen and Parks had said their goodbyes, and now they stood on the stairs, watching their family with false cheer. George and Shonny played with a top near the cold fireplace.

"George, time to weigh anchor, son."

"Aye, sir," he said—at nine, a free man once again. He handed the top to Shonny. "You work on this while I'm gone. I'll bring you back some more toys next time I come."

Camisha hastily wiped her cheeks free of tears and blew her nose. She made a distasteful face at her wrinkled wad of a handkerchief, stuffing it in her pocket as both women rose.

Marley took her hand and led her to the door.

"Ray, why don't you leave George here with Taleeb and me? He'd be so much safer." This from Helen.

Rashall sent her a look. "He's mine. He'll stay with me."

Marley glanced at Bronson, raising her eyebrows. He nodded—and that quickly, she understood it was time to go.

"I want to go, too," Shonny said, upset by the signals he'd seen too often in his young life. He knew what these goodbyes meant—crying women—and he was certain that, wherever he went, the uncle he adored did not have to put up with crying women.

Rashall bent to his nephew's height. "Shonny, I need for you to take care of your mother for me while the other menfolk are gone. Can you do that for me, young man?"

The little boy—eyes as large as saucers, with long, thickly curling black lashes, looked at the floor. "I want to go, sir," he whispered, his chin trembling. He held out his toy to Rashall. "I'll share my top. I don't eat much."

Ray drew the boy into his arms, hugged him hard—nearly losing it himself. He rose to his feet, passing him up to Taleeb, who'd joined his wife at the bottom of the stairs.

Marley expected a scene, but Shonny merely hugged his father and turned to watch his uncle.

"Well, that went better than expected." Camisha gave an awkward laugh.

Rashall took his mother's hand from Marley, then put his arms around her and let her cry for a long while.

At last, she stepped back. "Soon as you're gone, I'll be fine. It's the goodbyes. They never get easier, somehow. And this one—" She shook her head. "We'll pray for you, son. Please pray for us."

"Every day."

At last, they left, and the *Immortal* was en route to Bermuda.

&

The last few nights of the journey, they all three lay in hammocks in the captain's cabin, gazing up at the stars— Marley and her husband sharing one, Rashall in the other. The men sipped rum.

"Mmm," Marley murmured. "I'm craving a cigar."

Bronson hugged her. "As am I."

Rashall used a stick to set his hammock to swaying. "I thought women of a delicate disposition ordinarily craved unholy foods like anchovies dipped in chocolate sauce."

"Never let it be said that my wife is any kind of ordinary."

"Ray, why don't you want to marry my sister?"

He laughed, her old co-conspirator again. "What brought this on?"

"I know she likes you. I know you like her. You're handsome enough. This isn't the twenty-first century where we're worried about how green our grass is, or how European our car, or all the ungodly things women worry about just in staying groomed so they can stack up against whichever Hollywood starlet is showing off her bottom on the Internet."

"I understood nothing you said after 'handsome enough.'"

"That's all right. Neither do those people."

"Your point?"

"Life is short enough already, but here it's even shorter. You don't have time to waste on twenty-first century problems like 'does she like me?' or 'is there somebody better out there?'"

"I'm certain I should never find anyone finer—although I'm not sure what 'better' means. She's kind, intelligent, and beautiful. She's intellectually curious. She is an altogether exquisite woman. What kind of mate shopping do they do in your old time?"

"You don't want to know. Please, let's go back to Stonefield now and get her—before something happens to her."

"What does that mean?"

"I don't know. Neither one of us were born in this century. I'm still not sure what might happen from one moment to the next."

"Oh, that passes."

This from a new voice in the room, and instinctively Bronson drew his dirk from his waist as a man—vaguely familiar to all of them—appeared beside Rashall.

"Careful, son. You don't want to slice your lovely bride. Fear not."

The man, familiar to Marley, was dressed in a charcoal coat, waistcoat, and breeches, with a bright white shirt, ruffles at the throat and cuffs, and a white stock at his throat. Black hair was tied in a queue at the nape of his neck.

"Who are you? I swear, if you're an ally of Manning's, you shall die." Bronson placed his arm in front of Marley as he deftly climbed out of the hammock.

Rashall, too, was on his feet, but he had drawn no weapon. Marley had noticed weeks ago that, in fact, he had worn no weapons since they left Williamsburg.

The man smiled, his hands raised easily. His gaze was a light gray—almost silver—and guileless. "Don't you know me? Don't I resemble anyone you know?"

Bronson replied grudgingly. "You look like my father did when I was a boy."

"Oh! You're Grey." Marley whispered. "I saw you through the portal at Rosalie."

He touched his nose. "On the nosey."

Bronson's knife clattered to the deck as his face paled. Grey retrieved it and held it out to him, lightly handling the blade.

"Prove it to me." This from Bronson.

"Goodness. The lovely lass just vouched for me. Does her word mean nothing to you?"

"Sir?"

"All right then. The young lady is Merrilea, my own wife's sister. Let me think. Ah. Something only she and Rachel would know is that Merrilea purloined a necklace that belonged to their mother, and is now quite dear to my own granddaughter. You can just see the small scar she has, like that of my wife, at the corner of her eye, as a heartbreaking reminder of the worst night of her life. And she adores her older sister and still misses her."

Tears fell from Marley's eyes as she stared at him.

"And you, sir, are my younger brother. Your mother passed needlessly at your birth because of the poor medicine of this era—but her kin, including perhaps your own father—incorrectly blamed a backwoods curse for her death. As you arrive on the eve of your birthday, even you wonder if your life is drawing to a close by some fate yet unknown to you. You have lived your life taunting death, believing that makes you more firmly ensconced in life. And your father is … well, he's a hard man to know, but his passion and loyalty are true.

"And you, sir, are the son of a proud Boston free man and his even prouder Virginian wife, who thirty years ago in a trial no doubt still spoken of in the drinking establishments of Williamsburg's lawyers, saved my life. You have grown up with a father who can be dour—although I'm certain three decades with your mother have softened him—and a brilliant, beautiful mother who enjoys every moment of life, and lets nothing escape her. And there's something puzzling about her—a way she has of knowing things that she shouldn't know—that has mystified you your entire life. Oh—and you don't tell many people this, but you were named after my wife, Rachel."

Both men stared silently. Bronson watched his older brother, uncertain—until, finally, he extended his hand. "I no longer have faith in the limitations I've trusted my entire life. I rely on you to teach me."

Grey gave a slight bow and shook his brother's hand, then Rashall's. "I'm no longer a man to teach about limitations. For thirty years now I've taught people about possibilities—of improving the future by learning from the past. Well, Bronson, Rashall, Merrilea—today my desire is to improve the past with learning from the future."

"Does Malcolm know you're here?"

He laughed and waved his hand in dismissal. "Do you think I should be here, if not?"

"Good point. By the way, I go by Marley now."

"Different, but quite lovely."

"Apparently I was a simple child and couldn't pronounce the name, and my grandmother thought it charming."

He laughed. My heavens, he was handsome. She saw a little of Bronson in him when he smiled—she'd never realized how much Bronson resembled their father. Perhaps he had the same impressive bone structure, with his delicate mother's light coloring and large, tilted eyes.

"Tell us, then, what's this scheme to improve the past?" Bronson gestured to the table, and they all sat there. "How do you like the ship, by the way?"

"I see old Crowell has done a first rate job in exorcising the demons I invited into the poor old girl thirty-five years ago. She's indeed restored—rather like I was, after I found Rachel."

Bronson offered rum, and he accepted.

"Did Crowell see you…er, arrive?"

"No."

"He's talked about your ghost visiting the ship countless times over the years."

"Well, I can't speak to that. Or at least, I won't. Malcolm would have my head if he thought I was randomly rambling down days long gone."

He gave them a cryptic, Mona Lisa smile, leaving Marley certain that he'd haunted his own ship. His mischief was intoxicating. At last, the men settled down, listening to him.

"You see, the future is a place with a vast amount of information. My employer is a center for historical research. I have at my fingertips almost any kind of data or records imaginable—those that aren't classified, of course."

"You work for the historic foundation in Williamsburg, don't you? How did I not know you?" Marley asked. "I worked there for years. I was on the dig for … well, never mind that."

"Marley, you know why. Neither Rachel's time travel nor mine occurred until after yours. I didn't live in the twenty-first century until you vanished."

"Oh, of course. Right. Sorry, go on."

"So—along with teaching visitors about my life and historic events in the eighteenth century—I've spent the past thirty years studying other events and how they interlock, and any possible repercussions—good or bad—from those events. For example, the Miller sisters suffered a heartbreaking loss—but out of that, presumably, came some good. Rachel met Camisha when Rachel was adopted, and we all met our loved ones.

"And so one looks at the eventual good that came, long after the tragedy, and one can't help but wonder whether it was worth it."

Marley interrupted. "What's to say the good wouldn't occur, anyway? I read your ship log, so I know you're aware my parents both were born in the eighteenth century. Perhaps our traveling in time is a result of that—if an explanation can be found at all. And if no logical explanation exists, which certainly makes far more sense than anything we've experienced, then what's to be said for the logical progression of cause and effect?"

"A compelling argument indeed. But you know the importance of, as we've all come to appreciate—in fact Malcolm's insistence on—doing nothing to alter historic events, regardless of how much improved we believe they might be.

"So, for the moment, let's set that aside. I'm not allowed much time here tonight, by the way—only an hour—and so I need to get out what I came to say."

"Please, go on." This, from Bronson.

"In my research, I learned much about the man who—well, who committed the crimes against the Millers. And many questions remain.

"For example, nothing—and I do mean *nothing*, not only on the man who did the evil deeds, but on his brother, who protected him—nothing exists in their lives before the year 1976.

"I feel as if I owe something to young Robert—who was the son of my own seaman, Gideon—and his bride, Cassandra.

You must know, Marley, that I did not realize who Gideon was until Rachel and I were married and living in the twenty-first century."

"How did you figure it out?"

"I found them. Well, not them—they had passed away years earlier, but, again, I did a records search, expecting perhaps to read ancestry items. Instead, I found their death certificates. They passed away in the early 1990s. At that point I realized that they had traveled in time. I demanded to know from Malcolm the ever-widening scope of this time-travel scheme, and he said that the Millers—Gideon and Sarita, that is—were the first who brought children from another time, setting off the possibility of chain reactions. All I could think was what poor Hastings would say of all this. He always thought it so unseemly."

"He still does. He's still the same—well, I didn't know him, but for a man in his eighties, he's filled with energy and affection."

"I'm so glad to hear that. Truly my life improved the moment he, with his conscience and kindness, entered it."

"But what about the Millers and Malcolm?" Bronson asked, steering the conversation back.

"Yes, well. Malcolm explained to me that the scope of the time-travel instability was marked in time from the date Gideon and Sarita traveled back in time to the date of their destination. Thus, between 1753 and 1953, intentional time travel exists as a precarious thread throughout the lineage of the Millers—and, now, the Adamses as well."

"Say what?" Ray asked—his first interruption.

"Your mother was implicated for some reason with Rachel. That, you see, is an example of the instability. Mary and Malcolm have within their power the ability to allow others this method of experiencing other times. Malcolm has apparently allowed it liberally with the Millers. Still, I am grateful he found a place where Gideon and Sarita could abide peacefully, although even in this time period, where they were safer, they were not allowed to marry—legally, at least—for another fifteen years.

"I always worried about their children. Mixed-race children often had trouble finding acceptance from either community in my era, and mixed couples were certainly not allowed to marry—at least in church weddings."

"Uh-huh. Imagine that." Rashall looked from Grey to Marley.

"Perhaps now. It's not that way in the twenty-first century," Marley said. "That era has its own ridiculous set of problems."

Grey nodded. "'Tis true."

"You know, it's interesting how your accent is still colonial."

"Because of my work as an interpreter."

Bronson grew short. "Please! Can we let him continue with his story? I wish to hear his plan before he vanishes again into the atmosphere."

"'Tis simple. Malcolm Henderson allowed Gideon and Sarita in 1753 to travel to 1953."

"That's the same year Nan put Juliana through the portal."

"Juliana? Went back to 1753?"

Marley cast her husband an apologetic glance and hurried to summarize. "Yes. After our parents were killed. Nan put us both back there, to keep us safe, but I followed her back into the twentieth century before the portal closed. Nan—our grandmother, our mother's mother, raised me. And she was at least culpable for the murders, in that she explained to Manning how to use the portal."

"I don't understand. James Manning? What does he have to do with it?"

"The men who call themselves Sheppard—they're James Manning's sons. The younger one is a lunatic. The older one dotes on his brother and is quite intelligent."

"That explains their missing history. The first documentation of their existence appears on July 4, 1976 in Boston when the younger accosted a woman. They grew up with the help of state aid and the man now called Max Sheppard—"

"Formerly Maxwell Sheppard Manning. And 1976 was the date of my father's Phi Beta Kappa key."

"Sheppard has the sort of wealth to make Solomon blush."

"He's a computer genius. I remember his name."

"Marley!" Bronson exclaimed.

"I don't think I can stop interrupting." She sent him a nervous look.

"That's all right, I'm almost finished. What got me thinking, you see, was Rachel talking about Camisha. She told me that Helen, Camisha's mother, came to work for Max Sheppard only a few weeks before Rachel came to live there. It struck me as curious, because by then I knew that both Camisha and Rachel were in fact from the Richmond area as children. And yet they both wound up in Texas, with Max Sheppard? Quite an odd coincidence. So we were visiting Helen one day, and she mentioned that her husband's beat had been out there in the area near Stonefield. That in fact at one time they'd lived in the house nearest the Millers. Oh—Rashall, do you know what your grandfather did for a living?"

"He was a sheriff of some sort, Mother said."

"Yes, he was a Richmond police officer. And he was killed at home one night only a few weeks before the Millers, when Camisha and her mother went to visit Helen's mother in Yorktown.

"And at the visitation before his funeral, Helen met a man who came to pay his respects, telling her how her husband was an old friend of his. He learned she was obsessed to find the drug addict who'd robbed and killed her husband for no more than a few hundred dollars."

"But that *wasn't* why he was killed, of course! Jack came there to kill Camisha. That's what Manning had told him to do. He'd thought Camisha was in another time," Bronson said. He glanced at his wife then gave her a double-take, noticing her satisfied smirk at his own interruption.

"Exactly," Grey exclaimed. "Jack was in fact quite drug-addled, though, and perhaps he found 'Cameron Carlyle' in the phone book—don't ask, men—and grew confused about his mission there.

"At any rate, in that moment, there at the visitation, Helen told us, the man—Max Sheppard—offered her a well-paying job for very little work, just helping out around the house. She was persuaded that it would help her daughter have a better life.

"So I began wondering—why would a man come all the way from Texas to do that? And I looked at the facts surrounding Cameron Carlyle's death, and they were quite similar to the facts surrounding the Millers' deaths. What they now call a home invasion occurred—someone attacking people who are in a house. The attacks were both unthinkably violent, and the killer used a knife in both crimes.

"I've come to believe that Jack Sheppard—Manning, I suppose—killed Camisha's father, and that his brother knew it and protected him. He certainly was never even arrested for the murder of the Millers; it's still unsolved, and there had to have been DNA at the scene. I also believe that had he been discovered, or even arrested, he would not have killed the Millers. Only *after* their murder did Sheppard finally institutionalize him."

Bronson waited.

Grey glanced at his pocket watch. "I need your help. I cannot do it alone."

"Do what?"

"As dangerous as this time may be for you in terms of disease, my family live in a time where the man who killed Rachel's parents still lives and has at his disposal someone who protects him. Both of them with a great deal of money to bribe authorities for freedom.

"Malcolm has agreed to let me go to that night—the night Camisha's father died—and defend Carlyle against his killer—to the death. And to convince him that he must remain in Richmond, at the home near Stonefield. This, I believe, will help ensure that the good aspects of consequences from that unholy night will still occur."

"I will help however I can," Bronson said.

"Do not give your promise in haste, for its consequences are sweeping. You and I will have but 24 hours in that time to do what we need to do and to get out—otherwise we both shall remain in that time—as did the Mannings. I shall be an old man and Rachel but six. You, a man of nearly thirty, and Marley a child of three."

"I am not yet certain I understand all of these events."

"I think I do," Marley said. At Bronson's glance, she shrugged. "Well, that's what happens when you ask questions. But I do wonder one more thing—and it's a big one. What makes you believe that things will still fall into place as they have already—if my husband helps you? If my parents live, why will Juliana be in this era?"

"Why are you, now?"

"Only to love my husband. And perhaps to find my sister. Unlike you, I should never wish to leave this time."

He hesitated, misgiving plain on his face. "It is as the grace that flowed down from heaven and saved my own life, my very soul. I have no *cause* for belief—only belief. I have seen the miracles from my faith in my own life. I have seen the death that history assigned to me become life and freedom for two hundred men and women and all the many thousands and tens of thousands of the children who were their descendants. You must have seen that firsthand in your time there—along with the good that Camisha surely does, being the woman she is.

"Marley, I trust in goodness that I have seen come to pass. I don't believe goodness is repaid with heartache and evil.

"Bronson, I shall return at the right time. When I come, I will have but an hour to stay here with you and plan, if you will join me. Rashall, I see in your face an uncertainty, a crisis of faith perhaps equal to that of my own when God first blessed me with Rachel. I urge you: simply look up, recognize God's blessings raining down on you, and accept them. Marley, I send you my dear wife's deepest affection and hope for that day when we're all back together in Glory. 'And God shall wipe away all tears from their eyes; and there shall be no more death, neither sorrow, nor crying, neither shall there be any more pain: for the former things are passed away.'

"Tonight, I bid you all adieu and fair sailing."

On his way out of his old cabin, he stopped and touched the wall, gliding his hand lightly along the glassy surface of the polished teak. He inhaled deeply and turned, observing the others. He opened the door and walked to the ladder leading to the quarterdeck, and vanished above deck.

The three exchanged looks, and then Rashall silently followed Grey Trelawney up the ladder. They heard him pacing the quarterdeck overhead, and Bronson closed the door.

"So," he said, looking at his watch. "Midnight approaches—and with it my thirtieth birthday."

Marley stubbornly slipped her fingertips inside his open collar and withdrew the cross and dove. She kissed the symbols, and then her husband's chest. She lay her head there, listening to the steady beat of his heart.

"My darling, you know I am a Miller."

He rested his cheek against the top of her head, rubbing his face contentedly against her hair. "You are a Trelawney. But I recall your family, yes."

"And you know in the first moments you knew me, you, the son of a Dandridge woman, saved my life."

He crushed her hard against him, as if recalling that moment. "I know I thank God each day that I was there."

"In that moment, my dearest friend, the curse was broken. In this moment, I shatter it again and consider it conquered. If I must do this each night to reassure you, it is a task I will do gladly. Come and lie with me in our bed and let us ring in a new life together. A new world, free of curses."

And they did. Later, as they drifted to sleep, he whispered— not wishing to awaken her lest she slept, not wishing to mislead her lest she didn't. "You know I must help my brother."

The words drew her from her slumber, and she inhaled deeply. "You know I have a habit of walking through time portals when people try to leave me behind."

"You will not."

She laughed softly. "I will consider your feelings, but I am not fond of the idea of you wandering into a befuddled era, where anarchy and unbridled lust are confused with freedom."

"Unbridled lust? How so?"

"'If it feels good, do it.' That's the slogan of their time."

He chuckled softly, then gave a lecherous, "Aha!" Softening, he said, "Well, the slogan of my time is worshipping thee with my body. I will look forward to doing that 24 hours after I leave. I cannot promise what will happen then, but I will promise you this. Nothing—no moon, no stars, no ship of fools—can make me forget all the blessings that came my way the day I found you. Nor will I allow any of them to keep me from returning to my beloved. God has blessed us, Marley, and we owe Him the celebration of those blessings."

She heard the quiet chime of a clock at the captain's table.

"Happy birthday, my darling."

And with that, they celebrated with a good night's sleep, as a few dozen men, hundreds of miles away—a few of them good friends of theirs—and in a land they both loved, prepared to affix their names to a treasonous document that called into account those who would deny others freedom.

While overhead, their dearest brother paced in the silent July night, seeking himself God's will.

NOTE FROM THE AUTHOR

Crispus Attucks is treated as a footnote in history—possibly because, like most of us who have few buildings named after us, little is known about him. The details included in the prologue about his family are fictitious, written to help humanize him as the heroic figure I believe him to have been, based on the actions we do know. That he was hardworking is known, for he was believed to be a sailor for many years. That he loved freedom is beyond question, for he was thought to be an escaped slave, the son of a mixed union—an enslaved father and a mother from the Massachusetts tribe, evangelized and known as "Natick Praying Indians."

And we know that he was a man of courage. He didn't show up that night to be a hero of a new nation. He simply stood up to a group of heavily armed men to defend a wigmaker's apprentice attempting to collect payment for his master. He didn't have to take a stand. He was headed back out to the freedom of the sea and a life he loved. His act was a matchless opening to the American Revolution, and I hope this story encourages you to learn more about the real heroes of that time period who came to be part of the American story.

I also hope it encourages us all to be courageous in our own lives, in these sometimes troubling times.

Anne Meredith is a native Texan and the author of *Love's Timeless Hope*, *Love Across Time*, and *Tender (The Trelawneys of Williamsburg, Book One)*. Contact her via Twitter @_AnneMeredith or at annemeredithbooks@gmail.com. Reviews of this book are welcome on Amazon and Goodreads. For more information:
www.annemeredithbooks.com
www.amazon.com/author/annemeredith
https://www.facebook.com/AMRomance

Look for FOREVER (The Trelawneys of Williamsburg, Book Three) due out July 4, 2018.

MAJOR CHARACTERS IN THE TRELAWNEYS
OF WILLIAMSBURG (SPOILER FREE)

In alphabetical order

Ashanti Adams (Series). Husband of Camisha and a leader for freedom for blacks.

Bronson Trelawney (Series). Thomas's son, sea captain, hero of *Immortal*.

Camisha Carlyle (Series). Rachel's fabulous lifelong friend and champion as well as her conscience—an attorney.

Cassandra Miller (Series). Mother of Rachel, Marley, and Juliana Miller.

Dan Freeman Trelawney (Series). Married to Ruth, the pastor and leader of the Trelawney extended family.

Emily Trelawney (Series). Daughter of Grey Trelawney, said to haunt the Trelawney home in modern-day Colonial Williamsburg.

Godfrey Hastings (Series). Second in command to Grey Trelawney, Hastings manages Rosalie.

Grey Trelawney (Series). The son of Thomas Trelawney, hero of *Tender*, undergoing a conscience of crisis.

Hannah "Nan" Hastings (*Immortal*). Grandmother of Rachel, Marley, and Juliana Miller. Cassandra Miller's mother, once married to Godfrey Hastings' son, William.

James Manning (Series). Overseer at Rosalie, later a successful sea merchant.

Jennie Dandridge Trelawney (*Tender*). Wife of Thomas, mother of Bronson.

Jim "Jimmy" Bainbridge (*Immortal*). Nan's abusive, long-term partner, the man who traumatized Marley.

Juliana Miller (Series). Rachel and Marley's sister, Hastings' great-granddaughter.

Malcolm Henderson, Mary Van Kirk (Series). Guides for those who travel in time.

Max Sheppard (Series). Adopted father of Rachel, and the wealthy owner of a computer empire.

Merrilea "Marley" Hastings (*Immortal*). Heroine of *Immortal*, younger sister of Rachel. An archaeologist and historian at Colonial Williamsburg.

Rachel Sheppard (Series). Camisha Carlyle's best friend and the heroine of *Tender*—a marketing director.

Rashall Adams (*Immortal, Forever*). Camisha and Ashanti's son, a sea captain.

Robert Miller (Series). Father of Rachel, Marley, and Juliana Miller. A William & Mary history professor.

Ruth Freeman Trelawney (Series). Enslaved on Rosalie, a good friend to the Miller sisters, the Trelawney's schoolmistress and the chronicler of *The Trelawneys of Williamsburg*.

Thomas Trelawney (Series). Patriarch of the Trelawney clan, civic leader, and father of Grey and Bronson.

WILLIAMSBURG

THE TRELAWNEYS OF

WILLIAMSBURG